Praise for Jilliane Hoffman

'Hugely readable' *Daily Mirror*

'Fast-paced and action-packed, this thriller was one of the best I've read for some time. In a word: absorbing'
Herald Sun

'Jilliane Hoffman's first effort at crime writing shows she has a very promising future. The bottom line: chilling and compelling' *NW Magazine*

'Decidedly unputdownable' *Woman & Home*

'Slick, intensely readable. A tale of personal horror, thrills and vengeance guaranteed to follow in the bestselling footsteps of Patricia Cornwell, Kathy Reichs, Tess Gerritsen and Karin Slaughter. Strong, compelling stuff' *Guardian*

'Hoffman writes like an angel. Well worth a trip to the bookshop for an outstanding debut from a writer who may turn out to be a female Grisham' *Independent on Sunday*

'A gripping, well-crafted suspense story . . . an absolute delight. Shades of Grisham, nuances of McDermid, traces of McBain . . . a belter of a book. Charge your glass and enjoy this book. Do not permit anything to distract you from drinking it straight down' *Sunday Express*

ABOUT THE AUTHOR

Jilliane Hoffman was an Assistant State Attorney between 1992 and 1996. Until 2001 she was the Regional Legal Advisor for the Florida Department of Law Enforcement advising special agents on complex investigations including narcotics, homicide and organized crime. She lives in Florida. *Last Witness* is her second novel, following her bestselling debut, *Retribution*.

Last Witness

JILLIANE HOFFMAN

PENGUIN BOOKS

PENGUIN BOOKS

Published by the Penguin Group
Penguin Books Ltd, 80 Strand, London WC2R ORL, England
Penguin Group (USA) Inc., 375 Hudson Street, New York, New York 10014, USA
Penguin Group (Canada), 90 Eglinton Avenue East, Suite 700, Toronto, Ontario, Canada M4P 2Y3
(a division of Pearson Penguin Canada Inc.)
Penguin Ireland, 25 St Stephen's Green, Dublin 2, Ireland (a division of Penguin Books Ltd)
Penguin Group (Australia), 250 Camberwell Road,
Camberwell, Victoria 3124, Australia (a division of Pearson Australia Group Pty Ltd)
Penguin Books India Pvt Ltd, 11 Community Centre,
Panchsheel Park, New Delhi – 110 017, India
Penguin Group (NZ), cnr Airborne and Rosedale Roads, Albany,
Auckland 1310, New Zealand (a division of Pearson New Zealand Ltd)
Penguin Books (South Africa) (Pty) Ltd, 24 Sturdee Avenue,
Rosebank, Johannesburg 2196, South Africa

Penguin Books Ltd, Registered Offices: 80 Strand, London WC2R ORL, England

www.penguin.com

First published by Michael Joseph 2005
Published in Penguin Books 2005

2

Set in 11/13 pt Monotype Garamond
Typeset by Rowland Phototypesetting Ltd, Bury St Edmunds, Suffolk
Printed in England by Clays Ltd, St Ives plc

ISBN–13: 978-0-141-01712-9
ISBN–10: 0-141-01712-0

For Rich, the one who still never doubts.
And, of course, for Amanda and Katarina.

In memory of Hank Hoffman

I

The heavy wooden doors to courtroom 4-8 swung open again, tapping the back of the chair where the corrections officer sat fiddling with the bottom snap on his department-issued green windbreaker. The plainclothes detective entered and walked slowly up the center aisle, his dress shoes thudding softly on the tired tan carpet, past the excited crowd, before finally taking a seat on the witness stand to the left of Judge Leopold Chaskel's mahogany throne.

Miami Assistant State Attorney C. J. Townsend felt her mouth go dry. She rubbed her lips together, to keep them moist and to hide her anxious expression from the cameras, sketch artists and reporters that monitored her every move. Her heart began to pound furiously in her chest. But she could not run, could not just get up and leave – that was not an option. So she forced her eyes to look straight ahead of her. She didn't even glance at the man who sat at the opposite table across the gallery wearing an expensive Italian suit and a pained expression on his handsome face.

She knew he watched her, though, waiting for her reaction. For her, he wore a bemused smile beneath his feigned look of anguish, his fingers drumming patiently on the table before him.

'State, are you ready to proceed?' asked Judge Chaskel, perturbed that this case was once again *his* problem. He had run an almost-perfect trial. It should never have come back. Not for this reason.

'I am,' replied ASA Rose Harris, C.J.'s friend and colleague in the Major Crimes Unit at the State Attorney's Office. After a moment she rose from her seat and said, 'Please state your name for the record.'

'Special Agent Dominick Falconetti, Florida Department of Law Enforcement.'

'How long have you been so employed?'

'Fifteen years with FDLE. Four years with the NYPD in the Bronx before that.'

'Agent Falconetti, allow me to direct your attention to the year 2000. At that time, were you the lead agent on the case of *The State of Florida vs. William Rupert Bantling*?'

'Yes, Ma'am. The department headed up a task force – the Cupid Task Force, it was known by. It was comprised of detectives from multiple South Florida law enforcement agencies. In 1999 the task force was formed in response to a series of abductions and brutal murders that took place on Miami Beach. The subject had been nicknamed Cupid because of what he had done to the hearts of his victims, and the name stuck. I was the agent assigned initially from FDLE, so I, ultimately, led the investigation.'

Rose Harris gestured to the man at the table across from C.J. 'And that investigation ended with the arrest of a subject, namely William Rupert Bantling, on September 19, 2000?'

'Yes,' Dominick looked over where Rose had gestured, where William Rupert Bantling sat nibbling on his lip now, looking as if he might cry. 'Mr Bantling was arrested by Miami Beach police officers over on the McArthur Causeway. The body of victim Anna Prado was discovered in the trunk of his vehicle.'

'And Mr Bantling was subsequently brought to trial later that year for her murder?'

'Yes.'

'Who was the prosecutor in that case, Agent Falconetti?' The tone of her voice hardened slightly.

Dominick hesitated just a moment and looked in C.J.'s direction. 'Assistant State Attorney C. J. Townsend,' he said softly. 'She'd been the SAO Legal Advisor on the task force for more than a year.'

'During the course of this trial, you became romantically involved with Ms Townsend, is that correct?'

'Yes,' he said, looking awkwardly down at his lap, 'we developed a relationship.'

'And Mr Bantling was convicted after a trial, correct?'

'Yes. Convicted and sentenced to death.'

Rose Harris had moved behind Bantling at the table. Now she placed a hand on his shoulder, and he bowed his head meekly.

'But you came to discover that Mr Bantling was not guilty of this crime, was he Agent Falconetti?'

'I don't know that for certain,' Dominick squirmed uncomfortably in his seat. C.J. felt his eyes searching the courtroom for hers, but she continued to stare straight ahead. Her legs had started to shake underneath the table.

'You came to discover facts, Agent Falconetti, that caused you to question Mr Bantling's guilt, is that true? That he perhaps had been set up?'

'I discovered facts that caused me to question some things, yes.'

'That caused you to believe that Mr Bantling had been set up?'

'Yes, I have wondered,' Dominick finally said, his

voice resigned, his eyes finally giving up the search and casting downward instead.

'Show the court, please, what fact you discovered that led you to question the guilt of Mr Bantling – that led you to believe that he had been set up, as he had alleged all along?' Rose Harris was like a dog with a bone. 'Show the court the evidence you discovered, the evidence that had been withheld in the first trial, that evidence which told you an innocent man had been falsely accused and placed on death row!'

Dominick somberly nodded his head. He looked defeated, as if he wanted to cry himself. He reached down underneath the witness stand, his hands emerging seconds later with a black plastic garbage bag that was sealed with red evidence tape. Using latex gloves and a jagged knife, he slit open the tape and with a pair of evidentiary steel tongs, reached inside. The smiling, white rubber face of a clown emerged from the bag, the tongs holding it at a distance by its fuzzy tufts of red hair, its blood-red twisted smile dangling in front of the jury, twirling and spinning slowly back and forth, posing for every camera. An enormous collective gasp sounded through the crowd.

She could take it no more. C.J. sprang to her feet, screaming. 'He is *not* innocent! He's guilty! He's guilty!'

'Order! Ms Townsend! As an officer of the court you know full well how to behave yourself in front of me. The jury will disregard that outburst!' shouted Judge Chaskel.

C.J. sat back down, her face buried in her hands. She felt the man watching her, smiling at her downfall, wishing he could get a hold of the knife Dominick held in his hands, so he could make some new scars on her body. Maybe borrow the mask back for just an hour or so.

'It was in Ms Townsend's closet. Stuffed in a box at the top with some old Miami Beach police reports,' finished Dominick.

Rose Harris let the shocked murmurs finish their ripple through the crowd. 'Agent Falconetti, is Ms Townsend present in the courtroom today?'

'Yes.'

'Please identify her for the record.'

Dominick raised his head. The clown mask still dangled from the tongs in his left hand. With his other hand, he pointed across the gallery where C.J. sat. The click and whir of cameras filled the air, following his finger. 'That's her. Sitting at the table.'

Rose nodded somberly. 'Let the record reflect that Agent Falconetti has correctly identified the defendant, C. J. Townsend.'

C.J. sat upright with a start in bed, her face drenched in sweat and tears. The silence of the black room screamed in her head and she clutched her chest, trying to control her racing heart. The clock on the dresser read 4:07 a.m. Her hand reached out and she felt Dominick beside her, his back warm, rising and falling with his breathing as he slept.

It's okay. Everything's alright, everything's gonna be fine. It was just a nightmare. It's not real, she told herself, looking around the bedroom, her eyes struggling to see.

But just then, as if on cue, her beeper went off in the darkness on the nightstand beside her.

And that was when the nightmare really began.

2

'Fuck you, you fuckin' cracker-assed pig!' yelled the fat hooker. She still had the rubber tube wrapped around her arm, just above the elbow, from her last fix and it whipped about as she waved her arms in defiance.

'Ain't that special? You kiss your mother with that mouth?' Officer Victor Chavez was in no mood. He was already cutting the bitch a break by not arresting her, and now she had the nerve to actually complain about it. God, sometimes he hated this job. 'Now, you still need to move yourself out of here.'

'Ain't got no right. Jus' makin' some money. You want a blow, Officer? Twenty bucks. Maybe loosen your tight white ass right up,' she cackled.

'I'm gonna count to ten. If you're still here, I'll assume you want to crash at DCJ tonight.' DCJ was the Dade County Jail and the last place he wanted to be on this fine evening. Spending two hours filling out paperwork in that shithouse for some ho' who inevitably would be sprung first thing in the a.m. by an overworked, cranky judge.

'Don't want no jail, master cracker,' she mumbled, her eyes half closed, and she finally stumbled off down the street, narrowly missing a speeding Mustang. A screech of brakes was followed by a horn and a number of loud expletives.

'Kiss my ass!' the hooker yelled back behind her as she wobbled down the block and out of sight.

Chavez watched her teeter off, just as the small radio pack on his shoulder crackled to life. 'Alpha 816. Thirty-eight, thirty-five with a knife in an alleyway at NE 79th Street and Biarritz Drive, behind the Atlantic Cable Company. White male, fifties, gray beard. Complainant advises subject causing a disturbance.'

Thirty-eight was a suspicious person. Thirty-five was a drunk. Put the two together and you have politically correct cop lingo for homeless person. A bottom-feeder call, which of course meant that Victor Chavez would get it.

Victor looked around at the boring mess which was now his daily life. Chasing hookers off the street, nickel and dime junkies back into their holes, homeless people to their next park bench. When he was done doing that, he could expect to pull a husband off of his wife after pummeling her face in, and maybe respond to a car wreck caused by some overindulged idiot trying to find his way home off the Beach. It was barely one in the morning, and he had been on the job for just two hours.

Victor hated midnights. He hated being babysat by the Miami Beach PD's powers-that-be practically every minute of his ten-hour shift. He hated shit patrols and vagrants pissing in the back seat of his car, and he wondered when-oh-when his penance would be paid and the account with his sergeant settled.

Ever since the Cupid case he had been stuck on midnights, denied overtime, and passed over for the prime vacation times. When was it supposed to end? He was almost at *his* end, though, that was for sure. He was going to have to sit down with Sergeant Ribero next week and demand a normal schedule, a normal career. Not this piddly babysitting-the-homeless-and-fruitcake job. That was not what he signed up for when he became a cop almost four years ago. If need be, he would go to the Hialeah PD, where his brother worked. Get a job as a cop and then maybe move up to detective after a few years. Fuck the fun of the Beach. It wasn't fun anymore, anyway.

He clicked back on the shoulder pack to respond. 'Alpha 816. QSL from 20th and Collins.' The literal translation for QSL was 'I receive,' though in Victor's case, it always meant 'Shit rolls downhill and I'm at the bottom.'

No more. He could take no more. He actually had not even fucked up the Cupid case, when you thought about it. He had been the one to *stop* the son of a bitch as he tore over the McArthur Causeway with a dead girl in his trunk. Just one of the eleven women that the psycho had carved up. But in the eyes of his sergeant and the bitchy prosecutor, a carved-up dead body in a trunk meant shit. The stop – *his stop* – was 'bad,' and he had spent three long years trying to make amends. Well, no more.

Victor Chavez climbed into his squad car, happy he'd come to this decision. Happy to think that maybe, in a month or so, he would actually begin to *like* this job again. *Let the chips fall where they may*, he thought. Then he activated his blue lights and headed over to 79th and Biarritz to rustle some poor guy from the alley he probably called home.

3

Even though the man in the shadows could not see it, he thought that if he listened hard enough, he could actually *hear* the partiers over on Ocean Drive, just a few short miles down the road. The collective charged murmur of hundreds of voices floating on the hot, humid air, the clatter of dozens of outdoor restaurants, the loud thumping of heavy bass music escaping the bars and clubs, and, of course, the irritating beeps and revved-up engines from the Porsches, Benzes, and Bentleys that lined Ocean and Washington searching for the impossible on a Friday night – a place to park.

Just because you can't see something, doesn't mean it's not there.

Miami Beach, where anything goes and the rich and famous – and not-so-famous – come to play. And, of course, be noticed. The beautiful girls with their fake breasts and tight low, low-cut shirts and warm brown tans, *sans* those annoying tan lines, naturally. The beautiful boys, their hard, sculpted bodies decked out in Lycra, leather, snakeskin, spandex. They all mixed and mingled, drinking Cosmopolitans and Chocolate Martinis or chic tropical drinks like Mojitos. The exciting sexual energy that hangs in the heavy air is almost palpable.

He closed his eyes for a moment and simply listened.

Just a few miles away from all the decadence, here he was in this rotting shithole. The floor of the alley was littered with trash and garbage, old beer cans and liquor bottles, discarded condoms and empty fast-food bags.

Most of the streetlights had been broken out long ago, and the city just never bothered fixing them, because this was not the end of town where tourists spent their money. The alley was a refuge for drunks and dopers. Though, right now, it was empty. The Miami Beach cops had already made a pass through, shooing away the homeless and the undesirables.

Just because you can't see something, doesn't mean it's not there.

He heard the sound before he saw the car. The crunching of tires on cement, as they rolled slowly over glass and garbage. The purr of the engine followed by the squeal of a car door. The squawk of a radio and the slam of the door, and then footsteps falling heavy on cement. The sound echoed down the alley and off the walls of the closed businesses that surrounded it, sounding larger than life. But the footsteps quickly faded in the distance as the person turned and walked in the other direction, ignoring the alley and what lay in wait.

His heart raced with excitement and he breathed in the very scent of the night. The humid air filled his lungs, the oxygen pulsing through his bloodstream, rushing to invigorate his mind. He waited patiently until the footsteps disappeared before he unwrapped himself from the shadows. He was careful as he came upon the car, his silent footsteps deftly maneuvering past the rusty cans and broken bottles. Inside his jacket, his latexed fingers found the blade and he fingered it lightly and smiled. Electric blue and red lights danced silently off the walls of the alley in an almost mesmerizing sequence.

Let the games begin.

4

'Alpha 816,' Victor said into his shoulder pack, as he looked around the deserted alley in disgust. 'I am at the location of 79th and Biarritz, responding to a thirty-eight, but there's no one on scene.'

'Alpha 816. Location was Atlantic Cable Company. NE 79th Street and Biarritz Drive. White male with a knife; request for a unit to respond.' The crackling static of the dispatcher's voice filled the alley, but then just as quickly dissipated when he hit the button to respond, reminding him that he was alone.

'Alpha 816,' he said, 'there's no one here. I've also checked the parking facility and both businesses at that location, but they are also clear. The scene is secure.'

'Alpha 816. Will advise,' dispatch responded.

'Alpha 816. I'll be at twelve then.' It was 1:30 in the morning, and 'twelve' meant that it was time for a dinner break. A nice, greasy burger to help him get through the rest of this shitty night was in order. Tomorrow was his day off – he'd just work it off with a few extra sets at the gym.

'Alpha 816. I'll have you at twelve until 0230,' dispatch crackled back.

The radio went silent and he was alone again. He headed back to his squad car, thinking maybe he'd head back down to SoBe and The Diner on 11th and Washington for a bite. Maybe get a good look at the *mamis* while he

11

ate. Watch as they sauntered into Mynt from their limos in leopard-print catsuits and leather minis.

He opened the car door and sat inside. He had left the car running while he walked through the mess in the alley, so that the AC would keep the car cool. Though it was November, the temperatures were still in the 80s; the humidity at 90 percent. It was enough to make even a nice Cuban boy like himself gasp for drier air.

In September, MBPD Chief Jordan had ordered new-fangled laptops be installed in all marked Beach cruisers – a sign of how progressive the department was. Never mind that the Florida Highway Patrol and the Miami Dade PD had both had them for more than two years. They were supposed to speed things up – tag searches, drivers' license searches, BOLOs (be on the lookout), wanteds, report writing, obtaining interstate criminal information and FCIC criminal warrants. The laptops scanned, e-mailed and had internet access to everything, including CJNet – the Criminal Justice Network. Broad-reaching technology that provided, in Victor's opinion, the ability to retrieve almost too much information, and hence – when someone like himself fucked up and missed something – the perfect excuse for an ass-reaming by a member of the brass for not looking hard enough in the first place.

He hit the button on the pad to write yet another useless report on what he had *not* found in the alley and the MBPD badge screensaver disappeared. When he read the words that stared back at him in bold-faced capital letters, glowing white in the darkness of his squad car, he was at first puzzled. Within a moment, though, they became all too clear to him. But by then it was just too late.

5

HELLO VICTOR. LOOK BEHIND YOU.

The back of Victor's close-shaved head and his thick olive neck were meaty targets in the white glow from the computer screen. The piece of plexiglas that separated the front seat from the back seat slipped quietly to the floor, and his latexed hand slid out. Victor stared quizzically at the screen, the wheels in his mind turning slowly. Like a boa constrictor, the man wrapped his hand deftly around the left side of Victor's head, until it came under his chin. Then he yanked back hard and quick, just as Victor turned his face away from the laptop to see what, if anything, lurked behind him.

Victor's head slammed back, pinned fast against the seat. Then the man wrapped his arm around Victor's throat, pulling him up and his head back through the cut plexiglas. The knife sliced through the back of Victor's uniform, but did not cut him. Instead, it pinned his shirt to the back of the vinyl seat, so that Victor's head hung off the neck rest, his face staring up at the roll bar on the roof of the car, his throat exposed. Victor's body jerked about, and instinctively, his hand went for his gun, snapped in a holster to his right side, but the man in the back seat had already anticipated that. While one hand squeezed Victor's larynx closed, the other reached down past him to the SIG-Sauer P-226 at his side. Within seconds, the gun was his, and Victor's one hand flailed uselessly in search of it, as his other desperately tried to pry the fingers from his throat. His legs began to shake and kick out, and the horn beeped loudly when his foot hit it. The laptop toppled off the stand to the floor of the squad car. He writhed violently, trying to free himself from the seat, but the angle was awkward and the knife held him fast.

Then the muzzle of the SIG-Sauer pressed hard against Victor's right temple, and the latexed hand slowly released his throat.

'Shhh,' he whispered.

The heavy weight of cold metal against Victor's head instantly stopped the struggle. He listened to Victor's frantic panting, and could almost hear the thought as it sprang from Victor's head.

'You won't make it. I'll blow your head off before your leg is even halfway to the seat.' He knew all about the surprise Victor had strapped to his left ankle. Victor's scared eyes darted furiously about, but he could not see the face behind him.

The police radio next to the officer's head squawked to life. 'Alpha 922, Alpha 459. 1530 Collins. Forty-one down. Possible three thirty-two. Black male unresponsive on the side of the road. Fire rescue responding.' The radio crackled with assorted responses from other units in police jargon. Units that were, at that very moment, racing across the Beach to the scene of the emergency. Unfortunately for Victor, it just wasn't *his* emergency.

'What . . . do . . . you want?' Victor stammered. His voice was choked, and the man knew that big, bad Victor was about to cry.

'Don't cry just yet, Victor. We've got some things to discuss first.' Behind the seat, the man pulled out another

14

knife from underneath his jacket. This one was special. He brought it around the left side of Victor's head to where Victor could see it now.

Victor Chavez's eyes grew wide with fear. He felt the wet warmth of his own piss spread across the front of his pants. He kicked his legs out again furiously, uselessly.

'Okay, Victor,' the man said and smiled. 'Now open wide.'

6

The sound of her beeper startled her and C.J. groped at the nightstand beside her in the darkness to find it and quickly silence it.

'Is that you?' murmured Dominick groggily in the darkness. He nudged her gently as he rolled over, facing her, his eyes still closed.

'Sorry it woke you. I've got it,' C.J. said softly, her fingers finally finding the beeper and pressing the button to turn it off.

'Are you on duty this week?' he murmured, his arm reaching out under the covers for her.

But she pulled away and swung her legs out of bed, pulling her hair, still damp with perspiration from the nightmare, back off her face. She didn't want him to know she'd had another. 'That's me. I'm the lucky winner.'

Beeper duty, as it was called, was part of her job, assisting police officers after 5:00 p.m. with questions about probable cause, searches, warrants, and arrests. It was the policy of the State Attorney, Jerry Tigler, that prosecutors be available 24/7 to help cops with their cases, particularly since – unlike District Attorney's offices and complaint rooms in other major metropolitan cities, which operated around the clock with prosecutors handling complaints – the Miami SAO shut down pretty much at five. So the county was divided up logistically into two response regions – north and south – and every one of the 240 felony prosecutors in the office saw week-long felony beeper duty more than a few times a year.

The office's A, B and C prosecutors, those assigned to trial divisions and responsible for prosecuting first-, second- and third-degree felonies, handled the more generic felony questions: *Do I need a warrant to search this guy's house if his wife lets me in? Do I need to tell the parents of a juvenile that I'm questioning their delinquent son about a robbery I know he committed last year? Can I search a car if I think the driver's got a 357 under the seat?* Some questions were more basic than others, some more involved. The tricky ones were when a cop regurgitated a series of facts and events, and then asked the sleepy-eyed prosecutor if he had enough probable cause to make an arrest. Tricky, because probable cause – an elusive and difficult-to-quantify amount of facts needed to justify the arrest of a person – was a cop's decision to make on a scene, not a prosecutor's. Was it more probable than not that a crime was committed and that this is the guy who committed it? Tricky, because officers, on occasion, were known to stretch the facts to fit the crime. Or, alternately, to delete a few crucial ones.

The prosecutor's legal function was to come in *after* an arrest was made and prosecute the offender. To allow each office to operate without the constant threat of being sued, the Florida legislature conferred qualified immunity on the police for their discretionary actions in policing, and to the State Attorney's Office and individual prosecutors for their discretionary actions in prosecuting. But the two were not interchangeable, and Tigler's office policy often forced a prosecutor to walk that fine, treacherous line between giving out friendly advice at three in the morning and actually playing cop.

Specialized crimes were handled by specialized prosecutors, which required specialized beepers. Sexual batteries were responded to by Sex Bat prosecutors; felony domestic violence crimes by DVU prosecutors; major drug cases by Narcotics prosecutors; major fraud questions by Economic Crimes (ECU) prosecutors; and all homicides were rotated between the office's Division Chiefs and the senior trial attorneys in Major Crimes. And the media cases, the O. J. Simpsons in their white Broncos – those readily apparent to even a rookie five minutes out of the academy as a mess just waiting to happen – were handled exclusively by Major Crimes. The elite ten prosecutors assigned to Major Crimes handled a smaller caseload compared to other prosecutors and Division Chiefs, but they were the most sensational of homicide cases, their facts horrific and brutal, their issues complex and involved. Most, if not all, of their defendants faced death as their ultimate penalty, either by lethal injection or electric chair. C.J. had been with the office twelve years, assigned to Major Crimes for the past seven.

No one ever had a major fraud question at three in the morning, but there certainly were enough homicides in the city to consistently chime a homicide beeper in the middle of the night. And another Jerry Tigler policy was that every homicide had to be responded to on the scene. So when the beeper went off, you knew you were not just getting up – you were going out. As a Major Crimes prosecutor, C.J. saw homicide beeper duty at least once every eight weeks, and as the Assistant Division Chief of Major Crimes, she was assigned to permanent beeper duty for all police shootings and use-of-force cases. An added bonus. Thoughts of a transfer to ECU often drifted into her head after a 3:00 a.m. beep.

'Uh-oh. You better stay down and cover your eyes,' she said before flicking on the light switch. Dominick groaned and pulled a pillow over his head.

As she dialed the number, he asked, 'What are you on? Homicide duty?'

'Both this week,' she replied as the phone rang in her ear. 'Go back to sleep. I'll probably have to go to the scene, whatever it is.'

The line picked up in her ear and a male voice answered, 'Nicholsby.'

She recognized the name. Miami Beach Homicide. 'Detective, this is ASA C. J. Townsend. I just received a beep —'

'Yeah, yeah, Ms Townsend. I just called Criminal Intake. They said you're the prosecutor handling homicides tonight. You're Major Crimes, right?' The detective's voice sounded more anxious than she expected, given that a dead body at four in the morning was nothing unusual for a homicide detective. C.J. had learned that pretty much nothing fazed most homicide detectives. In fact, they usually liked to have a little fun with the more squeamish prosecutors in the office, loading up on the grisly details of their cases right before sitting down to lunch.

'Yes, that's right, Detective,' she replied. 'I'm on homicide and also on police shooting duty. What have you got, a homicide or a police shooting?'

'Well, it's a homicide.' He hesitated slightly. 'But this one's a little more than that.'

'Is it a multiple?'

'Nope. Just one – but it's . . . well, it's pretty bad.' In the background she heard the continued high-pitched sounds of multiple police sirens approaching. From the number responding, it sounded like a pretty big scene. She heard Nicholsby suck in a deep drag on his cigarette before continuing. 'I've got a dead cop down here on the Beach, Ms Townsend, and he's one helluva mess.'

7

'Shit,' she said softly, her fingers massaging her temples, rubbing away the headache which she knew was about to come on. She gently rubbed Dominick's back. 'I've got to go, hon.'

Dominick Falconetti could immediately tell by the change in her voice that the news was not good. He unburied his head from under the pillow. 'What is it? What's happened?'

She looked at him. His chestnut eyes squinted up at her in the harsh bedroom light, his salty brown hair tousled on the top of his head. She shook her head. 'It's a cop,' she said quietly.

'A shooting? Where? What department?'

'No, not a police shooting.' She took a breath. She knew this would be hard for him. It was always hard on a cop to hear that one of their own just took one for the team. They took it personal, even if they didn't know the guy. 'It's a homicide, Dom. On duty. I'm sorry. I don't know anything else, not even an ID.'

Dominick sat upright in bed. 'Holy shit. A cop? What the hell – how? Where?'

'That was Nicholsby with the Beach,' she said, up and moving now toward the closet. 'He didn't say how, he just said to get down there.' She emerged from the walk-in, a pair of tan pants in hand, buttoning a cream silk blouse.

Dominick rubbed the sleep from his eyes and ran his

hands through the top of his hair. 'I'll come with you. Just let me get dressed,' he said, watching as she pulled on her pants, then sat on the bench at the foot of the bed to put on her shoes.

'Now why would you come with me? Beach Homicide is there. They'll handle it.'

'Because a dead cop means FDLE will probably be called out to assist anyway. Because it's four in the morning and you're headed to what I'll bet is a real crappy part of the Beach.' He paused for a moment. 'Because I don't want you to go alone at this hour.'

She stopped putting on her shoes and smiled at him across the foot of the bed. 'Thanks, but an escort's not necessary, Prince Charming. I can handle myself. Besides, there will probably be about a hundred other Glocks attached to blue uniforms swarming all over that crappy part of the beach. It sounded like a pretty big scene. Sleep. Maybe the call won't come and you can actually get eight hours tonight.' She headed into the bathroom to brush her teeth.

He knew it was useless to argue with her. C.J. was an independent and headstrong woman. And even though plenty of things had happened in her life that could spook her from being alone at four in the morning, he knew she would do what needed to get done, silently bulldozing aside any fear she might encounter along the way. They had been together for three years, and remarkably, he found her to be stronger now than when they had first met. In his years in law enforcement, he had seen many a victim get swallowed up by their crime, too paralyzed by fear to even open their doors, to live their lives, always mistaking the backfire of a car for the blast of a shotgun and ducking for cover. But not C.J. It was as if she challenged her fears to defy her every day, not just by walking out the door, but by then driving herself to a job where she would surround herself with the worst criminals society had to offer up, taking on more cases, more tragedy. Like a parachute jumper who has had a bad accident when the chute doesn't open, instead of walking away from the sport, C.J. simply jumped from a higher altitude each time.

'A dead cop, huh? Jesus! The Beach must be a zoo. And Nicholsby didn't say who or how?'

'No. He was very tight-lipped. And he sounded pretty anxious, though, so I'd better go.' She leaned over him on the bed. Their lips touched, a soft, lingering kiss. Hers were cool and she tasted minty. His hand wrapped around the back of her neck, his fingers lost in her dark-blonde hair, pulling her closer to him. The other gently touched her face, his thumb lightly rubbing her cheek. He still missed her whenever she left. He still worried whenever she left.

'I'm sorry,' she said softly in his ear. 'I'll call you when I know more.' She rose to leave. 'It's Saturday. I'll pick up bagels on my way home.'

'Be careful, please. Call me when you get there, and stay on 95.' I95 was an interstate that carried Fort Lauderdale to Miami, a thirty-mile trip. Many a bad thing had been known to happen to those who ventured off the wrong exit, lost in the middle of the night.

'Yes, Dad,' she said lightly, heading for the bedroom door. 'Go back to sleep. Tell me what it feels like over breakfast. And don't forget to let out Lucy.' Lucy was her deaf basset hound, who, at the moment, was curled into a very tight brown ball right next to Dominick, where C.J. had been not five minutes earlier. She patted

Lucy's head. 'Opportunity knocked, huh, Lucy girl? The bed never even got cold.'

'Where exactly are you going, anyway?'

'Some alley off of 79th Street.' She blew a soft kiss at him. 'Love you,' she whispered. 'See you soon.'

The bedroom door closed softly behind her and then she was gone.

8

Dominick threw the covers aside and gently slid Lucy's snoring, curled-up body to the inside of the bed. C.J.'s ancient fat cat, Tibby, jumped up and sprawled out next to her. He pulled on his shirt and rose to get dressed and make some coffee. Sleep would not come again tonight. It was simply a matter of time before his own cellphone rang with the news.

A dead cop. Jesus Christ! *One of his own.*

He felt incredibly angry. Angry and outraged and inexplicably sad all at the same time. Even though he had no idea who this cop was or how he had died – hell, chances were he probably didn't even know the guy, there were that many cops in Miami – but still . . . *one of his own had lost the battle.* In the kitchen's bright track lights, he shook his head in disgust while he waited for the coffee to finish brewing.

There existed a unique camaraderie among law enforcement officers. As early as a rookie's first week in the police academy, the groundwork for the 'us against them' mentality was already carefully being laid by highly experienced, and therefore, highly pessimistic sergeants and lieutenants. Field Training Officers – FTOs – and fellow cadets became a rookie's only friends for a grueling and intense nine months, and the academy's maxim was 'prepare for the worst.' And so you do. You shoot at moving paper bad guys every day and are instructed to call for back-up if you have to as much as sneeze in a bad hood. You practice raids on mopes' houses where, inevitably, a few innocent hostages are sure to be found inside, and no paper target escapes without coming under heavy fire. Then, after dropping thirty rounds of ammunition and being beaten blue by the Redman in Defensive Tactics, you cap off the day having a few beers with the boys. Your life revolves around the job: You eat, sleep, breathe and socialize with other cops. You speak cop, 24/7, and your trained cop eyes now see bad shit everywhere, just waiting to happen. And no one knows you better than your partner. Death defied on your behalf by someone not even related to you breeds unwavering and unconditional loyalty to the men wearing the blue jacket. When one fell, every cop felt the hit, somewhere deep inside.

As a cop who originally launched his own career assigned to the crappiest house in the South Bronx, Dominick had felt that hit too many times. And, unfortunately, he had seen too many jackets fall with his own eyes.

He had moved up to detective within twelve months. Homicide in another six, but they still wouldn't let him out of the Bronx, no matter how many asses he kissed. He was good at what he did, finding answers. Probably too good. But after a few years, the bad guys all started to look the same, even when they weren't bad, and he knew it was time to go. On a cold, rainy, and particularly miserable New York day, he had pulled out his US map, closed his eyes and hoped his finger fell somewhere where even the criminals wore short-sleeved shirts. It landed on Miami – a bustling, metropolitan city, but with a more exotic and tropical flair. He'd gotten several offers with large departments – Miami-Dade PD, the City of

Miami PD, Miami Beach PD, Broward Sheriff's Office – but as a Special Agent with the Florida Department of Law Enforcement he would be doing more than just changing the scenery. He would be refocusing his career. At least that's what the FDLE Commissioner had told him sixteen years ago when he had offered Dominick a job as a Special Agent.

Florida's equivalent to the FBI, FDLE used highly specialized and experienced agents to work major state-wide investigations – those that crossed police department and county jurisdictions – and to assist both the feds and the locals with their more involved cases. State resources provided cutting-edge crime labs in each of the department's five regions, easily equaling the FBI's at Quantico. They were not a primary response agency, but rather an investigative agency, which promised Dominick no more midnight search warrants. Of course, that was the sales pitch. Then the Regional Director at the FDLE Miami Regional Operations Center took one look at Dominick's resume and promptly assigned him to the Violent Crime Squad, working homicide investigations. And although that didn't necessarily mean working vampire's hours every night, it also didn't mean leaving with the Fraud Squad and the five o'clock whistle.

The coffee pot chortled to a stop and the rich aroma filled the air. Lucy meandered out of the bedroom, sniffing for a handout. Dominick poured himself a cup and tossed Lucy a Pupperoni stick. She let out a happy howl and lay down, nibbling the treat at his feet.

The job had its dangers. Every cop knew that, accepted it. They put on the vest at the start of every shift – a cumbersome and constant reminder of the potential perils. The problem was, no cop ever really thought his badge would be the next number called to the frontlines. His number forever 10-7'd out of service on the radio by a somber Chief, a bugler playing *Taps* in the background. When the bullet came, Dominick supposed, even for a cop it was a total surprise.

Lucy followed him out to the balcony, curling up again at his feet while he leaned on the railing and somberly sipped his coffee. The black waters of the Intercoastal churned twelve stories below him, gently lapping against the seawall. A light breeze blew, tinkling the wind chimes. It was beginning to cool off, you could feel it now, just barely, in the air. Winter was almost here. Time for crowded beaches and traffic and two-hour waits at restaurants. He could almost hear the simultaneous mad squeal of tires as the snowbirds peeled out of their icy driveways up north and headed down to the Sunshine State.

Across the Intercoastal, behind the many condos and cheap hotels and high-rises that dotted Pompano Beach and Fort Lauderdale, slivers of pink and orange would soon begin to slice across the dark sky. Another magnificent Florida sunrise was just ahead.

Dominick sipped at his coffee and just waited for the phone to ring.

9

At four in the morning, the thirty-mile trip to Miami Beach took just a little over twenty minutes, though in rush hour it could take days. C.J. exited 95 at 79th Street and drove through the dark fringes of Liberty City, where many of the modest homes and businesses wore heavy iron bars on their doors and windows. Even at this hour, a couple of brightly lit pawn shops remained open and she spotted a few faceless figures still working the shadows. A few miles down, 79th turned into the John F. Kennedy Causeway, and quiet North Bay Village, before finally carrying her over the black waters of Biscayne Bay and onto the middle of Miami Beach.

As she came over the causeway, she immediately saw the flashing blue and red lights, converged on what looked to be at least a two-block radius behind a closed Chevron station. *This must be pretty bad.* In her twelve years with the office, twenty cops had been killed in the line of duty in Miami. And the intense reaction that followed was always the same: *No one will rest until someone has paid.* That included uniforms, detectives and prosecutors, from every house in every department in every jurisdiction. Official commands became personal vendettas.

She found a spot behind an empty, flashing cruiser in the gas station parking lot, and headed into the crowd of uniforms that sat up ahead. Miami Beach PD, and Metro-Dade PD were on scene, and C.J. spotted a few

Florida Highway Patrol cruisers as well. Behind the station was a large empty field surrounded by a six-foot chain link fence. Past the field, yellow crime scene tape was being strung around the back of a closed AC business, cordoning off the alley that sat behind it.

The jabber and squawk of dozens of police radios crackled around her. She approached a circle of MBPD cops, who were chatting among themselves at the edge of the field. The first string.

She flashed her badge. 'Anyone know where I can find Nicholsby, Beach Homicide? I'm with the State.'

The circle silently parted, allowing her to pass through. A small unnamed street ran beside the AC business, running perpendicular to the alley. C.J. could see an MBPD cruiser parked up in the alley, its blue and red lights silently spinning atop the car. They bounced off a high wooden fence that ran behind the back doors of the AC shop and the Atlantic Cable Company next door. Flanking the other side of the alley, behind barbwire-topped chain link fencing were three huge satellites and a reception tower, that belonged to the cable company.

One young cop nodded grimly behind him. 'That's Nicholsby over by the car, talking with Crime Scene.'

'Thanks.' At the lip of the alley on the other side of the yellow tape, stood two investigators in blue wind-breakers, 'Crime Scene' written across their backs in bold fluorescent yellow lettering. Between the two, a middle-aged detective in a polo shirt and khakis puffed away on a cigarette. In his early fifties, with sagging eyes and sagging shoulders, he looked like he needed a drink.

C.J. extended her hand. 'Detective Nicholsby? C. J. Townsend. State Attorney's Office.'

'Townsend. You got here quick.'

'What's going on?' She looked to the cruiser.

''Bout four this morning, somebody called in about a cop maybe sleeping in his car. Dispatch sends out a uniform, this rookie, Schrader. He opens the front door to wake the guy, and . . .' Nicholsby's voice trailed off. 'Crime Scene's photo'd outside, but we're waiting for the ME. He lives up in Coral Springs someplace.'

The cruiser sat just in the lip of the alley. The driver's door was open only slightly, and the edge of a white sheet spilled out. The windows appeared strangely opaque. Even the windshield.

'What's with the windows?' she asked. 'Is that tint?'

'They've been painted.'

'Painted? With what?'

'Blood. The sick fuck painted the inside of the car with the poor guy's own blood. That's why no one called it in at first. They couldn't even see in the car. Maybe thought the cop was on a snooze break and had left his lights on, put on a cover so no one could bust up his nap.'

'Listen,' Nicholsby said, grabbing her softly by her arm and spinning her attention away from the car and onto his face. His eyes were dark, intense. He almost looked frightened. 'This is bad, Ms Townsend.'

'I've seen bad before, Detective,' she said, shrugging back slightly from his touch.

'No,' he said, not yet letting go of her, 'I mean this is *really* bad. The worst I've ever seen and I've seen a lot. A few of my guys have not yet recovered.' He looked away from her and nodded behind him. A young cop in a Beach uniform was throwing up into the bushes that dotted the edge of the field. 'Probably going to have to visit the department shrink over this one.'

She pulled away from his touch and stared him straight in the eye. 'Thanks for the warning, Detective. I'll be fine.'

'Okay,' he shrugged, finally releasing her arm. 'Be my guest. The ME should be here any minute.'

'Who is the cop? Do we have an ID yet?'

'No. There was a mix-up with the sign-out on the cruisers tonight. Car 8354 was supposed to go with Gilroy, Vincent Gilroy. But that ain't him.'

'What about his badge?'

'Gone. So was his name badge on his uniform. Bastard cut it right off him.'

'And no one here knows him?'

'There are close to four hundred cops at the Miami Beach PD. Do you know them all? Besides, this guy's own mother would have trouble recognizing him now. The only way we knew it wasn't Gilroy is that Gilroy's blond.'

She started toward the cruiser. It was impossible to see inside the windows. Only that one piece of white sheet that crept out the bottom of the door told her of the grisly contents she would find inside. She pulled on the latex gloves that Nicholsby had handed her and slowly reached for the handle, covered in black soot.

'They've dusted for prints,' she called out behind her.

'Yeah, but only on the outside so far. So don't touch nothing inside, please.'

Slowly she pulled open the door and the rest of the white sheet, stained red, tumbled out at her feet, like a carpet.

Her latexed fingers hesitated for just a second and then pulled back the sheet that covered the figure in the front seat. She exhaled a quick breath and then covered her mouth with her hands, spinning herself away from the car, away from the horror that sat before her, chained with his own handcuffs to the steering wheel.

'Jesus Christ!' she exclaimed, panting, her fingers draped across her mouth.

'I told you it was bad,' said Nicholsby.

'No, no,' she murmured, her voice low, almost a whisper, speaking to herself, as much as to him.

A voice from the parking lot of cop cars called out just then. He was running toward them, a white piece of paper in hand. 'Detective! We've got an ID. We heard from the property clerk who assigned the cars tonight. He just got home from some bar. Looks like dispatch inverted the numbers on the car assignments by mistake on the paperwork. Gilroy was supposed to have 8354, but he's got 8534.'

'So who's supposed to have 8354?'

Before the uniform could respond, C.J. spoke. Her voice was weak, shocked with disbelief. 'Chavez,' she said quietly. 'I know who he is. Victor Chavez.'

IO

Her mind struggled to make sense of the frenzied thoughts and images that now rushed her brain. She was not prepared to handle seeing a dead cop, not savagely violated and in this condition. And she was certainly not prepared to handle seeing one she had worked closely with at one time. One who was more than just your average patrolman . . .

Victor Chavez's body sat upright in the blood-soaked driver's seat, his head slumped against the steering wheel. The engine had been turned off, the body left to swelter inside the car. Approaching full rigor mortis now, his handcuffed hands still held the wheel fast, so hard the knuckles were white. What remained of his face had been turned to the side, presumably by Schrader, the cop that had found him, and his terrified brown eyes now stared out the driver's side window at nothing. It was those eyes that C.J. had recognized instantly. 'Lyin' eyes,' she had once called them, pools of soft brown that spoke volumes more than his words ever did.

Now they gaped at her, the horror of the last few moments of his short life forever captured there. It was easy to see why others would have difficulty recognizing him. From the nose down he had been torn apart. The radio pack on his shoulder crackled with the dispatcher's voice, who, ironically, was at that very moment dispatching additional units to Victor's own homicide scene.

C.J. had moved away from the cruiser and back

behind the crime scene tape. She sat on the bumper of Nicholsby's unmarked Taurus and slowly sipped at the bottled water she'd finally accepted, hoping the wave of nausea she was experiencing would soon pass. A hand fell softly on her shoulder. It was Marlon Dorsett, another homicide detective with Miami Beach. C.J. had worked several murder investigations with Marlon over the years and knew he was one of the best. He smiled a mouthful of white teeth. 'C.J.? Lieutenant told me you were the on-call. I was wondering when you'd show.'

'Me?' C.J. smiled weakly. 'I've been here since the party started. I even beat the band.' She nodded in the direction of the cruiser. The ME had finally arrived and, at that moment, was measuring the very deep cut that sliced across Victor Chavez's throat with a fluorescent orange tape measure, while crime scene techs waited anxiously in the wings. When the ME was done they would descend on the car like hungry vultures, dissecting the cruiser down to its frame. 'How're you doing, Marlon?'

'Me? Not so bad. Wife is good, kids are a pain in the ass, job sucks. But, enough. I sound like every other guy in America.' He paused for a moment and shook his head somberly. 'This is a mess. Can you believe this shit? To go out this way?' He nodded at the bottle of water in her hand, acknowledging it. 'You don't look so good, C.J. Are you okay with all this?'

'Yeah, yeah. I just knew him, Chavez, from a case he worked. It surprised me, I guess.'

Marlon nodded and looked around. 'It's a shock for everyone. How's Dom doing? Is he here?'

Before C.J. could answer, Nicholsby finished up the very heated conversation he was having with his Nextel, the two-way cellphone/walkie-talkie radio. He turned both his attention and his mounting anger on Detective Dorsett.

'This is such bullshit. Dispatch has Chavez at this location for a thirty-eight at 0130. He cleared the scene and went twelve. That's the last communication with him we have. And no one thinks to tell us that very fucking important fact for thirty goddamn minutes while we try to work an ID?' He looked toward the car door, which was open wide. 'He's in rigor now, so we know he's been dead for at least a couple of hours. That pretty much makes our perimeter useless —'

'Unless the fuck hung around to watch the response,' Marlon cut in.

Nicholsby looked around him at the sea of blue uniforms. 'Not likely. At this time in the morning we're not attracting much of a crowd.'

'Witnesses?' C.J. asked.

'Nobody,' grunted Nicholsby.

'What was the thirty-eight he was called in on?' she asked.

'Homeless guy. No description. Waving a weapon. That's it. I'm getting the tape as we speak.' Nicholsby lit a cigarette and blew out a frustrated sigh.

'Who was the caller?' C.J. asked.

'Don't know. Didn't leave a name.'

'They never do. Nobody ever wants to get involved,' said Marlon. He paused for a moment before adding quietly, 'Unless it was a set-up.'

'What?' asked C.J.

Nicholsby nodded. 'That's what we're gonna look at. This guy, Chavez, from the shit I've just been hearing, was not short of enemies. The cage in his car was cut, and it looks like he got it from behind. So we've got to look at this from all directions. But right now, I'm hoping Mr Badass fucked up and left me his calling card in that car. A print, a hair, his cum for all I care. Anything. It would certainly make my life easier. I've got guys all over the Beach asking questions.'

'The County is in,' said Marlon. 'And the City.' The County was the Miami-Dade Police Department. The City was the City of Miami Police Department. 'Chief Jordan spoke with command at the City. Dees says he'll send the whole fucking Homicide Squad if we need it.'

'Everyone's phone's been ringing,' said Nicholsby. 'I got a call five minutes ago from Tallahassee, asking if they could help out. The Governor just got word. Everyone has been pulled out of bed and trees will start shaking before the sun comes up. I'm having Costidas pull me every perp who's ever been busted on the Beach. Every junkie, hooker, doper, gang-banger. Everyone and anything. We'll start with that.'

'Somebody will talk. It's just a matter of time,' Marlon said with a deep sigh. 'We'll get him.'

'Or them.' Nicholsby grunted again, then stomped out his cigarette.

All three sat in tense silence, watching as investigators with the Medical Examiner's Office pried Victor's stiff body out of the front seat of his patrol car. The body was rapidly approaching full rigor, and the muscles had frozen in the exact position they were in when he was killed. It would be another twelve to twenty-four hours before the rigor cycle would be complete and the muscles would relax and again become moveable. Now, draped under the cover of a white sheet, Victor's frozen, contorted body looked macabre as ME investigators carried it to a waiting gurney.

C.J. watched as the body was loaded into the van. The emerald-green tag that the Medical Examiner had placed on Victor's big toe peeked out slightly from under the white sheet, swaying gently back and forth. The technicians then covered him with a black body bag, zipped it closed, and the toe disappeared. 'I saw what was done to his face,' she said slowly, not really wanting to confirm her more irrational thoughts just yet, but finding herself asking the question just the same. 'What do you think that was about?'

'Well,' began Marlon, 'the slice across his neck that pretty much took his head off? That? That was to kill him. But the removal of his tongue? We're figuring that one was a message.'

'*That* was to shut him up,' finished Nicholsby as he fished the last cigarette out of his pack of Newports.

Then the back door to the Miami-Dade County Medical Examiner's van slammed shut, and the crowd of silent, flashing cruisers somberly parted to let it go by.

The overripe smell of death permeates even the best of fabrics, and no detergent or bleach or dry-cleaning fluid can rid clothing of the scent; just as nothing can remove the odor, once experienced, from a person's memory banks. Perhaps it was simply a psychosomatic reaction – a phantom smell that forever attached itself to a certain image. Whatever the case, C.J. knew from experience better than to even try to get rid of it, so she dropped the plastic bag that contained her tan pants and cream silk blouse down the twelfth-floor garbage chute and padded down the hall back to her apartment.

Fortunately, soap, water, and some serious elbow grease – as her father would call it – worked well enough to at least remove the offensive scent from skin. Of course, C.J. was pretty sure that that was not quite the scenario her dad probably ever envisioned when he passed down his words of wisdom to her as a kid, calling down from the front porch of their house while she scrubbed windows during his annual spring-cleaning frenzy, which consumed at least three of her Saturdays each May. The thought reminded her that she had forgotten to call her mom back yesterday and she made a mental note to drop them both a line. She'd have to tell her dad that she was thinking of his spring scrub fests. She'd just delete the why part.

The note from Dominick sat on the counter and she stared at it blankly for just a moment. The FDLE

Regional Director had called, and just as Dominick had predicted, everyone was being brought in on this one. The Cop Killer. She and Dominick had probably passed each other on I95. He, heading straight for the frontlines just as she finally made it back home, the bag of bagels she had promised in hand. She wished he were here.

The *Sun Sentinel* sat on top of the breakfast bar. Conspicuously absent from the headlines was the news everyone would soon be talking about, having just missed press time. She moved to the kitchen table and poured herself a mug of freshly brewed coffee. Homicide scenes were never easy, but this one rattled her somewhere deep down inside. And not just because tonight's victim was a cop, or because she had known him in passing from some case they had worked, as she had told Marlon.

Alone with her thoughts now, the apartment seemed uncomfortably quiet. She picked up the phone to call her parents, but then just as quickly put it back down. It wasn't even seven yet in California. She'd have to wait at least an hour or so.

Victor Chavez. The cocky rookie cop who had arrested the most notorious serial killer in modern American history. A killer so ferocious as to have earned him the macabre nickname Cupid. For eighteen months beginning in the spring of 1999, he had hunted the beautiful women that frequented SoBe's trendy nightspots. All of them young and exquisitely beautiful. All of them blonde. And all of them now long dead, their hearts methodically torn from their chests by a savage madman.

A routine traffic stop by Victor Chavez had ended the terror spree, and had finally put a name and a face on a killer: William Rupert Bantling. A successful businessman, with ice-blue eyes and chiseled good looks, to many

Bantling did not look the part of a madman. But the cold, stiff corpse that he carried in his trunk told a different story. A 22-year-old aspiring model, Anna Prado was young, blonde, exceptionally beautiful and conspicuously missing a heart when MBPD Officer Chavez and friends popped the Jaguar's trunk.

A seemingly perfect case had then been passed off to C.J., who, at the time, had been the Assistant Division Chief of Major Crimes, and for more than a year, the one prosecutor assigned to assist the Cupid Task Force. Subsequent search warrants and diligent police work by the task force had uncovered even more damning evidence – more sure-fire proof that the system had worked its magic, that the guilty had been caught and would not go free. But, if life had taught any lessons to C. J. Townsend, it was that things don't always work out like they should.

She closed her eyes now, trying to black out the image of William Rupert Bantling in that hot, overcrowded courtroom, packed with the media and their cameras, and her office's top brass. Back when she had first realized that he was far more than just a defendant. In that courtroom she had listened as Bantling bellowed angry words at Judge Katz, and watched the courtroom erupt in chaos around her. But she had not been able to move as silent alarms tore through her body and her mind, transporting her back in time to a stormy night in June of 1988. The night a faceless monster had brutally raped and tortured her in her own bedroom, leaving her for dead on blood-soaked sheets. The monster had worn a rubber clown mask to hide his face, but he could not hide his voice – his whispered, knowing words that night yet another weapon of torture.

41

She had been Chloe Larson back then, when she'd first heard that voice. Young and pretty and easygoing, a 24-year-old, soon-to-be-lawyer. About to embark on a promising career as a medical malpractice attorney, about to become engaged to a successful, handsome man, about to start a wonderfully normal life. The 'about-to-be's abruptly ended, though, and Chloe had found herself watching helplessly while the world around her went on as if nothing bad or horrific or senseless had ever happened. For her, time had stopped and she was trapped like a prisoner in a dark moment, bone-chilling fear coursing through her veins, the sound of rain beating against her windows while a madman with a blood-red smile sliced her to ribbons. The monster had never been caught, and after years of turning every corner in New York City scared out of her mind, she had moved on to Miami, leaving Chloe Larson far behind. And although the name had changed to Townsend, and the scenery had become greener, she had quickly learned you can't leave the memories behind.

In that courtroom almost three years ago, the past had finally caught up with C. J. Townsend's present. Justice had taken its course full circle and was now in her sights. Justice not only for herself, but now for the eleven young, beautiful women who screamed for it from their dark graves six feet under. And the perfect case was hers.

For all her years of experience as a prosecutor, she should have known, though, that sure-fire cases are never that. The ones with the million eyewitnesses, the twelve-page confessions and the veritable mountain of DNA inevitably became nail-biting verdicts with years of appeals in the making. Her perfect case, she had quickly discovered, was not so perfect. It seemed that justice might very well be evaded once again.

In your average felony case – cocaine possession, grand theft, burglary – a mistake by the police had its consequences under the law. Evidence may be suppressed, statements may be thrown out, the jury may not hear certain testimony. The Fourth Amendment protects the rights of defendants, and in that effort, sometimes the guilty do go free. But in the average felony case, the consequence of suppressed evidence, of discarded statements, of the case being lost and the defendant walking is not life-threatening. In this instance, though, a mistake would lead to a deadly outcome: a savage madman would go free forever. And that was a consequence that C. J. Townsend – Assistant Division Chief of Major Crimes, hardball prosecutor and victim – just could not allow.

C.J. sat at her kitchen table, the memories like a domino effect. One triggered another, and then another, and then another until the picture was vividly complete.

Young Victor Chavez may not have been short of enemies, but he also was not short of secrets. And Nicholsby's final words to her that morning echoed in her mind, like a soundtrack to her memories.

That was to shut him up.

12

'We've got trouble,' Dominick said on her cellphone.

It was Monday morning and C.J. was making her way back from court. She'd spent the last two hours arguing to prevent a grumpy and overworked Judge Goldstein from granting a first-degree murder defendant, accused of gunning down his three co-workers with an AK-47, a day pass to visit his dying mother in her nursing home. It was the third such motion in six months, and Mom remarkably always seemed to turn the corner when Sonny Boy lost his motions. She stepped out of the Richard E. Gerstein Criminal Justice Building and weaved her way down the handicap ramp, a cart of files in tow.

'That's not something I like to hear on a Monday morning,' she responded, trying hard to balance her oversized leather briefcase in one hand, the pull cart in the other, the cellphone buried in the crook of her shoulder. 'Where are you? Tell me they finally let you go home.'

'Nah, not yet. I'm still at the Beach. Black and Fulton and I just came from an operational meeting on this Chavez murder. So far FDLE's just helping out . . . or should I say *I'm* helping out. But they're thinking of setting up a task force if they don't get some leads soon. I'm going to head back home in an hour or so and catch a few Zs.'

'So what's the trouble?' she asked, darting across 13th

Street to the Graham Building, home of the Miami-Dade State Attorney's Office.

'The tox screens just came back on Chavez. He had coke in his blood and urine. He also had arterial sclerosis, a premature hardening of the arteries. Nothing unusual for a 70-year-old man, but sufficient evidence of long-term cocaine or heroin use in a 22-year-old kid.'

'Damn,' C.J. sighed. 'So he was using. Did it contribute to his death?' From the mess she had seen in the patrol car on Saturday morning, she strongly doubted it.

'Nope. Unfortunately for him, he did not die of a heart attack before his head was almost taken off his body. And that's another thing. Neilson found something else. Chavez's lungs were spotted red and filled with blood, indicating the guy actually drowned.'

Joe Neilson was the ME on many of C.J.'s cases. A little eccentric, perhaps, leaning toward odd, but he was always careful and deliberate in his work. Sometimes his findings proved very interesting. 'I take it that is not what you normally find with a throat slice?'

'Well, once Neilson saw the lungs, he went back and looked at the cut marks on the throat. He'd originally thought it was one slice that severed the carotid, windpipe and jugular all at the same time. But the guy would have bled out then, not drowned, and there would be little or no blood in the lungs. Looking more carefully at the cut marks, Neilson actually saw two sets. Only the jugular and the windpipe were severed in the initial cut. The jugular carries blood from the brain back to the heart and apparently runs slower than the carotid. When it's severed, it oozes blood, as opposed to the carotid, which spurts. So Chavez oozed into his severed windpipe and actually drowned to death. Unfortunately for him, drowning takes longer and is more traumatic than bleeding out.'

'Couldn't it be that the killer didn't get it right the first time, and had to go back and finish the smile?' A smile was a throat slice that went from ear to ear.

'Maybe, but Neilson doesn't think so. Based on the depth and width and placement of the first cut, he thinks the carotid was missed intentionally.'

C.J. had reached the second-floor elevator bay at the State Attorney's Office and was about to swipe her access card through the security doors that led to Major Crimes. She stopped and asked, 'What about the tongue? Was that injury pre- or post-mortem?'

'Neilson says the tongue was cut first. Chavez was probably struggling, moving his head when it happened, explaining the cuts, bruising and lacerations around the mouth and tear wounds through the cheeks. Then the jugular and windpipe were cut, finally followed by the smile.'

'Jesus Christ!' She was silent for a long moment. 'Did forensics turn up anything in the car?'

'The cruiser had a million prints, all of which belonged to subjects who conveniently deposited them on file when they crawled out of the back seat for booking. Same with hair and fiber. The cruiser is three years old and transports mopes. So we've got a million guys to talk to, but nobody to really question. Because of the tox screens, I need to look at Chavez's employee files, and probably rip his apartment apart.'

'You? Isn't Beach Homicide still officially handling this?'

'Yeah, but now they mistakenly feel there's a conflict and that FDLE is a neutral party. Black is best buddies with Jordan at the Beach, so I'm the plumber assigned to fix this shit.' Black was the Regional Director for FDLE, Dominick's boss. Jordan was the Chief of the Miami Beach PD. 'Chavez lived with his brother, a Hialeah PO. He might not give consent for a search, so I may need a warrant.'

'Okay. I was the on-call, so if your sweet talk doesn't work and you need anything, let me know.' She was still speaking when behind her she heard a very loud, very exasperated, 'Tsk.' It was not necessary for her to turn around to know that her secretary, Marisol, now waited impatiently behind her, purple nails on pink Lycra hips. She moved to allow the tsker to pass. It was Marisol alright, only the situation was worse than C.J. had initially thought. Today it was a flowered fluorescent mini.

'Good morning, Marisol.'

With a toss of her hair, Marisol ignored C.J.'s greeting and marched past, a bag of Doritos and a Diet Coke in hand.

Turning her attention back to the phone, C.J. asked, 'Any leads?'

'Yeah. Too many. But none of consequence yet. Seems Chavez was on a bunch of people's hit lists, particularly the women that he dated. Or should I say screwed and cheated on. Those are too numerous to count. Then there was the bevy of friends that he had borrowed money from and never returned, and the old high school chums who are blood-members of the Latin Kings. Who-ever did it had a bone to pick with this guy, and that's a mighty long list.'

C.J. felt the tension in her heart ease up just a bit. Apparently Victor was in the habit of keeping secrets. Or telling a few. And he kept mighty bad company.

Perhaps the one secret she feared most was not the one that had gotten him killed.

Dominick's tone changed now. 'How are you doing with all this?' he asked softly. 'I know it's got you upset.'

It was incredible, this power that Dominick had over her. His simple presence in a room made her feel safe, protected; his voice, even on the phone, reassuring. Dominick was the reason for her sanity – the light that glowed through the madness that had almost snatched her away again. And so she had opened up a door in the hard-faced façade that she wore for the rest of the world – just a tiny crack – and had let him in, before quickly slamming it shut. Their love affair had started in friend-ship, slowly ripening into love, and her feelings for him ran deep, deeper than she ever thought it possible to love a man. Sometimes, when she let him, he simply took her breath away.

They had never officially decided to live together, but sometime in the past three years he had stopped going back to his apartment and she had donated half her closet space. She looked down now at the brilliant round diamond that sat on her left hand and smiled. As a child might with a special blanket, her thumb moved between her fingers to touch the exquisite stone. Just feeling it assured her of reality, reminded her of the moment he had slipped it on her finger and asked her to share her life with him forever. The moment she finally was able to tell him yes.

'The shock has worn off,' she said. 'Chavez was not the brightest bulb, that's for sure, but who would ever imagine . . .' her voice trailed off, the private happy moment she had just experienced tackled by disturbing images. As the lead investigator on the Cupid Task Force,

Dominick was quite familiar with the cocky antics of Victor Chavez. *Most* of them, anyway. C.J. quickly pushed those thoughts aside. Instead, she softly said, 'I miss you. Any chance you can make it out of there tonight?'

'I gotta see what Black has me doing. I miss you, too. Aren't you hooking up with the caterer this afternoon?'

In the draining excitement of the past few days, she had completely forgot about the meeting with the catering manager at Turnberry Isles. Forgot, or, as Freud might say if given the chance, purposely failed to remember. Their wedding was a little more than six months off, but as the manager had excitedly told her in a recent conversation, 'It's a crunch time!' C.J. wished it were here already. That it was just the two of them going through life, not one hundred and fifty people going through a wedding. She hated the attention, the fanfare and hoopla that enveloped a prospective bride and groom. In particular, the bright spotlight that shines down and focuses on the bride. She had wanted simple and brilliant, like her engagement ring, but that was quickly drifting off course with the help of well-intentioned family and friends to, in her view, extravagant and overstated. It would be impossible to elope now, just hop on a plane to Vegas and come back enormously happy, with a marriage certificate and a tan, even though that's what she quietly yearned for.

'I completely forgot. I'll call him and reschedule so that we can enjoy that meeting together. And you can personally pick just the right shade of red napkin that you want,' she mused.

He laughed softly into the phone. 'Lucky me. Well, misery does love company, so save that dance for me. I'll call you later. Love you.'

'Love you, too,' she said and hung up the cellphone. She looked around the elevator bay, watching as other prosecutors hustled with carts and briefcases full of files down the maze of hallways that ran out from the elevators. Joined by them were the cops and defense attorneys, victims and witnesses on their cases. Their days carried on as normal – hurried and tense – a million things to do. She blew out a slow breath, an unseen weight lifted softly from her shoulders, and she slipped the security card through the door lock.

It certainly was a relief to learn that Victor had kept quite a few secrets from quite a few people. Maybe that was because she still kept a few of her own.

13

One look at Victor Chavez's personnel file at MBPD, and Dominick's list of individuals to question had instantly doubled. It seemed that Victor got along with no one, and no one got along with Victor. Neither inside the department nor out. He was described by his sergeant as 'surly and insolent,' and those were his good points. He had several complaints for excessive use of force, though they'd been dropped because most of the complainants were either homeless and transient and made useless witnesses, or they were tourists, who couldn't be found when IA finally got around to cracking open the complaint file six weeks later.

In the weeks since Chavez's death, Dominick had leafed umpteen times through a file that was suspiciously thick for a four-year rookie. Obviously, Victor had stayed right where he was because he had pissed off all the wrong people, and if he'd lived, he wasn't gonna get off midnights until the next ice age hit Miami. Or a new administration came and forgave him all his sins.

It was clear from the countless interviews Dominick had now conducted, that by all accounts, Victor Chavez held onto his job only because he had once pulled over a serial killer by chance on the McArthur. What really amazed Dominick, though, was that, according to his brother, Ernesto, Chavez was going to be offered another one in the very near future with Hialeah. Nepotism aside, was the PD that hard up for good help nowadays, or was it something more sinister? Perhaps the fear of the very large lawsuit that would surely be filed if the City actually fired a civil servant?

Ernesto Chavez had kept both his apartment and his story squeaky clean when Dominick knocked on his door the day before Victor's funeral. *Of course Dominick could look around. It was bullshit that a dead cop – a fucking hero, no less – had to have his house searched like some fucking criminal. FDLE and the fucking scum that made Victor's life miserable at Miami Beach had no respect for a dead fucking hero!* The tree had apparently sired two bad apples. It went on and on like that for the hour that Dominick and Marlon Dorsett, with three MDPD uniforms in tow, searched the cramped, two-bedroom apartment off the Palmetto Expressway. They didn't find any drugs.

For days after the funeral, Ernesto continued to deny any knowledge of his brother's cocaine use. But he changed his tune when his own tox screen, a surprise visited on him by his lieutenant at Dominick's suggestion, came back dirty. He'd signed up for the department's Drug and Alcohol Abuse Early Intervention Program to save himself a visit to the unemployment line, and he'd finally admitted that Victor and he had liked to party on the Beach, and that Victor had gotten in a bit of a pinch with his supplier. The doper went by the name of Lil' Baby J, a.k.a. LBJ. His given name was Jerome Sylvester Lightner and Victor had gone to high school with him.

In typical Victor fashion, rather than doing the smart thing and borrowing from one of the twenty or so girls he was screwing, he went to his friend Ricardo Brueto, a captain in the Latin Kings. Ricky gave him the five thousand that he needed to get LBJ and friends off his back. For the time being, anyway. In the gang world, though, payback can be a real bitch and interest is compounded on the hour.

After Victor had been placed in the ground – a 21-gun salute and all – the picture had become quite clear. Dominick suspected that once they found LBJ – who had gone into hiding the day after Victor died – they would find that Victor's tab had simply come due, or perhaps, to save his ass, Victor had even flapped his gums about his buddy in the Kings, and the news had traveled across town. The possibilities were endless and not at all pleasant, because when you lay down with dogs, you get up with fleas. If you ever even get up.

Ricardo had decided early on that it was in his best interest not to speak with detectives, and given his lengthy arrest record, Dominick could understand his apprehension. As there was nothing to bring him in on, the game became a wait and see. Wait until LBJ finally surfaced. Wait and see what he says when he's facing death row for killing a cop.

Victor's death was looking more and more like a gangland execution, rather than the random act of a homeless person, or the calculated brutality of a scorned lover, and that took some of the intense heat and pressure off of the detectives working the investigation. While it was still a number one priority to find the people responsible, it now became a drug death and slipped several notches on the importance list. Unlike other boys in blue killed in the line of duty, Victor had earned his one-way trip to see St Peter.

The drug information had leaked to the press, and so even they, with their ruthless appetite for blood and scandal, had gotten bored. The daily reportings on the *Cop Killer Investigation!* had moved off of the front page and into the local section, and were finally shelved together after a week or so. The spinning MBPD badge and knife logo had also disappeared from the Channel Seven News Team lead-in headline stories.

Poor Victor. Allowed to walk this world for only a short time, he'd accomplished just the bare minimum with his life while he was here, and hadn't gotten another chance to become something more. The funeral had been packed with uniforms, but Dominick knew their attendance at these functions was out of obligation more than affection or admiration. Most of the five hundred cops in attendance did not even know Victor, and those who did were kind enough not to comment on their real thoughts as to why he left this world the way that he did. The bagpiper played to a packed church, yet to Dominick, who had attended with the FDLE command staff, the cathedral felt empty. The tears of Victor's sobbing mother were, sadly enough, the only cries heard that day.

Dominick dropped the latest investigative report he had just typed out into the squad secretary's 'Pending Investigations' box, and headed for the deserted office's nearest exit. He tried to shake free the cobwebs of fatigue that clouded his brain, running his hands through his hair, hoping to stay awake long enough to steer the car home.

He knew the late nights and seven-day workweeks would end soon enough. With an entire police force out looking for Baby Jerome, it looked like simply a matter of time before Victor's murder would be officially solved and justice could finally be served.

14

Hidden behind a small grove of palm trees, the waiting man watched the cop through the driver's side of the marked cruiser. Miami-Dade Police Officer Bruce Angelillo looked tired and bored. Sporadic, heavy rain had pelted the car throughout the night, and water on the roof of the cruiser still trickled down the windows. Off in the not-so-distant Everglades, jagged purple streaks lit the sky.

The man who watched breathed in the smell of the rain and the wet cement that surrounded Miami's newest ultra-mall. To the west of the mall, where the lightning met the earth, was the seemingly ever-expanding Florida's Turnpike. But past that, pines soared high and deer continued to run. For now. Until they cut the saw grass and chased away the alligators and started building. And build they would: New homes, new condos, new townhouses – all dubbed 'estates' in massive marketing campaigns. They'd fit snugly together in rows surrounded by walls and a gatehouse. It was Florida's answer to modern-day crime.

The mall developer had put in a small grove of thick and lush tropical plantings to soften the appearance of the four thousand parking spaces' worth of black asphalt. Two hundred yards away, bright lights illuminated the mall's anchor stores – Burdines, Bloomingdale's, Dillard's – but in this far corner of the parking lot it was dark, with only the moon, barely visible under the thick cloud cover, creating long shadows through the palm trees. From his spot behind a tall and thick California date palm, nestled between two overgrown elephant ear plants, the man watched as the officer typed on his laptop in the dim glow of the cruiser's interior light, pausing to catch a yawn with the palm of his hand.

It was almost time. He could practically set his watch by it.

The wind picked up slightly and a dead palm leaf, brown and decayed, crawled across the deserted parking lot. The dry, scraping sound mixed with the rustle and sway of the palm trees, the wind dancing between their fronds. With a fury, the rain would shortly return.

It had been three weeks since the man had touched death, felt it pulse, warm and sticky through his fingers. His whole body awash in the lifeblood of another. He remembered Victor's meaty throat in his hands, the color red as it drained before him, drenching the cheap blue vinyl seats. And Victor's brown eyes, wide and round, pleading for understanding, his final words just a raspy, garbled choke. And now there was Officer Bruce. Another who wore his badge with a corrupt smile. Another who brought shame upon the jacket just by virtue of wearing it. His existence would certainly be missed, but hardly mourned. Not when the truth about Officer Bruce was discovered.

Like clockwork, Officer Angelillo opened the cruiser's door and stepped out into the night, stretching. He pulled out his pack of Marlboro Lights and lit one up. Smoking in the squad car was not an option. Not with a cancer-surviving ex-smoker for a sergeant. *If the job don't kill ya, them death sticks sure as hell will*, he preached at nightly roll call.

The man stepped out of the lush bushes and through the haze of smoke. It was funny, the look of surprise that crossed Officer Bruce's full face when his indolent brain finally translated the sound of footsteps behind him as a potential problem. Funny, because as a police officer, Bruce should have been more prepared for surprises. But, like Officer Chavez, he could still use some on-the-job training.

'Got a light, Officer?' the man from the shadows asked. The question seemed rather pointless, for Officer Bruce had already dropped his cigarette when he saw the man. His terrified eyes desperately searched the deserted parking lot. The sound that actually made it out of his throat sounded more like the squeal of a pig than the scream of a man, and his fingers fumbled uselessly to unsnap the Glock 40 at his side.

But it was too late. The jagged blade took him down, and, with almost inhuman strength, the man began to drag the officer's useless body back to the cruiser. And Bruce Angelillo's final thought, strange as it was, was that the sarge was right: Smoking would definitely kill him.

The cigarette rolled on the pavement, away from the car, shedding orange cinders like tears, before it drowned in a waiting puddle and finally flickered out.

15

At 5:00 a.m., the Nextel on the dresser began to chirp.

'Dom, pick up. It's Fulton.' Jimmy Fulton was the Special Agent Supervisor of the Violent Crime Squad. Dominick's squad. His gruff voice, complete with the heavy twang of a southern accent, crackled to life in the dark bedroom. Police sirens sounded in the background through the Nextel speaker.

Dominick was instantly awake. C.J. sat up next to him in bed. Rain pounded outside, beating violently against the windows.

He clicked the Nextel. 'Fulton. Dom here.' He was already out of the bed, pulling on pants with one hand, holding the phone in the other. Just by the sound of Fulton's voice, he knew he would be going out. 'What's up?'

'We got another one, Dom,' Fulton said, his voice shaking, tinged with angry disgust. And with unmistakable fright. Fulton had been an agent with FDLE for twenty-eight years, nineteen of which he had spent as an SAS of various squads, including Narcotics, Public Corruption and Organized Crime, and for the past two years, Violent Crime. He was a seasoned veteran, having seen it all and done it all. And in the fifteen years that Dominick had known him he had never heard that sound, that fear in his voice. 'Another dead fuckin' cop,' he said. 'Right here, Dom, right under our goddamn noses!'

Dominick stopped putting on his shirt. A raw, sick

feeling began to churn the acid in the pit of his stomach. 'What?'

'Looks like maybe the same bastard that nailed that Beach boy. This one's Miami-Dade. He's been tore up bad, Dom. Real bad. I ain't seen nothing like this shit in all my years. Not to a fuckin' cop!' His voice caught and Dominick heard him pull away from the Nextel. 'Jesus . . .'

Another one. Another man down. Polish up the bugle and break out the bagpipes.

'Christ,' Dominick said, sitting for a moment on the bed. 'Who, Jimmy? Who is he?'

'Dom, this guy's fucking face looks like hamburger meat. Tentative is a Bruce Angelillo. You know him?'

Dominick shook his head, thinking. Trying to place a face. He rose again and crossed the room. 'No, don't think I know the name.' He parted the bedroom's wood blinds and looked out the window. Sheets of rain whipped against the glass and the Intercoastal churned below. Across the water, the lights of Pompano Beach blurred rather than twinkled. Even though the clock said the sun would soon be up, Dominick doubted he'd see it. A mass of clouds had sat on South Florida for three days, drowning Miami in floods and causing accident after accident on slick highways. 'I'm on my way, then. Where to, Jimmy?'

'Just get to the office,' said Fulton. 'Be sure to take the 12th Street exit on the Turnpike.'

'Aren't you on scene?' Sirens still blasted in the background. Louder now, more of them.

'Yep, I am. I'm standing in the parking lot of the Dolphin Mall, Dom. Across the street from MROC, and the goddamn Florida Highway Patrol. Like I said, this one happened in our own friggin' backyard.' He let out a frustrated sigh and then finished quietly, 'Jesus, if I cut down a few pine trees I could tell you if you left the friggin' light on in your office, Dom.'

Dominick's stomach dropped. MROC was the acronym for FDLE's Miami Regional Operations Center. Headquarters. Just a few years ago, the state had bought up a chunk of land as far west in Miami as they could and last year had built a large, technologically advanced complex for all state law enforcement. That included new local headquarters not just for FDLE, but also for the Florida Highway Patrol and the Office of State-wide Prosecution. A communications center for all state radios from Palm Beach to the Keys was also erected, complete with powerful fifty-foot radio towers and a satellite system. A veritable fortress of police officers and troopers and prosecutors, that operated twenty-four hours of every day.

He shook his head, trying to shake the dizzying feeling. MROC was surrounded by pine tree preserves, but just to the north on the other side of the pines began the enormous parking lot of the Dolphin Mall. Now it was a crime scene for one of their own.

C.J. still sat on the bed – her head down, her face pale, rubbing her temples with her fingers. Words were not necessary; she had heard the whole tale from Fulton's mouth, courtesy of the Nextel. Like him, she was trying again to comprehend the incomprehensible.

'Alright. I'm there.' He clicked out and a deafening silence hung in the room, broken only by the patter of rain on the windows.

Tonight it was C.J.'s turn. 'Do you want me to come out with you?' she asked after a moment.

'No. The on-call will get it. You saw enough last month.'

'I may get called anyway since I handled Chavez.'

'Let's see if that happens. Sit tight. I'll call you when I know more.'

'Okay,' she said quietly.

He headed for the bedroom door, then stopped and turned back. A wave of emotion came over him all too suddenly and he sat on the edge of the bed, pulling her close to him, feeling her warm breath against his cheek. He kissed the curve of her soft, familiar neck, lightly scented with Gardenia Lily body lotion, and buried his head for a moment in her hair.

Then, without another word, he stood and slipped out the door, carefully sidestepping the still-sleeping Lucy on his way out.

16

Dominick had only to look at the mutilated, bloody body of Officer Bruce Angelillo in the front seat of the white and green Miami-Dade cruiser to know that it was the same killer. Or a copycat with a great eye for detail, and a mole in the MBPD – because most of the horrible details of Chavez's brutal death had been kept under wraps to prevent just that. The windows were caked red with drying blood; the throat left raw and exposed, the macabre smile now recognized as the signature of a vicious killer. Handcuffed hands still held the wheel fast, the name 'Angelillo' ripped from his uniform, stolen along with his badge and ID. All the facts told the same story. With one exception. Officer Angelillo still had his tongue, although it had been rearranged.

The media had descended upon the scene like raven-ous wolves, forcing FHP and Miami-Dade to close the exits off of the Turnpike and the Dolphin Expressway during, of all times, Monday morning rush-hour traffic. News choppers hovered overhead, taking pictures from a thousand different angles of the mob of poncho-wearing detectives below, and news vans stopped wherever they could on the roadways, raising their forty-foot satellite antennas, straining to get a better look for their live feeds to New York and LA. The result was, for the fortu-nate, a two-hour commute into downtown. The not-so-fortunate ended up victims in the string of accidents, caused by mindless rubberneckers and the unending rain.

The rain had drowned out any hope of discovering trace evidence in the parking lot or the surrounding area. Gone were potential tire tracks, footprints and bloodstains. Hair, fiber, and DNA that ordinarily might have lingered behind – caught on a branch or stuck on a cigarette butt or left on a piece of gum – were forever washed away in the violent storms.

The ME had come and gone by 8:30 that morning, taking Angelillo's body – along with a few news vans – with him back to the morgue. The parking lot, though, remained infested throughout the day with patrol cars and cops. The yellow crime scene tape hung like crêpe paper at a party – all over everything – battered by the weather and trampled by investigators.

The cruiser had been discovered at 4:45 that morning by an FHP trooper who had passed a couple of times and noticed the Miami-Dade cruiser sitting motionless, its engine running. Irked that the officer inside might be catching Zs while he was catching speeders up and down Florida's Turnpike, he had decided to give the lazy shit a piece of his mind when he opened the cruiser's door in the pouring rain. Dominick suspected the twenty-year veteran would be putting in for retirement by the end of the day.

At 10:00 a.m., the press conferences began. Everywhere. MDPD, MBPD, FDLE, FHP – and practically every other police department in Miami, including the 24-man department of Surfside PD – assuaged the fears of the citizens in their jurisdiction with reports of the investigation and the precautions their officers were taking. Facts were misspoken and, even worse, accurate facts were leaked in detail. The result was a mess. Lines at all departments were jammed with calls from worried citizens as the rumors spread. *Is it the work of terrorists? Is it gangs? Is it a serial killer?* And the reports of suspects and suspicious persons piled up, everyone now feeling compelled to turn in that strange neighbor with the dog that barks all night, or the co-worker with the beady eyes who complained over lunch that all cops were assholes after he got a speeding ticket.

By noon the real infighting began – each department ticked off at the other for blabbing to the press, for ignoring that unspoken code of conduct of the blue jacket: United we stand, divided we fall. Chaos had ensued. Two departments had jurisdiction over two separate, but obviously related, murders, and no one wanted to now share their information. And just as Dominick had expected, all the squabbling attracted the unwanted attention of a mighty large predator, one who waited to scoop up the juicy meat left behind when the others killed each other off.

The call came a little after 1:00 p.m., when RD Black was handed the phone in FDLE's state-of-the-art new conference room, and told to hold the line for the FBI's Miami Special Agent in Charge, Mark Gracker. While he was holding, Fulton chirped in on the Nextel to advise the Director that a few carloads of FBI Special Agents had just arrived on scene to see if they could be of any assistance.

With the mall as a backdrop in the pouring rain, a somber, but still wide-eyed, reporter held the microphone tightly. She struggled to contain her obvious excitement as she relayed in detail the latest handiwork of a killer who seemingly held a grudge against police officers. 'Are these cold-blooded executions actually the calculated retaliation of vindictive gang members, as has been theorized in the Miami Beach slaying? Or is it something worse – perhaps, a link between the drug cartels and PD corruption? Or can it be simply a perverse madman who has Miami's police departments – the designated protectors of society themselves – scrambling now to protect their own from a killer?

'Whoever it is has now got South Florida's finest exchanging their blue jackets for black mourning suits, at what will surely be yet another somber send-off for an officer killed in the line of duty.' She threw in the appropriate two-second pause before frowning sincerely and then signing off. 'This is Katie Cocuy for CNN News.'

Miami was back in the spotlight, at the forefront of breaking news. And everyone was going to be working overtime to nail the killer with the now-catchy, macabre nickname.

The Black Jacket.

17

C.J. sat at her desk, looking down at the mammoth puddles on 13th Street. The driving rain fell equally hard on the private defense attorneys in their expensive tailored suits, and the more conservatively dressed civil servants – the ASAs and Public Defenders.

Directly across the street from the courthouse sat the Dade County Jail – DCJ as it was known – a nightmarish mass of dull gray and steel mesh. Under a short overhang, people milled about, waiting for a loved one, or an associate, or their pimp, to make bond and get released. Green-uniformed corrections officers periodically shooed the undesirables away from the jail's entrance, but they kept drifting back.

C.J. plotted the path that she herself would need to take in just a few moments. Jury selection in her first-degree murder trial was scheduled for 9:00 a.m. before the Honorable Judge Sy Penney and it was already 8:42. In the corner of her office, on a metal cart, sat four heavy trial boxes that somehow needed to make it across the street in a dry condition.

Atop her metal file cabinet, a portable TV spewed seemingly unending coverage of the cop killings, as was the case for the past forty-eight hours. Matt and Katie, Diane and Charlie – even Kelly and Regis would probably comment about it before introducing their next heart-throb guest and his latest movie. And, of course, crime scene footage ran with every mention of the story. Mobs of flashing police cruisers, angry faces of police officers on scene, and of course, the black body bags and gratuitous shot of the brick-faced Medical Examiner's Office. It all served as an excitable reminder to the press of the last time they had needed to camp out on the Miami Courthouse steps, so canned footage of the Cupid murders and the Bantling trial took over when the cop murder footage ran out.

Before sadness or outrage – it was initially a small sense of relief C.J. had felt when Dominick had called. He'd told her the ID was positive: Bruce Angelillo. A rough-and-tumble but basically do-nothing cop, Angelillo had been on the job for six years with Miami-Dade and had worked the Kendall station, far from headline-making news of Cupid. She had not known him, had never worked with him. Dominick had supplied some sketchy details, but for C.J., the details did not matter inasmuch as her original paranoia could not dissipate.

With his turbulent personal life, by the ripe old age of twenty-eight, Angelillo had already been divorced twice and had two young kids, one of whom wasn't by either of his two ex-wives. And then there was his personnel file. Like Chavez, he had more complaints than commendations, and the parallels between the work ethics of both officers – or lack thereof – were already being drawn. It would take a day or so for the tox screens to come back, to see just how far those parallels ran.

It looked like the murders were going to be C.J.'s, though. Even though it was another Major Crimes prosecutor who had been called to the grisly scene at the Dolphin Mall – the former Chief of the SAO Gang Unit, no less – it was C.J. who the State Attorney himself called at home late Monday.

Much to the chagrin of the media, the on-air squabbling between departments had pretty much subsided by Monday night. Although no department really wanted to share their investigation with the other, it was clear that no department wanted to share anything with the FBI. C.J. knew that was not because the feds weren't effective. The Bureau certainly had the resources and advanced technology, and on an important, headline-making case such as this, they would offer up the manpower to make things happen. But, their hard-earned reputation among the locals for stealing thunder and passing blame was enough for everyone to take a pass on the money and the manpower, and the Chiefs finally agreed to circle the wagons. By 11:00 p.m. that night, a joint press conference was called by FDLE, the Miami Beach Police Department and the Miami-Dade PD. They were joined at the dais in the FDLE conference room by Chiefs from around the county. They presented a united front, everyone nodding somberly as FDLE announced the formation of a multi-agency task force at the request of the Governor that would operate out of MROC. Seated in the last seat on the dais was Jerry Tigler, the State Attorney. C.J.'s boss. When he stood to speak, he vowed the full support of the State Attorney's Office.

Her phone rang ten minutes later.

She was one of the top prosecutors in the office. She had task force experience, having served as Legal Advisor to the Cupid Task Force since its inception a year before a subject was ever even apprehended. More importantly, she had the respect of the law enforcement community, and homicide detectives in particular. She also had significant experience with serial homicides and spree killings, should that experience be necessary now. It was C.J. who Tigler wanted assigned to the task force. He knew, too, the personal hell she had gone through on Cupid, so his tone of voice was more pleading than an actual command. She told him she was starting trial in the morning and would get back to him with an answer.

Now the morning was here and her mind was made up. She quickly wrapped her entire metal cart in plastic sheeting left behind when the office was last painted, grabbed her umbrella from the stand and headed for the door.

She felt a fierce loyalty to police officers. Not just because of her relationship with Dominick, but because of what she did every day. What she, herself, often saw only in grisly crime scene pictures and bloody autopsy photos days later, they always witnessed first-hand. First on the scene to break up an angry fight, rescue a beaten wife, save an abused child. First to see the carnage left behind when the human mind suddenly snaps, and a depressed dad becomes an executioner, or a co-worker exacts revenge. She held an enormous respect for police officers, and for the bravery that they exhibited on a daily basis, willing to take a bullet for a complete stranger when the job called for it.

And prosecutor and cop worked together to accomplish the same goal – justice. For the most part, she worked now with the most experienced detectives in Miami and mistakes were hard to come by. And the homicide detectives who she worked with had become familiar, friendly faces. She knew of their personal problems at home, their kids' names, upcoming celebrations, and family tragedies. And she understood the heavy weight of responsibility that they silently shouldered on a daily basis. Surrounded by death and seeking answers, they were constantly being asked to work more quickly, because another one was always coming down the pike. It was a never-ending cycle, and it often made one forget that there were good guys in the world. 'We all wear glasses,' one detective had told her, 'and they're the color jade.'

Because of that intense loyalty to the badge, of course she would help out in any way that she could. How could she say no? And she might not have known this Angelillo, but Victor Chavez ... Even if he wasn't the smartest cop or the best witness, still she had known him personally. She had worked with him, talked with him in this very office, directed him on the stand. Unlike other murder victims on her cases, this time she had a face, a scent, a personal moment, to reflect upon and always remember. And she would do what she could to assist the task force in legally nailing his killer. She owed him that.

But inside she was worried. She knew the twisted mind of a serial killer, of a sadist – one who derives pleasure by inflicting pain on his victims. So she prayed a silent prayer, as she made her way to the elevator bay, that the murders were the work of vindictive gang members, just as Dominick had suggested and the reporter on CNN had gleefully speculated last night. And she hoped that this was not the handiwork of one who knew no reason.

18

'What is it with the fall season and fucking psychopaths?' asked the gruff, familiar voice behind Dominick. 'The Dolphins lose and everyone goes friggin' crazy.'

Dominick, standing in what just three hours before was the MROC Fraud Unit's squad bay for eight, but now was task force headquarters for twenty, turned around to face his old friend, Detective Manny Alvarez. Actually, he faced Manny's chin, which is about where Dominick stood against the Bear's beefy six-foot-five frame. 'Hey there, Bear,' Dominick smiled. 'Did you volunteer for duty, or were you drafted?'

'Fuck no, I didn't volunteer.' Manny pulled down on his thick black mustache, through which several silver strands had started to poke their way. Even though it was barely 10:00 in the morning, Manny already wore a five o'clock shadow. In fact, the only place on Manny where hair did not seem to magically sprout by nightfall was his tan Cuban head, which he kept smooth and shiny, atop an 18-inch-thick neck. 'I must've pissed off my lieutenant last month when I asked if his daughter was single. She didn't *look* fifteen in that outfit,' he chuckled. 'Now he figures he'll screw me with a fucking ninety-hour workweek, but I'll be laughing those OT checks right into the bank.'

'That's the spirit,' said Dominick.

'Not that I'm gonna mind squeezing the fucking *cojones* off a cop killer – there'll be a real sense of satisfaction when the lights flicker in ten years. But another fucking task force was not my idea of a good time. No offense, Dommy Boy.'

'None taken.'

Manny looked around the room, bustling with activity. Detectives from different departments and FDLE agents – all of whom wore plainclothes – moved in and out of the room, and unless you knew the person, it was impossible to tell which agency anyone was from. He hailed from the City of Miami PD himself. 'Two questions,' he said. 'Who else got sent to purgatory and are you the head of this posse?'

'You may know Marlon Dorsett and Ted Nicholsby with the Beach; Steve Yanni with Miami-Dade is coming, too, and of course there's Fulton and me. The rest I'm not too sure of yet. As far as leaders goes, it's an equal opportunity task force. Technically, there is none. I'm more of a mediator. I get to make sure everyone is on the up and up and no one steals the limelight from the others.'

'That means you're the boss,' Manny said with a laugh, landing his hairy paw on top of Dominick's shoulder. 'And I guess that also means the Fibbies are not in on this one. I heard about them all over that crime scene last night. God knows they can't bear to share news on the weather unless they take all the credit for the sun shining.'

'Don't count your chickens just yet,' Dominick said cautiously. 'The Miami SAC has been pledging his support all over town this morning.'

'Gracker is a fat shit,' Manny snorted. 'On that, everyone can agree.'

'You're preaching to the choir, Bear. Everyone

stopped fighting long enough to collectively tell the Bureau to go home, but they don't give up easy. Like a cockroach, they'll try and find some way under the door, and I would bet that at this very moment, Gracker and friends are having a cup of Joe with the pinheads at the US Attorney's Office, trying to figure out a way to get federal jurisdiction over crimes that have no federal jurisdiction. I'm expecting them to be creative.' Dominick already had a history with Mark Gracker and it went back far. If the FBI had a reputation for undercutting the locals and stealing the credit for solving cases they never even worked on, Gracker had helped them earn it. And for that, the Bureau had made him the Miami SAC. Dominick now never invited Gracker anywhere without first bathing in holy water and stringing wreaths of garlic over the door.

'Well, let me say now that it was fun while it lasted. Look at this place,' Manny nodded approvingly. 'It's a lot better than our last crib.'

FDLE was allocating an entire squad bay in the new building to the task force. The individual desks of the Special Agents assigned to Fraud had been moved out and down the hall to share the squad bay with POS – Protective Operational Services. A large, new cherry conference table had been brought in in their place, and three individual computer stations had been set up in the corners of the room, along with two copiers and two fax machines. The room still smelled faintly of new carpet.

'You're looking at tax dollars, hard at work. I'm not complaining. I got a new desk. And a view this time,' Dominick said.

Manny gestured out the window that Dominick stood in front of. Angelillo's Miami-Dade cruiser was long gone now from the parking lot across the street, though battered yellow crime scene tape was still visible through the thick pines. A dwindling number of uniforms continued to hunt for unseen evidence, hours after hope had been lost of really finding any. 'I hope that's not the view you got.'

Dominick shook his head somberly. 'Same window, down the hall.'

Manny looked now at the wall opposite the windows. 'And now you've got this fucking scenery to keep you company. Looks familiar, in a fucked-up sort of way.'

A massive corkboard had been mounted on the length of the wall, already decorated with gruesome crime scene photos from both officers' slayings. Directly in the center of the corkboard sat a two-foot colorized wanted poster featuring a grainy old booking photo of Miami's number one, most-wanted man: Jerome Sylvester Lightner, a.k.a. 'Lil' Baby J' a.k.a. 'LBJ.' Jerome wore a look of surprise on his hardened baby face, though this was the tenth such time he'd had to go before the cameras. His short, unkempt dreads sprouted from his head like a fern, and the camera had caught the glint of the many gold teeth hiding in his surly expression. If his round baby face made him appear even younger than his twenty-one years, it was his distant, cold, almost dead brown eyes that aged him. With a juvenile arrest record an arm long, he had already amassed an impressive adult record that was peppered with drug arrests, misdemeanor assaults and a felony Aggravated Battery, which was dropped when the guy whose face he had smashed in with a set of brass knuckles suddenly did not remember who had hit him or why. He'd also been busted twice for CCF – Carrying a Concealed Firearm. It was oftentimes difficult to explain to the average tax-paying, law-abiding citizen how Florida law worked, but never more so than when a guy with a three-page rap sheet was still walking around the streets of Miami taking ecstasy orders instead of making license plates at South Florida Reception.

'Before he told me to get the fuck out of his office, my LT brought me up to speed. So this is the *hijo de puta*?'

'A face only a mother could love. We've got everyone out looking for him . . . and his friends.'

Sharing some of his limelight on the wall were five of Jerome's closest buddies, top guns in his gang, the BB Posse – BB standing for Bad Boys – also wanted for questioning in the Black Jacket slayings. None looked friendly. All were considered armed and extremely dangerous and all had gone into hiding after Chavez was killed. On the other side of Jerome's glossy mug were pictures of Ricardo Brueto and company from the Latin Kings. Although Ricardo was not named officially as a suspect – at least not until Jerome was found – he was already under constant surveillance. No dummy, he kept on his best behavior while detectives followed him all over town.

'Well, brother, we'd better look fast, because I'm guessing a few other people might be looking to get their hands on this bastard before we do,' the Bear said, eyeing Brueto's picture thoughtfully. Then he stopped, lost for a moment as he looked at the corkboard, and in particular the grisly pictures of Victor Chavez's open throat, the blood-painted windows as a backdrop. 'Unless . . .' he paused, not wanting to finish his sentence.

Dominick read his friend's mind. 'Internal Affairs called down this morning to tell us that Angelillo was on their watch-list. They were looking into complaints that he was fronting muscle for dopers at some off-duties he was working. Thoughts were he had found it lucrative to mix the two jobs.' Many cops worked as off-duty uniformed security for the nightclubs and bars that dotted Miami Beach.

'And IA just called you with that very important info this morning? Almost three days after the guy is whacked in his own car?'

'Like I told you, until eleven o'clock last night, no one wanted to play in the sandbox with the others.'

Manny sighed. 'So we've got two dirty cops. Both tied to dope. Great. Makes us look like we're in a very worthy fucking profession. This is gonna give my ex-wives something else to bitch about in front of a judge when the alimony check's late.' His eyes returned to the crime scene photos. 'Okay, it's dopers. And they're obviously pissed and in the mood to send a message.' He paused and looked at his friend. 'So why don't you look convinced?'

'No one's taken the credit yet,' Dominick said slowly.

'We haven't found no one yet.'

'True . . .'

Dominick didn't finish the thought, and neither said anything further as they stared at the massive corkboard in front of them, hoping that no more pictures took up the space.

19

Ricardo Brueto stared out his window in Little Havana, down at the two undercover clowns in the black Grand Prix. At the other end of the block sat two more in a green Ford Expedition. *If they thought they was being sly by switching cars on him today*, Rico thought, *they was fuckin' wrong*. He could spot an undercover a mile away, even if they had their cop asses in a friggin' Porsche.

It had been like this every fuckin' day for the past four weeks. He couldn't take a goddamn leak without a cop pissin' next to him. They were breathing down his neck, hoping to catch him packing so that they could bust him up for a probation violation. Everywhere he turned, and on his fuckin' family, too. Not to mention his boys. The heat had been so intense that the street had cooled down like ice, no one wanting to do nothing until the cops stopped sitting on them. And that meant there was no money coming in. And with no money, Rico certainly had bigger worries to think about than some fat-assed *cochino* in a blue suit eating donuts down the block. No money meant trouble from above, and the voices were already starting to grumble. No one cared if he didn't have it – the message was clear: Get it. But the streets in Miami were cold, and nothing could come in or go out until this whole cop killing shit was settled. Until someone threw some meat on the fire to satisfy those hungry coppers and make them go home.

Fucking Chavez. That dumb-ass piece of shit. Being led

around by his nose like a street junkie, buying shit that he couldn't afford. And if it wasn't his nose that trotted him into the worst parts of town, then it was his dick, which he had buried in every cheap ho' all over town. Buying shit like he was Rockefeller or something, then having to come to the bank for a loan to pay for it all. Not once, not twice, but more times than Rico could count. Victor with his hand out, looking for a break, with soggy-assed eyes and a guilt trip because they were *hermanos*. Of course he couldn't make the payments, not on that shit salary of his. But there were solutions to every problem. Rico had thought it a nice arrangement, until . . .

Their brotherhood had been forged in high school and then both had gone their separate ways. Victor, always on a fucking power trip, had picked showing off his muscles in a tight blue uniform, thinking it made him all tough and shit. Rico knew better. It ain't the uniform that makes you tough. If you looked under his shirt, you'd see muscles that were a lot fucking bigger than Victor Chavez's, he just didn't need to show them off. Everyone already knew. And if you looked in the back of his pants, you'd see a Magnum that'd put a fucking hole right through that Kevlar Victor wore. Blow right through that shiny badge. *Now who's the fucking tough guy?* So it was kind of amusing at first to see a cop in his tight uniform knocking on his door in the middle of the night, all worried about what might happen to him, who might protect him from the big, bad brothers in Liberty City? Begging for help from the Kings. *Brotherhood, shit.* Rico had a business to run, people to answer to. You want something, you pay for it. One way or another.

Rico watched as another cop pulled up alongside the

Grand Prix, this one in a shiny new rented Altima. The Altima passed the Grand Prix a brown bag and then took off down the block, to join the Expedition. The light went on in the Grand Prix, and the driver opened the bag, while the passenger spoke into his handheld Motorola. The driver took out a sandwich and started to eat it, then stopped. He raised it up toward Rico's window and smiled like a prick, then laughed with his partner.

Rico closed the drape and punched the wall hard. Drywall crumbled, leaving a hole where his fist had been. Pain exploded in his hand, and blood began to seep from his knuckles and down his wrist. Rico ignored it. In the other room, the baby started to cry. Angelina called to him. 'Rico? Qué paso? Todo está bien?'

'Nothin'. Go back to bed.'

Fucking cops. Deserved everything they got coming to them. Ain't no tears flowing at their funerals.

He sucked the blood off of one knuckle, and looked around for a towel to stop the bleeding. Then the cellphone at his side rang, and an uncomfortable, anxious feeling settled in his stomach. He knew instantly from the number that he had bigger things to worry about than the sandwich-eating cops outside his door.

A lot bigger.

20

Internal Affairs, or IA as it is known to most, is a peculiar and isolated department within any police agency. Viewed as a separate enforcement agency unto itself, it is responsible for policing its own. For weeding out the bad. And any detective assigned to IA knew that such an assignment would be the last of his or her career, for they were now considered outcasts by all others in the fraternal society. Even a police department's top brass, while proclaiming IA to be a vital tool in fighting corruption, considered the department a necessary evil at best. Adding to the air of distrust was the fact that IA worked the investigations of their fellow employees in complete secret. Oftentimes an arrest came as a total shock, even to the command staff. And sometimes to fellow IA detectives.

So it really did not surprise Dominick that it took Miami-Dade's IA division almost two days to fork over their info on Bruce Angelillo. It didn't surprise him – but it did frustrate him beyond belief. The world had started to descend once again on Miami, on *his* investigation, and playing with IA would be like cleaning the teeth of a tiger. Without warning, the jaws would snap closed on his hand, and no amount of coaxing would get them to open again.

In MDPD, one complaint led to a preliminary investigation by the IA Reactive Squad, otherwise known as the Stop and Curse Squad. Two complaints, or a substantiation of the initial complaint, transferred the file next door to the Criminal Conspiracy Section, or CCS. CCS kept what was known as an IA Profile on every officer that they'd ever investigated or received a complaint about. In some agencies it was called the Dirty List, the laundry list of cops suspected of going bad for one reason or another. Some were suspected of being on the take, some of sexual advances on subjects in custody, some of improper use of authority. One of the reasons officers feared IA so much was the list, which was easy to get on, and impossible to get off. Once a name was handed to IA, they kept it in their files, forever subscribed in permanent marker. Even when they said they didn't.

Dominick wanted that list.

There was an obvious dope connection in the Black Jacket slayings. And while IA was willing, albeit reluctantly, to share info on a dead cop, they didn't want to risk blowing undercover operations on the live ones. It took the threat of a subpoena and the fear of an anonymous tip-off to the *Herald* about dissent among the ranks before Dominick got what he wanted. And even so, he was sure it was a very watered down Dirty List.

It came in a sealed manila envelope, delivered by a messenger who Dominick assumed was an undercover IA sergeant. He wouldn't say. Now at 9:30 at night, Dominick unsealed it, his tired eyes straining under the glare of the fluorescent light over the cherry conference table. Most everyone else had left the building long ago.

He pulled out the thick packet from inside the envelope, covered with a warning from MDPD legal:

Inside was an IA profile of every cop on the MDPD Dirty List.

Knowing that IA held their cards close to the chest and that Dominick was looking only at those officers which IA thought he needed to see, he was still shocked when he turned the page.

Shocked to see how many names had made the list.

21

C.J. had fallen asleep on her couch, the jumble of notes she had written out for tomorrow morning's cross exam in a heap underneath Tibby on the floor right next to her. Her glass of wine sat unfinished on the coffee table, and an infomercial had replaced Conan O'Brien on the TV screen. She sat up, startled, and looked around her.

She had been stuck in trial all week with Judge Penney and his odd court clerk. And twelve jurors who were getting increasingly annoyed that the case was dragging on far longer than the three days the overly optimistic Judge Penney had originally speculated it would. She and Dominick had passed in the shower all week, basically keeping in touch through hurried phone calls and love notes posted on the fridge. She had thought she might try and wait up for him . . .

It took a moment to shake the fog of sleep that enveloped her; for her ears to recognize and decipher the sound she was hearing. She hit the mute button on the TV. Nothing. *Was it real, or was it just the dream?* Then it started up again.

The phone was ringing in the kitchen.

She looked for the wall clock. 4:12 a.m. She rose to answer the phone and then she heard the other sound coming from the bedroom, the buzz of her beeper. It must be Criminal Intake on the phone now, trying her at home because she hadn't responded. When did the beep come in?

She stumbled into the kitchen, pulling the hair back off her face and rubbing the sleep from her eyes. She picked up the phone. 'Hello?'

She did not immediately recognize the voice on the other end, although she should have. Barely audible, it was soft, but strained. The all-too-familiar sound of sirens blared in the background, against the crackle of police radios. The voice was hesitant, as though the words he needed to speak were painful to utter.

'C.J. It's Dominick. I'm afraid I've got bad news . . .'

She raced down I95 at breakneck speed, taking the 395 exit onto the McArthur Causeway, which connected downtown Miami to the Beach. Over Biscayne Bay, the brilliant citrus skyline rose on her right, looming over the Causeway and the expansive Port of Miami, home to many cruise lines and their massive floating hotels.

She did not need directions. All she had to do was follow the shriek of sirens. Up ahead, off of the Watson Island exit, a mass of blue and red lights appeared. Watson Island was a small slice of county-owned land, which sat directly across the water from the cruise ships and towering industrial smokestacks of the port. With downtown Miami and the People Mover as a backdrop, it offered a potential million-dollar view, but the County wasn't selling it. But for the Parrot Jungle and the Miami Children's Museum recently making homes here, most of Watson would remain undeveloped and desolate. Only a few tiny fish peddlers were rented space. Their small shacks sat on the edge of the water, surrounded by a gravel and dirt parking lot and an eight-foot chain link fence. A one-pump marina gas station sat beside them, offering live bait on signs scrawled in fluorescent paint.

C.J. had been to Watson before. Watson Park, which actually snaked under the McArthur, offered fast and easy access to the bay waters and a desolate location. That made it a favorite spot for smuggling pick-ups and body dumping. More than a few floaters had made an appearance here over the years, sucked back in by the strong tide and snagged on the seawall.

She felt her stomach churn the wine she had drunk earlier in the night, and she swallowed hard as she got out of the car. News vans from every channel were already on scene, satellite antennas raised high in the cool night sky. She flashed her credentials as she approached the police barricade, and heard the whir and click of the cameras behind her as the buzz began. *Townsend! State Attorney's Office! Major Crimes! The Cupid Prosecutor!* She pulled her black Jeep Cherokee next to the swarm of flashing cruisers, representing every department in South Florida. She noted the mass of empty City of Miami cars, crowded together. *One of their own.* She slammed the door and made her way through the sea of cruisers.

It seemed that there were at least a hundred cops on scene. Radios crackled together, a million voices chattered incoherently all at once. This scene was crazier than even Chavez's. She had never seen so many cops before. She scanned the crowd for Dominick, but then her eyes spotted the telltale protective circle of blue uniforms, clumped together outside the white graveled parking lot of the gas station. She walked toward the circle, inexplicably both drawn to and repulsed by what she knew lay behind the uniforms. Again she flashed her credentials.

'Special Agent Falconetti?' she asked. The uniform

shook his head. 'FDLE? Task Force Operations?' As the rookie pointed to his left, she saw it now, behind him. The lone City of Miami cruiser, its lights still flashing, in the parking lot that abutted the gas station. The uniform said words to her that she didn't hear, but she nodded anyway.

'Thanks,' she said, moving past him, toward the car, her SAO credentials still in hand. Crime Scene had already begun its work, technicians combing through the contents of the trunk, with the towering skyline of Miami as a backdrop. Other techs took pictures of the ground from every conceivable angle, so that this moment in time could be relived second for second, angle for angle one day in a courtroom. Their flashbulbs erupted around her, and from the corner of her eye she spotted the ME's van, the steel gurney out and fully assembled. Waiting to pick up its cargo.

The cruiser's driver door was open, and from it hung a white sheet stirring uneasily in the breeze that blew off the water. Even from a distance of twenty feet, she saw the familiar caked dark streaks on the windows. As if in a dream, she walked toward the car, credentials held out for all who might otherwise have stopped her.

The outline of the body under the crisp white linen was like that of the other two. She could see the slumped head where it met the steering wheel, the bent elbows and clenched pointed knuckles. A detective who she recognized, but whose name she suddenly could not recall, stood by the door, presumably waiting for the ME to signal that it was time to remove the body.

'Lift the sheet,' she said, her voice a commanding, throaty whisper. Then she caught herself. 'Please,' she added.

Without a word, the detective did as he was told. The wind caught it for a moment, and C.J. was reminded of the billowing white sails on the boats that floated down the Intercoastal on any given day. Normally a calming thought, a relaxing image.

Not on this night. Never again . . .

Dominick's voice broke the vacuum, and voices rushed together around her. 'C.J.! Hold up!' She heard the sound of his footsteps, hurrying to meet her. Perhaps to stop her. But it was too late.

The sheet was off and the horror before her was now all too clear.

22

What she was staring at could not be possible . . .

The killer had left his barbaric signature. The body sat in the front seat, white knuckles grasping the wheel, steel handcuffs on his wrists, the familiar vicious smile across the throat. As with Angelillo, the tongue had been re-arranged, and hung exposed from the open gullet. But there was something different, something that made C.J. shudder.

'I wanted to talk to you first,' Dominick began, as he ran up to her side, his arm grasping her shoulder, lightly rubbing it. 'Before —'

'Is this a City of Miami cop?' C.J. interrupted, shrugging away slightly from the touch, unable to tear her eyes away from the gruesome sight.

'What?' Dominick replied, puzzled. 'It's a city cop. City uniform, city car —'

'Do we have an ID?' she asked, her voice rising. 'Who is he? Where is his name?'

She looked at the spot above the breast pocket, but the name had been cut off his uniform. Only a ragged hole remained. *Those eyes . . . she knew those vacant, dead eyes. But it couldn't be . . .*

'Yeah, we've got an ID,' Dominick replied slowly. 'Lindeman. Sonny Lindeman. Only been with the City about a year, though. Came over from another department.'

Her stomach dropped, as if she had fallen three stories

on a roller coaster. 'I'll be right back,' she said suddenly.

'Where are you going?'

'I need a moment.' And then she was gone.

Before he could respond, Manny Alvarez, accompanied by FDLE Special Agent Chris Masterson, walked up to the car.

'Look what the wind blew in,' Manny said to Dominick. 'I found him actually doing work. I think he may be hiding a report in that small head of his.'

Masterson had been assigned for more than a year to the Cupid Task Force when he was with Violent Crime. He now worked narcotics. He was one of FDLE's younger agents, and his youthful face kept him working long hours undercover.

'Hey, Chris,' Dominick said, still distracted by C.J.'s question and somewhat strange behavior. 'Did Fulton call you in?'

'Yep. I think he's calling anyone who's available. And even those that ain't.'

'Welcome,' said Dominick.

'Thanks, Days Inn, but I don't know if I'll be staying past the night. Depends on what Black says. I'm on OT as it is.'

'I don't mean to take the air out of the tires on your welcome wagon, Dommy Boy,' said Manny, 'but it looks like you have other guests to attend to.' He nodded behind him. Mark Gracker stood with two other dark-suited, obviously federal agents, his five-foot-six pudgy frame sandwiched between two slim six-plus-footers. Even from a distance, Dominick could tell Gracker was barking orders.

'It's up to you to save us all,' the Bear finished in a low voice that was not low enough.

As if on cue, Gracker looked in Dominick's direction. What could only be described as a snarl bloomed on his face, and he pointed his finger at them. That, in turn, caused Mutt and Jeff by his side to look over too, along with the press and their high-powered cameras.

'I have a feeling he's not gonna go away this time,' said Dominick.

'I thought you said there was no federal jurisdiction on these murders,' said the Bear.

'I also said I thought they'd get creative,' replied Dominick. He looked at Masterson. 'Have you seen photos of the other two Black Jacket victims?'

'Nah. I went to the Metro cop's funeral, though. I got a buddy there.' Metro referred to the MDPD.

'Well, you're here now. Don't be shy.' Dominick stepped aside, ushering Chris closer to the cruiser. From the corner of his eye he spotted C.J. She stood near the ME's van, not talking to anyone. She didn't look well. 'Give me a sec, guys. I'll be right back,' he said, starting toward her, and ignoring an obviously unhappy Mark Gracker in the other direction.

'Whoa! A necktie!' Chris said suddenly behind him.

Dominick stopped and turned back to face Chris. 'What? What did you say?'

'This is a necktie. A Colombian necktie.'

'What the fuck is a necktie, Junior?' asked Manny.

'It's when the throat is slit and the entire tongue muscle is pulled down the inside of the throat and out the slit, so that it hangs out and looks like —'

'A necktie,' Manny finished. 'I see it now. How do you know this shit?'

'I was with DEA for six years before joining FDLE, undercover stints in Bogotá, Cali. I've seen a lot.

Although this,' he said, motioning toward Lindeman's body, '*this* is more legend. Even in Colombia, where it was supposedly thought up by the powerful Cali cartel, you don't see neckties. In fact, I've only seen it twice before. Late Eighties, when I was working a case on the outskirts of Bogotá, two informants popped up wearing just a tie and their birthday suits.'

'Why a necktie?' Dominick asked, looking at Lindeman's body. 'Does it mean anything?'

'It means someone's talking, and the boys on high don't like that.'

'Why's this one missing a set of ears? What does that mean?'

'Someone heard something, too. Maybe something they shouldn't have.'

'So it's definitely drug related?'

'I've never heard of one happening outside narcotics, so I'd say it's safe to assume you're dealing with high-level dopers. Angry ones, at that.'

'Excuse me,' said the ME tech with the steel gurney. All three parted and then watched silently as the investigators in the Medical Examiner's jackets began the task of zipping the body into a black bag and removing it from the cruiser.

'Well, Chris, guess that?' said Dominick. 'This is Days Inn calling. You're gonna be spending more than the night. Go pack your bags.'

Chris shook his head. 'Me and my big mouth.'

'And let's just keep this in-house for a while. See if our federal friends can figure it out on their own before they steal the damn chalk off our blackboard.'

Gracker was still waiting impatiently for Dominick to approach him. Just to fuck with him, Dominick started in his direction, then stopped, smiled and turned on his heel the other way. *Fuck him. He can wait.* He found C.J. still standing where the ME investigators had been moments before. 'Hey, are you okay?' he asked. She seemed more than a world away. Although he wanted to put a comforting hand across her shoulders, after that last reaction, he did not even try. It was strange. They had been together now for such a long time and some moments he still felt as if he didn't know her.

'Fine, I guess. How about you?' she replied, her voice distant and detached.

'This is tough. Three down. But we may have something. Chris Masterson just showed up. Followed by the feds.'

C.J. nodded.

'Chris was DEA a while back,' he continued. 'He looked at the body and says it's definitely dopers, in case there was any doubt.'

'How's that?' she asked.

I gotta get Chris to look at the photos we have of the other two cops, but it looks like the last two got what's known as a Colombian necktie.'

'A necktie? What the hell is that?'

'A message. Apparently it's a nasty signature of the Colombian cartels. Chris says he's never heard of it happening here and only saw it twice on a case he worked in Bogotá.'

'What's the message?'

Dominick looked over at the ME's van as it pulled away from the barricade. A storm of flashbulbs erupted, following in its wake. 'Somebody's been talking, and somebody else wants it to stop. And the missing ears means he heard something he wasn't meant to hear.'

C.J. grew pale. Fortunately, Dominick was still watching the press pounce on their moving prey.

'I bet when we dig up the past on this guy,' he continued, 'we're gonna find out he's been running with a bad crowd, just like Angelillo and Chavez. But I'm also beginning to think that maybe this isn't just local bad-boy shit. Maybe someone higher up is pulling LBJ's strings.'

On those final words, C.J. felt her stomach tighten. Even though she had quit six months ago, she knew she'd be picking up a pack of Marlboros just as soon as she got away from here.

'Did you know him? Lindeman?' Dominick asked her suddenly.

'No,' she lied. 'Why?'

He shrugged. 'Just wondering.'

23

'Falconetti. Nice of you to come say hello.' Gracker had obviously given up on the stand-off and walked over to where Dominick stood next to Manny and the crime scene techs.

'Hey, Mark. I guess I didn't notice you over there,' Dominick replied, smiling. Maybe it was juvenile, but he also knew how much Gracker hated being called by his first name once he made SAC, so Dominick made a point of using it. Every opportunity that he got.

Gracker turned red. 'Well, *Dom*, here we go. Looks like we're both working the same scene. Déjà vu.'

'Yeah? Which one is that?' said Dominick, looking around. 'I don't think there's a federal crime that's occurred on my scene.'

Now it was Gracker's turn to smile. 'No? I guess you're the last to know then. I've got a federal obstruction investigation going on here. My men are gonna need you to pack up all that crime scene evidence you've just been gathering for us.'

'What the hell are you talking about? What obstruction?'

'Your victims ran on the wild side. The Bureau has opened an investigation into their criminal activity while on the job, and possible Title 18 violations.' Title 18 referred to the section of the United States Code that dealt with criminal drug offenses.

'Help me out here, Mark. The guys are dead.'

'Doesn't matter under the law.'

'This is a homicide scene. Not a drug deal,' said Manny.

'I don't know why we all just can't get along,' Gracker said with a shake of his head. 'You see, someone has killed the subjects of our investigation, Dom. Potential witnesses. And that means that the person or persons responsible have just committed the very federal crime of Tampering with a Witness, Victim or Informant under Section 1512, Chapter 73 of the United States Code. And this,' he finished, looking around, '*this* is now a federal crime scene.'

Dominick had expected them to be creative, but not this creative. There was another three-letter acronym he could think of to describe the SAC at that moment, and it also began with the letter S. He paused before uttering his next words, which he knew could not be taken back once spoken. 'You know, Mark, I'll bet you ran this very weak theory before your very busy legal department before you actually had the nerve to traipse out here and try and bully me with it. God knows you tried to get your foot in the door on this before and no one would open it. So I'll assume for a moment that you have a valid federal investigation into the very heinous crimes of obstruction of justice and witness tampering. But I've got three homicides, none of which are going to be turned over to the Bureau and the US Attorney's Office, no matter what wild-assed legal theory you throw at me. So when we are done here, go gather your own evidence. Because, with all due respect, *Mark*, without more than your bullshit, you'll be needing a court order before I hand you a fucking nose hair from this scene.'

With that, Dominick turned and walked away, leaving

Manny to deal with the fallout. He reached for his Nextel and chirped RD Black to give him a heads-up about the very nasty, very public shitstorm that was sure to come his way via telephone. In about two minutes.

It was funny, the politics of politics. You never really knew whose favor you were in, even in your own party, until the play had been called. And while Dominick knew that his boss despised Gracker and the feds as much as he did, he also knew he couldn't and wouldn't say so from his position. To the public, all of law enforcement was happily united in one cause – ensuring the safety of its citizens. So what Black would say when Gracker called to complain that FDLE was obstructing a federal investigation – his uncensored, grating voice on decibel level ten – Dominick was not quite sure.

He could only hope that the play was called in his favor.

24

C.J. unwrapped the thin film of plastic that encased the pack of Marlboros in her hand, and peeled back the wrapper, as the fresh scent of tobacco filled the car. It took only a puff for her body and brain to welcome back an old friend, and her nerves instantly relaxed as she blew a smoke ring through the steering wheel.

Her car was still parked in the empty 7-Eleven parking lot. The sun was just beginning its ascent into the sky, and soft colors of purple and tangerine warmed the skyline. She exhaled and closed her eyes, leaning back in the seat. Trying to think. Trying hard not to let panic overrun every rational thought in her brain. In her mind's eye, she saw a young Victor Chavez – sitting in the fake leather chair in front of her desk at the State Attorney's Office, in his crisp blue uniform and shiny black shoes, with bulging biceps and an ankle holster strapped to his leg.

September, 2000 – Victor's pre-file. The post-arrest conference where a prosecutor takes sworn witness testimony to determine what charges can and should be filed against a defendant, either by Felony Information, or, in the case of first-degree murder, by Grand Jury Indictment. Only those charges which, in an ASA's good-faith judgment, are able to be proved beyond a reasonable doubt, can be filed.

C.J. was the check in the safety-valve system, the rational, prudent balance against the sometimes overzealous and hot-tempered police. One of the last inspectors on the line as the system spit out defendant after defendant, churning out justice on a daily basis. And sitting in her high-back leather chair, her window looking out upon the steel and concrete of the Dade County Jail across the street where William Rupert Bantling was being held without bond at that very moment on a charge of murder, she had listened to the cocky rookie tell his tale of finding the young model's body in Bantling's car. But the tale was full of thinly veiled fibs, and C.J. was smart, and Victor was a bad liar. And so, within minutes, his arrogant smile had been thoroughly dismantled. In its place was a scared and worried pout, as it should have been.

The stop had been illegal, based on an anonymous tip that was devoid of probable cause. Victor had recognized his screw-up too late – after the trunk had been popped, revealing its ugly contents under the bright lights of the McArthur. The search was revealing and horrific, but still no more legal, for it had been predicated on an illegal stop. That's how the law read. With the help of his sergeant, Victor had then tried to fix it all by changing his story to a faulty equipment stop – making the facts fit the crime by taking out the Jaguar's taillight with his foot – and C.J. had almost been able to hear the lock spring on Bantling's cell as she paced her office, trying her best to figure out what the hell to do.

She'd made a decision on that day. To help transform a bad lie into a plausible reality – to ensure that justice would happen – she had sacrificed her own ethics. A new story was created. One that would stand up to legal muster and justify the stop of the Jaguar and the subsequent search of the trunk. Once that was fixed, then the search warrants that authorized the search of Bantling's home and cars would also be safe, all the damning evidence admissible. And so the house of cards was carefully constructed.

C.J. sucked in a deep drag now on the cigarette and nibbled on a thumbnail, looking out the window as a well-tanned homeless man settled in on his breakfast of a Krispy Kreme and a pint of Jack Daniel's.

The problem with conspiracies was self-evident. The more people that share a secret, the harder it is to keep control of. And in that office, in that high-back, she now heard herself, demanding answers from the fallen officer.

'So it's you and Ribero?' she'd asked.

And then Victor Chavez's shaky voice in response. *'Lindeman knew about the call, too.'*

Chavez's voice now whispered that name over and over again in her head. Three people had shared the truth about that night on the McArthur before they so graciously let her into their dark coven. Two of those people had been methodically executed. And a message had been violently relayed through their deaths: *Someone's been talking and it has to stop.*

Justified paranoia or simple coincidence?

She pulled out of the parking lot and headed home. In less than three hours she had to be back in court before an ill-tempered judge and a restless jury, and she still had to shower and change. And finish prepping her cross.

Her thoughts tumbled over one another until they were simply a mass of confusion. What if the Black Jacket slayings were not the work of gang members or drug cartels, or even a warped corruption-fighting vigilante? What if, instead, someone was systematically eliminating those who knew the secret that she now shared with only one other person? Who would want to silence the keepers of that secret, and why?

She thought of Chavez's sergeant, Lou Ribero, the remaining living member of the corrupt cop trio, and wondered: *What if?* But then thought again of the question: *Why?* And to that there was really no answer. She also wondered about Officer Angelillo, the Metro cop executed out at the Dolphin Mall. As far as she knew, there was no connection with him. She had never even met the man, and he wasn't in on any of this. What to make of that? Perhaps, she thought, with an exhausted sigh, as she slid her Jeep into its assigned spot, she really was just being paranoid. She closed her eyes. If only she weren't so alone in all this . . .

A problem always seems a lot bigger in your own head, her father had once said. *Chances are if you share it, you'll see that.*

She looked at her watch again and let out a low whistle of alarm as she grabbed her purse and notebook and Marlboros off the front seat and dashed upstairs to her apartment. There was no more time left to ponder unanswerable questions. She had to get to court.

25

'We need to talk,' Dominick began. It was seven o'clock at night and C.J. sat alone in her office, disturbing thoughts interrupting her concentration, as she stared at the Westlaw computer screen in front of her.

He had appeared suddenly in her doorway, his words making her jump slightly in her chair. It bothered her that she hadn't heard him enter. That she had been taken by surprise, but she said nothing.

'Hey, there,' she replied. 'What brings you here?'

'You. Now, what's keeping you here, and why haven't you been answering your phone?' He looked concerned, maybe even angry. He had moved into the office from the doorframe, but did not sit.

'I've been in trial, remember? I was waiting on a verdict.' The answer was partially correct. 'I called you back and left a message —'

'Yeah. I got it. Congratulations on your guilty.' His voice softened somewhat. 'But this is not like you. It's not like us. I've barely seen you lately and now it's three days since we've even talked. What's happening here?'

'You've been busy, I've been busy, Dominick. Time got away from us, I suppose.' He had been coming home after she was asleep. She had been leaving before he woke up.

'No, no,' he said, shaking his head. 'That's not the answer. This has been happening for a while. *I've* been trying to reach you. *I've* been trying to speak with you.

I'm here.' He paused, and a deafening silence hung heavy in the air.

'I'm sorry,' she finally replied. There was no way to tell him the thoughts that had consumed her mind since Sonny Lindeman's body was discovered Monday night. *Even the closest of lovers keep secrets*, she had rationalized. The responsibility of this one was heavy enough for her to carry. She didn't need to weigh Dominick and his career down with it as well just to ease her own burden. And there was the distinct and troublesome possibility that he would not feel as she did. That his conscience would not keep as silent as hers, and he would feel compelled to disclose to the proper authorities that which could never be revealed.

'Why? What's going on with you?' He leaned his hands across the front of her desk now, his eyes searching to find hers and read them. 'Is it this trial? Is it Black Jacket? I need to know, C.J. You've been a million miles away, and I can't reach you. No matter how hard I try.'

'Dominick, you've worked sixteen-hour days since the first Black Jacket murder. When and where is it you would like to reach me?' She paused before continuing. 'I'm sorry,' she said again. 'My mind has been taken up with this trial for a month. You've been busy, I've been busy. We'll both try harder.'

She looked straight up at him then and his probing brown eyes continued their search. She knew sometimes how it felt to be a suspect in his custody. He missed nothing.

Instead of sitting, he walked around her desk to where she sat. He spun the chair around to face him, and taking her hands in his, pulled her up to him. Without a word, he kissed her on the mouth, his goatee gently tickling her chin in a familiar, comforting way. Yet to feel him this close – physically, emotionally – inexplicably frightened her at that moment.

'I'm sorry, too,' he finally said, holding her close. 'It's been hard, these murders. Not just work-wise.' His voice lowered, as if he were speaking only to himself. 'I feel like I owe it to them. More than anyone else on the task force. *I* have to find the person responsible, and I'm not doing a very good job. Because no matter what they did, they didn't do anything to deserve going out like that. They were on the job, for Christ's sake. In their friggin' uniforms . . .'

'You'll find him,' she said quietly.

C.J. knew that becoming a cop was not simply an option imagined at career day for Dominick. Although he didn't talk much about them, she knew pretty much everyone in his family was a cop somewhere. His uncles and cousins were with the NYPD, his brother-in-law, a robbery detective with the Nassau County PD on Long Island. His grandfather had been a cop in the Bronx for thirty years, and his father had walked a beat for twenty. She should have realized just how personally Dominick would take these murders, but she had been too busy distancing herself, and for that she now felt incredibly guilty.

'I should have been honest with you,' he said. 'This case has really gotten to me. Maybe I've been looking to reach out, and we, well, we haven't connected lately.'

She heard her voice catch on those final words. Dominick had been there for her so many times, to help her deal with the emotional baggage she carted around. Now he needed her and she had abandoned him. She had not sensed his mounting desperation, because she had been keeping him at arm's length, pushing him away. Because, unlike him, she could never be completely honest.

'Look,' she said softly. 'You're right. Judge Penney has been demanding and I've been distracted. And then Monday . . .' her voice drifted off. She looked down. 'And I'm sorry, baby. I should have come home earlier. I should have—'

But he cut her off. His mouth met hers with another kiss. This one, though, was slow. She felt his hand run up her back, over her silk camisole. His fingers wrapped around her neck pulling her closer, making her skin tingle. His breath was warm on her cheek, and then his tongue met hers. He tasted like beer, but sweet, the bitterness gone. She wrapped her own arms around his back, her fingers floating over hard muscle, pulling him closer. Even at forty-two, he still had the perfect body.

'Can we go home now?' was all he asked.

26

Without a word, he came up behind her as she closed and locked the apartment door, his body finding hers and pressing tightly up against it. His arms wrapped around her, hugging her close, his face buried in her hair. For a few minutes they stood like that in the dark hall of the apartment, his body against hers, her hands holding on to his arms, letting them envelop her. She closed her eyes and felt his breath, warm against her ear, and his goatee tickle her neck. Her fingertips traveled over his forearms, feeling the smooth definition of muscle that reached up past his biceps, onto his shoulders and neck.

She imagined for a moment that it was just the two of them in this world. No cranky judges or screaming public or high-profile cases. That work was no longer about death and what caused it, and that funeral attendance was not listed as part of either of their job descriptions. She imagined that it was just her and Dominick, living out completely different, uncomplicated lives, with no pasts and no secrets to wedge a silent, growing gap between them.

He would not let go and she would not let him. His hand pressed against her stomach, keeping her close to him, so close she could feel him now, hard against her thigh. His breathing became quicker, more deliberate and his tongue wandered out, over her ear, his open mouth traveling slowly down the curve of her neck. The fingers of his other hand crawled deliberately over her chest, moving to open the buttons on her blouse and expose her. Within seconds all were open, and his warm hand slipped inside her bra, pushing it aside, cupping her breast in his palm.

There existed an intense chemistry between them that could never be denied. C.J. knew that when she was with him, when they became one, a side of her involuntarily opened up, like a window, and he could not only see in, but could reach in and touch her very being. The skin on their naked bodies as they moved together, was simply a glorious, but insignificant barrier between their souls. They breathed as one, and for a moment in time, without words, he knew everything about her, things she herself did not even know. Perhaps that complete feeling of oneness was what also frightened her so badly at times. When they were this close emotionally, the flaws were easy to spot.

She moved her arms up, running her fingers through the short hairs on the back of his neck and pulling his head down, deeper into her neck. She arched her back into him, wanting to experience more of him, needing to touch him, taste him, right there in the hall. She let his fingers explore her breasts, his mouth on her neck, and felt her breath catch when his hand moved slowly down, over her belly until he found the button on her pants and opened them.

They had made love a thousand times in their relationship, but she still felt the same anxious butterflies whenever he touched her. A sensation that she had never had with any other man. She heard herself moan as his hands pulled her pants off her hips with a quick tug and they fell to the floor in a heap, and his fingers moved down the front of her panties.

'Oh God, I love you,' she said softly, her hands still wrapped around his neck, her fingertips digging into the back of his shoulders.

'I want to make love to you,' he whispered back into her ear. 'Right now. Right here.'

'Yes,' she said, her eyes still closed.

He took off his shirt while her hands moved behind her, over his hips, pulling down his slacks, until they crumpled into a heap next to hers.

He spun her around gently so that she faced him now. She felt his naked skin warm against hers, the hair on his chest curling against her breasts as he pressed her to him, his arms wrapping around her protectively, like a cloak. Then his hand gently traced underneath her chin and he tilted her face to look up at him. She opened her eyes. Soft light from the patio outside filtered in through the sliding glass doors, slicing through the living-room blinds.

'I'm sorry,' she began softly, fearing she might cry. The moment was overwhelming her. 'For tonight, for everything. For not being there for you . . .'

But he cut her off. 'Sshh,' he said softly. 'I love you. Don't ever doubt that.'

Then he kissed her gently on the lips and laid her down on the living-room rug and made love to her in the patio light.

27

Sonny Lindeman's funeral was held on a windy Friday afternoon at the Church of the Little Flower in downtown Coral Gables. From four blocks away, C.J. could see that it would be useless for her and Dominick to try and get a spot closer to the majestic Spanish cathedral. Cars lined the streets, and people dressed in black somberly walked past their car as it waited at the light on Red Road. Motorcycle cops with Coral Gables PD directed traffic and parking. Dominick ignored the uniforms, and instead slid the car into a small swale on the side of the road with a prominent NO PARKING sign next to it. As the officer strode up to begin the inevitable confrontation, Dominick placed the FDLE identification shield on the dashboard and walked around the side of the car to C.J.'s door. The cop said nothing and turned and walked away.

Hand-in-hand they walked in silence to the church, footsteps on the pavement the only sound on the somber processional. Voices were hushed as they made their way to the front of the church.

She had not wanted to come today, but she had done so out of respect. Respect for Dominick, who she knew needed her there. And respect for his profession, which had, in the past seventy-two hours, suffered yet another professional black eye. Dominick had been right; within hours of Sonny Lindeman's murder, nasty information had oozed out of the City of Miami's Internal Affairs

Department like a clogged drain. Sonny had been a recent addition to their Dirty List, fingered by a flip informant who wanted to cut a deal in his trafficking case. Elijah Jackson handed out names like birthday party invitations, and walked out of DCJ without posting one red cent as bond.

Two days later Elijah's body had floated by a fisherman in the Miami River. The Medical Examiner was pretty sure the cause of death was his severed carotid, but since Elijah's stomach had also been sliced open – leading to a fish feeding frenzy and swifter decomposition – it was impossible to say for certain.

What had proven to be even more interesting than the name of a bad City of Miami police officer, were the other names that Elijah, a former BB Posse member, had coughed up before floating downstream. Valle was the magic word that had actually sprung the lock on his cell. The head of one of the wealthiest families in Miami, Roberto Valle owned half of the real estate in the county and half of the SoBe nightclubs. Nightclubs where, coincidentally, each of the Black Jacket victims had worked an off-duty. A respected family man, Valle had been honored many times over for his philanthropic gifts to society and charitable donations, but it made no matter. The actions of anyone and everyone in the nightclub business inevitably raised the cynical eyebrows of law enforcement, who had looked at Valle for years for money laundering. Elijah Jackson had finally given them what they needed.

Marked and unmarked police cars from every department lined Sevilla, further than the eye could even see. Melbourne, Lakeland, Orlando – even Tallahassee and Jacksonville PD cruisers were there. From near and far, the blue wall attended, even for an unknown brother. Even for yet another who had fallen from grace.

A swarm of uniforms and dark-suited detectives crowded outside the tremendous glass and wrought-iron church doors, nervously smoking and chatting. All waited until the last possible second to actually enter the church and hear the final goodbyes. Dominick found Manny, Marlon Dorsett and Chris Masterson talking with several others. 'Hey, guys,' he said, looking around. 'Chris, is Fulton here?'

'Yeah,' Chris replied. 'He went inside with Black and Jordan from the Beach to get a seat. Said he'd hold one for you.'

'Hola, Counselor,' said the Bear to C.J. with a grin. He wore a tweed jacket with a solid brown collar that was about two inches too short at the wrists. Either Manny had put on a few pounds since the last time he had broken it out, or, as was more likely the case, it was borrowed. His black tie was scattered with little teal and white Florida Marlins emblems. 'We didn't get a chance to chat the other day. How's those wedding plans coming?'

'They're coming, Manny. Dominick just booked the salsa band.'

'I love it.' He rubbed his stomach, which protruded over his pants just enough to be noticed. 'And the food . . .' He turned to Dominick. 'Hey, Dommy Boy, you gonna shake that small Italian ass of yours on the dance floor with me?'

'I might slip a disc, Bear,' Dominick mused. 'And I'm gonna need that small Italian ass intact for my honeymoon.' C.J. felt him rub the back of her hand softly.

The Bear turned to her. 'Hey, that reminds me,

Counselor. You got a friend for me for the wedding?'

'Marisol? We've been down that road before, Manny. And she still won't talk to me after the last time you broke her heart.' Although a silent Marisol was not necessarily a bad thing. 'She hasn't given me an accurate phone message in months.'

'She misses me, does she? Psycho-witch.' He paused for a moment, pulling down on his thick mustache, as if remembering something. 'Maybe I'll call her.'

C.J. winced, trying hard not to imagine the work ethic of a twice-scorned Marisol.

'C.J.,' Chris Masterson said. 'Long time, no see. How you been?'

'Okay, Chris,' she smiled, looking around her. They had worked together on the Cupid investigation, and had always gotten along well. He was sweet, but quiet. No match for Manny Alvarez in a conversation. 'I've had better days than this, though,' she said.

'Haven't we all? I hear you're on this Black Jacket Task Force, too. I just got sucked in.'

C.J. swallowed hard. 'I was. I'm not sure if I'll still be able to do it. I've got a lot going on. Trials and motions . . .' Her voice tapered off. 'I think Maus may help out. He has the gang expertise.' She had not yet shared with the State Attorney the suggestion she had been quietly nursing over the past few days – that she be taken off the task force and replaced with Andy Maus, the former Chief of the SAO Gang Unit and the Major Crimes prosecutor who had responded to Angelillo's crime scene. Nor had she shared the idea with Andy, although his reputation as a back-stabbing press hound made her think he'd be more than happy to take the reins.

'Really? Any thought, then, before you leave us?' Chris asked.

'No. Dominick did tell me your tale on the mutilation. A Colombian necktie?'

'Nasty, isn't it? Great way to send a thoughtful message to the masses.'

On that note, she decided it was time for a cigarette. 'Yes. Excuse me for a moment, won't you?' She walked off into the crowd and then behind the church. Out of sight of the task force crew and Dominick, who didn't yet know that she was back on the butts.

Several officers in dark brown MDPD uniforms stood chatting with the dark blues of Miami Beach and the City, none of whom she recognized, under the droopy umbrella of a hundred-year-old eucalyptus tree nearby. She lit her Marlboro, trying hard not to think about what Chris has just said.

She heard the low voice of one of the officers behind her. 'Isn't that the Cupid prosecutor?'

And after a moment, another. 'Yeah, yeah. That's her, I think. Townsend. She's on this, now. I heard it on the news.' She felt their eyes on her.

Another voice, this one with a heavy, immediately recognizable New York accent. 'Hey, Carl, did you know that first guy? Chavez? The one who pulled that sick fuck over?'

'Yeah, a little. He was an asshole. Didn't deserve what he got, but he was still an asshole.' A pause. 'I knew Sonny, too. Before he was with the City, he was road patrol on the Beach. Worked with him once.'

'No shit?'

'Yeah. I think he might also have worked Cupid.'

C.J. felt her heart stop.

Another voice. 'Everyone worked Cupid.'

The New Yorker piped back in. 'Damn straight. I put in so much OT on that case, I bought me a new boat!' Laughter.

And another. 'I was tracking FI cards, following up on all that shit.'

'You must have done more Cupid bullshit than us, Carl,' said another voice.

'Night and day. That's what I'm saying. Everyone, every department worked on Cupid. It's no surprise that Sonny did.'

'How long was he with the Beach?'

'Only a year or so. Couldn't take the administration. Or the midnights. So he left for Miami. And when does he get it? On a fucking midnight shift.'

'I'm doing midnights.' A thick Cuban accent. 'They asked me if I want to ride with somebody now. I said fuck no, I don't need no babysitter. That safety in numbers shit is for my five-year-old. Just let that fucking Black Jacket try shit with old Papa here. I'll blow his fucking head off faster than he can smile.' A collective murmur of agreement sounded.

She crushed out her cigarette and hurried back past the group to the front of the church.

The loud electronic whoop of a police siren sounded. Down Sevilla, a motorcade of at least thirty police motorcycles, riding together in two straight rows, their blue and red lights silently flashing, led a black hearse, followed by a trio of limousines, to the curb in front of the church. Somber, reverent silence immediately descended upon the crowd. Some took it as their cue to enter the church, others turned to watch as the back of the hearse was opened, the shiny pine casket revealed. The distinct whir of helicopters was heard overhead. The press had no respect for the living and certainly none for the dead, and choppers from five different news agencies hovered up above, having followed the processional block by block from the funeral home.

C.J. again found Dominick and Manny in the crowd. The others apparently had already gone inside. Dominick looked at her for a moment, then smiled softly – a *knowing* smile – nodding his head slightly as a sign that he understood, then turned his attention back to the hearse. She immediately felt guilty. Breath mint and perfume notwithstanding, he knew.

The doors on the three limousines opened. From the first one a young woman in her early thirties – obviously the wife – exited; even her dark sunglasses could not hide her complete devastation. Family members that had spilled from the other limos helped her up the walkway, but she continued to turn back, as if looking for answers through the open hearse door, where her husband lay inside. She was ushered into the church, so close C.J. could see the dark streaks of mascara that trickled down like black rivers from under her sunglasses.

Another young woman followed, an infant in her arms, along with several men. All wore a similar desperate, confused expression. Back by the hearse, C.J. spotted a little girl, whose hand was held tight by an old woman.

'Damn. A wife and two kids. Can you believe that shit?' Manny said in a low voice, shaking his head.

C.J. felt her stomach churn. Her eyes remained glued to the little girl who passed before her, clutching her grandma's hand.

She heard the small, unsure voice. 'Nana, is Daddy in that car?'

The old woman paused. 'Yes, Lisa,' she whispered, 'but that's only his body. Daddy's in heaven now.'

The little girl whispered back in that tiny voice, 'I don't like heaven.' Then they both walked into the church, and the heavy glass and wrought iron doors of the cathedral closed with a dull thud behind them.

Unfortunately, though, the day didn't end there. After an emotional eulogy and draining two-hour church service, a police motorcade escorted a miles-long processional to the graveside services, where the Honor Guard in full dress blues met Sonny's flag-draped casket with a 21-gun salute. Officers took turns stoically remembering not just Sonny, but others who had fallen in the line of duty.

C.J. stood on the lawn in the hot sun flanked by Dominick and the FDLE command staff. A hand tapped her then on her shoulder. 'Ms Townsend?'

She turned and faced Lou Ribero. C.J. remembered the Miami Beach street sergeant as, Dominick had once called him, 'full of piss and vinegar.' Now he looked small and uncertain. It was apparent that he – like her – had questioned the coincidence of both Chavez and Lindeman's deaths at the hands of the same killer. He was the only other person who knew of the dark secret forged under the fluorescent lights in her office some three years ago. Or so she thought. His face was pale and drawn. He stared at her for a long moment, his eyes now searching hers.

While they had run into each other at the State Attorney's Office and periodically at the courthouse over the past three years, they'd both avoided conversation. Neither ever needed to discuss again the lie that had forged their permanent bond. A rookie – *his* rookie –

had screwed up a simple stop, but they both knew that fact did not make a guilty man innocent.

She expected him to say something now, to demand an explanation or an answer for the paranoia they both so obviously shared. But he said nothing, her troubled eyes confirming to him that she, too, had no answer.

'I'm sorry,' she said after the moment had passed. It was all she could say.

He looked disappointed that there would be no comforting words, only confirmation of his own anxiety. He nodded absently. 'Me, too,' he said, his voice final and flat. Then he just walked away, lost in thought.

Under the ten code system used by many police departments, '10-7' means 'out of service.' When an officer 10-7's his number over the radio, it signifies to dispatch that his shift has ended and that he is now off duty. On the portable steel dais, City of Miami Chief Bobby Dees, a line of blue officers in salute behind him, bowed his head as he pressed the button on the sound system. A grainy recording of Sonny Lindeman's voice, identifying himself with his badge number, crackled over the speakers. It was simultaneously broadcast over police radios across the country.

'*Miami, this is 1720,*' he said.

'*1720?*' replied dispatch in a monotone.

'*I'll be 10-7 at home.*'

'*1720, I'll show you 10-7 then, at 0700.*'

'*Have a good morning, Miami.*'

Then sound clicked out and Sonny Lindeman's number was forever placed out of service.

28

'Miami leaked. Gracker and his boys hit Roberto Valle up this morning,' said Dominick, just as Manny walked in the door. It was barely 10:00 a.m., and already the faces gathered around the task-force conference table were looking grey. A simple cast-status meeting had become a full-blown powwow.

'I hope you brought some for us,' Jimmy Fulton said, referring to the plastic shot cup of *café Cubano* that Manny held in his hand. It had taken Manny his first two days on the task force to make nice with the homely, crotchety secretary in Public Corruption. Now she brewed a special pot of the stuff just for him each morning.

'Get the fuck out,' said Manny, bewildered by the news. 'As for this,' he said – throwing back the shot with a big 'Aaahh' – 'you're all on your own. Make sure you compliment Marta's hair, though, if you want her to make it just right.' He made it into the room and took a seat next to Fulton at the other end of the long confer-ence table. He opened the window beside the *Please, No Smoking!* sign and lit a cigarette. 'When did this happen?'

'The leak or the chat?' quipped Marlon Dorsett.

'Both.'

'The City was leaking like a sieve before Lindeman's body even got cold,' said Dominick. 'The press knew he was on the Dirty List two days before he got hit. But Valle's name was off-limits to everyone. Only a select few in the departments knew his name had come up, and all were warned to shut up. He's a touchy subject.'

'No one wants to get scratched off his Christmas list just yet,' scoffed Manny. Roberto Valle may have been suspected for years of laundering illegal money through his many nightclubs and hotels, but all that was somehow forgotten and forgiven when someone needed a new cancer wing. The checks didn't just go to hospitals, either. The Fraternal Order of Police had used a few to help establish a scholarship fund. 'At least not until he's actually indicted.'

'Someone didn't listen,' added a tired-looking Ted Nicholsby, who had earned the nickname Grim for a reason.

'I think gums were flapping at the funeral,' Dominick continued. 'Elijah Jackson's prosecutor has been trying to get in with the feds as an AUSA for the past year.' An AUSA was an Assistant United States Attorney, a federal prosecutor. An esteemed position that paid far better than the State for what was bitterly viewed by some as fewer hours and less work.

'And Valle was the key,' said Fulton.

'I think so,' Dominick said. 'We'll see if Jackson's prosecutor hangs a "for rent" sign on his office door at the State Attorney's and gets a longer acronym before his name next week.'

'The *Enquirer* will find the source before anyone in command coughs up a name. Especially that wimp, Tigler, who'd have to find his balls first. That's a tough job for a State Attorney who's a eunuch,' Manny said. 'What's the damage now?'

'From what I hear,' said Dominick, 'Valle pretty much called Gracker a fat piece of shit and told him to pound sand until he had a warrant signed by one of the many federal judges here in Miami who Valle himself helped get appointed. Or, alternatively, a state warrant from one of the many state judges Valle's ultra-generous contributions helped get elected. Then he kicked him and his Mutt and Jeff friends out of his very well-appointed SoBe penthouse.'

'Ouch,' Manny chuckled. 'That I would've liked to have seen. I bet Gracker's whole fucking bald head turned red.'

Everyone looked at the Bear quizzically for a moment.

'The difference is, boys, I ain't losing it. I shave,' Manny said, defensively rubbing his own naked scalp.

Dominick nodded skeptically. 'Still, in a short five minutes, that asshole has managed to fuck up any future informal sit-downs we might have had with Roberto Valle.'

'So what's next, Dom?' asked Manny.

'Elijah Jackson ran the floor at Maniac, Valle's club on Collins where Lindeman worked an off-duty more than a few times last year. No club experience besides tipping back a few on the weekends, just friends with the right people. Namely Fat Mack, a top gun with Jackson's own former Boy Scout club – the BB Posse, whose members in the past three years alone have collectively been charged with trafficking over 200 kilos of cocaine in separate arrests. Jackson himself's got three priors for possession, one for sale. One withhold and three walks. Before he met his maker, he bragged Maniac was pulling in well over three mill a year in revenue. Perhaps I'm being cynical, but methinks Jackson earned his salary more for what he did off the books than on.'

'Or what he did *to* them books,' added Manny. 'Isn't there some law that says that if you want to keep your liquor license, you can't employ felons? If not, there sure as hell should be.'

'Jackson was never adjudicated. No conviction,' said Marlon.

'So he was supplying dope?' asked Manny.

'Three million is a lot of money. Money that perhaps needs a good bath first,' said Dominick. Money laundering went hand-in-hand with drug dealing. And of course, there was a value to cleaning money.

'That's why they pay you the big bucks, Dommy. You have an evil mind. If you're right, Valle could be scrubbing a lot of soap on a lot of Colombian backsides all over town.'

'His six nightclubs and three hotels on the Beach brought in over eighty million last year.'

Manny let out a low whistle. 'And you found out that figure how?'

'Miami isn't the only leak; the feds have equally big mouths. I have a friend, believe it or not, at the Bureau, and he owes me a favor. A look at Valle's personal tax return for 2001 opened my eyes to just how severely underpaid I really am. Don't fret, the warrant is snaking its way through the federal system to deliver me official copies of his 1040 and 1120s.'

'What did the City of Miami do, Dom, with all this sordid information in the past twelve days since Elijah handed them Valle's name on a platter?' asked Fulton.

'Met. They met and had meetings and then more meetings to discuss the meetings with Maus, the City, IA and the Chiefs to figure out exactly what should be done.'

'In other words, nothing,' finished Chris Masterson.

'That is correct,' said Dominick.

'So no surveillance on Lindeman, Valle?' asked Matt Lobelsky, a detective with MDPD.

'They were getting around to it. No one thought of a connection to the Black Jacket slayings, because nobody wanted to give up their poker hand before a monumental national news-making arrest. Letting the task force know about another dirty cop on an off-duty never occurred to Miami IA. Or so they say,' said Dominick.

'Eighty million is a lot of *dinero*,' Manny said. 'If Vale is operating a few laundromats, then I'll bet he's got some grateful clientele. Unless you think he's running the drugs himself, bringing in a little something for Fat Mack and friends to pick up at the Port of Miami and distribute to the needy.'

'It's possible. But, to borrow a phrase from my favorite hot dog company,' said Dominick, 'I think Valle answers to a much higher authority. Nighclubs make for the perfect cleaners, and there are some powerful people in this world who have an awful lot of laundry to do.'

'Okay. Then assuming Chavez, Angelillo and Lindeman were dirty muscle and knew what was going on, why would Valle have them killed and risk attracting attention? What purpose does it serve?' asked Marlon.

'All three cops worked at different Valle hotspots. Maniac and Place were under the thumb of Elijah Jackson and his ex-friends from the BB Posse. But Channel is a frequent stomping ground for Ricardo Brueto. At least it was until his pal Victor Chavez stopped showing up for work,' said Dominick.

'I see where you're taking this. The mantra for effective capitalism – eliminate the competition?' said Manny.

'Eighty million is a lot of money. Maybe Jackson or Brueto didn't want to share,' added Chris.

'So LBJ kills Chavez not just because he's a prick and owes him money, but so BB Posse can move in on Channel and move out the Kings?' asked Manny.

'Channel brought in almost five million last year. The fee for running that kind of cash through the washing machine is well into seven figures, and a cut to the Posse would net some serious six digits. That's worth killing for. And that's just Channel. Brueto's got three other clubs in his pocket, with some mighty majestic-sounding names on Valle's payroll,' theorized Dominick.

'So we're back to a gang turf war?' asked Manny.

'Funded by a big fish,' said Chris.

'And I think that big fish himself is sitting in the stomach of a large whale,' said Dominick.

'Namely?'

'Chris and Jimmy have the experience in narcotics. And according to them, only a couple of names come to mind.'

'Let me guess. Cali and Medellín. The cartels are funding a war. Oh, fuck.' Marlon let out a low whistle. He had worked homicides on the Beach for ten years, and while drugs were involved in a lot of his cases – because either the defendant or the victim was buying or selling or using or had used – the cartels didn't figure prominently in most of his equations. None in fact. Those types of investigations were handled by the feds: FBI, CIA, DEA, US Customs, Border Patrol. And that was a good thing, since drug wars could get very nasty and very personal.

'Since Pablo Escobar was taken down, Medellín is no more,' said Chris. 'And Cali faces extinction with the fate of the Ochoa brothers. We've seen a change in how the cartels operate. In '97, Colombia finally signed on the bottom line of the US extradition treaty, and now the fear of being shipped back to the States has forced the giants to subcontract some of the shipping and laundering to minimize their risk.'

'They've lost control, so maybe someone decided the time is right for a hostile corporate takeover,' said Fulton.

'Now the North Valley Cartel and Domingo Montoyo are making a power play to take over where Escobar left off. And with the help of FARC, the Colombian revolutionaries who provide security for the fields and transportation, Cali is still alive,' said Chris.

'This has been in the making, then, for some time,' sighed Marlon.

'Those neckties were no coincidence,' said Chris. 'Gang-bangers don't just learn that shit on the streets.'

'But which one is it? Who's the supplier?' asked Manny.

'That, my friends,' Dominick said, 'is the question of the day.' He slipped several thick manila folders marked SOUTH FLORIDA IMPACT — CASE-SENSITIVE MATERIAL across the conference table.

IMPACT was a multi-agency task force, that for the past ten years had worked exclusively on major money laundering and narcotics smuggling operations in South Florida from an undercover Miami location. FDLE was a member of IMPACT, and, by legal agreement, transferred their statewide jurisdiction to other task-force members while working on an investigation.

Then Dominick looked down at the table. 'So, gentlemen, start your reading.'

29

'I just don't have the time right now, Jerry,' C.J. said, watching as Jerry Tigler slumped down even further into his high-back burgundy chair. 'I've got a full caseload as it is and Black Jacket would just be too demanding.' She had practiced this speech a hundred times in her head before making it and was sure she had a reasonable excuse for every frantic plea she knew the State Attorney would throw at her.

'We can make the time, C.J. We can lighten your caseload. Why don't you give the Frison case to Bernie? He doesn't seem to have enough to do. I've watched him go home at 4:30 for the past month.'

'Jerry, Frison is a triple homicide set for trial in four weeks. I can't just pass it off on someone.' Especially not Bernard Hobbs, a fellow Major Crimes prosecutor, who actually had been heading home early for a lot longer than the past month. The only reason Tigler was on to him now was because someone had probably handed him a clock and told him to look out the window as Bernie's crimson-colored Honda Accord zipped off into the sunset with the mad rush of secretaries whose days ended at precisely 4:30 p.m.

'C.J., I need your experience on this one. I'll assign Andy Maus, too, but I want you to do it with him. Split the time. I'll make sure that Guillermo cuts back on new cases for a while.'

'Jerry, I've never said no to you before, but I am going

to now,' she said, her voice sounding hard and edgy, even to her own ears. She had already thought this through as well: Insubordination might just have its consequences. So be it. She could not be on this case anymore, waiting for another beep to come or phone to ring to notify her of the carnage. Even though the task force had linked Roberto Valle to the drug cartels and dirty cops, the paranoid part of her still did not want to be the first one on the next scene, wondering if under the mess was a face she was supposed to recognize. Like Lou Ribero's.

The faint sound of Christmas music from the office holiday party downstairs permeated the otherwise heavy silence between them. It was Tigler who blinked first, squirming finally in his seat.

'Fine, then,' he grumbled and sighed. 'I know you've been through a lot, C.J., and I knew that prosecuting another serial killer might prove difficult for you . . .'

A cheap shot. She felt a defiant surge of anger swell in her and, as he paused, she sat up stiffly on the edge of her seat.

Then he continued. 'But you're the best. You're *my* best and, I guess I'll just have to respect your decision concerning the division of your time. However, if Andy needs help, you give it to him. He can be very focused. Too focused. And I don't want him painting those boys on the task force into a corner because someone fits his idea of who a suspect should be. The public is getting anxious that there have been no arrests and I don't want to just throw them a bone to shut them up. I don't need this office making mistakes this year.'

Of course not. Tigler had won re-election by a mere 600 votes. And a lot of people – even his own – saw opportunity in 2004.

'Thank you for understanding, Jerry. Emotionally, I'm fine,' she said coolly, 'Time-wise, I'm strapped. If Andy needs assistance, he knows he can ask me.' Fat chance that would ever happen – that Andy and his ego would take a trip down the hall to *ask* for help.

'Well, then, C.J., I guess I'll wish you a Merry Christmas. Are you going to the party downstairs?'

'For a little while. Until someone breaks out the lampshades.'

'I'll see you there, then.'

She walked out of his office and took the stairs down to the second floor. She had hoped that she would feel more relieved when she slammed the door shut on this case.

The party had spilled out of Major Crimes and into the elevator bay. Like a cold, it was spreading down the halls of the Felony Divisions, and by 4:30, the whole building would be infected. Cocktail franks and cookie platters would make their way from the Legal Department on five to the Felony Screening Unit on one, and those in the know would congregate in the offices that had a little something special stashed in their desks to add to the holiday punch.

C.J. spotted Marisol, clothed head-to-toe in pink stretch denim, near the rolling file cart that had been converted to a dessert tray and now blocked the entrance to C.J.'s office. With a red Santa hat on her head and a large flashing Christmas tree pin between her breasts, she was hard to miss.

'Merry Christmas, Marisol,' C.J. said as she approached the door. Marisol's eyes caught on the stack of files in C.J.'s arms and her whole face fell.

'Don't worry. These aren't for you,' C.J. said. 'In fact,

126

we're getting rid of them. Andy Maus will be handling Black Jacket and assisting the task force. That falls into Alyssa's division.'

'Oh,' said Marisol as her face relaxed, puffing round and soft again.

'Have a happy holiday, then. I left something for you—'

'Yeah. I got it. Thanks,' Marisol managed, with some difficulty. She cracked her gum, and then paused before adding, 'I have something for you, too. It's on your desk,' she said, half smiling.

C.J. hoped it was not a pipe bomb. Things had been rocky since Marisol had gotten in trouble with her supervisor a few weeks back for cheating on her time sheet. She had immediately suspected that it was C.J. who had handed her up, but it hadn't been.

'Well, thank you. Enjoy *Noche Buena*, then, if I don't see you,' C.J. said, rolling the dessert tray away from her door. *Noche Buena* was Christmas Eve, and for most Cubans in Miami, that meant great, festive parties and dancing till 2:00 a.m.

'Yeah. Merry Christmas,' Marisol said, her pink hips finding the music once again. She dipped a long sparkly fingernail into her drink and swirled it around, before popping it in her mouth for a taste. Just as C.J. cleared the door, Marisol called out behind her, 'Do you know if Manny Alvarez is going to the PD's tonight?'

Following the relatively conservative gathering at the SAO, would be the annual Christmas Party hosted by the liberal Public Defender's Office, a party that had been blamed in the past for more than one ruined career and broken marriage. Most of this afternoon's SAO attendees – cops, defense attorneys, and more than a few prosecutors and judges – would not remember their own names come morning. Or want to, for that matter. The worst of adversaries in court became the best of buddies for just a few hours of every year.

C.J. shrugged, even though she knew the answer. Manny was a fixture there every year. The PD party had led to the demise of marriage *numero uno*.

'Well, maybe I'll see him there,' said Marisol thoughtfully.

C.J. nodded and then closed the door behind her, making a mental note to call Manny and give him a heads-up. Not that he would be warned off. Manny was attracted to problem women like a dieter to the buffet lines.

She turned on the light in her office and quickly placed the Black Jacket files into a cardboard file box. She closed the lid tightly and taped it shut with packing tape, scribbling Andy Maus's name across the top and placing it far away from her desk.

A typical three-day cold snap in December had plummeted temperatures outside from a balmy 73 to a chilly 52, dropping into the 40s at night. Tonight, the TV news would carry footage of orange groves and flower beds all bundled up and preparing for the night's freeze. The gloom and doom prospect of lost crops and lost jobs would propel the anchor excitedly for at least a good five minutes.

C.J. grabbed her black overcoat, which she broke out maybe twice a year, and placed her two file boxes marked *State of Florida vs. Joey Frison* on a hand-cart. A brutal triple homicide that started out as the premeditated death of one – Joey's girlfriend, Denise Kopp – but became three when Denise's sister and her friend tagged along to the courthouse to help Denise get her restraining order. Joey now faced the death penalty for shooting all three women in the head with a sawed-off shotgun as they waited at a light. C.J. would spend the holidays preparing to make sure he got it.

She felt weary. Weary and overwhelmed and inexplicably frightened by her job. She was no miracle worker, but she was good at what she did – taking a case before a jury and painting the picture they needed to see, one witness, one piece of evidence at a time. She had become a prosecutor to be a voice for those who had none, in a system that listened only to its lawyers, a system that strived to protect the Constitutional rights of the accused, oftentimes at the expense of their victims. And she did that job every day, taking it home with her on weekends and on vacations, never really putting it aside. There they were, always nibbling at her thoughts at a traffic light or in the shower or at the beach. Like a general, her mind always forming a plan of attack on how to do battle, how to put the enemy away, how to keep them there, contained. In criminal law, until the sentence has been served, the phone can ring at any time, an assistant from the Attorney General's Office on the other line telling you to keep a heads-up because it's coming back. Even years later – *it's coming back*. So no case ever really goes away. It stays forever stacked in the recesses of your mind, like a warehouse, piled neatly next to the rest. C.J.'s warehouse was nearing capacity. And the feeling of vindication, of giving back something to society, had waned. The difference she had hoped to make in this world was not seeming to be enough in the end.

She fingered the present left behind on her desk calendar by Marisol. A black coffee mug filled with hard candy that carried Marisol's message of peace in white bold-faced letters: BEHIND THIS BOSS IS A BETTER SECRETARY. C.J. left it behind on top of her file cabinet.

She headed for the door, with Joey Frison and his shotgun – her bedtime reading this coming Christmas Eve. Her fiancé was too busy hunting another monster to sit beside her and help her strategize on how to put this one away. Or at least in storage, where she could never forget him.

30

Drugs. It all came down to drugs and money and that's why three cops were dead. Dominick rubbed his temples. How much money did it take to look the other way? To strong-arm a couple of people? A few hundred here and there? A cut of the take? What was their price? Dominick wondered. Angelillo, Chavez, Lindeman? What was the going rate to betray the badge?

They probably thought that there would be no harm. After all, it's just money. *I'm not hurting anyone. All I'm doing is sending a message in the uniform. I just have to stand here and pretend to be on their side. Tomorrow, when I'm on duty, I'll bust some mopes. I'll take in the guy who hits his wife and the loser smoking crack in front of a school bus. I'm not really one of them.*

Dominick sat in his car, one hand still rubbing away the throb in his aching head, the other drumming fingertips against the hard plastic of the steering wheel. Underneath the music on the radio, the state police dispatch crackled and hummed with information and emergencies. Most were intended for FHP troopers, who shared the same frequency, called to respond at this time of night – 1:30 a.m. – to a DUI or an accident on the highways. On another channel, FDLE agents on surveillance sat on a house in Florida City chatting occasionally with agents working the Governor's protection detail and other agents up on a wire. On yet another, Beverage Agents with ABT – Alcohol, Beverage and Tobacco –

worked a sting inside a bar in Pembroke Pines known for its underage drinking. As light faded from day, and most normal people turned off their engines, had dinner with their families and went to bed, a whole other world was just waking, their business best done in the dark. And the cops that followed them into the night just watched and listened and waited. In undercovers that smelled of Burger King and old coffee, they chatted and joked amongst each other, watching with night-vision binoculars set on dark doorways. Always listening, always waiting for the right phone call or conversation to come through the static on the tap or the bug and wake them with a jolt of pure adrenaline. Afraid to blink or sneeze or go to the bathroom because they might miss *it* – the defendant sneaking out a window, the exchange, the conversation – the one act that would prove the bad guy bad. The night held many secrets, but it gave up just as many.

Dominick sat now on Washington Avenue, his eyes on the strip of busy nightclubs that dotted the SoBe street before him. In Versace catsuits and Roberto Cavalli body stockings, the nightlife spilled onto the streets, in and out of expensive cars, leaving expensive tips behind. He had spotted a couple of uniforms working off-duties outside, but he knew there were others inside, mingling, even though they shouldn't, with the VIPs and celebrities. Dominick had the list of who worked where, right there on the seat next to him, as all off-duties have to be signed off on by the department. The off-duty lists had been the first thing forked over by each PD, right after their Dirty Lists. But even though his own car smelled of stale coffee and fast-food grease, Dominick was not on surveillance tonight. There was no call for it yet, as the wire would hopefully go up on Valle soon – assuming that after FDLE Legal was done with it, that the judge and SAO would okay it – and maybe that would lead to some more names and some more answers.

Tonight was simply about an inability to set it aside, to stop the search and resume life as normal when the clock told him he was no longer on duty. He had not even realized it drove him here till he threw the car in park and sipped at his coffee.

The answer was out there. It always was, you just had to know where to look. And this case was no different. But it was worse. The Black Jacket. The cop killer. It never let him sleep. It never let him out. It never stopped screaming, forcing him to look for answers by himself in the night.

Dominick thought of his father now. *What was your price, Dad? How much did it take for you to look the other way? And was it worth it?* He closed his eyes for a moment and leaned his head against the seatback. In the darkness he saw his father now, coming home late at night in his blue uniform, gun holstered to his side, shiny handcuffs dangling next to a cold black baton. Dominick lay in bed, watching shadows from the rooftop party across the alley dance on his ceiling, waiting until he finally heard that rattle and jingle of keys, the slow creak of the door in the jam, the final twist and click of the deadbolts – his father home from the beat, as his mother had called it. The cracked linoleum felt cold beneath his bare feet as he crept lightly past his parents' bedroom, toward the kitchen where he knew his father would be sitting with his cold Miller and pack of Marlboro Reds.

The crisp bills, held tight in his father's hand, rustled like soft whispers as they slipped off one another, his father's nervous grunts barely audible as he counted them into a neat, small stack. Even at twelve, Dominick had known what he was witnessing was somehow wrong, but did not know why; the air somehow smelled different, felt different. He listened as his father counted the small stack of money before him over and over and over again, as if the number could not possibly be right, gulping at his Miller High Life and chain-smoking cigarette after cigarette. Dominick never waited up for him to come home again.

And now, in the darkness of his undercover, under the streetlights of SoBe, Dominick forced open his eyes. He banished for the moment the image of a man who he had once idolized, who he sometimes despised. He stared now at the people crossing Washington, milling about, trying to beg or flirt or bribe their way past the red ropes of the Mansion. Strangely enough, though, there was no more sound, no music, no whispers on the radio to fill the car. All Dominick could hear was the hollow and familiar voice in his head screaming for an answer he would never find, to a question that he would always ask.

31

'*Cafecito*,' Rico said to the short, round man behind the counter. Chatter in mixtures of English and Spanish sounded all around him and the robust, sweet scent of cigars hung heavy in the air, which was, for January, unseasonably warm and sticky. Tantalizing, fragrant smells of paella and fried steak wafted onto the sidewalk on Eighth Street. Old men dressed in their best *guayavera* shirts gathered in small groups on the patio and outside the bakery next door, enjoying their coffees and conversations. Although the busy scene played the same at any other Little Havana cafeteria, *Versailles* had been chosen today for a reason.

The voice came now from Rico's left. He did not look over. 'What, you bring company with you wherever you go?' A reference to the surveillance team that followed Rico around everywhere.

'Motherfuckers won't get off my ass. I can't do shit,' Rico groused, knowing enough not to turn around, lest the *cochinos* in the Taurus down the block catch his lips moving on film or something. Hell, they could probably read lips. He couldn't fuck up now. Too much was at stake.

'We're not here to talk about you,' said the man with no accent. 'We were paid a visit.'

'I heard.' Rico swallowed hard.

'These events . . .' the voice paused for a second, cognizant that parabolic mikes could be placed anywhere and in anything. Cops could be very creative – with or without a warrant – and his words would need to be carefully crafted. 'These *events* have brought a great deal of attention. There is concern. Mouths have opened.'

'That was taken care of,' said Rico. He knew for a fact that Elijah Jackson would say no more. Someone had made sure of that, feeding Elijah right back to the fucking river as fish food. Made Rico's job easier. Let the Posse kill each other off for ratting, it saved him time and trouble.

'Everyone wants to be a hero, though,' said the man. 'Certainly enough incentive.'

Crimestoppers was offering a $100,000 reward for information in the Black Jacket slayings all over billboards in the worst neighborhoods in South Florida. That sort of *dinero* motivated people to say the wrong things sometimes.

'Not at my end,' said Rico nervously, downing his shot with one gulp. He whipped out a cigarette and lit it quickly. He still did not look behind him. 'Money ain't opening no one's mouth. I'll make sure of it.'

'Well, we're not so sure. It's a motivator.' The voice paused again. 'Nothing is coming in, Rico. The well is drying and no one wants that. Everyone has been hit hard since this Black Jacket. There needs to be a peace offer. Put the baby to rest, once and for all.'

Rico gulped, knowing what the man was about to propose. 'In a minute, a minute. But, if you're thinking about . . .' Rico looked around. 'Shit. That . . . that could be difficult.'

'It shouldn't be that hard. You're gonna find that dead president for us, Rico, and you're gonna send him our thanks and our regards. You do that and it's double what the pooch would pay.' The pooch was a reference to the Crimestoppers poster dog, Detective McGruff. He was being offered a $200,000 bounty for LBJ's missing head.

'Okay. Okay. I can take care of that,' Rico said after a moment. 'But I don't know where he is. No one does. He's been hiding out like a fucking scared-ass, and the brothers won't give him up.'

'No one's untouchable. Remember that, Rico. Wait for the call. No one but you does it. Understood?'

'Ain't he gonna move?'

'Don't you worry about that. You just wait till you get that call. Tomorrow or next year. You do what you're told.'

'Yeah,' Rico said.

'Oh, and Rico. When the time comes, don't bring your friends along wit' you,' the voice said, referring to the Taurus that had crept up the block. Then he disappeared into the busy crowd, leaving Rico all alone at the counter.

32

The man waited in the shadows of the gray stairwell trying hard not to breathe in the stench of old piss and vomit and stale beer. Four stories below, the brilliant lights and glitter and neon of South Beach spread out before him. The hour was late, and the freestanding parking garage on 13th was empty, as it had been for hours, its purpose really to accommodate the shoppers and beachgoers that trolled Washington Avenue in the daytime. He had already checked to make sure that there were no undesirables haunting the many dark corners and crevices on each level, looking to sleep off the day's drink or get in a quickie in the shadows before heading home to the wife and kids. Only a single car sat alone now on the rooftop of the fourth floor, its engine on, the AC dripping condensation that ran out from underneath its belly trickling into a slow-growing, oily-looking puddle. The car faced east, toward Ocean Drive and the shores of Miami Beach, its windows closed tight against the night, its distracted driver oblivious to what waited for him in the dark stairwell only a few yards away.

It was ironic, really. The same super-ego that would win a cop a gold medal for bravery would be the very same one that would ultimately drive the steel nail into his own coffin. It caused him to join the SWAT team and bust blindly through doors looking for hostages, but it also told him he was invincible, impenetrable to bullets and knives, no matter how many funerals he had attended. *The motherfuckers ain't taking me* attitude got a cop through the shift, through the next twenty years. It made them detectives and sergeants, and it drove them here, alone, to a deserted parking lot late on a Saturday night to park and do paperwork just like they've always done in the middle of their shift, in silent defiance of department recommendations and of their own fears. *Because no mope is gonna make me change my routine, make me change my life. No motherfucker is making me run or taking me down. Just fucking try it. I'll be waiting. I dare you . . .*

The man walked out of the shadows of the stairwell behind him, inhaling the scent of the sea and suntan lotion that lingered somehow in the beach air even in the dead of night. He walked confidently toward the cruiser, rising to the silent challenge made by the man seated in the front seat.

You're on, Sergeant, thought the monster as he fingered the blade in his jacket pocket. Then he tapped lightly on the window and, with a smile, introduced himself to the man inside.

33

Just eight more years. Eight more and he would be free from doing this shit every night. Shit that he loved and shit that he hated. It had started not to matter anymore, and for the first time in his career, Lou Ribero had begun to count the time. The time till he was off his shift. The time before he had to go back. The time before he was done with the whole fucking job. He used to think he would do this forever, maybe take the Lieutenant's test next, then maybe even one day, Captain. Who the hell knows? His wife, she wanted to move up to Mount Dora and antique shop for the rest of her life and he had thought, well, maybe that would be a great job to go out with. Retire after twenty with the MBPD and sign on as a captain with the six-man force of the Mount Dora Police, where the biggest things he would have to worry about would be parking on the swales and people paying for their antiques with invalid credit cards. But he would still be a cop and he would still be on the job, even if the paycheck wasn't so hot and the crimes weren't so interesting. He would still be a part of it.

But now ... now it was different. Everything was different. He swallowed a chunk of his roast beef hoagie and slugged down a gulp of Coke as he moved the cursor over the right box on the laptop and began to type out yet another detailed report in the dim light of his squad car. His growing ulcer threatened to burn a black hole straight through to his intestines, and he rubbed his stomach trying to ease the pain. Even the pills didn't help with the stress no more. The past couple of months, the tension at the department over this Black Jacket was so thick you couldn't breathe sometimes. Now everything had to be perfectly documented, every second accounted for. There was lots of pressure to find the guy, find his motive, weed out the cops who don't walk the straight and narrow, attack the ones who were victims because that's where the problem must be. They must have been targeted for a reason. Off-duties were bad, cops could be bought.

It pissed him off, the manipulation of the facts by the press and the hypocritical reaction of indignation from the public. Because the truth be told, people didn't really *want* to know what needed to be done to catch the bad guys. Just do it. Find the murderer, get the confession, clean the street, get rid of the dopers, just don't tell us *how* – because it might be ugly. The department, well, they preached the rules, but everyone knew what had to be done when roll call was over. As a sergeant, Lou himself had done the preaching.

He had done this job for twelve years, and he had never really given a shit about the press or the bleeding hearts at the ACLU or the hypocritical idiots who wrote editorials in the paper. He'd always slept soundly at night. Of course, he didn't okay guys on the take. That was different and that was bullshit. And so if it did turn out that Chavez and Lindeman were really dirty and were taking home on the side – not that they deserved to get whacked – but, well, then let the truth come out. The only problem was, Lou Ribero didn't really think that was why they had been hunted.

He had talked to that prosecutor at Sonny's funeral

and she knew, too, even though she had said nothing. Couldn't bring herself to say shit to him except sorry. *What the fuck was that about? Sorry?* She had realized the connection, just like he did, and she was definitely afraid. But of what? Afraid for herself? Afraid for him? Afraid to get caught? Afraid that the secret would get out and she would lose her job? Or maybe she was worried that that psycho Cupid would get out of jail if anyone besides them figured a connection between Chavez and Lindeman.

Lou remembered the headlines back then, how that sick fuck had to be restrained and gagged in court, held back by Corrections all the while vowing to kill the prosecutor, claiming he had raped her, claiming he had been framed, claiming she had set him up, that the police had set him up. That was bullshit. The guy was fucking guilty. Lou remembered that girl's body, Anna Prado, stuffed like a rag in the back of that Jag's trunk, eyes wide open and missing a heart. That was an image you never forgot. And bodies don't just crawl into trunks by themselves. People have to put them there. Maybe the stop wasn't perfect, but that was just a bullshit technicality and that dead girl *was* in that trunk and that guy *was* fucking guilty. Even if there had been a reason to doubt before, then there were those hearts, the hearts of all those dead girls that the task force had found later, linked back to Bantling. There was no coincidence. So they had done the right thing after all.

And in three years, Lou Ribero had never looked back. Cupid had been just another case where a bad outcome had been averted by quick thinking. But now . . . someone was making him look back, making him take it home, making him wonder, and all Lou could ask himself every single fucking day of this never-ending job was *why*?

The light tap at the passenger window quickly pulled him out of his troubling thoughts with a start. At the sound, his fingers moved to unsnap the SIG-Sauer P-226 at his side, but when he saw the familiar face smiling at the window he relaxed and unlocked the door.

34

Dominick raced down 395 and the McArthur Causeway with lights and siren on, the tremendous cruise ships in the Port of Miami and the glow of downtown blurring past on his right. He felt the unsettling familiarity of déjà vu creep over his consciousness.

Police cars already lined Washington. Patrons were being escorted out of clubs and hurried away from the crazy scene that unfolded on the streets, the crowds excitedly looking around to see where the commotion was coming from. Their eyes settled on the top of the four-story parking garage, which had exploded in a mass of flashing blue and red and white lights. Dominick counted no less than five helicopters that dangled from the sky, searchlights criss-crossing the streets below like the opening of a five-star casino in Vegas, while the MDPD helicopter kept them back, shooing their cameras away from the scene that developed on the roof below.

Crime Scene was dusting the elevator for prints, so Dominick took the stairs two at a time instead, pushing past more techs who photographed and videoed each level of the stairwell from every conceivable angle. He burst out of the stairwell and onto the fourth floor. No less than twenty cruisers were parked haphazardly across the lot. An ambulance and fire truck waited nearby, their lights on as well, but there was no need for either. One cruiser stood alone, its windows painted black from the inside. Just the driver's door was open, and the heavy white sheet trailed out onto the asphalt.

Handhelds and radios exploded around him, cops reporting back and forth on the status of the wide-reaching perimeter that had been set up, hoping to ensnare a killer who might still be within their grasp. The frantic energy bordered on chaos, as sergeants and lieutenants from different departments barked different orders to those in their charge. Mark Gracker, who had apparently just arrived on scene as well, also barked orders to the FBI agents he had brought with him.

Manny and Ted Nicholsby stood talking with three men in MBPD uniforms, two of whom looked like they had been crying. The third looked sick, and Dominick noticed vomit on the tips of his black shoes. Manny looked in Gracker's direction and Dominick could tell the Bear wanted to kill him, maybe throw him off the roof to the hungry wolves in uniform below who would love to feast on an asshole – any asshole – right now.

Dominick headed immediately for the lone cruiser, the one no one else wanted to get too close to. The painted windows glistened, as if they might still be wet. He lifted the sheet with gloved hands and cringed. 'Jesus Christ,' he whispered.

'This is bad, Dom,' said the voice behind him. It was Marlon. He looked shaken up. 'We've got a ten-block perimeter set up and FHP is blocking off—'

'What the fuck is this?' Dominick barked, his voice shaking as he stared at the sight below. 'What the fuck is this?'

'Looks like the others,' started Marlon, but Dominick shook him off.

'Where's Chris? Where's Masterson?' he demanded,

his eyes searching through the commotion on the rooftop.

'He's here. Let me raise him,' Marlon said, stepping back to talk into the Nextel.

Dominick spotted her then. C.J., standing by herself next to the entrance to the stairwell. Even through the flash of the red emergency lights that spun across her face Dominick could tell she was pale. Her arms wrapped tightly around her chest, she stared blankly through him at the cruiser.

What the hell was she doing here?

He walked toward her, searching the crowd of uniforms and plainclothes for ASA Andy Maus, but he was nowhere to be found.

'Dom? Hey, Marlon raised me.' Chris Masterson appeared suddenly in front of him.

'What the fuck happened here?'

Chris looked at the cruiser. 'Sergeant with the Beach. ID'd as Louis Ribero, age thirty-six.'

'What the fuck happened?'

'Looks like the same killer,' Chris started, confused. 'It's another necktie, that's for sure. Throat was slit and then the whole tongue muscle was pulled—'

'What the fuck happened to his eyes?' Dominick demanded, his voice rising to almost a shout. 'What is this freak trying to tell us? You're the goddamned expert! What the hell is his message and what does he want?'

'The eyes were gouged. From all this blood, it may be pre-mortem. I can't tell you what the message is for certain but given the necktie and probable cartel connections we've found I'd say the message is this guy saw something. Something he shouldn't have seen.'

'And now he'll never talk about it.' C.J. was suddenly

beside them both now, her eyes still glued on the cruiser. Her voice was distant and flat.

'Are you okay?' Dominick asked, taking off his FDLE windbreaker and wrapping it around her shoulders. She looked so cold, even though the air was mild. Chris looked embarrassed, as if he had intruded on an intimate moment, and he backed up a few feet, turning his attention to one of the crime scene techs who had begun to photograph the car.

'What are you doing here?' Dominick asked after Chris had walked away. She looked awful. He knew she wanted nothing to do with the Black Jacket case, did not even want to discuss it with him since she had asked to be removed from the task force. 'You're not on this anymore. Where the hell's Maus?' he asked, looking around past her.

'I was beeped,' she said softly.

'What? Here? Who beeped you?'

'I don't know who. I called back the number and got the Miami Beach Police Department's homicide unit. When I asked who had beeped me, no one knew. The detective who answered said everyone had just gotten called out, here, to another Black Jacket murder that had been tipped on the nine-eleven line.'

'So it must have been a homicide detective. Are you the on-call?'

'That's just it. I'm not on homicide duty this week. Gail Brill is. And it wasn't the homicide beeper that went off. I don't even have it.'

Dominick looked confused.

'Apparently someone wanted me to know, too,' she said wearily, pulling her hands through her hair. Her eyes finally looked away from the cruiser and up at him, and he knew then that she was more than just frightened. She was terrified.

'Dominick,' she whispered, 'the page came through my cell.'

35

'Now this is interesting – he used a different knife on the throat. This one was serrated, with a significant dip and curve on the end, before the blade met the handle. I'm thinking, Detectives, that you're looking for a hunting knife in all likelihood,' said Dr Joe Neilson, the breath from his words fogging the clear, plastic shield that covered his face. His nose twitched several times, and he looked as if he were about to sneeze. Then his eyes blinked rapidly and he looked back down at the nude, still body laid out on a gurney that ran off next to a stainless steel farm sink.

'Incredibly sharp and efficient. And here we have the same situation that we found on Officer Chavez,' he continued with a smile, the nose twitch finally subsiding. Both his face and his stainless steel ruler were now almost lost in Lou Ribero's ragged throat. 'Here,' he said, without looking up, his bloodied latexed fingers motioning for them to come closer. 'There is an overlap of tears, the first of which initially severs the jugular and the windpipe only. Blood spots in the lungs indicate this guy drowned in his own blood. Again, this overlap appears deliberate. The second went smoothly, straight across from ear to ear, no hesitation.'

Dominick, Manny and C.J. stood in the white-tiled laboratory at the Miami-Dade Medical Examiner's. Britney Spears cooed lightly on the radio in the background and the room smelled of fresh coffee and disinfectant and death, a scent C.J. knew never left these walls, lurking in cold storage or sliced up into tissue samples and placed in heat-sealed plastic bags in file folders next to X-rays and death certificates.

Normally, ASAs did not have to attend autopsies, even if they were on homicide duty, as that was the lead detective's job, but Black Jacket was no ordinary case. Unfortunately, it would take at least another four to five hours for Andy Maus to make it back from a three-day weekend across the state at his nephew's christening in Tampa. Jerry Tigler had refused to send out Gail Brill, the on-call ASA covering for him, secretly relieved, C.J. was sure, that someone from the MBPD had been smart enough to beep C.J. first instead of him. There was no room for argument, not unless she was prepared to quit right there and then over the phone, so she had stayed on scene, just a few feet away from the cruiser, its lights still flashing against the backdrop of the city, answering legal questions.

Tigler had also informed her she needed to attend the autopsy. Then, she supposed, he had hung up and gone back to bed. And so here she was, standing as close to the exit door as possible without being conspicuous, arms wrapped tightly around her chest, watching, detached, as this whole macabre scene played itself out. She was trapped, watching the autopsy of a man whose murder – her now frightened and crazed mind told her – she might very well be responsible for.

Sweetheart, Dominick had said, *someone in Beach homicide probably remembered you were the original ASA assigned to Black Jacket. They got your cell number from Nicholsby or Dorsett's Rolodex, or from SAO Criminal Intake, or your secretary, or they had it already, C.J. Maybe they're embarrassed they beeped the wrong person at 3:00 a.m. and now won't own up. Honey, you can't keep seeing ghosts.*

Without further explanation, she appeared paranoid. And there would be no further explanation. It was then that she insisted on driving herself to the Medical Examiner's, and left the rooftop long before Dominick could have the chance to play protector and hop behind her wheel, taking direction of yet another tragedy in the making, his probing questions and soft brown eyes demanding answers that she could not give him. And now she knew he was angry with her, avoiding her when they had met upstairs in the reception area, refusing to look at her now during the autopsy. But the truth was, she had needed to be alone – not because she wanted to be, but because she had to be. She could not trust herself – in a rush to clear her own conscience – not to drag him into this conspiracy.

Dominick was jotting notes as Neilson moved about Ribero's body, making incisions and taking measurements and weighing organs, mumbling excitedly to himself under his breath. A pale-faced Manny moved back even further from the steel gurney and rubbed another gob of Vicks VapoRub under his nose. He shot C.J. a weak grimace and then twirled his finger in a circle by his temple. The Vicks made the silver strands in his mustache shine under the fluorescents.

'What about the eyes?' asked Dominick.

'Definitely pre-mortem. We can tell because of the bleeding. If the eyes had been removed after he had died, then there would be minimal bleeding at the incision sites. Most likely sent the poor bastard into shock.' Neilson paused for thought. 'Well, hopefully.' Then he continued excitedly, 'Here, look at this, Detectives!' the fingers of one hand probing the inside of Ribero's empty socket, the other again beckoning excitedly for someone to come closer for a better look. And again, there were no takers. Joe Neilson was more enthusiastic than most MEs and it took working with him a few times to figure out what really needed to be seen. Manny and Dominick had worked with him enough over the past decade to know this was one of those times they could stay put. 'The blade he used on the eyes was smooth – look at the way the optic nerve was severed! And I'm guessing now at the width, but I'd say we're looking at a one- to one-and-a-quarter-inch diameter. Impossible to tell on the length. Maybe a scalpel, but I don't think so. Swiss Army, possibly.'

'Excuse me, Doc,' said the man in green scrubs who stood atop a stepladder over Lou Ribero's naked body. He held a Minolta Maxxum 3000 in hand.

'Oh, okay.' Neilson backed up slightly, his fingers holding the ruler steady inside the empty black socket. White flash exploded on Ribero's face.

'We'll send the photos to the FDLE crime lab in Tallahassee. Rieck is an expert on knife patterns,' said Dominick.

'Quantico also has excellent facilities,' added Neilson. 'I know that—'

'This is a state case. We've got it,' said Dominick, his tone instantly communicating that the subject was not up for discussion.

'Okay, then,' said Neilson with a shrug. He flipped up the protective mask and waited impatiently while the tech finished up with the pictures, his foot tapping anxiously under the gurney. 'Ceasar?' he called to the technician in green scrubs reading the morning edition of *El Nuevo Herald* across the room. 'Can you finish?'

The man nodded, putting aside his paper and grabbing a metal bowl, a washcloth, liquid soap and a large spool of black thread from the white Formica cabinet overhead. Neilson rinsed off cross-sectioned slices of gray matter with a rubber hose and then slid them off of the counter into a plastic evidence container. Then he pulled off his gloves and threw them in the wastebasket marked BIOHAZARD.

'What about drugs, Doc? This guy got anything in him like Chavez and Angelillo?' asked Manny, looking anywhere but Neilson's face when he asked the question.

'The preliminary tox results show no drugs in his system, but it will take a few days for the rest to come back. His heart was strong, no sign of long-term drug use. This guy would've lived to be a hundred maybe, but I guess someone else had other plans,' he said, reaching over Ribero's gray feet for his coffee cup on the counter behind him. His arm hit the toe tag, and it swung gently back and forth for a few moments. 'Detectives, coffee? I'll make fresh.'

'No, thanks,' said Dominick, heading for the door, averting his eyes from C.J.

'How much of that shit do you drink every day?' asked Manny in amazement with an eyebrow raised as he followed Dominick to the exit sign.

'Not enough. I've got another four lined up this morning, Detective,' Neilson said over his shoulder, while he busied about making fresh coffee. 'My next damsel in distress – meet Dawn.' He nodded behind him at another gurney that had been wheeled into the far corner, where a naked woman lay, her lips and protruding tongue swollen and blue. He pulled on a new pair of gloves with a snap and crossed the room to another steel farm sink with an extended rubber hose. 'The ladies down here, Detective Alvarez, well they're all just dying to meet me,' he joked then with a smile, and either a wink or a twitch. No one was quite sure.

Then the doors to the lab swung open and Dominick walked past C.J. in silence, heading straight down the hall for the elevator.

36

It was impossible to deny the connection any longer. Four men were dead and three of them she'd shared a secret with. Three of them had received a brutal Colombian necktie, and the three she had conspired with had been mutilated in a more symbolic way.

Victor Chavez's tongue had been cut from his mouth.
That was to shut him up.
Sonny Lindeman's ears had been sliced off.
He obviously heard something he wasn't meant to hear.
Lou Ribero's eyes had been gouged.
The guy saw something. Something he shouldn't have seen.

And she knew she was not the only one to note the symbolism. The task force still frantically worked the drug angle, but Dominick now had them re-running every case, every traffic ticket, every goddamn FI card each officer had worked, written or assisted on to see if there was any other link. For what it was worth – considering each now knew they were being investigated, thanks in part to the feds – the taps were up on Valle and Brueto, but had so far yielded nothing. Ribero's last off-duty was more than six months ago and it was supervising the traffic at a public roadway construction site. He had done a few off-duty stints at clubs on the Beach when Miami hosted the Source Awards, but there was no clear link yet to Valle, the Posse or the Kings. No one could even place him at a Walgreens, much less tie him to a drug cartel.

And it wasn't just the task force that was searching through the rubble, either. The FBI had descended with not just the court order Dominick had demanded, but backed now by the very-much-pissed-off muscle power of the US Attorney's Office for the Southern District and the legal manpower of the Department of Justice. And though everyone in law enforcement had been ordered to cooperate, no one really did, which meant that no stone would be left unturned. Twice.

The shortlist of those to be interviewed was anyone who had worked with, associated with, had been arrested by, or was related to any of the slain officers. That included family, friends, associates, defendants, defense attorneys, judges, and prosecutors. The longlist included everyone else. There was no doubt she had made that first list. She thought she had buried Lindeman's name, but Ribero and Chavez had both testified in the Cupid case.

She had stayed home on Monday, the phone pulled from the wall, the cell off, claiming the need to work on a motion without distraction, when the truth was, she had sat out on her patio all day, smoking cigarettes and drinking wine and staring down at the lapping waters of the Intercoastal, trying desperately to figure out what to do. What even *could* be done. And after three days, she still had no answers. Because she could not answer the core question: *Why?* Why would someone want all three men silenced? And what the hell did Bruce Angelillo have to do with anything?

Jerry Tigler was pissed off at her because she still would not work Black Jacket, and Andy Maus, now back from Tampa, was pissed that he had not been the one on scene Saturday morning, and that Tigler still wanted her to work it. She knew that Dominick was angry and hurt, and worst of all, frustrated with her. He was the one person who could read her, who she could not fool when she lied and told him everything was fine. So she had avoided him and his phone calls. Sleep was difficult, to say the least, as her brain worked overtime trying to answer the same questions that had consumed her for months now.

She had accepted the consequences of her decision three years back. But she had not been prepared for this.

She had not been prepared for her decision to cost others their lives. And still she could not figure out why. She had dug a trench in heavy sand, and it was now collapsing in on itself. It was burying her alive.

But she couldn't just hide out in her apartment any longer hoping the answers would come to her. She had a file cabinet full of other cases to attend to. Motions, trials, arraignments, pre-trial conferences, pre-file screenings, First Appearances, Arthur Hearings. And the list kept getting longer.

The package was waiting for her on her desk on Tuesday morning when she arrived at work at 7:00 a.m., on top of a stack of other mail. It bore no return address, but C.J. had not noticed that until she had sliced through the packing tape and parted the flaps.

Styrofoam peanuts spilled out on her desk when she dug her hand inside the box to pull out what she initially had presumed were depos or maybe audio- or videotapes sent over by inter-office mail or perhaps a court-reporting service. When her fingers touched on the cold, smooth, hard object inside, she was at first puzzled. But as she pulled it from the box, the horror of the moment became all too clear. But only to her.

In her hand she held a small statue that she recognized instantly, although she had not laid eyes on it in fifteen years. The three wise monkeys, carved in green jade, sat next to each other in a row, their eyes large and their teeth bared. The hands of one covered his ears, the hands of another, his eyes, and the hands of the third, his mouth.

Hear no evil. See no evil. Speak no evil.

It was a message, personally addressed to her and delivered right here, to her office – the very place that had spawned the conspiracy. The conspiracy that she now knew definitely had killed three men. But as the delicate statue slipped from her hands and shattered into pieces across her desk, she also knew something else.

She also thought she knew who had sent it.

37

In 1987 her parents had traveled to the Orient for two weeks, her father hoping to walk the Great Wall of China, her mother hoping to take a picture from the snack bar of him doing just that. On their return, they had given her a small statue of the three wise monkeys that they had picked up at a souvenir stand in Beijing. Her mother had said it would bring good luck to her home.

It was carved from green jade.

It had sat on the end table in her living room when she lived in Bayside, back when she was a law student, back when she was twenty-four and pretty, with lots of friends and a cute boyfriend, back when her biggest fear was taking the New York State Bar Exam. Once upon a lifetime ago, before William Bantling had forever changed the course of her future.

He had known everything about her, from her favorite TV show to her favorite restaurant. He knew where her parents lived, when they had called, when they were visiting, the nickname of Beany that her father had given her as a child because of her sweet tooth for jelly beans. He knew all about Michael, her lousy ex-boyfriend, from where they had vacationed in Mexico to what position they had made love in the night before. And he had been there, in her apartment, not just on that night, but, she had realized afterward, many times before – reading her mail, thumbing through her books and photo albums, fingering her clothes, maybe eating out of her refrigerator, drinking from her milk carton. He had hunted her, stalked her, and then he had whispered her secrets back into her ear, his voice a throaty sing-song, letting her know that he was the one in complete control. And from that there would prove to be no escape, not even in her dreams.

Everything about that night, about that apartment, she had thrown away, from the toothbrushes to the furniture. Anything that he might have touched or tasted or played with or studied she never wanted to see again – ever. And she had not looked back, struggling instead for years to forget the past and grasp hold of a future.

Until now.

Bantling had sent her a message from behind iron bars and barbed, electrified fences, locked away and waiting for his final phone call on death row. *He* had been in her apartment. *He* had seen the jade monkeys, she was sure of it. No one else would have known of them, or their significance to her. Unless . . .

Unless he had told someone.

Her heart was pounding as she pulled her hands through her hair, pulling back the thoughts that threatened to again derail her sanity. The prosecutor screamed questions inside her head, trying hard to slap her awake, before she slipped again. *Wait, wait . . . If it is Bantling who sent this, and he knows about the lies each officer uttered to put him on death row, why would he kill the very people who could possibly one day free him? Who could help prove he was not Cupid? Why would he eliminate witnesses?*

Because he is sick and deranged! She answered herself back in her head, screaming just as loudly at the prosecutor. *Because he'd love nothing more than to let me know that he's watching and he knows what I've done and that he's still in control, and that I'm not safe. I'm next. He is picking them off right in front of me so that I'll go insane first . . .*

No, no, no, she shook her head, muttering the words aloud now. Her thoughts raced back and forth.

Unless he had told someone . . .

Wait, wait, wait. Let's analyze this, C.J. Just like any other case. What if the opposite were true? What if someone else didn't want him to ever get out of jail? What if someone didn't want him to prove he was not Cupid?

But who would want that? Who, besides her, would want to make sure Bantling never got off death row? That he died for crimes he did not commit?

And the answer to that frightened her even more than the question itself.

The very person who had committed them.

Or persons.

38

'Something has happened and I have to go away for a while.'

'You've got to be kidding me, right? C.J. what is this, some sort of joke?' Dominick stood in her living room, staring at the suitcase on the living-room floor.

She moved around the room as if she did not want to stop, clearing off her coffee table and tidying up. 'It's no joke, Dominick. And I'm sorry. God, am I sorry. I don't want to do this, but I have to go. I have to.'

'What the hell happened, C.J.?' he said, grabbing her arm as she passed him, to stop her from moving away from him. 'What the hell has been going on?'

She did not pull away, but she would not look at him. Her voice was all but a whisper. 'Things aren't the same.'

'What are you saying? Between us? I know we've both been busy – I've been tied up these past few weeks, but,' he paused for a moment, his voice choked with either anger or sadness. Maybe both. She couldn't quite tell. 'Where the hell is this coming from?'

She still couldn't look at him. She just shook her head and sucked in a sniffle. 'It's just a leave of absence. A couple of weeks, a month, maybe. I don't know. I just know I need to get away from Miami, from work for a while. I'm burnt.'

He let her answer hang in the air. His hand still grasped her arm by the elbow, but his grip had slackened. She felt him study her now, his mind gather up the thoughts in his brain and then line them up, posturing them into stinging questions, as he would for an interview with a subject. And then he said it.

'Why did you lie to me about Sonny Lindeman?'

'What?'

'You heard me. Why did you lie to me and tell me you didn't know Sonny Lindeman? He was one of your Cupid witnesses on the original A-form.'

'Dominick, I don't remember—'

'Bullshit. You have a mind like a steel trap. I knew from the look on your face that night that you knew him. And you knew Chavez and you knew that last guy, Ribero. I remember you talking to him at Lindeman's funeral. You have been freaked out since Chavez popped up missing his tongue and don't think I'm the only one who has noticed. Your boss might be an idiot, but even he knows this is not you. This is not C. J. Townsend, the prosecutor with balls bigger than mine who has witnessed more shit in her career and in her life than the very fucking veteran homicide detectives she's been assigned to help out. She doesn't walk away from an investigation, she doesn't refuse to come to scenes or discuss cases. So what gives, C.J.? Now you're walking out on *us* and I want to know – what the fuck gives?'

'I wish I could, Dominick. I do. But there's nothing now that you can do. Or me, either.'

'Try me.'

She sat silent for a moment longer, just listening to the controlled sound of his breathing, staring at the gold badge with the state of Florida on it that was clipped to his belt. 'I got a package yesterday. Something in the mail.'

'Where is it? Where is it?'

'It was a statue. A small statue. I dropped it and it shattered, but it wouldn't make a difference. The box was plain, no return address. I'm sure it was clean.' She paused, carefully considering her next choice of words. 'It was a message, a personal message, intended for me.'

'What was the statue?'

'The three monkeys. You've probably seen them somewhere before. Hear no evil, see no evil—'

'Speak no evil,' his voice drifted off and he paused in thought. She could see the light flick on, making the connection. 'Black Jacket. Jesus Christ! The eyes, the ears – maybe that was meant for the task force, C.J. Maybe that statue was meant for us!' he said excitedly. This could be the break they needed, an attempt at communication by the killer. 'You were at the last scene, you were the one initially assigned, your name was in all the papers. Maybe whoever sent it thinks you're still with the task force and they're sending us a message through you. Was there anything else with it? A note? Where are the pieces?'

'No, there was nothing and it's gone. Dominick, look, it was not some oversight by a gang-banger who has attention deficit and can't read the paper to know I'm not handling it anymore. Listen to me. I used to have the *same* statue, carved in green jade, in my apartment in New York. I got rid of it, I got rid of everything after the rape. But he, he was there, and he saw it . . .' Her voice caught and she stopped. Tears began to stream down her face. 'I'm not being paranoid. I'm not.'

'Because of that you think it's from him? You think it's from Bantling?' She had never admitted to him that it was Bantling who had raped her. She had never admitted it to anyone. In fact, she had denied it was Bantling when Judge Chaskel asked her point blank after Bantling's murder conviction. And Dominick had never pushed her for any other answer. Never.

'C.J.,' he continued, his voice soft, but firm, as though there was no room for argument. 'I know it was Bantling who raped you.' There. It was out. 'I *know* it was him, honey. And so if he was the one who was in your apartment and he was the one who saw that statue, *why* would he send it back to you now? Wait, let's not even get that far. How *could* he send the monkeys to you? He's on death row.' Before he even asked it, though, Dominick already knew the answer to his own last question. Where there's a will, there's a way. And where there's money – which Bantling once had plenty of – there was a long line of people on the inside and the outside who would do a favor.

'Things just are so complicated, Dominick. I never wanted them to be, but they are. I thought I was,' she caught herself before she finished the sentence. *I thought I was doing the right thing at the time. I thought I was saving society from a killer, but somewhere along the way, the lines got blurred. Now I may be responsible for the deaths of three cops. I may have taken a daddy from his kids.*

'What would Bantling have to do, though, with the Black Jacket murders, C.J.?' She could see him thinking, sorting through information that was always in his possession, looking for the link, that in his mind, his trained eyes should not have missed. 'Is that why you're running? Those cops all worked Bantling's case, all of them. We know that even Angelillo followed up Cupid leads. Bantling's now sending *you* messages. Why? What happened with those cops?'

He took a breath, remembering now how his foot had crunched over pieces of taillight on the McArthur the night Cupid was pulled over. A taillight that Victor Chavez later said was broken out miles before he pulled over Bantling's Jag. It wouldn't have been beyond that moron Chavez to flub a fact or two, make the facts fit the crime . . . but, C.J.? She said nothing, and he knew from her lack of response that he was unfortunately headed in the right direction. Then he quietly asked his final question. 'Did you fix it? Was it fixed?'

She was not going to drag him into this. She would not make him an accessory to her crime. She shook her head. 'No.'

'Then tell me what it is. It won't change things.'

'Yes. Yes, it will.'

'Goddamn it, C.J.! I love you. You know that.'

'But it will change *how* you love me, Dominick. It will change *how* you love me. And I can't take that, seeing that look in your eyes, knowing something is different even though you tell me it's not. I would rather end this now – knowing that you love me – than stay, wondering if you don't.'

'That's a cop-out. A fucking cop-out and you know it. Let me be the judge of my own feelings!'

She said nothing, just looked down at the floor.

'So this is it? The wedding, it's off? Everything is —'

'Postponed.' She pulled her hand through her hair, still looking at the floor. 'I don't know, Dominick. I've got to figure this out and I can't make you a part of it. You can't help me now.'

He backed up, away from her, simply nodding his head, wondering how everything had changed so fast and why he hadn't seen it coming. Or why he hadn't wanted to. He turned and opened the front door.

'I'm sorry,' she said, crying.

He closed the door behind him without looking at her again. He headed toward the elevator feeling sad, angry, bewildered, fooled, betrayed. A dozen emotions he hadn't expected when he pulled his car into the parking lot downstairs. While one part of him wanted to find a bar and lose consciousness with a bottle of J&B, the cop in him wanted to find answers. Answers to questions he should have been asking all along.

The answer was always out there. You just had to know where to look.

He opened the car door and slid in, looking up at her bedroom window twelve stories above, where she finished preparing to leave. The answers he should have known months – even years – before started coming to him now. He hung his head against the steering wheel before mumbling his one final question aloud.

'Jesus, C.J. What have you done?'

39

William Rupert Bantling, Florida State Prison inmate number 578884526, lay on the thin, plastic mattress and stared up at the bubbles in the ceiling. A while back, some genius in jail administration, who had nothing better to do with the state's money, had thought that painting the prison's cement ceilings, floors and walls a pasty, industrial gray would be a brilliant idea. Maybe cheer up the forty-four death row inmates who sat alone in their six-by-eight cells twenty-two hours out of each goddamn day practicing their goodbyes. Maybe it would help calm them back down after their lawyer called to tell them not to make any plans after 6:01 p.m., Eastern Standard Time. Now the humidity that made life unbearable had swelled pockets in the paint, the genius had either been promoted or fired, and flecks of gray paint rained down on Bill Bantling every fucking night.

Normally he hated this time in his already unending, incessantly boring day. The time spent staring up at the peeling ceiling, just waiting for the dumpy guard with a control issue to flick the lights before time, while guys were still reading or brushing their teeth or shitting, and then yell 'Lights out!' with a wheezy chuckle before moving on to his next Hershey Bar. Any idiot should know that it's coming, and to put down the toothbrush and get off the pot fifteen minutes before time, but these were not just any idiots. These were the best of the lot. The shouts of the pissed-off animals that surrounded him would start and then go on for another twenty minutes or so. But tonight, none of this would bother him. Tonight, let it rain, because nothing could take away the smile that consumed Bill Bantling's handsome face.

He closed his eyes and saw her, her once *extraordinary* face, hovering over his. Her long honey-blonde hair with the delicate curls at the ends, draped past sculpted cheekbones and over tanned naked shoulders. Red luscious lips that never lost their pout, even after all these years. He had conquered her once, and she had submitted – those pretty eyes no longer defiant, but terrified – weeping salty tears that ran down her perfect cheeks onto the silk panties that he had stuffed in that very luscious, red mouth.

He had had her again. Running, defeated, terrified. In that courtroom 992 days ago, he had seen that look in those eyes again. First defiance, when she thought she could win, that she could play this game with him, because she was a prosecutor and sat in the powerhouse seat and could whisper in the judge's ear while he was chained to the fucking table in a red jumpsuit. Then fear, when she finally realized that it took more than a title to fuck with him. And that she couldn't run from him in her nightmares. Because that's where he was, every night. She still went to bed with him. And by the end of that farce the press called a trial three years ago, he had known that she was his once again. Those weepy eyes had come to court, crinkled with age lines and sunken in dark circles, and they couldn't look at him. That moment he knew he had won.

And he would again. Now he knew that and it made him smile. He clutched the letter in his hand, the one that told him he was back in her nightmares once more.

It's not over, oh no. In fact, the fun's just beginning, he thought to himself. He smiled again just as the guard shouted, 'Time!' and those perfect eyelashes fluttered above him, raining down flecks of gray paint that felt like tears.

40

As the plane touched down, C.J. looked out the window at the pasty, gray sky and wondered if it was going to snow. That would be bad. It had been years since she had driven in snow, let alone the kind on twisty mountain roads.

She boarded the Alamo Rent-a-Car bus with a dozen other people, all of whom carried large duffle bags and ski-totes. Just like on the plane, it looked like everyone was heading to the powder. A young family, a group of friends, a loopy-eyed couple. Pictures of excitement and happiness and good times to come, ripped right out of some Vail brochure or a *Condé Nast Traveler* article. Everyone except C.J. She carried no skis, no heavy parkas, just a simple bag with a sweater, a pair of jeans and a tube of toothpaste – enough for one night.

She had practiced what she would say a thousand times before even booking her ticket. Then another thousand times on the five-hour plane ride. And she would use every minute of the two-and-a-half-hour drive to Breckenridge, an old, small ski town, to rehearse a thousand more. But it still did not sound right, what she needed to say. It probably never would.

She had not spoken to Lourdes Rubio in the three years since the Bantling trial. Their parting after his sentencing was civilized, but cold, and shortly thereafter Lourdes had closed down her criminal law practice in Miami, picked up and left town without any goodbyes.

Previously, Lourdes and C.J. had worked together on other homicides, and she had always found Lourdes to be straightforward and ethical. Her opinion, of course, had since changed.

There were times in the years since that C.J. had thought about Lourdes, wondering what had happened to her, where she might have headed, if she were still practicing, but that was where her curiosity ended. Because she knew there would be no warm and fuzzy reunions or 'let's catch up' chats between them. Ever. And Lourdes knew it, too. She had said as much the last time they had spoken in that courtroom. Right after her client was dragged out by three corrections officers, kicking and screaming under a gag and shipped off to face the needle on Florida's death row in Raiford.

She sipped at her coffee, probably her tenth of the day, and turned the Blazer out of the Alamo lot, headed for 170.

It's coming back. Whatever the reason, get those files out of storage, because it's coming back.

Only this time, C.J. knew the reason.

There was one more person who knew why Victor Chavez had pulled over Bantling's Jaguar on the McArthur that night. And she was still alive, practicing personal injury law in a small town where most people were ski bums, and it was all too easy to get lost and forgotten in the seasonal transience of the population.

C.J. had never forgotten their last conversation in that quiet, deserted courtroom, after the press had left and the judge had gone back to his chambers and the jurors had all gone home. When it was just the two of them, separated by more than just the physical distance of the empty gallery. She had never forgotten what had been said, just closed the lid tight on the memory and shoved it into storage in the warehouse in her head, hoping never to have to open it again.

C.J. flicked the wipers on full speed to keep up with the heavy, wet flakes that assaulted her windshield, and turned on her headlights. After many phone calls and an exhaustive public records search, she had finally found Lourdes, a woman who obviously did not want to be found, living in the mountains two thousand miles away from the familiar fronds of a palm tree and practicing the type of law she had once claimed to detest. C.J. had finally conjured up the balls to make the phone call and tell Lourdes that they needed to meet, and that's when it had gotten strange. Strange because Lourdes did not seem particularly surprised or shocked to hear C.J.'s voice on the other end of her phone, and she certainly did not miss a beat when C.J. suggested they meet to discuss something. She asked no further questions, just gave her a date and directions from the Denver International Airport.

The entire call lasted less than two minutes, and after C.J. had hung up, she couldn't help but think that it was odd, Lourdes' reaction to her phone call. Or lack thereof.

It was as if she had known C.J. would be calling.

41

A light jingle, like that in a candy or dress shop, chimed when C.J. opened the wood door with the small peek-a-boo window. Outside the two-story building, in simple gold letters above the door was the name L. RUBIO, ESQ. It was so unobtrusive, C.J. had almost missed it, and she wondered if Lourdes really wanted to run a law practice up here after all.

She stepped into the modest office, furnished in Southwest colors of turquoise and indigo and copper, and looked around. A large, hand-knit Indian throw rug was mounted on the wall above a plain oak desk, and a simple bookcase filled with Colorado Revised Statutes and personal injury treatises lined the far wall. Lourdes' law degree from the University of Miami hung alongside the throw rug, next to her State of Colorado law license, but there was nothing else commemorating her many years as a criminal defense lawyer down in Miami, not even an acknowledgment that she was admitted to practice in Florida. No plaques or awards from any of the associations that C.J. knew Lourdes had been recognized by. No framed newspaper articles or pictures with Jeb Bush or other political cronies she had won over with her brains and tight connections. There was nothing. Nothing besides a carved wooden moose that stood with a smile next to a few family pictures.

Lourdes stood, quietly watching C.J. look around her office, a cup of coffee in hand.

'Hello, C.J.,' she finally said, and it made C.J. jump, as if she had been caught doing something she shouldn't have. She turned from the pictures and faced Lourdes for the first time in three years. Lourdes did not move toward her, but stood still in the doorway that led to a back room, just watching her. She blended right into the walls in her cream oversized sweater, which she wore over blue jeans and boots. A big change from tailored suits, three-inch heels and $30 per square foot rental space in posh Coral Gables.

'Hello, Lourdes,' C.J. replied slowly. 'Nice office.' Small talk would be a waste. 'I think you might know why it is I needed to talk to you,' she began.

'Bill Bantling, I figured. Have a seat, C.J.,' she said, moving quickly from the doorway and behind her desk, her hand ushering C.J. to one of the two chairs in front.

C.J. nodded deliberately. The irony was not lost on her, as she took her seat in the client's chair, before what once was one of the most powerful criminal defense attorneys in Miami.

'What else but him? Let's face it, C.J., there's not a lot else that's left between us to talk about.' Her tone was edgy and harsh, as if she had been thinking of what she was going to say for years, and each time she had rehearsed it aloud to no one but the mirror, she had gotten even angrier. So now even her hello sounded like a hiss.

'Something has happened,' C.J. said slowly.

'Is Bill dead yet?' Lourdes asked, the sarcasm dripping from her voice.

'Obviously, you and I have unresolved issues.'

'There's a line C.J.,' said Lourdes. 'And you crossed it.'

'Who draws that line, Lourdes? Who?' C.J. could feel

the anger in her swell as well. 'We all did our job. Every one of us. The police, the State. He got a great defense.'

'Bullshit. He never had a chance. *I* dropped the ball. *I* screwed up. And I live with that thought every single day of my life.'

'The system worked its magic. The guilty paid for their crimes.'

'He paid for someone else's, though.'

'As if his weren't bad enough to warrant the punishment? You sit here, Lourdes, full of remorse for your perceived role in this? For who? For a man who viciously raped fourteen women around the world, probably more? Not just raped – but tortured and maimed and almost killed them? A man who would do the same to his own attorney if he got the chance? Save your guilt for someone who deserves it.'

'He got the death penalty, C.J. He's going to die. A human being is going to die for something he did not do. Doesn't that have any effect on you?'

C.J. paused for a moment, then said quietly, 'I did my job, Lourdes. He would've raped others by now. Three, four, maybe more, if he had gotten off. Maybe he would have killed them. I did my job, and I made a choice. The lesser, I believe, of two evils. You ask if it affects me?' C.J. leaned forward in her chair, her hands on the edge of Lourdes' desk, her stare locking onto Lourdes', forcing her, for a long moment, to see the damage with her own two eyes, the scars that words never adequately explained. 'Think about it. How could it *not* affect me?'

'You're justifying,' said Lourdes, coldly.

'And you're denying,' said C.J. as she sat back in her chair. 'Four cops are dead, Lourdes. Four cops, in case you didn't read it in the papers while up here saving society from the likes of people like me, one slip and fall at a time. Now I want to know – do you still talk to him? What did he tell you? What did he tell you about me?'

That was it. She knew that the anger in her voice had been replaced ever so slightly with desperation, and she knew Lourdes had heard it also.

'Hold on,' Lourdes said, her hand raised in front of her. 'Just wait. If this is about the cop killings in Miami, yes, I have heard about them. But now you want to come into my office and insult me, and then beg me to divulge privileged attorney–client information? Just so that you can assuage your own fears and guilty conscience? You can forget about it.'

'I'm not trying to allay my fears, nor am I asking for penance. But I need to know what this is about. I need to know if these killings are somehow related, Lourdes. People are dying.'

'And that matters to you suddenly?'

'Innocent people.'

'Not from what I've read. Seems all those good cops whose characters couldn't be impugned on the stand were all good-for-nothing dopers. That's what I've been reading. They were working for the cartels, those saints.'

'A task force is still working that angle,' C.J. paused. There was no sense in bluffing. It was time to show her cards and see what Lourdes was holding. 'You knew about the tip.'

No one had ever claimed ownership to the phone call that had set all the dominos in motion more than three years ago on the McArthur. Rather than search for an identity, C.J. had buried the 911 tape's existence, initially rationalizing the call could have originated in anything from road rage to misidentification. Later, after Bantling had been convicted, after the truth had almost killed her, she had assumed that the caller was dead. Now she wasn't so sure.

Lourdes smiled, a bitter, frozen smile that was not at all friendly. 'The tip? You mean the piece of evidence that the jury never got to hear? The evidence that was withheld from the defendant?' She watched C.J. for a long moment. And without another word, she knew.

'So now it becomes clear. You think there's another killer out there, C.J., don't you? Now you're a little more than worried – you're desperate. It was okay when you thought the real Cupid was dead and buried, but now there might just be another killer. And this one likes cops, is that it? He likes cops,' she paused for just a second, 'or maybe *witnesses* would be better term?'

'I'm going to be honest here, Lourdes. I got something in the mail. A jade statue just like one I used to own when I lived in New York. When, he ...' her voice drifted off. 'You know what he's capable of! I need to know who he told. Someone he's talked to must have sent it to me!'

'I'm not going to presume to know what any one person is capable of, C.J. I'm also not going to give you any privileged information. I have spent three years running away from what I've done, trying to make my-self believe that the ends somehow justified the means. And now I know for sure that that was not the case. We both do.'

'He's a madman, Lourdes. Remember that.'

'I felt bad for you, C.J., about what you'd been through, about what he did to you. I still do. And I had a hard time with that, balancing my feelings with my job, with the oath I took to zealously defend my client. I let my feelings manipulate me, and I compromised myself in that trial, thinking it might make me a bad lawyer, but a better person. And I live with that damn decision every single day of my life. And every day, believe it or not, gets even harder. I feel bad for you, for what happened, but you're alive. He didn't kill you. And I'm not going to help you kill him.'

That was it. There was nothing left between them to discuss. C.J. stood and blinked back tears. She gave one final nod to Lourdes, then walked out the door and into a nasty snowstorm. The soft jingle of the door chime was quickly silenced when a cold gust of wind slammed the door closed behind her.

42

Lourdes sat at her desk for a long, long time after C.J. had left, listening to the tick of her wall clock and the familiar burp and hiccup of the old coffee pot in the back kitchen, her face buried in the open palms of both hands.

Who draws that line, Lourdes?

C.J.'s words sounded again and again in her head. She knew that she had not given her an answer, because Lourdes honestly didn't have one. It was her embattled conscience that had driven her out of Miami, away from a successful practice, from friends and family, to hide from her sins up here in the mountains, hoping time would ease its suffering. But it simply made the condition worse. Her conscience – was that friend made or born? Or was hers skewed with the help of a mother who'd read from the Bible every night before dinner, even when there was no food on the table to eat? Some people supposedly didn't even have a conscience – failing to develop one by the age of three or four, and sunk for life. Some had one and ignored it constantly. Others had one, but it didn't always work right. So what made the conscience, the friend, always right, anyway? *Who draws that line, Lourdes?*

Bill Bantling had been her friend before he'd become her client. She hadn't seen the sociopath in his startlingly blue eyes before he sat her down and told her he was a rapist. And even then, it hadn't clicked. It must be a mistake, she had thought. A 'he-said-yes/she-said-no' toss-up that he had lost one night after things got a little hot and heavy. But then she had read them – the police reports out of New York that described in vivid detail all the brutal things Bill Bantling had done with his sharp knife, his face disguised by a rubber clown mask. It was not just hard to read – it was agonizing. And the unspeakable injuries . . . Lourdes knew C.J. would never recover, physically or emotionally. How could any woman?

She couldn't blame C.J. for her feelings, but her conscience would not allow her to excuse her actions. *Why?* Why wasn't it right to put him behind bars forever for his crimes, even if it was ultimately for one he did not commit? Why did her fickle conscience scream and buck at that, but not when faced with the hard realization that Bill would do it again and again if the lock was ever sprung on his cell?

She knew he would too. C.J. was right in that regard. The real William Bantling was a predator. Once he had let her in on his explosive little secret past, she had seen it, and he had no longer cared if she did. The ruse of their friendship was up and her purpose now in the relationship was to simply get him off. And she had agreed. She had agreed to represent him. She had agreed to use the best of her abilities to give him a zealous defense. And, she knew, that was where she had failed. And that was why her conscience throbbed. And that was why she had run.

She knew now what had to be done, and time was again of the essence. She could not let him die because of her own ineptitude. Even the worst criminals deserved a passionate defense – it was the foundation of the legal system. And if she were to stand accused one day, she would expect no less from her own attorney. Yet, she had failed him on purpose. She fingered the cassette tape in her hand, the one marked *911-9/19/2000 8:12 P.M.* The one that she had gotten from the Miami Beach Police Department's Records Department three years ago, before the original master was destroyed. She had carried it around in her top desk drawer, its presence a constant reminder of her failure. She slipped it in the yellow bubble mailer with the other information, and sealed the clasp shut on the back then placed it in her outbox. She would mail it on the way home to her TV dinner.

The light jingle of the door sounded just then and Lourdes looked up. Above the door, the wall clock read 4:30. Where had the time gone? Beyond the vinyl blinds at the window, she could see practically nothing but white now. The news had said last night to prepare for the worst but, of course, she hadn't. And she should've left the office two hours ago when C.J. had, because now the roads would surely be a nightmare.

Now the 4:30 prospective client that she had forgotten all about was here. He'd braved the treacherous weather to meet with her, and she hadn't even looked at her appointment book. She composed herself, then rose with a smile from behind her desk and came out to meet him.

'Ms Rubio? Whew! I wasn't too sure if you'd be here with this weather and all,' he said as he shook off the cold. 'But I figured you'da called me.' His voice had the soft twang of a Midwestern accent.

Damn. She couldn't even remember his name. Unger? Something like that. 'It looks pretty bad out there, Mr . . . ?'

'Uustal, Al Uustal. Remember? We talked on the phone?' The man brushed the snow off his black overcoat and draped it over his arm, but kept his black wool beret on.

She nodded. 'Yes. I'm sorry, Mr Uustal. It does look pretty nasty out.' She glanced out the window again, and saw that the snow drifts were already up to her window and the street looked empty of the usual line of parked cars. 'I'm surprised you made it through.'

'Oh, I wouldn't have missed this appointment.'

She motioned for him to have a seat in front of her desk, then she moved behind it and sat down, searching for a legal pad to take notes. Now that he was here, she couldn't send him away. 'I had some pressing business this afternoon and lost track of time. Forgive me for not being more organized.'

'That's alright. I understand.'

'Now,' she said, finally catching her breath, and looking at him with a serious smile over her glasses. 'Let's talk about why you're here.'

'Well, I think that's pretty obvious. I need your services. I . . . well. This is very difficult for me.' He looked around nervously, then leaned in close to her desk and said in a hushed voice. 'Is what I tell you – can you tell anyone else?'

'No, Mr Uustal. What you tell me is protected by the attorney–client privilege. It can't be divulged to anyone. And the privilege extends to my support personnel as well. Although,' she added to reassure him, 'there's no one else here at the moment, so you can speak freely.'

He nodded, then sat back in his chair. 'There's been a murder. This girl, she—'

'Oh, I'm sorry,' she said, her hand up. 'I don't want to interrupt, but I don't handle criminal cases, sir. I used to, but . . . not anymore. The most criminal work I do now is limited to DUI.' Her hands pulled the Rolodex on her desk closer. 'I'm pretty much strictly personal injury, but I can recommend someone who handles criminal defense.'

He looked concerned and pulled down on his mustache, cupping his mouth in his hand. With that cap on and the tint in his glasses, it was hard to see his eyes. 'Well, I don't know if I need a defense lawyer,' he said. 'See, it hasn't actually happened, this murder. Yet.'

Lourdes again held up her hand to stop him from saying any more. 'Future crimes are not protected by the attorney–client privilege, Mr Uustal. Before you say any more, if you have knowledge of a crime that is going to be committed, and you divulge it to me, that information is not protected and I would need to report that to the authorities.'

A strange and uneasy feeling came over Lourdes Rubio at that moment. Behind the man, she could see that the front window was almost completely frosted now with snow from the gusty storm outside. Night had begun its slow and steady creep over day, and the light was almost gone.

The pause hung in the air for a moment, and just like that, she knew who he was and why he was here.

His long fingers slid down his mustache, revealing the friendly, now familiar grin underneath.

'Oh, I'm not too worried about that,' he said, rising. He pulled a strange-looking knife from underneath his jacket. 'I don't think my attorney will be telling any more tales out of school,' he whispered, as he came around the desk to meet her.

Then the snow settled in on them and the light disappeared from the mountain sky.

43

He watched her struggle for air, her hands at her throat. Her eyes were open, staring up at him, begging him – *the very person who had split it open* – for help. He just watched.

That was the most fascinating part of death, he found. Watching it come. It was different for everyone. Some became calm, as if you'd done them a favor by ending it all a little earlier than they had planned. Others were composed, as if to appear as anything but would be completely undignified. And others, well, some went nuts – flailing and thrashing in full swing, fighting with all they had left. Those, he suspected, were the ones who knew they had fucked up. That knew they still had some unfinished business on this earth, and were not yet ready to present themselves to their maker.

He never kidded any of them into thinking this wasn't the end, into thinking they weren't going to die. He didn't believe that was fair, leading them to believe they'd be closing their eyes for a bit, expecting to wake up in a hospital with a new grasp on the preciousness of life. No, he didn't think that death under false pretenses was the right thing to do. So he'd told them, each and every one over the years, that they were going to die. It gave those who believed something to pray for, and for those who didn't, well, it gave them some time to reflect and maybe start believing.

It was incredible this power that he had over life. He supposed every human being had it, but only a select few chose to use it. In his hands, he could make the ultimate decision. The ultimate one. Would someone go home to their honey, or close their eyes forever?

He had discovered that power, the weighty *thrill* of bringing death, that first time, quite by accident. His gun had discharged and left a hole the size of a dime in the chest of another man. He had watched the man – a boy, really, all of about seventeen or eighteen – he had watched him stagger back when the shot hit him, square in the center of the chest. He could tell that the boy hadn't even felt it at first, because his face, initially surprised, quickly grew dark and surly, and he moved forward as if to lunge. But then his body disobeyed him and he dropped to his knees. 'Fuck!' he yelled, his hand to his chest. Then the coughing began. And the gasping. And the pleading. 'Motherfucker, man! Call someone!' He had barked before the words stopped coming.

But he had just watched, like some villain in a bad dream, mesmerized that this asshole – who would've killed him first if he'd had the opportunity – was now on his knees begging for help. 'I think you're going to die,' was all he had said to the boy. That was when the thrashing and flailing started, as the boy fought off that final meeting with a God who would surely be more than just disappointed when they met.

He had thought himself a monster, then. And he was frightened by what he had done and, worse, by what he had not done. It had been disturbing what he had felt watching someone die – the surge of excitement that was unexpected and almost erotic. But then they had come and patted him on the back and said, 'Congratulations!' as they zipped the boy up tight in a body bag. Because to them, the boy was the enemy, and that made him a brave man who had done what he was taught to do by killing. It was okay to kill certain people – the bad ones, they had said. In fact, it was welcomed.

That day had changed him forever. It had stirred something in him that perhaps had always lain dormant. Like some mythical vampire or ghoul, he had become addicted to death, craving that rush, the taste of power that he held in his hands, wondering for many years if he was some sort of freak, but believing deep down that he was not. He had only to read the morning paper to know that there were, indeed, others out there like him. All over the country. All over the world. Like other addicts, he had taken comfort in that knowledge. That was when he had set out on a strange journey to find his own kind.

The blood had seeped into the rug like a sponge and was creeping its way slowly across the room. He was careful to step over it as he walked around her desk to her outbox. The yellow bubble mailer sat on top, already stamped and just waiting to be sent off to Neil Mann, Esq. of Coral Gables, Florida.

Almost done now, he thought as he picked up the mailer and tossed it into the duffle. He flicked off the light with his gloved hand and closed the blinds on her window. Then he slung the duffle across his shoulder and walked out into the snowstorm to finish the job that he had set out to do.

44

'So, just like that, the crazy bitch wants to get together again. The same lunatic who almost ate my nuts for breakfast when she caught me talking to that *mami* from Walgreens. "That wasn't no witness!" she'd said then. Now she wants to get married and have my baby. Can you believe that shit?' Manny said, with a yawn and then a puff on his cigarette. 'I should never have gone to that PD party. Never. It fucks me up, Dom, and I lose my head. A few drinks and a roll in the sack for old times' sake has now got me trading in my balls for a living-room set from Rooms To Go.'

'You were warned, buddy.' Dominick had hoped to spend the five-hour drive to Raiford in silence, contemplating all the things C.J. had said, or, more importantly, all the things she had not said. But then Manny had insisted on coming along, and Dominick had spent the hours listening to the Bear either yap or snore. Perhaps it was a good distraction, after all. Too much thought about what he had to do next would rip him apart. He needed to be calm.

'That's true. The Counselor did send me a heads-up, and she knows better than anybody what a nutcase her secretary is.' The Bear grew quiet for a few long seconds. Everyone on the task force knew that C.J. had left the office and left Miami. It didn't take a brain surgeon to figure out that since Dominick was still showing up to work every day, she'd also left him. Most had cut him a wide path, leaving him alone to lick his wounds in private. But not Manny, who'd felt obliged to do just the opposite. Manny had enough experience in the field of exes to know that what Dominick really needed was a few laughs, a good friend, and a lot of drinks to make it through the first couple of weeks and get back on the horse. He certainly didn't need to be zipping off to no death row by himself to re-interview the psycho serial killer who had once claimed in open court to have raped and tortured the poor guy's now ex-girlfriend. No, Manny figured, that wouldn't be a smart move at all, when he'd heard Dom making plans over the phone with the warden for a visit to FSP.

'It's okay, Bear,' Dominick now said, when the silence hung on a little too long. 'I can stand to talk about her. I'm a big boy.'

'Women, Dommy. I'm no expert – look at me, dating a freaking psycho who wants to be Mrs Alvarez number four and I'm actually considering it, too – but, well, what can I say? Soft and smelling sweet. Then they look at you with those eyes and they wiggle their ass and it gets me. Each and every time.'

'Are we talking about your troubles or mine now?'

'You're not alone is all I'm saying. We've all lost one that hurt.'

Dominick's tally was now up to two. The tall pines that lined the quiet highway streaked by in a blaze of green, broken intermittently by signs for a gas station or fast-food joint. He thought about Natalie, his first fiancée, his first love. Long, dusty brown hair that went on forever, with matching eyes that smiled at him from across the room, even when her mouth didn't move. 'Seven perfect people,' she had said. 'According to *Cosmo*, there are seven perfect people for everyone in this world and it's up to you to find them.' Then she had kissed him and mused with a laugh, 'Thank God you didn't live in China!'

It seemed like a lifetime ago when she had died. When he thought that nothing and no one would ever stop the pain, the physical pain, when she had slipped away from him as he held her in his arms in that hospital bed. He'd prayed that the bullet that had ripped through her brain had somehow missed the part that made up Natalie. But her eyes never smiled again, and three days later he had simply held her when the doctors had switched off the respirator, because there was nothing else he could do. He had just watched as her chest stopped rising and falling and she left his life forever. Then he had hunted down the animals who had put that bullet in her brain when she didn't fork over her purse fast enough in the Macy's parking lot. It had taken three officers and the chomp of a K9 to get the gun out of his hands, to prevent him from killing the two of them in the lobby of MDPD headquarters.

Seven perfect people. The remaining six might as well live in China, he had thought, because he swore that he would never even look again, never get that close to a woman again. Then he'd met Assistant State Attorney C. J. Townsend. Smart, funny, and a brassy whip in court with a natural, amazing beauty that she never wanted anyone to see. But glasses and a purposely drab hair color and conservative black suits just could not hide it.

He had not looked for it, rejecting the idea of a relationship before it had even begun. But there was more to C.J. than any other woman that he had met, and he wanted to find out what that was. He wanted her to let him in, so he could help fix whatever it was that troubled her. And he hadn't felt that way since Natalie. Before he could say no, he had fallen into a relationship with her, and even when she tried to push him away, he would not let go, holding on even tighter, because he knew it was what they both wanted. And he knew that he loved her.

Now the incredible ache was back. And it was a different one this time, because C.J. was not dead. Rather than a bullet tearing through her brain – this time, the man that had taken her from him had used a knife, and it had indeed hit the part that made up C.J.

What a twist of fate, really, the way history repeats itself. Nine years later, here he was again, hunting down the animal responsible. What would he do this time? Would he learn from experience and fire his weapon before Corrections could throw him to the ground? Maybe it was a good thing that Manny had come along. Because Dominick honestly didn't know what he'd do as a man, as a cop, when he came face to face with the monster who had readily admitted to raping the woman he loved and leaving her to die. He needed answers. Beyond that, he wasn't quite sure what he was capable of.

'Thanks for coming along, Bear,' was all he could manage to say.

'Anytime, *hermano*. Anytime. Now let's go see what this asshole knows,' the Bear replied, rolling down his window. The sweet, full smell of sugar pines and grass filled the car before Manny lit another cigarette.

They had left the commercial strip, and for the past nine miles had rambled down Route 16, a slim two-lane highway, past simple homes and lazy cow pastures and horse stables and small farms. It was hard to imagine that there was a prison out here, much less six of them in a ten-mile radius. But the one they were going to this afternoon was different from the others. Florida State Prison was a maximum security, 24-hour confinement facility for 1200 men, the one that had earned distinction from its neighbors by housing the absolute worst of the worst offenders in the state. All were psych-grade, and all so violent that they had to be separated twenty-four hours a day even from each other. They ate alone, slept alone. Even recreational time in the yard was now spent alone: Individual four-by-four chained pens called 'dog runs' separated them from each other for the three times a week they were permitted outside. A walk to the shower on their block required cuffs. To the clinic, shackles and leg irons. And, of course, the prison held yet another remarkable distinction from its state brethren. For forty-four of those men, FSP would be the final stop. The basement of Q-Wing was home to Florida's only electric chair and lethal injection room. The Death House.

'Who the hell lives out here?' said Manny in amazement, as they passed another newer-looking brick home.

'Corrections. The keeper's gotta live somewhere outside the zoo, right?' said Dominick as they came out of the sweet pines and onto land purposely shaved flat and left barren. He turned the car left now, down the smooth blacktop and into the waiting arms of a sprawling three-story complex. Straight past three posted WARNING signs, he drove into the glimmering silver of razor-sharp, roll-top barbwire fences that unfolded over a mile, past electronic motion detectors and five-story watchtowers, right under the imposing stone archway. Rusting metal letters welcomed them to Florida State Prison.

45

A raspy voice squawked over a dozen hand-held radios. 'Q-Wing walking! Clear E!'

From almost a quarter-mile of cement hallway away, Dominick and Manny could still hear the buzz of the steel bars sliding open on Corridor E, the final barrier that led to Q-Wing, the prison's death row. Then the buzz of doors at D-Area, and another squawk of the radio. 'Q-Wing walking! Clear D!'

Dominick heard him coming then. The prison guard's boots, heavy on the cement floor, and the jingle of keys, followed by the shuffle of a man in irons and shackles. Like a hundred steel rattlesnakes waving their tails in warning, the rhythmic metal hiss got louder and heavier and more deliberate with each step. It came to a stop, ten feet away, on the other side of the solid steel door that led into the hallway. Metal keys banged off the door, then the buzzer sounded, the lock clicked, and the door opened out.

Dominick looked up from where he sat on the edge of the small conference table. He had been to FSP a few times to interview prisoners, and he always felt his breath catch when that door swung open. In the next moment, he would get to see what these walls had sucked out of a man and what they would now spit back out. The transformation was always bad. More often than not, it was shocking.

He could see the beige and brown uniform of the

sergeant and mob of other COs surrounding the flicker of the orange shirt that identified a death row inmate. Then the door slammed shut and the sergeant barked, 'Q-Wing 10-97, Colonel's Room. Clear!'

It was against FDLE policy for an agent to get personally involved with a victim, a defendant or a witness in a case. A violation could lead to an investigation by EI – the Office of Executive Investigations – the FDLE equivalent of Internal Affairs. Given his relationship with C.J., Dominick was pushing the envelope by being here, subjecting himself to possible discipline, but he no longer cared. He could feel his heart pound suddenly in his throat, and the air became thick.

The hiss shuffled into the room, nudged by the CO behind him. 'Let's go, now! Move!'

He was leaner than the last time Dominick had seen him, but even with his orange shirt and baggy blue pants, he could see that Bantling had been working out religiously. The muscles on his forearms were defined, his neck thick and tight. He wore his salty blond hair slicked back off a handsome, clean-shaven face, but the lack of sunlight on his skin contrasted sharply with the orange, and made him appear pale and ghostlike. His eyes flickered with a look of bemused confusion and he searched the room for the reason he might have been brought down. Then he spotted Dominick and Manny, and a knowing smile worked the corners of his mouth.

'Call us when you're done,' barked the CO. His badge read *Sergeant Dick Plemmel*. A jumble of keys hung from his belt clip which had slipped underneath his enormous pot belly. He pointed to the phone on the table with dirty fingernails and added, 'We're right down the hall if he gives ya any trouble.' Then he jingled out of the room.

'He's such a Dick, isn't he, Agent Falconetti?' said Bantling, with a chuckle, after the sergeant had left. 'He likes the inmates to believe those are keys to the prison. That he has them all and they better not fuck with him, because he can open as many doors for them as he can close. A bit of psychological warfare. Might have been an interesting thought process back in 1950, when keys and not computers opened doors, and murderers might actually have been afraid of their jailors. But the boys all laugh at Dick when he jingles by, because they know that his life out there, ironically, is even worse than theirs in here.'

'How's life been treating ya?' asked the Bear as he settled his large frame into the seat. He pulled out a cigarette and offered one across the table to Bantling. 'Did you get to meet Ol' Sparky on the orientation tour?'

Bantling ignored Manny. 'Let's see, Agent Falconetti. What brings you here on this lovely, hmm, what day is it . . . Wednesday? Forgive me, I lose track, sometimes. So much to do around here.'

'I was wondering if you'd tell me,' said Dominick.

'Let's not be coy, now. I wouldn't tell you if you were on fire. But,' Bantling said, his stare drifting back and forth between Manny and Dominick, 'from the look on you and your big friend's faces, I'd say it must be something very serious. And considering all we have in common, I'd venture a guess that this might be about your girlfriend, Agent Falconetti.'

Dominick looked around the room, trying to hold in all emotion, as he would with any other subject. *Don't let him draw you in. This is your interview. Control it.* 'What do you do up here all day long?' he asked.

'I think. A lot,' Bantling said. 'How's it feel to be back

in the limelight again? Such a celebrity. You're the talk of the town around here.'

'I see you get the papers.'

'The boys on the block get very excited when they hear a cop's been killed. You know what they say about good news – it travels fast. What is the count up to now, Agent Falconetti? Four, was it? Sounds like the people are revolting, maybe. You'd better be careful.'

'Watch your goddamn mouth,' cautioned Manny.

'What are you going to do, Detective Alvarez? Arrest me? Charge me with threatening a police officer? Maybe I'm the one who needs protection. Seems like all those lying, drug-running cops had something in common before they ate a blade – me.'

'You want to share anything you know about those murders?' asked Manny.

'What I know? I know that the man who falsely arrested me was the first to die. I know that the sergeant who covered for him was the last. And the two in between, maybe they were freebies.'

'What do you know about a statue? A jade monkey statue?' Dominick asked.

'Now you want my professional decorating opinion?'

'Don't be a wise-ass,' Manny said.

'If I talk to you, what do I get in return?' asked Bantling, his eyes not leaving Dominick's.

'To feel better about yourself,' said the Bear, with an exasperated snort. 'Just tell the man what he wants to know and we'll leave you to your group therapy.'

'Save it. I feel fine already.'

'I want to know what you know about a monkey statue,' pressed Dominick. 'Green jade. The one where they're covering their eyes, ears and mouth.'

A moment passed and then a slick smile bloomed on Bantling's face. 'So now we get to the crux of the problem, Agent Falconetti. So this *is* about your girlfriend. Sweet Chloe Joanna. She is still your girlfriend, right? I mean, I don't see a wedding band.'

'That's enough,' shot Manny.

'Are you still plucking the little flower?'

'Who sent it to her?' demanded Dominick.

'I think maybe you're not,' Bantling cackled, answering his own question. 'But I bet you wish you still were. So she has another admirer, does she? Sending her gifts? Busy girl.'

'Who did you have send it to her?' Dominick shouted, his hands flat across the table, his angry face in Bantling's.

'She's exceptional, though, isn't she?' Bantling whispered, his blue eyes not so much as blinking, locked on Dominick's. 'One look at that face, that once-perfect face, and you can't get her off your mind. And then you take her and . . . mmmmm.' Bantling licked his lips. 'Feels good.'

'Watch your mouth, asshole!' shouted the Bear.

Dominick felt the hatred explode inside his head. If he had not checked his gun downstairs, he would have killed the man. His fist met Bantling's smiling face, smashing his mouth shut.

'Dom, no! Jesus Fucking Christ! What the fuck are you doing?' Manny threw his chair back and grabbed Dominick from behind, pulling him off.

Bantling pushed himself back off the table and fell, face down onto the floor. He slowly tried to stand back up, his chains rattling, blood dripping from his nose and mouth. Down the hall footsteps clambered and doors unlocked, as correction officers stormed the hall. They'd likely witnessed the scene on the room's video camera.

'You sick fuck!' Dominick yelled, his arms still held behind his back by the Bear.

Bantling calmly spit the blood out of his mouth onto the floor. 'Is that what's really bothering you, Agent Falconetti?' he asked.

The door opened and Sergeant Plemmel stormed in at the ready, with five COs behind him. 'What the hell happened?' Plemmel started. 'What did you do?' he yelled at Bantling.

'I bet that's it, isn't it?' Bantling said with a bloody smile, ignoring Plemmel. 'That sick thought creeps into your head every goddamn night, doesn't it? The idea that when you're fucking her, it's *my* face she still sees. Every single night. And you just hate that, don't you?'

'Get him the hell back to Q! Now!' screamed Plemmel at the other COs.

Bantling wiped his mouth with the back of his orange shirt. He looked at the blood on his hand and sleeve, and then up at the video camera in the corner of the room, before smiling once more. 'I guess I'll be seeing you all again,' he said as two COs pushed him to the door. 'Sergeant Dick, I think my nose might be broken. Save that tape, now!'

'Let's go, asshole!' yelled Plemmel, hurrying out the door.

'I should have fucking killed him. I should have,' Dominick said.

'Dom, easy. Calm down, man,' said Manny, his beefy arms still wrapped around his friend. 'He ain't worth your friggin' job.'

'Be sure to send Chloe my regards, Agent Falconetti,' Bantling called out behind him as he shuffled back down the hall. 'And be sure to tell her I'll be seeing her again, too. Real soon.' Then he laughed as the radio squawked, 'Clear!' And the steel-barred doors buzzed open and then slammed shut with a dull thud.

46

Bill Bantling couldn't help but smile. Hell, he was beaming right through his shattered nose and cracked tooth. And even when the nervous UF dental student pulled it before the novocaine set in, he still smiled.

He probably should be angry, given what he had just discovered. The ugly scenario that now, unfortunately, made perfect sense. He had been set up – railroaded – three years ago, of that there was never any doubt. And as the days had melted into months and then years inside this living hell, he thought he had it all figured out. But apparently he had been missing a few pieces to the puzzle.

Someone had put that fucking body in his trunk that night, and either through coincidence or something more sinister, a cop had pulled him over. The rest had played out in the hands of the woman he should've killed fifteen years ago. Once in her clutches, she had manipulated the system – the judge, the jury, the detectives, and finally, even his own useless attorney – and she had sent him up here to die, to death's waiting room, counting down his days.

At first he hadn't been able to figure out who had put that body in his trunk. And then, right after they had shaved his head and fitted him with a new wardrobe, the guard had slipped him a copy of yesterday's paper – her distraught face on the cover of it. She, C. J. Townsend, was being led out of *his* psychiatrist's office by an army of police officers to a waiting ambulance. He had read the article about how the world-famous Cupid prosecutor had almost become the victim of a brutal Cupid *copycat* killing. Right there in Miami. Right there in the office of *her* own psychiatrist. Thank God she'd been able to kill the bastard before he could make her his *first* victim.

That's how the papers saw it. And the cops and the courts. Dr Gregory Chambers was a sick work-in-progress, a wannabe who was obsessed with his colleague and patient, C. J. Townsend. The real Cupid, William Rupert Bantling, was still locked up safe and sound on death row just waiting his turn. *Whew, trusty citizens! We all just dodged another bullet!*

But he knew better. So did that bitch. He tried the argument in the courts when he went on trial for the murders of the other ten women he did not kill. But no one would listen, because he was already a convicted man. No one *could* listen because she had made sure they couldn't. Chambers was dead, and dead men tell no tales. And the fact remained that a fresh corpse was still found in *his* trunk and evidence was still found at *his* house and the hearts of the other Cupid victims were all linked back to *him* and *he* had already been convicted of the murder of one of them. And for some fucked-up legal reasons, it didn't matter that the good doctor was the real Cupid, and, he figured, had set him up to be the fall guy. That Chambers had done it all for the thrill of watching that bitch go the full round with her rapist, her claws out and heading straight for his jugular. Her conviction – *her victory* – had been used against him in the next trial, and it drove the final nail into his coffin.

Now, thanks to Useless Attorney Number One's

recent change of heart, professed to him in legalese in a two-page letter and sent right to his cell, he knew it wasn't just coincidence that told a cop to flip on the blue lights and pull him over that night. And thanks to Falconetti, he now also knew that someone else besides the deceased good doctor might not want that bit of info to get out. There was someone else besides sweet Chloe Joanne who might be very content to let him die for a crime he did not commit. And now he knew why.

It was easy to see now. Simple, actually. *Hear no evil. See no evil. Speak no evil.* Very clever, he had to admit. The perfect little telegram, sent right to her door. A warning of things to come. Things that happen to witnesses and those who lie.

He knew who C. J. Townsend's new secret admirer was, alright. And she had every reason in the world to be afraid. In fact, she should be terrified.

47

She had known from the very moment she left Miami there was nowhere to run. But she had tried, heading back to the familiar shores of California where she had grown up. Three thousand miles and two time zones away, to a weekly efficiency on the beach in Santa Monica, lost in a crowd of strangers. It was not the soothing comfort and familiarity of Mom and Dad and old friends in quiet Sacramento that she sought – rather it was anonymity. She needed space and time to think, away from the constant pressure that awaited her in Miami.

Everything had spiraled out of control once again. She honestly didn't know if her own judgment was so severely impaired that she was seeing ghosts where none existed. She was jaded by what she knew, what she had done, her perspective clouded, to a certain degree, by guilt. But to others who did not know of her lies, the facts pointed in another direction: There were other comfortable, plausible explanations that did not come back to her or William Bantling. Maybe what she needed was distance, to get herself out of the acidic environment of law enforcement, where she knew too many sordid, inside details about crimes and criminals and an imperfect legal system that could be compromised, the checks and balances department bypassed. Maybe there was no relation between the cop killings and Bantling, after all. She was sure Bantling had heard about the Black Jacket murders in prison. Maybe just to freak her out, he'd had someone send a monkey statue to her office. A sick forget-me-not. The prison now blocked the mail he still wrote her, his seething, hate-filled letters. Every once in a while, one still slipped through, stamped *From a Correctional Institution* across the front, and she would rip it into a thousand pieces, her hands wrapped in her jacket or the tail of her shirt, so that her fingers would not even touch the envelope he had written on and licked. A surprise package would be something she should expect from him, but it didn't necessarily mean that he *knew* she had lied with those cops. It could all be weird timing. Coincidence.

She knew she was rationalizing, avoiding, burying her head in the warm, California sand and hoping it would all just go away. But she relished the fantasy. She had even begun to look at long-term apartments and want ads in the paper, and had gotten some information on taking the California Bar. She missed Dominick intensely, but could not bring herself to pick up the phone, letting his calls go to voicemail, lest he update her on the Black Jacket investigation, or even worse, succeed in persuading her to come back. If she heard his voice, she knew it would make everything more difficult. She wanted to stay here and hide. Bantling's letters didn't reach her now. Her beeper didn't sound out here. There were no more bodies to discover in the middle of the night, to go home and dream about.

But even from the moment she had stepped off the plane at LAX, she had known it wouldn't last.

Now she sat in a worn, plastic lawn chair on her second-floor balcony, sipping another glass of wine, enjoying her cigarette and watching the boardwalk with the amazing, foamy dark-blue sea crashing in the distance. The sun was setting and the sky had erupted in glorious colors of orange and purple, descending for its slow and final kiss with the horizon. The Ferris wheel lit up the pier across the beach, and the sounds of laughter and screaming and carousel music floated onto her balcony like a symphony. And for a nice long minute, she had no other thoughts in her troubled head besides the crisp taste of the wine in the back of her throat, the smell of the ocean, and the sound of the night's music.

It was then that she made the unfortunate mistake of checking her voicemail. She had three messages – two from Jerry Tigler, and one from Rose Harris, her colleague in Major Crimes and Bantling's prosecutor in his subsequent trial on the murders of the other ten Cupid victims. Both said to call them as soon as possible. Both sounded upset.

She knew in her heart what it was about, who it was about. She should have ignored them. Made her decision right then and there to make a new life out here in California, whatever the cost.

But as she dialed Tigler's home number, she knew that her time out here was up. The fantasy escape from reality was over.

Miami was calling her back home.

48

Jerry Tigler's breathy, anxious voice answered the phone on the first ring. It was ten o'clock at night in Florida. Past his usual bedtime. 'Hello?'

'Jerry?'

'C.J. Where've you been?'

'Busy. I got your message. What's up?'

'Where are you? Everyone's been trying to reach you all day.'

'It sounded important.'

'Have you spoken with Rose yet?'

'No, I called you first.'

'C.J., we need you to cut short your vacation. I know you're going through a, um, rough time and I hate to do this to you, but we need you back.'

'Jerry, I'm not sure if I'm even coming back,' she replied slowly.

'You are now. He's filed a Rule Three, C.J. William Bantling. Cupid. It came in this morning. Rose has it.'

Her heart began to pound and she slugged down the last sip of wine, careful to cover the phone with her hand so he wouldn't hear her. A Rule Three. Shop talk for a post-conviction motion pursuant to Rules 3.850 and 3.851 of the Florida Rules of Criminal Procedure. The only legal mechanism at this point, at least through the state courts, that would allow Bantling to ever see daylight again. She began counting months and days off in her head, just to be sure her numbers were correct. 'A

Rule Three? He's already had his shot, Jerry. His judgment and sentence were final in 2001. His time's up. He's too late under 3.851 – on that the case law's clear.'

'Do you think I'd call you in the middle of the night if it was that simple, C.J.? Rose knows appellate procedure like the back of her hand. She says we've got a problem on this one.'

'What the hell is the problem? I know appellate procedure, too, Jerry. Procedurally, he's barred—'

'He says you withheld evidence. He's collaterally attacking the judgment and sentence.'

She felt her stomach flip-flop suddenly. She tried a voice that sounded normal. 'They all say that, Jerry. It's boilerplate language. And he tried that in his motion for a new trial and his last Rule Three, and it didn't fly. This doesn't sound like new facts to me, facts that couldn't have been discovered before with the exercise of due diligence by his attorney of record.' *Right out of the statute.*

'Neil Mann is handling his appeal. He attached an affidavit to the motion from Lourdes Rubio, attesting that she withheld evidence from her own client. That she was in collusion with you. He alleges there's an audiotape of some kind. A 911 tape. There's your newly discovered evidence.'

There was nothing she could say. Nothing. She wanted to drop the phone and run, but her legs just wouldn't move.

'You need to answer this, C.J. And Judge Chaskel wants it this week. He has it set down on his motion calendar to determine if he needs a full-blown evidentiary hearing.'

'Can't Rose handle—'

'Don't go there. If this is done right, this guy will walk

right out of Florida State. Rose's convictions were all predicated on your Williams Rule evidence. Everything is riding on your conviction. If it's overturned, her convictions will be tossed.' Not to mention, of course, that this was an election year, and if William Bantling – the most prolific serial killer in Florida history since Ted Bundy – walked out of those prison gates, Tigler could kiss his job and his political future goodbye.

Williams Rule. Normally speaking, a person's prior unrelated crimes and bad acts could not be used against them in trial, so as to avoid the 'he did it once, he must've done it again!' line of thinking in the jury room. And while it was frustrating to keep silent about a three-page-long rap sheet at the guy's fourteenth trial for burglary, C.J. understood the law's purpose. But there was an exception to that general rule of evidence, and it was known as Williams Rule. In Florida, prior convictions and evidence of prior crimes and bad acts will be deemed admissible if they go to show a defendant's identity, intent, knowledge, modus operandi, motive, opportunity or pattern of criminality in the new case.

Bantling's conviction in Anna Prado's murder, and the facts surrounding her homicide, were admitted as Williams Rule evidence in Rose Harris' trial late that summer on the ten other murder counts. The method of death, the mutilation of the hearts, the manner of abduction, the targeted type of victim were all the same in each of the eleven murders, and were admitted at trial to show modus operandi – method of operation – and identity. This time it was okay to jump to the conclusion that if he did it then, he must've done it now. In fact, it was welcomed by the law.

But that little bonus in the law also now caused a big

problem. If Bantling's conviction in the Prado murder was overturned because evidence had been obtained illegally, then the use of that evidence and his conviction in the subsequent trials would also be barred. And his convictions in the other ten murders would then be overturned as well. He would be entitled to a new trial on all of the murders, and it would all go back again to the illegal stop.

'Jerry, I . . .' she stammered, her head down and in her hands. The lights from the Ferris wheel reflected off the cars in the parking lot below, and she watched them spin around and around on the windshields. 'I was going to stay here. I wasn't coming back.'

'Get your ass on a plane, C.J., wherever you are,' Jerry Tigler finished in a firm and unsympathetic voice. 'You tried this case, and you of all people should be scared if this guy ever gets out of prison. From what the world saw in that courtroom three years ago, there is no place you can go on this green earth where he won't find you then.'

49

Dominick wasn't surprised when RD Black called him into his office for a chat a week after his visit to Raiford. He had been expecting it sooner. Black told him that EI was starting an investigation regarding Bantling's charges of battery and police brutality, standard procedure in excessive use of force complaints. It would take anywhere from days to weeks to months to finally complete. 'Keep your chin up,' was all Black had said as Dominick headed back into the hall. 'And next time, take a good, long look at your surroundings before you let some asshole get inside your head.' A reference to the infamous video that had now been played a dozen times over for the big and the brassy up in FDLE's Tallahassee Headquarters.

He was pissed off at himself for losing control. He could be suspended, maybe even lose his job over this. All for what? He had gained nothing. No information, nothing that could help either C.J. or the Black Jacket investigation. Now he had nothing except a big, dark cloud hanging over his head, a pissed-off administration, four unsolved murders, an anxious public breathing down his neck, and a fiancée who wasn't anymore. Not to mention a pounding headache that had gone on for days straight.

He *was* surprised, however, two days after he had walked out of Black's office, to be greeted by Mark Gracker and two carloads of FBI agents in the parking lot of MROC. When they flashed their badges at him, as if Dominick didn't know who they were, he almost laughed. Then Gracker stepped to the front of the pack.

'Agent Dominick Falconetti.'

'What the fuck is this, Mark?'

'I need you to come with me,' Gracker said.

'What kind of stupid-assed game are you playing?' Dominick said, looking around, his voice rising.

Gracker just gestured with his hand to the black fed mobile behind him. The door was open.

Dominick figured it would be best to just ignore him. After all, his temper had gotten him in enough trouble lately and if he stayed here just one minute longer, he was going to rearrange Pudgy's face. Although it would probably be an improvement, it would also be a bad idea. He moved to walk past him, but Gracker grabbed his elbow, and with a sneer in his voice, he said, 'Maybe you didn't hear me, *Dom*. I need you to come with us. Let's not make this any more difficult than it has to be.'

Dominick shrugged him off. 'I'm not going anywhere with you. You come to *my* building and tell me to get in *your* fucking car? Piss off, Mark. I'm having a shitty enough day without you in it.'

Dominick tried to walk away again, and two FBI agents blocked his path. One of them was Chuck Donofrio, an old friend Dominick had worked with years back on a joint cargo task force when the guy was with MDPD. He looked at Dominick, as if he were disappointed in him, then shook his head. 'Dom, man, let's not make this too hard.'

'What the hell are you doing, Chuck? What is this?' He looked around at the faces of men he once worked with, who once respected him. He saw the positions they had taken up around him, the open car door that led to the back seat, the defensive stand and brace that cops take when someone is about to be taken into custody. He knew the steely and unfriendly look in their eyes. The tables had turned. He was a subject.

'What is *this*, asshole?' Gracker said with a smirk, as if this was exactly the reaction he wanted, '*This* is payback. As for your already shitty day, I'm about to make it worse. Give me your firearm and get in the car, Agent Falconetti, because I have a warrant for your arrest. You have the right to remain silent. I think you know the rest.'

50

C.J. sat in the high-back burgundy chair in her office –
the same one she'd thought she might never sit in again
– and stared at the black and white truth of Bantling's
Motion for Post-conviction Relief.

It was not paranoia. It was not overreaction. It was
not a guilty conscience. It was real and it was fact and it
was right here in front of her. And the judge. And now
the world. This was just the sort of motion that a bored
clerk lives for. The Tom and Nicole divorce petition. The
Carmen Electra and Dennis Rodman marriage license
application. The Prosecutor In The Biggest Criminal
Case Miami Has Ever Seen Has Just Fucked Up motion.
They can smell media attention the moment the glass
doors swing open and the legal assistant/messenger
drops the file on their desk with a wink and a, 'Take
good care of this one. It's special.'

When the motion was filed by Neil Mann, the tip to
the press had probably come out of the clerk's office
before the ink was dry on the courthouse stamp. The
phone calls and messages from local media had started
before her plane even set down on the tarmac at MIA,
and were now a slow-growing mound of pink message
slips, piled on her desk. An exasperated Marisol had
threatened a disability claim due to either exhaustion or
carpal tunnel.

It didn't take a genius to make the same connections
that just days ago her stressed-out brain on a sandy

beach had justified as simple coincidence. *Defense Alleges Prosecutor in Cupid Trial Withheld Evidence – Miami Beach Cop Said to Have Lied Is Black Jacket Victim!* the headline ran in the local section of the *Sun-Sentinel*, right above an anxious picture of herself three years ago coming out of the courthouse. She should be thankful, she supposed, that it wasn't the front page, but she didn't need to read the rest. In fact, she threw the whole paper in the garbage on her way out of the 7-Eleven, before the clerk had even put her fifty cents in the drawer.

It was clear from Mann's motion that Lourdes had indeed suffered a change of heart and position. In her three-page affidavit she stated that she 'intentionally did not represent her own client to the best of her ability' and was 'derelict in her duties as defense counsel in a death penalty case.' She said she had 'failed to diligently cross-examine witnesses and did not present testimony or evidence that she knew would lead to a suppression of the evidence gathered against her client' and, in fact, 'purposely withheld exculpatory evidence from the court and from her own client's knowledge.' She also stated that she had lied on the record in the penalty phase when asked by the court if there was truth to the defendant's allegations that he had raped the prosecutor. For the grand finale, she dropped the bomb that she was in possession of a 911 tape that detailed the real reason Bantling's Jaguar was pulled over. She explained that Officer Victor Chavez had lied about the circumstances surrounding his stop of the vehicle, because it was based on an unverified anonymous tip and was therefore devoid of probable cause. For good measure, she had thrown in an allegation that C.J. had known about the tape's existence as well, and purposely had failed to disclose it to the defense as exculpatory evidence, thus committing what was known as a Brady violation.

It looked bad. But, as her father had said on more than one occasion, 'You can't unring a bell.' There was nothing C.J. could say to defend herself that wasn't a lie itself. A house of cards built on a false foundation. How long would it last before it all fell down?

The knock at the door pulled her out of her thoughts, and she ran her hands through her hair before rising to answer. The last thing in the world she needed was to see Jerry Tigler again, who had come into her office three times already to make the same angry and anxious observations.

'C.J.? Counselor? You in there?' It was Manny Alvarez. 'If you are, you better let me in before she sees me or no more *café con leches* for you.'

She opened the door and Manny entered, looking exhausted and stinking of cigarettes. In his hand he held two small styrofoam cups. 'Here,' he said, thrusting one at her. 'I figured you'd need a shot of something. Given the day I'm having, I'm sure yours must be worse.'

'You read the paper?'

'Who hasn't? Welcome back, I think. Sucks, doesn't it?'

She just nodded.

'So, is it a problem?' he said, plopping into one of the chairs in front of her desk. 'I mean these fucking mopes will say all sorts of shit to get off. And I never liked that attorney of his, Rubio. Too uptight and serious. Just a growl, never a smile, like she hadn't had any in a while.'

'Manny . . .' C.J. said, shaking her head.

'No offense, Counselor, but it does make a difference.' He stroked his mustache thoughtfully and popped off the top of his coffee. 'I read in the *Herald* what she says happened. That's such bullshit. Chavez was a crummy cop, but anyone stuck in a room with him for five minutes would never give him credit for finding the bathroom, much less orchestrating a departmental conspiracy. I was at the scene that night, and I talked to that kid – big balls, but nothing upstairs to match. Rubio picked the wrong cop to call smart. And to pull you into it, too. What is she trying to do with that?' He sucked down his coffee in two gulps, then let out a happy, *Aahh!* 'Goes to show you, Counselor, damn defense attorneys will say anything to get their clients off. I've learned that in my eighteen years in this business.'

'I'm filing an answer. Chaskel's got it set down for Friday for a Huff hearing.'

'What's that?'

'It's basically a hearing to determine if the motion is legally sufficient, enough to warrant a real hearing. An evidentiary hearing.'

'Uh-oh. What's this mean?'

'Yeah. Uh-oh is right. Witnesses. Testimony. Bantling will have to prove what he said in his motion – that there really is newly discovered evidence and that new evidence would probably produce an acquittal on retrial.'

'Retrial?' Manny sat up, a look of disbelief taking over his face.

'That's what he's hoping for. That's the remedy under the law.'

'Fuck.'

'You can say that again.'

'Fuck.'

'We don't want an evidentiary hearing, Manny. They'd have to bring him back down from Raiford. It will be another circus. And if he wins and gets a retrial . . .' Her voice faded off. Even she didn't want to face the answer to that question just yet.

'He'd come back?' Manny shook his head. 'You couldn't do this evidentiary hearing with just the lawyers?'

She shook her head.

'And you'd have to handle this shit? After all the things he said about you in court? About, well, you know,' the Bear squirmed in his seat, trying to find the right word, 'about, uh, *attacking* you and all. That don't seem right.'

'The burden is on him. I have to wait to see what Chaskel's going to make him do.'

'Fuck. This guy is like a freakin' bad penny. He just keeps popping back up.'

They both sat silent for a minute, contemplating what had just been said. Finally she asked the question that had been on her mind since her plane landed. Since she'd heard the knock on her door and hoped it was Dominick's voice on the other side. 'How's he doing, Manny? He must be upset about all this.'

'Have you seen him?'

'No. I . . .' she stammered, 'I screwed things up when I left, Manny.' She paused for a moment. 'He moved out, and I . . . I haven't even called him. Now, well, now he doesn't call me.'

'Whoa, whoa, wait a sec,' the Bear said, sitting up in his chair. He leaned forward. 'You and he haven't even talked? Since when?'

Now she was embarrassed. She thought that as friends, Dominick would have mentioned their break-up to Manny. 'Forget it,' she said. 'I'm sorry. I didn't mean to involve you.'

'So you don't know?'

Now her heart began to race just a bit. 'Don't know what?'

'Damn, Counselor. I thought you knew. I thought he would've called you.' He rubbed his bald head as he struggled to find the right words. 'Dom ain't working this case no more, C.J. He ain't working no cases, thanks to your bad penny. Dom's been arrested by the feds on civil rights violations. FDLE suspended him last week.'

She pulled into the Miami Beach complex, a former assisted living facility turned chic art deco condo. She found a rare spot in guest parking, unsure what to do next. His state car, the Grand Prix, was not in his assigned parking spot, replaced instead with his personal car, a Toyota 4Runner, which normally sat unused on the street. He must be home. The first thing to go, after his firearm, would have been his car.

Even with all the trouble renters bring, Dominick had thought it a wise investment in the hot South Florida real estate market to keep his condo and let it appreciate. The plan was that maybe after the wedding, they would cash in on both condos and then look for a house that could fit a pool and a barbecue in the back. Maybe even adopt a couple of kids to fill up the rest. Now it turned out that his shrewd thinking had another pragmatic benefit. C.J. looked up at his apartment on the fourth floor, the one she had spent more than a few nights at in the beginning of their relationship, and blinked back tears.

It was 4:00 on a Wednesday afternoon. A time she would never normally expect to find him at home, but then again, things were no longer normal anymore. She tried to think of what to say and how to say it, but nothing came. Although she knew this was a conversation that needed to be had in person, she wished he had picked up the phone when she called to tell him she was coming over.

She walked across the parking lot, through the glass doors, and took the elevator up to four. She had walked the same path a hundred times before, but now it felt strange. The hall smelled different, the air was cold and she felt unwelcome at that moment, like an intruder. She knocked on his door and waited, but there was no sound inside. She tried his phone on her cell, and heard it ring until the answering machine inside picked up. She hung up.

Going back home at that moment was not really an option. Her neighbor, Mrs Crombsy, who had been watching Lucy and Tibby, had warned her that a few reporters had taken her parking spot to set up camp. So she sat down in her pantsuit and settled up against the wall in his cold hall. With her head in her hands and her purse in her lap, she decided to wait.

Wait until he finally came home or came out – or until she finally gave up. Whichever one came first.

52

The soft sound of footsteps on carpet rounded the corner. C.J. had heard the ding of the elevator a hundred times in the three hours she had been there, and didn't bother looking up anymore from her spot on the floor. Then the footsteps slowed to a stop some ten feet away, and she knew it was him.

She looked up and saw his face. 'Hey,' she said with a smile, rising gingerly, stretching her stiff back. He did not move to help her, jut stood, glued fast to his spot. 'I was wondering when you'd finally come back.'

He wore running shorts and a tee shirt that looked damp. His dark hair was tousled on his head, his face unshaven for at least a few days. The salt-and-pepper goatee was turning into a full salt-and-pepper beard. He said nothing, just watched her, as if she were a ghost. Then he looked away and around the hall uncomfortably, as if looking for an escape route, jingling the keys he held in his hand.

'I saw Manny,' she said when he didn't respond. 'Why didn't you tell me?'

He looked at her in disbelief. 'You didn't even call,' he said finally, after allowing a few more awkward seconds to pass. 'Nothing. Not a word. You disappear on a sunny afternoon and I don't hear from you again. What the fuck is that, C.J.?'

'Dominick, please,' she said, her eyes starting to get

wet with tears she swore she wouldn't shed tonight. 'You know why I left.'

'Bullshit. Trying to figure out the reason you left has cost me my job and gotten me indicted.'

'I didn't ask you to be my hero,' she said, immediately regretting she had.

'Oh, that's nice. That's perfect.'

'Can we go inside to discuss this?' she said, her voice lowering as she looked around.

He said nothing.

After a moment she continued, 'Why the hell did you go up there, Dominick? Why? What purpose did it serve?'

'I wanted to know why,' he said, his voice low and controlled, as if he was trying very hard to hold back his emotions. 'Why, no matter what I do, he's there, he's always there, C.J., inside your head. And I've tried, ever since I met you, to help you, to be with you, to love you like no other woman, to get him the fuck out of your head . . .'

Her face grew dark. 'Don't play psychologist with me, Dominick – thank you very much. You can't *fix* me,' she said. 'It's not that simple and it never will be. I'm sorry if I come with a lot of baggage, but then again, I thought you knew that.'

He shook his head and looked down around his sneakers. The moment took forever to pass before he spoke again. 'I love you, C.J. And I can't seem to fix that either.' He looked up at her now. The emotions had won the battle, and she could see the pain in his eyes and not just the anger, the swell of tears he struggled to hold back. His fist clenched the keys tight in his hand.

She closed her eyes, but her cheeks were already wet. How she wished she had met him at a different time in her life. 'I'm back for you, Dominick,' she said, her voice barely a whisper, stepping closer. She wanted to hold him. But he moved away, his hands in front of him, as if to ward her off. The flash of anger was back again in his face.

'No, no, no . . . Don't give me any credit. You're back because of *him*, C.J. Not me. Let's make that clear. You came back because of him.'

'Don't do this, Dominick. Don't.'

'And that's what I can't figure out. That's what I just don't get. What is it with you and him?'

'I won't explain myself,' she said, shaking her head, clenching her jaw tight.

'Why, C.J.? Why did you come back to face the guy you hate, but not the one you said you loved? The one you were supposed to marry?'

'Listen,' she said, cutting his question off. 'I'm here to finish what needs to be finished. That's all I'll say. What you tried to do to him with a fist, I need to legally do in a courtroom. Permanently. And only *I* can do it. Got that? *Only me.* You think I want to be in a room with him? You think I want him in my head?'

'I don't know what to think anymore,' he said flatly. He had checked his emotions again.

She waited for what seemed like an eternity for him to say more, but nothing happened. 'I love you, Dominick. God, that's true. Whether you choose to believe it or not, that's up to you. But *I* know it's true. And I'll be there for you through all this in any way that I can. If you want me to.'

He wouldn't look at her, so she finally walked past him toward the elevator bay, her fingers lightly touching his motionless hand as she passed. Halfway down the hall she stopped and turned back to face him. 'I left because I was trying to save you. That's what you don't see. I can't drag you into this pit, because it's black and it's bottomless and there is no escape. And if I have to live in a nightmare alone for the rest of my life, then so be it. It's worth my sanity. I won't let him take that again, I'd rather die.'

Then she rounded the hall corner and hit the button down. Her arms were crossed against her chest. She felt so cold, so incredibly cold. When the bell rang and she still had not heard his footsteps come up on her, she knew it was over.

On legs that shook like jelly, she walked into the empty elevator and hit the lobby button. As the doors were closing, she collapsed in the corner, crying uncontrollably when the doors finally shut.

53

C.J. camped out at the NSU law library in Davie the entire weekend. She wore sweats, a Phillies baseball hat, a ponytail, and glasses, hoping her anxious face blended with every other stressed-out law student's. She pulled any and every case she could find that dealt with Rule Threes, Brady violations and newly discovered evidence. Then she spent two days holed up at the kitchen table in her apartment, pushing troubling thoughts of Dominick from her head, and carefully crafting her answer – the legal response to Bantling's motion.

In Florida, once you were convicted of a felony, a good appellate attorney and a Rule Three was pretty much your last chance to buy yourself a *Get Out of Jail* card. But the law was nothing if not particular, and the judges far too busy to hear every motion that came down the pike from a desperate defendant with a pen and paper and too much time on his hands. The cogs of justice would quickly become jammed with paper and backlogged calendars if there were no limits, so you had to play by the rules of the statute, or else you didn't play at all. If you wanted to see the inside of a courtroom, the motion had to be filed within a certain time period – one year after the judgment and sentence were final in a death penalty case. And to avoid an endless amount of do-overs, the motto was 'speak now or forever hold your peace.' One year and one shot was all you got.

Unless the claim was based on newly discovered

evidence. An incarcerated defendant's last hope at sunshine and a retrial, a new evidence claim was the only way for a Rule Three that's out of the time line to survive an outright dismissal as a matter of law. But claims of newly discovered evidence were not just buzzwords that automatically turned a lock. It was much more serious than that. "I didn't know about the evidence the first time because I didn't think to look" was not a good enough answer. "I didn't know because it was hidden from me" just might be a better one.

C.J. had racked her brain for four days, because she knew she would have just one shot herself. If she could stop Bantling at the Huff hearing, on his first assault, then he would never get his tank up the hill where it could do some real damage. He would not be present at the hearing, only his attorney. If she could shut down his motion on procedural or legal insufficiency grounds, then Corrections would never even have to bus him down from Raiford for a free vacation on the taxpayer's dime and a full-blown evidentiary hearing.

If she could do it by the book.

If she could get it dismissed without ever having to confront or address his 'new' evidence in court.

If she never had to craft another lie.

Or remember an old one.

If she could out-lawyer Neil Mann.

If, if, if . . . it all came down to *if* and she pushed herself now to find the cure – the legal miracle that would keep him out of the courtroom. She'd die trying, because she didn't think she could face him again, see him with that knowing grin, like an old lover that had stolen an intimate moment with her. She knew it was not so much *getting out*, but *getting even* that he wanted, and she knew it would be fun for him to watch her drown in the backwash of her own lies.

And, of course, there was one more reason to stop this now. If it should go to an evidentiary hearing – if detectives and crime scene techs and medical examiners became witnesses once again – she'd have to relive it all again, the tale of a murder that had almost been hers. The carefully planned abductions. The drugs. The rapes. The torture. The pictures. The death chamber. The smell of old champagne in her hair, the bitterness of the Haldol on the back of her tongue when the shot kicked in, the ice-coldness of the black room.

A few news trucks, their satellite antennas towering above 11th Street, sat in front of the courthouse Thursday morning when she had arrived for work. There were a few other big cases going on that morning, C.J. told herself. The mom who had shot her twin baby sons in the tub. The former city commissioner on trial for improper influence and taking a bribe. The sentencing of a former UM football star for DUI. It did not necessarily mean they were there for her. *Yet*. If it went to an evidentiary hearing, the press would heat up.

She piled three of the seven boxes which made up the *State of Florida vs. William Rupert Bantling* on her metal cart, and then topped it with the box full of case law that she had copied that weekend. She said a silent prayer to St Christopher, her mother's favorite saint, asking him to help her get through this day.

For the past few weeks, she had been dodging the phone calls and questions of her parents while she struggled to sort her life out. They had never even known she was in California, just a quick plane ride down the coast. C.J. knew they were probably worried about her.

Her mom always was, claiming it was a mother's duty. She didn't dare think of her father learning that his daughter had worked to put the wrong person on death row. A man who preached forgiveness, she knew he would not forgive that.

It was time to leave now, and no time to think of what would happen if she didn't win today. She put on her sunglasses and left her office via the building's side door, then she headed quickly across the street to the maintenance elevator in the courthouse, hoping to avoid the madness that she feared might be waiting just for her.

54

Courtroom 6-8 was not the most majestic of court-rooms. It was relatively new, but small, having replaced the old offices of the State Attorney, that had operated out of the sixth and ninth floors of the courthouse under Janet Reno, before the Graham Building was built. For years the space had then sat empty, finally put to good use in the late Nineties as desperately needed court-rooms.

In just a few short years, though, new and fresh had turned to old and weathered. Someone had picked mauve as the carpet color of choice, and it was already dotted with stains and worn in spots, the gray walls scuffed and picked over, written on in places by those who had a pen or a marker and nothing better to do.

Her prayers to St Christopher had worked. It turned out that only some of the attention downstairs was hers. Only a few reporters – nothing like the crowd drawn at Bantling's trial – waited outside the courtroom doors for her.

'Ms Townsend! Did you know about the tape? Have you seen it?'

'Did you know that Victor Chavez lied on stand? Did you ask him to do it? Do you think he was targeted by Black Jacket? Do you think these cases may be related?'

'Was this a conspiracy?'

'Is an innocent man on death row?'

The questions were the same as the ones scattered

about her office unanswered on pink message notes. Her answer was also the same. Silence.

'Aah, Ms Townsend,' Judge Leopold Chaskel III said, from atop his small throne in the packed courtroom, before it could close on the shouts outside in the hallway. 'I think we knew you were coming down the hall before you did. A few groupies outside, have we?'

'Good morning, Judge. I'm sorry to interrupt your calendar,' she said, looking around the room. Unfortunately for the press, Thursday mornings were Chaskel's plea days, so even if they wanted one, there wasn't an empty seat in the house. 'I'm on at—' she continued.

'Ten. I know. Find a seat. Mr Mann is here, somewhere. He checked in already. I'm going to finish up my calendar, but let me give you the same advice I gave Mr Mann, who attempted to give a press conference in my hall this morning. Don't. Got that? I hate finding out what I'm going to say before I say it. Especially when it turns out to be wrong. I won't have this fiasco turn into the circus it became last time.'

'I don't think you'll have to worry about me, Your Honor,' C.J. said. *Rule with me, dismiss this thing, and we won't have to worry about it at all, Judge.*

'Good. I'll finish up here and then the rest of the morning is yours, although I don't suspect it will take that long.' He held her stare with his own for a long second before turning back to his calendar.

The judge's final ad lib could be good or bad. Obviously somewhere along the line, Chaskel had made up his mind about a few things. He was a no-nonsense former state prosecutor and a great judge who did not like his cases coming back on appeal. For any reason. C.J. said another prayer to St Christopher.

She sat down in the gallery on the side reserved for the State and stared straight ahead at the jury box, or 'the box' as it was known. The line of defendants brought over from DCJ sat chained together in the same street clothes they wore to every court appearance, the same clothes they had been arrested in. Some looked nervous, others looked clueless, others defiant and angry. None of them cared about C. J. Townsend, Bill Bantling, Cupid or Black Jacket – they all just waited for the judge to call their name and make them an offer. Some would get no offer but the statutory max, having chosen the wrong victim – one who came to every court appearance and demanded to be heard. Others would get the deal of a lifetime – no victim to make a fuss, no family members who cared, no witnesses who wanted to be bothered.

C.J. watched the young B-prosecutor at the podium handle her cases. Out of law school maybe two years, she held the futures of so many in her hand as she offered up her pleas.

The defendant scores non-state prison sanctions. The State offers a withhold and two years' probation.

The State offers five years' state prison, followed by ten years' probation.

The defendant is a habitual offender. The offer is fifteen, concurrent on each count.

Twenty years.

Thirty years.

The offer is life.

Prosecutorial discretion allowed for plea offers anywhere between the score on the defendant's sentencing sheet and the statutory maximum for the crime he was charged with – sometimes a difference of many years. Some prosecutors were harder, some more liberal. It was just the luck of the draw for a defendant whose division they ended up in. Years were sometimes divvied-up over lunches with fellow prosecutors and Division Chiefs, like pennies at a poker game.

He scores to thirty-six months on a second-degree burglary. Two priors for grand theft. What should I offer?

The max is fifteen years. Hmmm . . . offer him five, then. Pass the ketchup, please.

Charlie, man, you're a fucking ball-buster. Five? Offer him three years, Tim, plus five probation. And I'll take the salt when you're done.

Alright, alright. I'll split the difference and offer four plus two probation if he takes it tomorrow. You think that's enough?

Deal done. Lunch over.

That had been C.J. just a few years ago. At a different podium, in a different courtroom, with a different judge, juggling one hundred cases set for trial, one hundred lives at a time. *Where were they all now?* she wondered. *Had she made a difference after all?*

Neil Mann, a tall man with a long, drawn and sad face, shuffled into the room and found the wall opposite C.J., on the side reserved for defense counsel. A former Assistant PD and one-time intern at the State Attorney's Office, Mann had disappeared into private practice for years, specializing mostly in criminal appellate work and avoiding the courtroom and litigation at all costs. He was no great shakes, but he was also easier on the pocket-book, C.J. assumed, than Lourdes Rubio had been at $300 an hour. Appeals were tedious and time-consuming and expensive and Bantling was gainfully unemployed now. The once-significant stash that had financed his trials was long gone, but unfortunately for him, he still had enough of it to disqualify him from the free services of the public defender. Just not enough to hire anyone really good.

'Alright then,' Judge Chaskel said finally at eleven thirty, after the last chained defendant was marched back out the jury door. He surveyed the courtroom. It had mostly emptied now, the prosecutor and the PD packing up their stacks of boxes. He spotted the few reporters who had actually decided to stick it out through his plea calendar, and his eyes narrowed.

'Mr Mann, State. I'll see you all in chambers now. With the court reporter,' he said, rising. He turned to his clerk and added, 'Janine, bring the *Bantling* file.' Then he disappeared off his throne in a puff of black, even before Hank the bailiff could shout, 'All rise!'

55

'It's late,' Judge Chaskel said, taking a seat at the head of the table. He looked at his watch. 'I didn't mean to run this late. I have a lunch appointment.' He motioned for everyone to sit. 'I know that you've all got a lot to say, most of which I don't want to see repeated on the front page tomorrow. There's no need for that now. I don't want the press speculating every day for the next couple of weeks, so I thought we'd let them sit this one out till then.'

C.J. felt the knot in her stomach grow as she took a seat across from Neil Mann, a bad feeling spread through her bones. She began to unpack her boxes off the cart anyway. 'Your Honor, did you get my answer?' she said slowly. 'I filed it on Monday.'

'Yes, yes I did. But after careful consideration and a review of the case law, I think it's clear we're gonna need a hearing.'

She stopped unpacking. 'I thought that's what we were here for,' she replied.

He looked at her strangely, as if they both knew a bad inside joke but couldn't share it. 'An evidentiary hearing,' he said slowly. 'To see what it is we've got here.'

'I don't think we need to go that far, Judge,' she opened up her legal folder. 'First off, the motion is untimely. He had his window and that closed.'

'Counselor, it's a new evidence claim. There's no time bar on that.'

'The defendant has raised the same grounds of ineffective assistance of counsel and new evidence that he did in his last Rule Three,' she pressed. 'And you ruled last summer that that was an issue that should have been, and was, raised by him on direct appeal. So he's procedurally barred from raising it again.'

'This claim of ineffective assistance is new,' Mann piped up. He twisted his Bic pen in sweaty fingers. 'It's now based on the newly discovered 911 tape that his own attorney confessed she failed to admit at trial.' He cleared his throat, then added, 'On purpose.'

'If Lourdes Rubio knew about such a tape at trial,' C.J. snapped back, 'then how can it be new evidence? Evidence that, and I quote from the rule, that was "unknown to the defendant or his attorney at the time of trial and could not have been ascertained by the exercise of due diligence"? The rule says if the attorney knew it, or could have found it, then she can't come back after conviction and complain when things don't go her way. Lourdes Rubio says she knew about it. Obviously, this was simply case strategy and *not* new evidence under the rule – this is sour grapes.'

'That's a good point,' said Chaskel thoughtfully. Then he opened his daybook. 'Make it at the hearing.'

For some reason she had not expected or truly believed it would come to this. She really had thought she could dodge another bullet – refusing to accept the reality that would come as a consequence of defeat today. 'Your Honor,' she continued, hoping to pull a rabbit out of a hat, her voice edgy and sharp, 'with all due respect, do you think it is in the public interest to bring Mr Bantling all the way down from Raiford for a hearing that you just agreed may not even be necessary?'

The judge's eyes narrowed again, and he looked at her coldly, as if he had just lost all respect for her and her argument. He did not like being challenged. Not from the very person who might have actually put him in this tenuous position. It was his reputation at stake now, with the public and the press and, of course, the appellate courts – a reputation he had carefully built over the years with sound and prudent rulings and a very low reversal rate. A reputation which he thought might earn him a nod one day to one of those appellate positions.

'Ms Townsend, Mr Bantling is alleging Brady violations. Very serious Brady violations, I might add. That you and your office purposely withheld evidence from him in a death penalty case. In *my* court. And he's arguing collusion, that you were in on this plot to withhold exculpatory evidence with Ms Rubio from the beginning. Now you want to argue semantics with me about when she knew what she was doing was bad?' He struggled to keep his voice low and devoid of anger, but he slipped. 'If Mr Mann proves collusion, I'll tell you right now, I don't see any weight in your argument. Now, I don't even know what this tape says. I don't know if it's exculpatory. I don't know what Ms Rubio's testimony will be, about what she actually knew and when she actually knew it, but I'll tell you, I'm damn anxious to hear it. Because I sat in that courtroom for four weeks trying that case with you, and I don't recall hearing anything about a 911 tape. I do, however, remember Mr Bantling's allegations that he had assaulted you when you were a law student, and the united thinking between you and his attorney that this court simply did not need to be burdened with the knowledge of such allegations during a death penalty trial. And let me just say, I did not appreciate being kept in the dark in *my* courtroom. It was a thin line you had both walked.

'So, Ms Townsend, this hearing could very well mean a wasted afternoon or two or ten for all of us, but that's what we're all going to do. And I'm gonna get to the bottom of this. The right way. Now let's all pick a date, shall we?' He matched her stare with his own until she finally looked down at her day timer.

'Yes, Your Honor,' she said quietly. Her head began to spin and she bit her cheek so the pain would bring her back.

His face. She saw his face smiling up at her from the open page.

'Ms Townsend? Is that date satisfactory with you?' It was the judge, and he was tapping his foot impatiently under the table while Mann, the clerk and the court reporter all stared at her, waiting for an answer.

'I'm sorry. I was thinking, Your Honor. What was that date again?'

'March first. It's a Monday. I'm going to clear my afternoon calendar for the week to try and finish this up, so that the defendant does not have to keep getting bused back and forth. He can remain at DCJ with extra security.'

One week. That's all she had left. 'Yes, Judge, I suppose that's fine,' she stammered.

'No. It *is* fine, then. No excuses. I want all your witnesses, Mr Mann. No hodgepodge. The first one I want to hear from is Ms Rubio.'

'No problem, Judge. She's very anxious to testify,' Mann said, nodding excitedly. His shoulders had picked up a bit, as if he, himself, hadn't really thought he might win today and the good news had put a little extra bounce in his step. 'This has weighed on her heavily,' he finished with a concerned frown.

'Spare me. Just have her here on the first. With that tape. And play nice – send a copy to the State. Just in case they don't have it already.'

'If he's alleging ineffective assistance, he's waived attorney–client privilege. I get access to Lourdes Rubio's defense files,' C.J. said. At least that would help her prepare for Lourdes' full frontal assault in the courtroom.

'Make a motion to compel, and they're yours,' said the Judge.

'I have them already, Judge,' said Mann. 'I'll provide the State with a copy. There's about four boxes full.'

'I love it when everyone gets along. As for your witnesses, Ms Townsend,' the Judge continued quietly, 'I think we have a problem. Officer Chavez is no longer with us. Nor is Officer Ribero, although I don't know how much his testimony matters for the purposes of this hearing.' He thought for a moment, then, as if having made up his mind, but deciding not to share, he finished with, 'Let's see where Ms Rubio leads us. Chavez's sworn trial testimony may be enough.' He turned to Janine. 'Order me the transcripts from Officer Chavez's trial testimony and his testimony from his motion to suppress. Check the court file for the dates. And order me Officer Ribero's as well. I want them for this hearing. And Corrections . . . Janine, make sure Corrections has the defendant down for that week. He's a death row inmate, so call the warden at Raiford and make sure the proper security precautions are put in place. We're gonna keep him down here for a while, so call DCJ as well and see if there is anything special they need to do to prepare.' He paused for a moment before adding, 'Bantling can be difficult. I've had problems with him before, and so has Corrections when he gets violent. Let's not have any more this time. Let's be prepared.'

He nodded at all of them, as if this was a good time for everyone to go home and for him to go to lunch. Then his eyes fell on the *Herald* under Neil Mann's accordion file.

'And that's another thing,' he continued, his eyes narrow slits that read caution once again, 'I saw the paper today. The rumors are already spreading and I don't try cases by rumor. I want them to stop. There will be no more leaks to the press, no speculation, nothing filed unless it's under seal. You are all gagged. Got it? If the press has a problem, which I am sure they will, they can go through the proper channels, but I won't have what happened last time happen again in my courtroom. They were practically swinging from the chandeliers with their cameras and microphones. Waiting for me in the parking lot,' he finished with disgust and shook his head, as if to rid his brain of that last vulgar image. 'Are we all clear on that?'

'Yes,' the room murmured in agreement. C.J. rose with Neil Mann, who practically danced out of chambers, anxious to use his cell phone, his thick files flopping under his arm. She watched him leave, knowing who he would be dialing in just a few minutes. She gathered her own files and her box of case law, which hadn't even been cracked open, and placed them back on the cart. She was still in a fog, stunned by the reality that she had only days to prepare for, her stomach a churning pit of acid.

It was just the two of them now, Janine having headed back to her desk in the outer office, the court reporter to another courtroom, Mann to brag of victory to his wife/secretary before placing his phone call to FSP. 'Good afternoon, Judge,' she said, as she wheeled her cart out of his conference room.

'This could be very interesting, Ms Townsend,' Judge Chaskel said quietly with a frown, taking off his robe and putting on his sports jacket. She turned to face him again in the doorway of his office. 'Too interesting, I'm afraid. Make sure your legal department is on hand. This could get very sticky for you. Just an FYI.'

Then, without another word, he walked past her out of his conference room, down the empty back hallway of judge's chambers, and headed off to lunch.

56

C.J. sat at her kitchen table, surrounded by stacks of legal treatises and boxes of file folders, and stared at the words she had just read. The words that leaped out at her from the endless pages of Lourdes' otherwise illegible chicken scratch.

Chloe, Larson? Bayside, NY, 1988, Rocky Hill Road, <u>sexual</u> <u>assault</u> – in home = vindictive?

She felt her heart pound fast and she reached for her wine glass.

Things had piled up in the two weeks she'd been gone from the office. The hearings that she'd missed had mostly just been reset, and her days were filled with motions, depos and pre-files to prep for on her other cases. So she'd dragged home Lourdes Rubio's client files that had been couriered over by Neil Mann, and had spent late nights all week, meticulously combing through every document and each word. It was unsettling, to say the least, to read the attorney–client notes that Lourdes had taken. Particularly the ones about her.

She rubbed the crick in her neck and pushed herself away from the table. It was time for a cigarette.

She took her glass, walked out onto the patio and lit up a Marlboro. A white moon filled the night and she watched the parade of boats float down the Intercoastal for a few minutes. She and Dominick had sat out here so many nights, in hard plastic chairs, just talking for hours over a bottle – or, on occasion, bottles – of wine. He had talked about getting a boat for the longest time, joking that when they finally retired, he would cruise her around the world. Or at least down to the Keys, since they would both have state pensions.

She dialed his cell phone and got his voicemail, but hung up without leaving a message. Missed calls would tell him that she had called again. He was probably out with Manny or Chris, or maybe by himself, drowning his sorrows – the very ones she was responsible for – in more than a few drinks. She pressed the phone against her forehead, wishing he had just answered. Wishing she had heard his voice tonight. Wishing he didn't hate her, but knowing she couldn't blame him.

It felt like everything was falling apart. Dominick. Her career. Her life. And even though she struggled to push the negative thoughts out of her head and focus on what needed to get done, the days seemed harder to get through. And she felt more and more isolated. Not a good sign.

At the lowest point of her depression years ago, when sleep had stopped coming, she had seen him everywhere – the stranger in a clown mask whose face could be anyone's. Therapy had saved her then, and for the next twelve years, it had kept her functioning, helping her control her fears so that they would not control her. The last ten of those years she had spent in the care of forensic psychiatrist Gregory Chambers. Greg had not been just her doctor, but her friend and colleague, as well, serving as an expert witness for the State on more cases than she could count. For those ten years, he had been there to make sure she didn't slip back into the darkness of depression. He had been her confidant, her consoler, her life rope when times were bleak and it was hard to just get out of bed some days. And then she suddenly found out, when she needed him most, he had also been treating the man she had been running from all along in her nightmares. That she hadn't been in therapy – she had been in a twisted experiment.

She didn't know exactly when their relationship had changed, if it had ever been what she thought it was, if Greg had ever really been her psychiatrist or her friend. Those were questions she would always ask and never be able to answer.

Dominick had been her therapy then, when it all fell apart, when nothing was as she had always believed. But now . . .

No, no. She shook her head, shaking the tears away that had started to well up again. She would not go there. She would not let herself slide into a depression. It would be too easy to do, and too hard to crawl back out. She pulled her hair back off her head, looked at the phone again. Then she dialed.

'Hello?'

'Hi, Mom,' she said when she heard her mother's voice on the other end, amidst what sounded like the running of water and clinking of dishes. 'It's me.' It had been more than a few days since she had last spoken to her parents. Try a few weeks.

'Hello, honey!' The water turned off and the clinking stopped. She could see her mom wiping her hands dry on her apron in the kitchen. She was probably cleaning up from dinner. 'Your ears must be burning. Your father and I were just talking about you. Dad,' she shouted, 'it's Florida on the phone. It's your girl! Where have you been?' she asked, her voice back to C.J. now.

'I know. I'm sorry. I've just been, well, busy.' She could smell the Liquid Joy soap bubbles through the phone, see the orange sun beginning to set outside the kitchen window above the sink. The image was comforting. Her parents still lived in the same house where she'd grown up. 'How have you two been? Busy? How's work?'

'Something's wrong. I hear it,' her mother said. She had fine-tuned worry radar. 'What is it? Is it work? Are you okay?'

'Nah, Mom, I—'

But her mother could hear no more. She worried so much about getting bad news, that she always made C.J.'s dad hear it first. 'Here's your father,' she said.

'Chloe?'

'Hi, Dad.'

'Something wrong?'

'That's Mom's words. Nothing's wrong, Daddy. I've just, well, I've got this case.' She rubbed her forehead. Even though she wasn't planning on talking about anything more serious than the weather and Aunt Pat, her father had that soft, non-judgmental tone of voice that just coaxed words right out of her. He should have been a psychologist. And right now, she supposed, she needed to talk. 'It's that serial killer I tried a few years ago. There's a hearing on Monday and, I guess, maybe I'm just anxious.'

He paused. She could feel his frown. The one that made him look old. 'Is that the one who made those allegations in court? About you? About your—'

'Yes,' she said, cutting him off before he had to say the words. 'Cupid. He's appealing, and the judge has now set down a hearing. And, well, he's going to be there, Dad. In court.'

'Can anyone else handle it, Chlo? Anyone in your office?'

'I wish. No,' she sighed. 'I'm it.'

'Well, what happens if you can't do it?'

'He may get a new trial. He may get off. I have to do it.'

'Then you have to do it. How long is this hearing?'

'A few days, I suppose.'

'Is it the same judge as the last time?'

'Yes.'

'Good. I liked him,' he said. 'He didn't take any bull. Will there be a lot of security?'

'Oh, yeah. It will be packed, I'm sure.'

'Are you afraid he can hurt you?'

She sighed. 'Only if he gets out.'

'Can Dominick be there with you?'

C.J. hesitated. 'Things are a bit rocky in that department, Daddy. It's a long story. We . . . we broke up.' She couldn't help it. She started to cry softly, holding her hand over the phone so that he wouldn't hear, but she knew he probably did.

'Because of this?'

'I can't get into it right now, Daddy.'

She heard him sigh. 'You're strong, Chloe. You can do this. I know you can.'

'Dad, can I come home?' she said with a dry laugh after a few moments and tears had passed.

'When you're done. Mom's already got the room made up. And then we'll celebrate.' He paused again. 'That's not what you wanted to hear, I bet.'

'No,' she sighed.

'Don't let him get you on the run, honey. If he senses that, he'll try to mess with your head the whole time.

And remember, you're the one who put him behind those bars. He fears *you*.'

'Thank you, Daddy. I should go. Tell Mom I said 'bye. Love you.'

'I love you, too. Listen, don't wait so long to call next time.'

C.J. hung up the phone and wiped the tears away defiantly with the back of her hand. Her father was right, as she knew he would be. She would not let him get her on the run, or see her shake, or hear her heart race tomorrow. She was stronger than that. She stubbed out her cigarette and finished her wine. Then she headed back into the kitchen to finish her reading.

Then you have to do it.

It was as simple as that.

57

'*United States vs. Dominick Falconetti*, case number 04-21034-CR-GUTHRIE.'

'Is the defendant present?' asked the Honorable Reginald Guthrie, as he stirred his coffee in a mug shaped like a gavel. He was a big man, with long jowls and just a soft hint of a southern drawl that he sometimes tried to hide, depending upon who was in front of him.

'Yes, Your Honor,' said the clerk.

'Have him come forward,' he motioned with his hand without looking up from his breakfast just yet. A staunch Democrat, Judge Guthrie had been appointed to the federal bench in 1976 by Jimmy Carter and had spent the last seventeen of those twenty-eight years with the same clerk and the same bailiff. He grabbed the indictment from the stack of paperwork on his desk and quickly scanned the charges while he gulped down a slug of his coffee. He frowned and bushy white eyebrows crawled together across his forehead. 'Hmmm . . .' he said, sounding thoroughly disappointed, as he did with every defendant, 'Title 18, Section 242. Deprivation of Rights Under the Color of Law, Mr Fal-coon-etti,' he said sounding out the syllables slowly as if they tasted bitter. It was definitely not a local name, so they probably did. He looked up, but not at Dominick. Only at his attorney. 'Okay, Mr Barquet, how does he plead?'

'Not guilty, of course,' said Les Barquet, with a dry smile and a drawl that matched the judge's. Lester

Franklin Barquet was old school himself, dressed to the nines in southern manners and a three-piece suit. He was a well-known criminal defense attorney and also a fixture in Judge Guthrie's courtroom. He'd brought the donuts.

'Of course,' said Judge Guthrie, smiling back. *They all say that*, was the look they shared.

It was strange being talked about in the third person, Dominick thought as he stood there before the judge in his best blue suit, hands folded in front of him. It was as if he did not exist. He had been in court at least a thousand times before in his career, but never as a defendant.

'Alright, then, let's get a date. I want to set down motions in the next thirty days and I want to keep this moving. I've got a tight schedule and an overdue vacation coming up in a few months. I don't want this hanging over our heads if it can be helped,' the judge said, slugging down a sip of coffee and reaching for a Krispy Kreme. 'Thanks, Les. I don't need one, but I'll take one.'

'My pleasure, Judge. Your Honor,' said Les with a smile again, 'I think we all want that. And if you'll let me indulge for a moment, I think I can give the court a bit of information that it might be lacking on this case.'

The Assistant US Attorney went to object, but the judge shooed him off, donut in hand. 'Let's hear what Mr Barquet has to say.'

'Judge, Mr Falconetti is not your ordinary defendant, if there is such a thing. He's a Special Agent with the Florida Department of Law Enforcement. He was up at Raiford interviewing a very violent death row inmate, the serial killer known as Cupid, who, I might add,' he said with an eyebrow raised, 'is the *victim* in this case, when the unfortunate misunderstanding occurred. Agent

Falconetti has been suspended from his job until this matter is resolved, so I'm sure you can understand his anxiousness to get this on your trial schedule as soon as possible and clear his name.'

'Cupid, huh?' said the judge, reaching again for the indictment which he hadn't really read the first time.

'Yes, Your Honor. Agent Falconetti was interviewing Mr Bantling about another series of homicides he might have information about when he got a little unruly.'

'Additional homicides?'

'Yes, Your Honor. The cop killings in Miami. Agent Falconetti has been working those as well.' Les turned to face the courtroom, sweeping his hand dramatically across the crowd behind the defense table, which included Manny, Chris, Fulton, Ted Nicholsby, Steve Yanni and Marlon Dorsett, along with a handful of agents from the FDLE Gainesville Field Office. 'These men, Judge, are just some of his colleagues from FDLE and Miami law enforcement who have come today to show their support.'

Now the judge finally looked at Dominick. He nodded. His face had softened. 'Sounds like an unfortunate incident indeed, Agent Falconetti.' Then he shot a skeptical look at the Assistant US Attorney, Nick Lowell, before turning his attention back to Les. 'What you gonna need on this, Les? Time-wise?'

Discovery – the right to know and access the evidence that the government has against a defendant and intends to use at trial – was not automatically granted to a defendant in federal court like it was in state court. Exculpatory evidence – evidence that tends to exonerate the defendant, otherwise known as Brady material – that *always* had to be handed over by the government. But that was it.

In federal court, the prosecutors played their hand close to the chest, and trial by surprise was the rule of the game. There were no depositions taken in federal court, no right to interview the witnesses and victim before trial. That's why their conviction rate was so high. It was hard to block the punch you don't see coming. And the government had enough money and manpower and resources to pack a mean punch.

'Not much, Judge. You know me. This whole thing shouldn't take very long,' Les said. 'I've already spoken to the boys down at the prison. They're very cooperative. Agent Falconetti acted in self-defense – that's the uniform opinion.'

'Self-defense?' shot the prosecutor.

'Injuries?' asked the judge, ignoring Lowell's exasperation.

'A bloody nose,' said Les.

'A federal indictment for a bloody nose?' asked the judge. The eyebrows went up and formed an arc of surprise.

'Try a *broken* nose and a cracked tooth,' said Lowell defensively.

'That's not what those boys down at the prison are saying, Mr Lowell,' said Les. 'Looks like your victim might have had a bit too much time alone to think of ways to even the score in his death row cell. They think a bloody nose was all it was, till he rearranged his own face.'

'That's crazy, Les,' said the prosecutor, shaking his head. 'There's a video.'

'Talk to the guards. That video doesn't show all that much. And it don't show him in his cell two hours later, now does it?'

'Why isn't this in state court?' asked Judge Guthrie, his brows crawling together again.

'They don't want it, Judge,' said Les.

Lowell shrugged. 'Mr Bantling does have rights, Judge,' he tried. 'No matter who he is.'

'So *I* get it? A federal indictment for a simple battery?' the judge shook his head in disgust and reached for another donut. 'Let's get this over with, then. Mr Barquet doesn't need much time. Let's get a date.'

Dominick stood stone-faced while they all settled on important dates for his future, hands folded meekly in front of him. Even though it sounded as if the tide had turned in his favor a bit, he was still very much the outsider in this legal clique. He knew from his experience in the courtroom that defendants should keep their mouths shut unless addressed.

He was so embarrassed standing there. Mortified, actually. Worse to him than appearing in front of a judge for his arraignment, was appearing in front of his friends and colleagues as a defendant. Ever since he had been suspended, his phone had rung off the hook with well-wishers and buddies wanting to drop by for a beer and a condolence. So much so, that he didn't stay home anymore. He jogged and worked out and went to the library and the coffee shop and didn't answer the phone. He knew he was lucky that they had all come to support him today, but, except for maybe Manny, he wished they hadn't. They would gather around him and pat his back and take him to lunch, where they would talk with him over a cold one about how much the system sucked. Then the hour would be up, and they'd go back to Miami, back on duty. And he . . . well, he would head back to the gym.

Les Barquet finished up schmoozing with the judge and chiding the AUSA and grabbed his briefcase. He then led Dominick back through the gallery and down the center of the courtroom, past his friends and his colleagues and his sister who had flown in from Long Island that morning. Dominick nodded a silent thanks at them all, hoping that his face was not obviously red from shame.

He saw her then – C.J. – sitting by herself on the aisle in the back by the doors. She smiled at him softly. She looked tired and even concealer could not erase the dark circles completely from underneath her beautiful green eyes. She mouthed something he couldn't make out as she rose.

It had been more than a week since their exchange in his hallway. She had called, but he hadn't answered, and this was the first time that he had seen her. At that moment, it felt like someone had punched him in the gut, stolen the air out of his chest. She must have slipped in after the arraignment had started, because she hadn't been there when he had looked for her before. He'd been wishing she wouldn't come, but hoping she would. Because if she didn't show he would be right. And he could be mad and bitter forever. And he could hate her.

But here she was.

Damn, he missed her. So much so that it physically hurt to see her now. For her to see him this way. And while one part of him wanted to grab her right there in the courtroom and shake her and hold her so that she would never need to run again, the other part of him knew that it was as she said. He could never fix her. He could never make it better or easier, he could never take away the pain or the nightmares. It had come to this – a standoff between her past and her present, and the past had won again. He now knew it always would. And he also knew why.

So he didn't stop, and he didn't hold her, like his body and soul ached to do. And it took all his strength as a man to keep walking past her into a waiting elevator and out of her life.

58

C.J. watched him from the back of the courtroom, his back to her as he stood in front of the judge. He wore the blue suit they had bought together last year from Brooks Brothers in the Sawgrass Mills outlet mall. His shoulders, though still strong and confident, sagged just a bit. He'd gotten a clean, short haircut. The scruffy beard he'd had when she last saw him was gone. Judges never trust defendants with facial hair, and he knew that. She knew he was more than embarrassed. His body language, the one she knew and felt down to a science, told her he was beaten.

She'd sat in Starbucks and seen Manny and Chris Masterson walk up the courthouse steps. She stayed put, sipping her coffee and waiting until they had gone in the building and through security before venturing out herself. She knew that there would probably be others that would show up for him, so she waited until after nine o'clock – after everyone would be seated in the courtroom and the calendar was being called and court was in session – and there would be no time for anyone in the back rows to chat, no time for anyone to ask her questions. The clerk had told her over the phone that Dominick was number nine on the calendar, so she knew she wouldn't miss him. She couldn't miss him. She had made a promise.

And I'll be there for you through all this in any way that I can. If you want me to.

Then she finished her coffee and headed across the street herself. He hadn't responded that night to her offer in his hallway, but it didn't matter. She had set this wheel in motion. She was the reason he was even here. She had left her messages, she had flown up to Jacksonville today. She would be there for him, even if he did not want her to be.

She hadn't believed that he would swoop her up in his arms like a character in a bad romance novel, that time would somehow stop and all would be forgiven. But she had hoped. She had hoped that he might forgive her for leaving, for not saying sorry or goodbye. For disappointing him. For hurting him.

She never really believed he would pass her by without hesitation, though. Without so much as a smile or a nod or an acknowledgment of the words she had whispered. When his eyes finally caught on hers, she saw first the flicker of surprise, before pain and anger betrayed them once again. Before they looked away from her, and her heart stopped. For a moment she thought she caught the same sweet intimate sparkle that only lovers have, when a simple look says a whole page full of words. But if it was there, it was gone before she had fully recognized it. He was past her and through the doors, and they knocked loudly together as they swung closed behind him.

She'd often heard people try and describe suffering a broken heart in books or movies or over lunch, and it all sounded like clichés. But at that moment, words she had long thought melodramatic suddenly came to life. And somewhere deep inside her, something physically ripped. She could feel it tear apart from her being, so deep and so entwined, that it could never be fixed.

Manny broke away from the circle of cops who had come to show their support a few rows up, who knew Dominick was here today because of her, and who now stood watching with downcast eyes as he walked away from her. The Bear headed toward her with a big smile and an embarrassed look of pity, one that said he had seen everything. 'Counselor!' he called.

But she was already gone.

She walked out of the courtroom and picked up speed, taking the first elevator down and then breaking out the courthouse doors into the sunshine. She raced down the stairs of the courthouse, hoping to make it to her car before she completely fell apart.

59

'I don't know about this, Tom. Judge Guthrie didn't look too convinced,' said the US Attorney for the Middle District of Florida into the phone. He swiveled his seat and stared out the window of his office onto downtown Jacksonville.

'You're gonna tell me, Jeff, that that's not a friggin' battery? That's not an abuse of one's civil rights there on goddamn video?' Tom de la Flors, the US Attorney for the Southern District yelled in exasperation at his colleague and law school friend on the other end of the line.

'This is a different town, up here, Tom. A different mindset.' The US Attorney scratched at his head and closed his eyes, wishing he didn't have to have this conversation. It felt unsavory. 'A lot of boys who live here work Corrections down in Raiford, Lawtey, New River CI, Union. FDLE headquarters is up the road in Tallahassee, along with all the other state agencies. You know how it is with juries when it's a cop.'

'There's a video, Jeff.'

'Think Rodney King, Tom. And now think Rodney Goes To Jacksonville.'

'This is not a race issue.'

'No, but it's a cop's word versus a scumbag.'

'Bad example anyway, Jeff. They nailed those cops on federal charges after the State screwed up.'

'Only because no one wanted to see LA burn twice. No one here is afraid of Jacksonville going up in smoke.

The point I was trying to make is that video don't mean diddly sometimes.'

Jeff sighed. Tom and he had been classmates at Duke, but that was about it, as far as he could remember, and he did not like having to explain himself to yet another loudmouth bully from Miami, classmate or not. Every lawyer he knew in South Florida thought they were hot shit. Give them a title and the condition worsened. Jeff was born and raised in Jacksonville, having left only for school at his dad's insistence and headed right back upon graduation. After forty-three years, he was sick and tired of the patronizing comments about the 'old south' from his pompous colleagues who lived and practiced south of Palm Beach, in the land of transplanted New Yorkers and raft migrants.

'I don't know about Miami,' Jeff continued defensively, 'but I can tell you, this is not a defendant's town, Tom. Not a death row defendant, and certainly not one who's a serial killer, who looks on that tape like he might eat his own mother. Just because Lowell got the indictment don't mean too much. Once Judge Guthrie and a jury made up of folks who live around here, hear the Special Agent with the impeccable record and no complaints on the stand, and see the man already convicted of eleven murders snarl in color on that tape – smiling after he takes a hook, like he knows he can play the system . . . Well, what I'm saying, Tom, is that around here, that's not necessarily a civil rights violation. That's just deserts. Add in the convicted serial murderer swearing up and down that he's a brutal rapist who once tried to kill the esteemed cop's pretty, prosecutor girlfriend and you've got them lining up outside that courthouse with Kleenex and potpies.'

'Fuck them,' de la Flors grumbled. 'Fuck him.'

'Excuse me?'

'Sorry about the language. Look, Jeff, take this as far as it will go, then, and let a jury decide. That "esteemed cop" had been interfering with a federal investigation the Bureau has been trying to run down here into those cop killings. And it's not the first time he's tried to trump this office. He's got some pretty big britches.' *Britches. There's a word that might get through.*

Tom de la Flors tapped his pen on his desk. Dominick Falconetti had an attitude. One that he did not like and one that had grown since the Cupid fiasco. He and his chain of command needed a wake-up call. They had fucked with him last time and it had cost him an appointment to a federal judgeship.

'Let him work off some steam at home for a while with the daytime soaps,' de la Flors continued. 'And let the Commissioner and his boss sit and stew about the soundness of their hot-tempered agent's judgment and all the good it's doing their task force now.'

'I won't push this, I'm telling you up front,' said Jeff wearily. 'Carson Trunt wouldn't touch this with a ten-foot pole.' Trunt was the State Attorney for the Eighth Judicial Circuit in Bradford County, home to Florida State Prison. He handled jurisdiction over state crimes, such as battery committed in state institutions. Jeff knew that it would be hard to explain to a jury in federal court why the US government wanted to prosecute a state cop for slapping the face of a state convict at a state penitentiary – when, for some reason, the State itself wanted no part of the case.

De la Flors gritted his teeth. 'There's a video of this cop pummeling the face of a defendant in custody and you're worried about people thinking you're pushing this too far?' He blew out a low breath and changed his tone before continuing. 'I think you're okay. You're doing your job is what you're doing. Carson Trunt is being derelict. But of course, it's election year, isn't it?'

He hung up the phone and shook his head in disbelief at Mark Gracker who sat in front of his desk, picking his fingernails clean with the tip of a business card. 'They're not too enthusiastic up there, let's just say that,' he said. Gracker nodded slowly, but knew enough at that moment to say nothing. 'You better move fast on what you've got down here.'

Damn southerners, de la Flors thought, running his hand through his thinning hair. No wonder they lost the fucking civil war. *Kleenex and potpies*. What the hell were they running up there – a courthouse or a county fair?

60

Bill Bantling smiled as the guards walked him back to his cell, down the hallway that somehow didn't seem as gray and as drab as it had an hour ago. The meeting with his lawyer had gone quite well. Better than expected, actually.

Apparently the odds of a trip back to court on a post-conviction motion – *any* post-conviction motion – were about 450–1. So said Bill's fellow inmates and the lazy-assed guards who worked the block. There were inmates who had filed ten, fifteen, thirty of their own Rule Threes over the years in state court, an equal number of 2254 motions in federal court, and countless public records requests, bogus habeas corpus motions and certiorari petitions, and a dozen other tongue-twisting Latin-named documents. Of course, Bill's own attorney had told him *his* chances were much better, but that was because, Bill knew, Neil Mann wanted his money up front.

Now his odds had dropped to 50–1 for a new trial after a hearing. Shave a few points again if your attorney's down on his rent. Still a long shot, but Bantling would take it any day of the week. Any day at all. Throw in a little vacation from this hellhole, a road trip through the Florida countryside, a sweet reunion with some old friends, and it would be a regular party. Then there was that little added bonus that he hadn't counted on – a federal indictment and a suspension for the lead detective and, *damn!* He was beating the house!

Oh this was going to be fun. He had the goods that would take his not-so-sweet Chloe down. That would lock her in her own little cell, with rats for roommates and visits from former friends and lovers once a week if she was lucky. If she didn't go nuts again, that is. Then her cell would be white and padded and there'd be no visits for a long time. *That might be even better*, he chuckled to himself. He knew he could do it, too, despite the odds. He had Lourdes Rubio praying for forgiveness on letterhead. He had that tape. Chloe had no one. No one at all. They were all dead, every one of her little flying monkeys, her henchmen. She was it. The last witness.

The door slammed on his six-by-eight cell, locking him back in. But not for long. Because it was time to pack. Pack up his toothbrush and put on his Sunday best. Because he was coming home.

And when he made it back downtown next week, he was gonna take care of some other little business. He knew there was another who would like nothing better than to see him rot in this prison for something he didn't do. One who had tried to manipulate his future up here as well. Once Bantling finally got to hear that tape, he knew it would confirm what he had just recently begun to suspect, and then he'd take care of this new player, too. He had a few cards left to deal at the State Attorney's Office and to his newfound friends at the US Attorney's. Interesting little tidbits that he could exchange on the legal bartering system if things didn't go his way this time.

Bantling didn't yet have a face to put with the name. But soon enough, the best and the brightest would be able to figure out the identity of the one he knew was one of their own. The one lurking within their own ranks. The man known in certain deadly circles simply by his nickname.

Cop Killer.

61

Then you have to do it.

Her father's words sounded in her head when the elevator doors opened on four. C.J. straightened her shoulders and pushed her way to the front of the car and into the usual mass of confusion that existed in the courthouse hallways at 1:00 p.m., right after lunch as afternoon calendars began to start up.

Judge Chaskel had commandeered one of the larger courtrooms in the building, 4-8, to accommodate the grumbling press. His gag order had been effective – too effective – and his last-minute duck into chambers for Bantling's Huff hearing did not win him any brownie points with the media. To avoid never-ending, lengthy Florida-in-the-sunshine hearings and right-of-access and freedom-of-the-press complaints, Chaskel had opened a larger door for the evidentiary hearing, but the gag order was still on. Thankfully, Neil Mann was too afraid of irritating the judge and not smart enough to jump on the *we've all been scorned* bandwagon with the press. It might have churned up some well-needed sympathy for his client, but he hadn't played that card.

C.J. made her way to the courtroom doors with Rose Harris at her side, her hand held up in front of her as a sign that she had no comment on anything. She was relieved to see that Rose had adopted the same policy. They'd been colleagues for ten years in the office – five together in Major Crimes – but they'd never been great friends. And the events of the last few weeks had put an even greater strain on their relationship. But a united front before Chaskel and the State Attorney and the press was necessary, so they walked together, each pushing a cart full of files. C.J. knew that Rose resented the fact that her case against Bantling hinged on C.J.'s, that if C.J.'s conviction was tossed, hers was sure to follow.

Rose was tough – both in and out of the courtroom – using both her claws and her brains to quickly climb the SAO ladder over men who had been there for years. She had tried the other ten Cupid murders because C.J. had passed them to her. It had been necessary for C.J. to try Bantling by herself on Prado, but it would have been emotional suicide for her to try him on the others. Four weeks in a courtroom with him was enough. Once she secured the conviction, Rose and Williams Rule had taken over. But now it looked like history might be rewritten, and no one was very happy with that prospect.

Travis Cormier with Corrections held the door open for C.J., and for just a moment she hesitated. Like a horse that knows instinctively not to attempt a jump, her legs bucked at walking in. She knew he was in there already. She could feel him.

'You coming, State?' said Travis impatiently. ''Cause this door's not holding itself.'

She would not let him mess with her head. She was stronger than that. 'Yeah,' she said, 'I thought I forgot something for a second.' Then she swallowed the fear that was climbing out of her stomach, and she walked in on legs that she willed not to tremble.

The room was almost full with onlookers and press, but she did not see them. All she saw was the back of Neil Mann and his stringy black hair that was in desperate need of a trim. He stood at the defense table, the back of his suit jacket pulling under the armpits, hunched over the man she could not yet see, but knew sat there waiting for her.

Mann had argued in a motion against irons and shackles and Judge Chaskel had agreed. So the Department of Corrections had outfitted their most famous inmate in the latest in electronic wear. Dressed in a suit, legs casually crossed, the electronic restraining device known as The Bandit dangled off his ankle. Around his waist, under the dress shirt, he'd be wearing a React Belt. Both of which would deliver an electric shock that would drop a 350-pound man to his knees in seconds should the CO from FSP push the button. Bantling had come down from Raiford with his own entourage of Corrections – four sergeants, one lieutenant and two corrections officers, plus a chase vehicle to follow his van. No one wanted to take the blame should he go missing, or come back with another notch on his belt. His escorts conspicuously lined the wall behind the defense table, back by the jury box. Courthouse corrections and court liaison officers secured the back door and judge's door.

C.J. slowly forced her glance up the table and saw the long white fingers on one hand, drumming slowly against the wooden table. The only thing that was missing was the face, still hidden behind his attorney's frame. Her eyes were drawn to those fingers, though. Even though she was too far away, she could have sworn she heard the clicking of his nails on the wood, a low whistle under his breath. Just biding time.

'All rise!' shouted Hank the bailiff suddenly.

There was no time to think. The door to the judge's back hallway flung open and Judge Chaskel appeared, sailing quickly to the bench. She scurried up the aisle.

'No cellphones, no beepers while court is in session. Use them, lose them. The Honorable Judge Leopold Chaskel III presiding. Be seated and be quiet!' Hank had been in the system for thirty plus years and somewhere along the way he had lost the manual on diplomacy. Now everyone was treated the same. Like shit.

The judge looked at his watch and then at C.J. as she hurried through the small gate into the gallery. He watched in silence as she made her way in front of his bench to the State's table next to Rose Harris.

He let her sit down and unpack her boxes. The room was quiet, everyone slightly eager to see if maybe the judge would yell at her to hurry. She heard the heavy sighs of a few in the rows behind her, as if they had been waiting hours instead of minutes. Rose tapped her pen and C.J. wanted to slug her.

How did it come to all this? To being the loathed kid in class? The one no one wants to sit next to? She and Rose might not have been the best of friends before this, but they certainly had respected each other. C.J. had been before Judge Chaskel a million times, and he had always liked her – or so she thought – never caring if she ran a few minutes behind schedule. Now he practically glared at her from the bench. *Was she being overly sensitive, or had everything changed?*

Her head in her boxes, she had yet to see Bantling's face, but she knew he was smiling. At least on the inside. Outside, she was sure he wore a pitiful, pained *Help me, I've been framed!* look for the press and the judge and his attorney and anyone else who was watching.

'I'm sorry, Judge,' C.J. said.

'Are we ready now, State?' asked the judge.

'Yes, Your Honor,' said Rose.

'Yes, Judge,' C.J. said quietly.

She could have waited. Waited until Bantling took the stand, waited until she was forced to look. But she didn't.

She'd hoped that maybe she'd steal a glimpse of a decrepit old man, a man who had been beaten.

She hoped wrong.

Those cold blue eyes were waiting for her when she turned and faced him. Eyes that cut into her. His face was colorless, but certainly not old and definitely not defeated. With his forehead resting somberly in his hand, he turned, so that the view of the judge and the camera was blocked. Then he mouthed his first words to her in three years.

Welcome back.

62

Neil Mann was nervous. So much so that his bottom lip was quivering slightly, an anxious habit that he'd had since he was a kid. It was one of the reasons he left trial work.

He needed this client. It wasn't much money, but it was certainly high exposure. Bill Bantling could do for him what William Kennedy Smith had done for Roy Black. Skyrocket him to the stratosphere of celebrity clients and $450 an hour and appearances on television as a legal expert.

But now that dream was in serious danger.

This case – the case that makes a career – had fallen in his lap. The letter from Bill had come in on a Wednesday, and Neil had recognized the name right away. Then Bill had forwarded him the handwritten apology letter from Rubio. That was when Neil knew he'd be investing in a new suit for today's hearing.

He had spoken with Rubio on the phone and she had told him all about her conversation with a drunk and horny Victor Chavez at a bar on South Beach, just a week or so after Bantling had been arrested. Victor hadn't yet known she had signed on as Bantling's defense counsel when he told her about the anonymous tip that made him think there were drugs in Bantling's Jag. Then, Rubio had told Neil about the 911 tape and about how she purposely threw the motion to suppress and ultimately the trial. Of course he had offered to fly out to see her

269

– the proper thing to do – but she didn't want any part of seeing him. He didn't want to push and spook her. She offered the affidavit – notarized and all – and a copy of the tape. And she said she'd come down for the hearing, when and if it was ever scheduled. At her own expense, she insisted. Neil wouldn't even have to pay.

It was a gift from the Gods. Or so he thought.

Now the Gods were playing a cruel joke on him.

The tape had not arrived. But he hadn't worried about that too much at first, because she was very guarded, very secretive about it to begin with. Neil had thought that she might just have decided to bring it down herself. She had told him exactly what it said, word for word, so actual possession wasn't such a big deal till the hearing. Which was, of course, today.

After the Huff hearing, he'd called and left a message on her voicemail to tell her of the date for the evidentiary hearing. But he'd heard nothing. Then he called again, but there was no voicemail, just a disconnected number. That was when Neil had started to panic. On Wednesday, he'd finally broken down and hired a PI, who'd called Neil back on Saturday with the news. Neil had spent the weekend trying to figure out how to salvage the case that was supposed to make his career.

'Alright then, everyone's here and time's a-wasting,' said Judge Chaskel, sitting back in his leather chair. The courtroom was far more majestic than his normal digs. 'Mr Mann, this is your show. So call your first witness.'

Neil Mann rose hesitantly, his fingers rubbing nervously on the edge of the defense table, leaving sweat marks. 'There's been a problem, Judge. I think we might need to go sidebar.'

Judge Chaskel sat back up stiffly in his seat. 'Are your

witnesses here, Mr Mann? I told you both last week that I was not in the mood on this case to play games. Especially not now that we've got the defendant present and special arrangements have been made.'

'It is a witness problem, Your Honor.' Neil's lip had begun to quake, and that was not a good sign. 'One I just found out about over this weekend, and I don't know how to proceed. I thought we'd go side—'

'What is it, Mr Mann?' snapped Chaskel.

'It's Lourdes Rubio, Your Honor. I received a call from my private investigator this weekend . . .'

'Let me guess,' the judge sighed. 'She's had a change of heart and is not coming.'

'Judge, she's been murdered.'

The flashbulbs erupted, the press ran out to call their editors, and the circus was back in town once again.

63

'Chambers, please,' said the judge, not even batting an eye. 'Now.' The press that remained in the courtroom stood to complain, but the judge could care less. He sailed off the bench, a nervous Neil Mann in tow, followed by the court reporter juggling her equipment, and the clerk. Two corrections officers moved in closer next to Bantling.

'This is unbelievable. Unbelievable. Murdered?' said Rose, shaking her head, her voice a shocked whisper. 'Let's go C.J.,' she said, rising from her seat and grabbing her file. 'The judge is in no mood. Let's find out what happened.'

But C.J. couldn't move. She sat there staring at her file in front of her and thought she would vomit if she stood. She blinked at the paper and saw Lourdes sitting in front of her across her desk, in her southwestern office in the middle of nowhere. She remembered the contempt Lourdes had had for her, when she tried to persuade her to divulge what was perhaps privileged information. Information, C.J. had suspected, that might lead her to yet another madman. But Lourdes had refused.

Murdered? Not just dead. Not car accident, not cancer, not a freak brain hemorrhage. *Murder.* When? Where? Did it have to do with her? With this? And did C.J. look like she was thinking just that to everyone who watched her now in the courtroom? Did she look guilty? She had not disclosed to the court her meeting with Lourdes more than two weeks ago, because legally she was not required to. And, she figured, Lourdes would have probably volunteered that herself today. Now what should she do?

'I guess Neil didn't think to spring the news on his client before telling the world,' said Rose, in a low voice, looking over at the defense table. 'Bantling looks like someone just knocked the wind out of him. Good,' she snorted.

Bantling stared at the judge's bench in front of him, elbows on the table, clenching and unclenching his fists, as if he were trying hard to control himself. The smile was gone. Another CO moved in to back up the two who had moved from the box.

'C.J., you're pale, girl. Come on, drink some water,' Rose said, impatiently, shoving a plastic cup at her. 'And let's get in there before Chaskel has a cow. It's a terrible thing to say, but this might not be a bad thing. For us anyway. Without Lourdes, there's no motion now. Bantling's new evidence just bit the dust, and we might all be going home a lot sooner than we thought.'

64

'What the hell just happened in there?' Chaskel barked at Neil Mann, as soon as C.J. closed the door behind her in the conference room.

'Judge, I just found—'

'No. *You* found out this weekend. *I* just found out in front of a courtroom full of cameras and people.' He looked at C.J., whose eyes were downcast on the floor. 'Were you in on this one?' She looked up at him in surprise and he·backed off, answering his own question. 'Apparently not. What happened then, Mr Mann?'

'I hadn't been able to reach Ms Rubio since the Huff hearing.'

'And you didn't think to tell me that before?'

'She was very reclusive, Judge. It didn't alarm me until this week. And, rather than ask for a continuance and delay justice any longer for Mr Bantling, I hired a private detective to locate Ms Rubio for me. So that I could secure a material witness bond if I had to from this court, and force her in, if that was what it took. On Saturday, the PI called to tell me she had passed away a couple of weeks ago, the victim of an apparent robbery gone bad in her office. The police are still investigating, but there's been no arrests. No one called anyone here, because she had severed all ties with the community when she left. Her mother died a year ago, and there was no other family she was in touch with. I'm sorry, Judge,' he finished, looking down again at his feet.

'I should've been told before I took the bench.'

'I wasn't sure how to proceed, Your Honor. I'm still not. This is Mr Bantling's last shot.'

'Before his federal appeals begin, that is.'

'The clock is up on his twenty-two fifty-four as well.' A 2254 was a federal motion for post-conviction relief based on Constitutional grounds, and it was even more strict, time-wise.

'Not my concern.' Chaskel sighed in frustration, 'Let me think this through. We have Rubio's affidavit.'

'It's hearsay. The State can't cross-examine an affidavit, Judge,' said Rose.

'She's dead, Ms Harris.'

'Exactly, and, I don't mean to be callous, but it's through no fault of the State. I'm sorry, but we still have the right to cross this witness. A witness whose testimony was being presented to undo eleven first-degree murder convictions.'

'I didn't hear the State objecting about hearsay when we talked about admitting Officer Chavez's trial testimony,' said the Judge.

'That's different. He was subject to vigorous cross-examination by the defense when he testified at trial. His testimony is admissible under the rules,' insisted Rose.

'What are you suggesting? I simply ignore the new evidence Mr Mann has presented and ship Mr Bantling back to die? Because the witness whose testimony could clear him – his very own trial attorney who has admitted malfeasance – has been murdered?' He turned to Neil Mann who had brightened a bit. 'The 911 tape is a business record, and the custodian of records at Miami Beach can bring that in. I'm sure that Mr Mann can figure out some hearsay exception so that we can listen to it, correct?'

Mann looked sheepishly back at the ground. 'I don't have it, Judge. The tape. She was supposed to bring it. The master was erased years ago, because originals are destroyed at the department after thirty days. She told me she got her copy on the twenty-ninth day.'

Chaskel's face froze. 'You've got to be kidding. You really have to be. I'm bending over backwards to give your client the benefit of every evidence rule and you don't have the goddamn tape that started this whole thing? How is that possible?' He turned to Rose and C.J. 'State, you had access to Rubio's defense file. Was it in there?'

'Not even the mention of a tape,' Rose volunteered.

C.J. felt her stomach flip-flop. 'No, Judge,' said C.J. 'There was no tape in the file.' At least that much was true.

'Christ, this is a mess,' said the judge. 'I'm damned if I do, damned if I don't.' He ran his hand through his hair and blew out a low breath. 'I have to do some research. We all do. Nine tomorrow, I want everyone here and I want some law on all this. This is a man's life that hangs in the balance, so we'd all better get it right.'

65

By the time C.J. had crossed the street to her office, she knew the grisly, frightening details. The press spilled them on every channel, even breaking into soap operas and game shows to keep the public informed, and the race was on to be the first to get and air the ugly crime scene photos. As a gesture of integrity, some media outlets would blur out Lourdes' twisted body, showing only the blood-stained carpet where her body lay. Others cared more for ratings than integrity, and of course, that alone would spawn another debate, causing the pictures to run all over again.

Lourdes' body had been discovered on a Friday afternoon, after she failed to show up in court all week. Not that anyone, besides perhaps her abandoned clients, had noticed. It was the cleaning lady who had found the body. Lourdes had died of multiple stab wounds, her purse and watch were missing, the earrings ripped from her ears, the rings torn from her fingers, the victim of an apparent robbery. She was last seen by a client in her office on the Friday morning before the long President's Day weekend, right before a major snowstorm hit the area that afternoon. Because the body had not been found for a week, and decomposition had begun, the date and time of death were impossible to specifically determine. Based on her absence from court, it was thought to be sometime between Friday afternoon and Tuesday morning.

C.J. had left Lourdes' office at 2:30 p.m. that very Friday, during that very snowstorm. She heard the wind in her ears as it wrapped around her, helping slam Lourdes' office door shut behind her.

She had checked and double checked the dates, but it was true. And now she was completely numb, afraid to think anymore. She asked no questions, made no phone calls. She didn't want anymore information, though, as a prosecutor, she could surely get it.

Did the 'multiple stab wounds' mean a sliced throat? Was the tongue muscle moved, was she given a Colombian necktie? Were any fingerprints or fibers found at the scene? Are they unidentified? Were they hers? Are there really any suspects? Were there any witnesses in the area, witnesses, perhaps, that spotted a dark-blonde female in a rented Blazer leaving the scene?

Accompanying each question, was the dark realization that *she* might be the answer. She had told no one of her meeting that afternoon with Lourdes, the angry words that had been exchanged, the topic of discussion: William Bantling and the controversial anonymous tip that had put him behind bars. Her silence, once discovered, would probably look very suspicious. Then again it would look suspicious that she had even been to Lourdes' office in the first place and hadn't told the court last week. Suspicious, and possibly contemptuous and maybe, now, worse. Every road out was a road back in, and it was getting harder and harder to breathe.

She put her head in her hands behind her closed and locked office door.

There was no more questioning it. Everyone was dead. Chavez, Lindeman, Ribero, and now, Lourdes, Everyone but her. She was it. The last witness to a deadly conspiracy that had turned on its conspirators. It wouldn't be much longer, she knew, before others would see the undeniable connection as well.

There was no point in looking for answers. Instead, she sat in her office and buried herself in legal issues, case law and Westlaw, ignoring the impatient knocks of Marisol and the calls of Jerry Tigler and the hungry press. Soon enough, she suspected, someone would figure out to ask the questions she herself could not, and fingers would begin to point at her. Then it would not be just Marisol at her door. It would be Manny or Chris Masterson or the Colorado State Police or the FBI.

Or worse.

There was one out there now who knew the answers she did not. One who had picked off witnesses, one by one by one. William Bantling would not have killed off Lourdes, his only chance at escaping a death sentence. But the man who did not want that tape out would. The man who, even without a tape, would not want Chavez to talk out of school, or Lindeman's guilty conscience to one day betray him, or Ribero's fear to send him running to court to tell the truth.

Because the truth meant Bantling had, indeed, been set up that night on the Causeway. Set up by someone who knew what would happen when Chavez and company popped the trunk and found a woman naked and missing a heart, a victim of the serial killer Cupid. Someone who had put that body in that trunk.

She remembered Greg Chambers' soliloquy in the darkness of his black-painted death chamber, her face pressed against the cold steel gurney. *Now don't go thinking that I'm going to reveal the secret family recipe, give a last-second detailed confession so that it all becomes clear, because I won't. Some things you will have to go to the grave wondering about.*

She had not gone to her grave, but he had gone to his. Chambers was dead, so that meant that it was *someone else* – someone still very much alive – who had called in that tip three years ago. She had always just assumed that it was him.

She heard the floor begin to empty. First, the rush of secretaries at 4:30 p.m., then the Major Crimes attorneys as one by one they packed up their briefcases and headed out past her door to the security doors and elevator bay. Nighttime gradually descended on the building, and by 9:00 p.m. she knew she was alone on the floor. By 11:00, she knew she was alone in the building.

She didn't want to go home alone. Not tonight, with the crazy, frightening thoughts that were running through her head. She couldn't go to Dominick. A hotel was an option, but it would be full of strangers and lax on security. Here, at least, there was a guard, and security-access doors and, other than prosecutors or police officers, no one was even allowed in the building after hours.

So at 1:00 a.m., she put on yet another pot of coffee to help her read through the mountain of case law she had collected, to write the legal brief of a lifetime. It would help get her through the darkness, before the early morning light enabled a trip back home and a quick change of clothes.

Then she would be back here. Back to stop one monster, before the other found her out.

66

Judge Leopold Chaskel sat at his desk in chambers, reading and re-reading the legal briefs before him, thick with attached case law from every court in the country. Only cases that were directly on point from Florida's Third District Court of Appeal, the Florida Supreme Court and the United States Supreme Court were binding on any decision he would make. But the decisions of other courts, even those outside the jurisdiction, that had faced the same or similar issue, were called 'legally persuasive.' In other words, if four out of five dentists say it's good, then he should, too.

His eyes burned from the strain of reading so much small print and from a lack of quality sleep, and he wiped them with the damp cloth that Janine had slipped in with his lunch order. At 2:00 in the morning he had decided to pack it in, but found he couldn't, tossing and turning all night, until Lucienne, his wife, finally made him move into the guest bedroom at 5:00. That's when he officially gave up on sleep and put back on the bifocals and started reading again. Capitol case Supreme Court opinions were never two pages, either. Try twenty and thirty and forty pages, with multiple, complex issues.

He knew the additional cases he had pulled himself would be the same that the defense and State would present to him in the morning. They, too, had probably been up all night at their computers researching, each pulling out all the stops – one to halt this train, the other to keep it moving forward – and he wanted to be prepared. He knew this was going to go up on appeal either way.

He had been right. The arguments had come at him like rapid rifle fire this morning, and those damn cameras and microphones and pushy reporters were there to lay watch to the entire thing. So even though he was exhausted, he was glad he had forgone sleep.

Damnit. Judge Chaskel slammed his reading glasses on the desk and rubbed his eyes again. He had run what he thought was one of the cleanest trials for a major media case this courthouse had ever seen. It was fast. It was smart. It was judicious. He had not pandered to the press to drag it out like a marathon or a bad soap and keep his face on the air, like some other media-saturated cases of the past. The defendant had been a problem, but he had solved it, accepting no bullshit or theatrics in his courtroom, and on that issue, the appellate courts had sided with him already. He had handled Bantling's initial *Motion for New Trial*, his first Rule Three, and put all those issues to bed neatly in a succinct, airtight opinion, and the appellate courts had agreed with him on that again. Now, when the end was near, when it seemed as if the plane had cleared the runway, it looked as if he had been sabotaged, the victim of subterfuge in the courtroom by the very people that he had trusted to help him run the system.

Eleven dead women. Even though the law was sometimes black and white, lives were not. That was what was so eternally frustrating about being a judge. The small print oftentimes forgot the human toll. It was easy to see things as numbers and dates when there was no face sitting in a witness box, looking up at you and asking you to do the right thing. Because justice as the law required and 'the right thing' were not synonymous. How could he not think of eleven dead women now, the brutal facts of their murders still fresh in his mind, the heart-wrenching screams of their mothers echoing in his courtroom, revisited in excruciating detail by the Medical Examiner in page after page of trial testimony that sat now before him on his desk? It was hard to just skip over that part and get to the legal questions, without tripping over those words, those pretty, dead faces reduced now to only a last name in an appellate brief.

If he allowed in the Lourdes Rubio affidavit as evidence, he would have no choice but to grant the motion for a new trial. The facts were clearly damning, and once he made that affidavit official – once he made it legal and part of the evidentiary record – he could not then legally ignore its content. Neither could the appellate courts. And there would be a ripple effect – the reverberations of his reversal on Prado would overturn the other ten convictions, he knew. A new trial was the remedy, the outcome of which would be a lot less certain than the first.

However, if he kept the affidavit out, unless the defendant could show an 'abuse of discretion by the trial court' – an almost impossible legal feat – it was never coming in and it was never coming back.

In other words, the ball was entirely in his court.

Despite Lourdes Rubio's last-minute effort to help her former client, Judge Chaskel had been in that courtroom and had heard the evidence, and there was no denying that Bantling was guilty. That was what was so damn frustrating. Even if everything she had said in her affidavit were taken as true, that the stop was predicated on a bad tip – a tip not recognized by a black and white reading of the law – he knew that *legally* it might take Anna Prado's body out of that trunk, but not *factually*. Her tale of a vengeful prosecutor seeking retribution for a decade-old crime was an eyebrow raiser as well, but then again, he was certainly having his doubts about C. J. Townsend lately. He used to be able to depend on her, take every word she told him as true. No more. She had been less than forthcoming regarding her prior assault and Bantling's absurd allegations, and that was one thing he did not appreciate in his courtroom – a lack of candor. It was something he might have expected from the defense bar, but not from a Major Crimes prosecutor. Obviously he had set the bar too high.

Now she had left him with a mess. They both had – she and Rubio – but only Townsend was around to pay the penalty.

He tapped his pen against his desk, wiped his eyes again and took a final sip of his cold coffee. He rose and put his black robe back on, his shoulders suddenly old and heavy under the weight of it, and walked out of chambers.

And as he slowly made his way down the quiet back hall to take the bench and confront the circus, he said a silent prayer that what he was about to do was the right thing. And that God would forgive him if it was not.

67

The door from the judge's hallway opened without warning, and Judge Chaskel swept to the bench. He surprised Hank, who stood chatting with one of the FSP sergeants by the box. 'All rise!' seemed rather pointless by then, so Hank just barked a flustered, 'Be seated!' even though most of the courtroom still was.

The media was officially back now in all its glory. With boom mikes and cameras and satellite trucks, every station had staked its claim as soon as the courtroom doors opened that morning. It was now late Tuesday afternoon, and even though the wait had stretched to seven and a half hours, no one was about to give up their hard-fought seat. They had hung around the entire day, ordering in lunch and hooking up live feeds from the courtroom. The legal arguments that would be made, C.J. had thought, would have put even the most diehard of Court TV fans to sleep in a matter of minutes.

The feeds alternated back and forth between the courtroom in sunny downtown Miami and outside Lourdes Rubio's office building in Breckenridge, Colorado. The cameras focused in dramatically on the small, white and black FOR RENT sign that sat now in the front window. It was supposed to look ominous and chilling and abandoned, but occasionally the cameras would inadvertently catch the other reporters doing the exact same thing, and the effect was lost.

Then there were the shots of the Breckenridge Police

Captain, trying to look somber, but equally as excited as the reporters, at a crowded press conference in police headquarters. Relishing his fifteen minutes, he said in a loud and surprisingly confident voice, 'It's still an open investigation. We have approached this as a robbery to date, but we are not discounting any theory. Lourdes died under very violent circumstances. We're asking the public to call in with any information they might have.' The use of the victim's first name was supposed to bring a hometown, 'we're all dealing with the loss,' feel to the investigation, but he pronounced Lourdes' name wrong. That clip ran every twenty minutes or so, or whenever the courtroom drama became too legal to be called exciting, spliced with old footage of Lourdes at Bantling's trial three years back.

Manny had shown up with Chris Masterson and Steve Yanni at about ten past nine, listened to the legal arguments for two minutes, yawned and, in a note passed to C.J., vowed to come back with reinforcements when the legal wrangling was officially over. C.J. had left a message for Marisol to beep him and tell him to come back this afternoon, realizing after the fact that was probably not the best of ideas. Now Marisol herself stood in the rear of the courtroom, sandwiched between the Bear and half the police force in Miami, a big toothy grin on her fuchsia-colored lips. C.J. looked, but of course Dominick was not there. He couldn't be, given who the defendant was.

Now the cameras were devoted solely to an obviously tired and troubled Judge Chaskel. He had announced at 1:00 p.m. that a ruling would be pronounced at 3:30, and he had made it to the bench, of course, right on time. It was 3:31 and even with the courtroom jammed to its paneled walls, you could hear a pin drop.

C.J., along with the rest of the courtroom, tried to read the heavy lines that crossed the judge's face, weighing down his brow and pulling at the corners of his mouth. Her head pounded and her hands were wet with sweat. Maybe she would be able to get a head-start out the door if he threw a scowl her way, one that told her his ominous warning to her was about to come true, that things would indeed be getting sticky for her. But his seasoned face divulged no clue. He looked out at his courtroom, like a king on a small throne, but focused on no one, no camera, in particular. Then his eyes dropped onto the prepared order he had in front of him.

C.J. had done her best that morning, and had made what she thought was a good, sound argument. Once she sat down, Rose stood up and made it all again. Neil Mann was no match for the two of them, or Judge Chaskel's quick hypothetical 'let's play devil's advocate for a moment' questions. He delivered a weak argument, his bottom lip shaking so badly at one point that C.J. thought he might actually cry.

But the law was a funny profession. Oftentimes even the strongest of arguments lost to the most emotional of cases. Judges in criminal cases were supposed to be impartial, looking only to the law, but C.J. knew that Chaskel could not just ignore a death sentence. So she crossed her fingers under her folder and dropped another prayer to St Christopher that the judge would finish this now.

'The defendant has made a motion for post-conviction relief pursuant to the Florida Rules of Criminal Procedures, Rules 3.851 and 3.850,' the judge continued, his words carefully chosen, not for the cameras but for the court reporter. 'He had asserted two grounds for which he seeks relief. The first is an ineffective assistance of counsel claim, where he alleges that the performance of his attorney of record, Lourdes Rubio, was so deficient that it deprived him of a fair trial. The second ground for relief is a newly discovered evidence claim. The defendant alleges that there is newly discovered evidence, only recently obtained, that if introduced at retrial would probably produce an acquittal. In support of these two claims, the defendant has attached a notarized affidavit from Lourdes Rubio.

'In this affidavit, Ms Rubio admits to coming into possession of certain evidence, namely a 911 tape, after Mr Bantling had been arrested and after she had been retained as counsel, but before his trial began. This 911 call, allegedly recorded on the emergency line by the Miami Beach Police Department on or about September 19, 2000, the night Mr Bantling was arrested, was allegedly placed just a few minutes before the defendant was pulled over by Miami Beach Police Officer Victor Chavez for traffic violations. The substance of the call is as follows:

'Operator: *"911. What's your emergency?"*

'Unidentified caller: *"There's a car. A late-model black Jaguar XJ8. Right now he's headed south on Washington from Lincoln Road. He's got two kilos of cocaine in his trunk and he's headed to the airport. He's going to take the McArthur to MIA, just in case you miss him on Washington."*

'Operator: *"What's your name, sir? Where are you calling from?"*

'After that, the line goes dead.

'Trial testimony from the arresting officer supports that Mr Bantling was driving a 2000 black Jaguar XJ8 when he was first seen driving recklessly on Washington at approximately 8:15 that evening. In her affidavit, Ms Rubio alleges that the anonymous 911 call formed the basis for the illegal stop of his vehicle, and in support thereof points to an out-of-court conversation that she had with the arresting officer, Victor Chavez, wherein he stated as such. She alleges that the tip was legally insufficient in detail to provide probable cause to pull over Mr Bantling. As such, the subsequent search of his vehicle was also illegal, and the fruits of that search – namely the discovery of the body of Anna Prado and then the physical evidence gathered from a search of Mr Bantling's home – were poisoned and thus inadmissible. Ms Rubio, in her affidavit, states that, because of compromised personal feelings of sympathy she had for the prosecutor, C. J. Townsend, who was herself a victim of a sexual assault years before, she purposely withheld this information from her client and the court. She asserts that she did not present this evidence, failed to effectively cross-examine witnesses and did not zealously defend her client.

'The defendant, through the affidavit of Ms Rubio, presents a very interesting, very disturbing theory, and one that certainly requires further examination. This court thus duly ordered an evidentiary hearing to be held to explore both the truth and the scope of Ms Rubio's allegations. Ms Rubio was to testify before this court, and be subject to vigorous cross-examination by the State. Any evidentiary attorney–client privileges that had once existed between her and Mr Bantling would be waived.

'The factual problem for the court is this: Between the time Mr Bantling's Rule 3.850 was filed and this evidentiary hearing, Ms Rubio has died. In legal terms, the witness is now unavailable. In addition, the arresting officer, whose testimony and motives she wishes to call into question now, is also deceased. However, his statements in Mr Bantling's trial are legally admissible as evidence in this hearing, and would be in a retrial, under the rules of evidence as former sworn testimony. And finally, the 911 tape which serves as the root of both grounds of the defendant's motion cannot be produced by either the defense, or the State, as the Miami Beach Police Department routinely destroys their 911 master reels thirty days after recording.

'The legal problem for the court is this: The allegations of Ms Rubio are serious and troubling and, if true, most certainly would constitute grounds for a new trial. But Ms Rubio's affidavit, while duly sworn and attested, is still an out-of-court statement sought to be admitted by the defense for the truth of its content. In other words, it is hearsay. Ms Rubio is unavailable to testify as a witness, to be cross-examined by the State, the veracity and reliability of her statements questioned, her credibility confronted in a court of law. The legal question then, that I have asked the State and defense counsel to research and have heard argument on all morning, is this: Can this hearsay be admitted in a post-conviction evidentiary hearing where the defendant is under a death sentence?'

The judge paused, and the courtroom air trembled with anticipation. He looked up at his kingdom once again, surveying the cameras that watched him for a moment, as if making one final, last-second mental check of his words before he released them. His brow furrowed and he looked back down at his notes, his eyes catching for a single, split second not on the cameras, not on the defendant, but on the State. On C.J. The look he gave her lasted only a moment, but its impact would be forever. She stood before him then, stripped of her status as a litigator, as an esteemed Major Crimes prosecutor. And he condemned her. For what she had done, and what he was now forced to do as a result.

'The admissibility of evidence in a post-conviction hearing lies in the sole discretion of the trial court. No exception to the hearsay rule exists to admit Ms Rubio's affidavit. The 911 tape cannot be produced, and as such, does not exist in the eyes of the law. That leaves this court with the undisputed testimony of Officer Victor Chavez, and the same issues it confronted and dismissed in the defendant's prior Rule. The circumstances, legally, are the same, given the unfortunate and untimely demise of Lourdes Rubio. There is no general catch-all hearsay exception in the state of Florida. If a statement does not fit into a recognized hearsay exception, it is inadmissible. This court has explored issues of fundamental fairness to the defendant, as the penalty is death, but in the end, it must consider that should it grant the defendant's motion and grant a new trial, his newly discovered evidence would probably not produce an acquittal at trial because it is inadmissible.

'The ineffective assistance of counsel ground must also fall for the same reasons. The State has the right to cross-examine Ms Rubio on issues concerning motive, preparedness and effectiveness. They are unable to do so, so the statements in the affidavit are not admissible for this purpose either.

'Therefore the defendant's motion for post-conviction relief is hereby denied. The sentence of death shall stand. This hearing is adjourned.'

Then the judge sailed off the bench just as quickly as he had come. And C.J. knew he would never look at her quite the same way ever again.

68

The courtroom seemingly exploded around him, cameras focused on his face, questions shouted at him across the room, reporters tripping over each other to run out into the hallway.

'I'm sorry, Bill,' was all Mann could manage to say, avoiding his client's eyes.

'Sorry? What the fuck just happened, Neil?' Bantling hissed.

'He denied it. It's over, Bill. I'm sorry.'

'What do you mean it's over?'

'Rubio's statements aren't coming in.'

'You said airtight, Neil. So I'll get another trial, right? One with a new lawyer?'

Neil hated this part. He really did. Telling a client that they had lost, that he had lost it for them. Usually it was a written opinion he had to translate over the phone, and he was able to soften harsh words a bit in his favor, but this had just happened live. *Didn't this guy just hear the goddamned judge speak?* 'No, Bill. The judge denied the whole motion. He ruled her statements can never be heard, that the tape can never be heard. They're hearsay. They died with her.'

'So what does this mean?' The FSP sergeants were untangling a set of leg irons. Through the noise of the courtroom, he could still hear their distinctive clang.

Neil sighed and shuffled papers in front of him. 'It means you go back to death row. It means another appeal from this order, but I frankly wouldn't hold out much hope.' At least not with him, anyway. Bantling's money was running out and, after today, it didn't look as if the phone at the law office of Neil Mann would be ringing off the hook with new clients or lucrative CNN legal correspondent offers, for that matter.

'The fuck I'm going back there. I want a hearing.'

'You just had it.'

'My own bitch attorney set me up and now that doesn't matter, Neil?'

'She's dead, Bill. Dead witnesses can't speak from the grave, they can't be cross-examined. It's a problem for a case. That's why the Mafia always wants to get rid of them in movies. Without witnesses, there can be no case.'

That was when a light snapped on somewhere in Bill Bantling's head. His eyes darted around, like a crazed animal in a cage. 'I need to speak with the detectives,' he said quickly. He watched as a CO in a brown uniform inspected a pair of shackles ten feet away, obviously waiting the appropriate few minutes necessary for Bill to finish up with his attorney before they packed the bus. 'Falconetti and Alvarez. The FDLE team police that worked my case. The ones looking for that cop killer now.'

Mann looked at him quizzically. 'Agent Falconetti is under suspension because of what happened with you. He's not on the task force anymore. What do you need to talk to them for?'

'Alvarez then, the big one who was with Falconetti. Any of those task force detectives. I want to talk to them.'

'What's this about, Bill?' Neil Mann's curiosity was

raised. 'You know anything you say to them can be used against you, should you get another hearing.' Then again, a last-minute repentant confession of how he killed those girls would surely get the cameras rolling again.

'Set it up,' Bantling said. 'Down here. They'll want to hear what I have to tell 'em. Don't let them move me back up to Raiford today.'

His eyes caught then on C.J. as she made her way past the bench to the door the judge had just left from, leaving her boxes and briefcase and press interviews behind with that other bitch prosecutor. Hoping, he was sure, to escape the press and to avoid one final confrontation with him. That maybe he would just get shipped back to hell by the time she was done hiding out in the bathroom, and she wouldn't have to watch it get ugly. It would all just go quietly away in a prison bus. But, unfortunately for her, the door was in lockdown now that the judge was gone and the proceedings over. She waited with her back to him, trying to blend quietly into the scenery, for the bailiff to open it. Doubly unfortunate, was that the bailiff was not quick enough.

'There's still one more monkey left,' he called to her. She didn't turn, but Hank did. So did the court reporter and the clerk.

'You're next, you know,' Bantling hissed, loud enough to draw everyone's attention.

Neil grabbed his client's arm, suddenly aware that it was not cuffed. 'Bill, this is definitely not helping. Don't talk to her.'

'Tell Alvarez I know who he's looking for,' Bantling said, knowing she could hear him. Everyone could. 'I know his Black Jacket. And I know why he's killing all those cops.'

'Jesus Christ!' said Neil, stepping back, his hand dropping reflexively off Bantling's arm.

'We both do, don't we, Chloe?'

Those left in the courtroom had now stopped to look in Bantling's direction. All except C.J. Conversations quickly drifted into awkward, stunned silence. Hank finally managed to tear his eyes away from the scene that unfolded in front of him and open the lock.

'Go to hell,' she said, turning to look at him. Her voice was low, but her words were strong. She would not allow herself to look away or break his stare. *Remember . . . he fears you.* She pulled open the door.

'Oh, I'll see you there, Beany. Only the way I'm going won't hurt as much. Three minutes max, I've heard. With you, I'm sure he'll take his time,' Bantling called, his voice rising to an angry shout.

He was quick. He moved past a shocked Neil Mann and toward the slow-closing door behind which she had just disappeared, knowing she could hear him breathing behind her as she ran from him. Again. The click of her heels betraying her on the hard floor all the way down the hall.

He made it as far as the witness box. That was when the FSP sergeant hit the remote button on the React Belt, and 50,000 volts of electricity immediately dropped Bill Bantling to his knees in agony, contracting his muscles, and robbing him of sight and hearing for a minute. Screams and shouts erupted around him, joined by the frightened squeak of his own useless attorney, and the collective cackle of radios declaring an emergency in 4-8. Then the pile of corrections officers and court liaison landed on his back, shackles and chains and squawking radios in hand. It took the struggles of five men to get him back under control. And as they packed him back up in cuffs and leg irons, and strapped his body into a transport chair, the crowd oohing in horror at the very twisted sight of him — it was finally, perfectly clear to him. He was indeed a man condemned. She had won. And when they stuck the bite belt in his mouth and wheeled him out of the courtroom and down the hallway, he had one final thought. Just one. And he'd hold onto it until the day when they finally strapped his body down tight on that gurney.

Oh, I'll see you there, Chloe. I'll be right behind you, following you all the way into hell.

69

She just ran. As fast as she could down the corridor, past closed courtrooms and Judge Sieban's bewildered clerk who happened to stick her head out of his chamber door as she passed. She couldn't hear the click-clack of her high heels, heavy on the terrazzo floor, or the frantic, petrified screams of Janine and the court reporter in the courtroom, or even the loud shouts of Corrections overtaking 4-8. All she heard was him behind her, breathing hard on her neck, in her ear, in her head. His long white fingers brushing her jacket, grazing her hair, reaching out to touch her for the very last time. And even though she wanted to stand strong before him, she ran.

She hit the double doors that led to the main hallway at full speed, realizing all too late that they were locked. Padlocked from the outside hall, because a death row inmate was in the courthouse and the building was officially in lockdown to prevent an escape attempt. She slammed into them, shaking them violently, breathless, afraid to stop, to turn and see him standing there with an almost-perfect smile, hands out and now able to reach her throat. Corrections too far back to do her any good.

There was no way out. None. She was trapped inside this hall, inside this building, inside this prison that she had built for herself. And it wasn't even over.

With her eyes shut tight, she shook the doors, willing them to open, finally collapsing against them. The angry shouts from the courtroom spilled into the hall, and into her head; the pounding steps, she recognized now, were running in the *opposite* direction.

'C.J.?'

It was Chris Masterson. He stood five feet away, a concerned and confused look on his face. His hands outstretched before him, like she was a wounded, frightened animal he had trapped and needed to calm.

'We got him, C.J.,' he said softly. 'We took him down.'

70

'Oh, you're gonna love this one, Dommy Boy. Just love it,' Manny said as he walked into Dominick's living room. 'Guess who wants to play friend of the police now?' He looked around the apartment, his lip curling. 'Damn, you need a maid. This place is sad, and that's coming from me.'

'Want a beer?' asked Dominick, ignoring the comment.

'If you can find one for me in this fucking mess, sure. Now listen up,' he said as Dominick headed to the fridge. 'I'm gonna solve your troubles. Cupid wants to deal.'

'What?'

'He wants off the row, which ain't never gonna happen, but it might just get your butt out of the hot seat when Judge Guthrie hears about it. Did you watch the hearing on TV?'

'Of course.' Dominick walked out of the kitchen, two bottles in hand. He paused for a moment, then asked what he had been thinking all day. 'Is she okay?'

'Counselor? She was out the door before it got bad. Masterson checked on her. She's okay. A bit shaky, considering. You should phone her.'

Dominick said nothing.

'It's your call,' Manny said and shrugged his shoulders. *Dear Abby* he was not. 'So you saw that asshole. Well, we all saw him live. Fifteen COs sitting on this guy, a crying court reporter and a screaming clerk. His attorney, that idiot Mann, waddles up to us, shaking, and says he thinks Bantling wants to deal. Says – get this – he knows who Black Jacket is.'

'What the hell?' Dominick sat up in his chair, leaning forward.

'Yep. That's what he says. Course, by now, Bantling's bound in so much iron, Superman couldn't pull him out. Talk about overboard – they got him chained to a wheelchair with a waist iron and shackles, and a bite belt so he don't nip at no one. The guys from FSP are all set to wheel his black and blue ass back to Raiford, when his attorney tells me and Chris this Black Jacket tidbit, loud enough for all the reporters to hear. So we put the kibosh on the trip and make hotel arrangements across the street at DCJ for one more night. Long story short, we gotta get the judge involved because Corrections won't budge on keeping him without approval. Another long story short, we had to put a "keep out" sign on the door so that prick Gracker couldn't come in with his Fibbie friends and fuck it up like he did with Valle. He wasn't happy. Let's put it this way, I may be sharing some down time with you, after all the four-letter words I called him,' the Bear chuckled.

'So what does Bantling say?'

'Sit down for this. Says that freak doctor of his, Chambers, turned him onto a club. A snuff club. Like the sex pervs who deal in kiddie porn, he says these are guys who like to trade pictures and stories, too, but instead of swapping kiddie pics, they trade snuff. Pictures of people getting whacked. Not already dead, but getting dead, got it?'

'I know what snuff is, Manny.'

'He says, of course, *he* never whacked nobody because

he's not Cupid. Says *they're* all crazy, though. Part of a club Chambers set up, each taking turns offing people for fun. Live. Says he saw their freakin' snuff pictures and video on the internet.'

'How did Bantling get involved in this?'

'He had his own sets of pictures to trade. Pictures of him raping women. I guess someone saw potential. They called him The Ladies' Man.'

Dominick looked past him at some spot on a far-off wall. His fingers clenched the beer in his hand and his jaw went tight. The Bear took a quick guzzle before continuing, feeling more than awkward at that very moment. 'Guy admits, Dom, with a smile on his face that he's a snap-happy rapist. But I'm supposed to give him some sort of brownie point because he's not as bad as the company he's been keeping? I thought Chris was gonna take his head off, but you've already tried that and, frankly, it's not the smartest thing with a video camera in the hall, so we just let the guy talk.'

There was a long silence as Dominick thought about God knows what and Manny took another slug of his beer. 'What's this club shit got to do with Black Jacket?' Dominick said finally.

'Move over, JFK fans, there's a new conspiracy theory in town. Bantling says he's been set up. Says Chambers was the real Cupid, and set him up the first time around as the fall guy for the chick murders. Now he says he's being set up by Chambers' *partner*.'

'Partner?'

'Yeah, you heard right. He thinks Chambers had a partner who helped him kill all those women. That the plan was for Bantling to fry in the death house for crimes he didn't do. That would, I guess, put an end to

Bantling's club membership card. Everything's smooth till Bantling's attorney, Rubio, sends her former client a love note this past fall that she was going to make things right because she did such a shit job at trial. Mentions an audiotape, this 911 tape no one ain't never heard of before. A few weeks later, everyone started up and dying on us.'

Dominick felt his stomach turn. He remembered his conversation with C.J. the night she left. Lourdes Rubio's sudden, violent death did not escape him. The pieces were starting to come together, only he didn't want them to. 'Witnesses?' he asked.

'I guess. He points out that Chavez and Ribero worked his case.'

'So did almost every uniform in Miami, and definitely every uniform on the Beach.'

'I know. I don't buy it either. Course, now Rubio turns up cold.'

'A robbery in her office,' Dominick said, almost defiantly.

'Coincidence? Bad luck?' the Bear said, shrugging his shoulders. 'I've heard stranger.'

'Why kill them?'

'To keep things status quo, I suppose.'

'So Bantling stays in jail?'

Manny nodded and finished his beer. 'Takes the walk. End of story. That's his theory.'

'That's too long-winded,' Dominick said shaking his head. 'If this is about letting Bantling die and this club kept a secret, why not just take Bantling out of the equation up at FSP?'

'My guess? Too much security. You can't touch someone in there, especially someone on the row. It's a 24-hour lockdown facility. And a hit just means another witness. Better to let him die out a natural death with Old Sparky or a needle. More poetic. But that's me talking. Bantling ain't that articulate, not with that thing in his mouth.'

'Shit,' said Dominick, sitting back in his chair. He rubbed the overgrown stubble of his goatee, which had just started to grow back, and would have to be shaved off again for court next week.

'Like I said, move over, conspiracy fans. Corrections was stamping their foot, itchy to get their most famous prisoner back home today, so we sent him on his merry way. Masterson's handling the internet shit. Knowing that bastard, though, he's probably checking out *Bitches Gone Bad* porno sites as we speak – on the State's time and dime,' he sighed. 'Your department will need to investigate the snuff shit.'

'Who else would have known about the tape?'

'I guess anyone either Rubio or Bantling might have told.'

Dominick was quiet for a moment. 'What do you think?'

'Me? I don't think Bantling really knows shit, to tell you the truth. First off, he's Cupid as sure as I'm breathing. I never bought into that pansy shrink Chambers as a real-life Hannibal Lecter. Chambers as a one-time whack job – yes. And everything we've got so far after months of investigation and hours of manpower points us in the direction of a gang war maybe, like you said, funded by the cartels. The neckties, the drug connections, the dirty cops linked back to dope and money laundering and IA investigations. We haven't cracked Black Jacket yet, but we're close, and Bantling knows that like everyone else who reads the fucking paper. So he's exploiting us. LBJ is still missing, but the wires are picking up shit going in and out of Valle's clubs. So it's a matter of time till someone slips. My bet is Brueto. Grim's been on him like stink on shit, and thinks he's gonna break or go broke.

'I do think the snuff club info is interesting, though,' he finished, rubbing the back of his head. 'And I certainly wouldn't put it past people to think one up.'

'That's heavy duty,' said Dominick softly, his brain unable to stop the images he was having now. A group of people sitting in their homes watching simultaneously as another human being was killed before them in real time. Someone they had never known, never met. Someone who might be a mother, a daughter, a dad or a grandpa – their life, their entire existence, disregarded and their death now simply a source of titillation. Dominick had seen snuff photos before. Those images never left you. Never. They crept into your dreams and they jaded your reality. Pretty soon it was hard to imagine just what a human being wouldn't do to another human being. What it was that had not yet been thought of. Now there might just be a club of them, learning and feeding off each other.

'Jesus,' Manny said, 'your fucking kid can rent *Faces of Death* – those movies where real people die on film, getting eaten by alligators and cracking into a million pieces when their parachutes don't open – at their neighborhood Blockbuster. Filmed by someone who watched it happen live, and then distributed by someone else who thought it was entertainment.

'People are whacked, Dom. Enough psychos in this world, the internet now just helps them find each other.

Customs has kiddie porn clubs with thousands world-wide swapping pictures of three-year-olds and each other's daughters. And not just one. Damn, there are hundreds of organizations, dealing in crap that would make you throw up. White slavery and child slavery rings that exist even today, right here in the US. So a snuff club wouldn't surprise me. And it wouldn't surprise me that Bantling would head up a local chapter.'

Dominick said nothing, just quietly peeled the label off his Michelob bottle, watching the paper pieces flutter to the floor.

'Bantling had so many fingers out and pointing in that interview that he damn near ran out of hands, everyone doing him wrong at the same time. The Counselor, Rubio, Chambers and now the phantom partner, who he admits he's never even gotten a look at. Look at the pattern, though. His *prosecutor*, his *defense attorney*, his *shrink*, and now, guess who he says the masked man is? It won't take a brain surgeon to see this one coming.'

'Let me guess,' Dominick said, with an eyebrow raised. 'Me.'

'Don't flatter yourself. Although, I guess it could be.'

'Did he give you a name?'

'Of course not, that's what I'm saying, he don't know shit. No names, Dommy, just another friggin' nickname, the nickname the partner went by online, supposedly. I feel like I'm in a *Sopranos* episode sometimes – everybody's got a friggin' nickname. Black Jacket, Cupid, Ladies' Man, Son of Sam, Big Joey, Little Joey, Louie Sack of Shit.' He shook his head. 'Ready?'

'Hit me.'

'Cop Killer. Ain't that one original?'

'Cop Killer? What the hell kind of name is that?'

'Bantling says Chambers' partner-in-crime took that name not because he kills cops, but because he *is* a cop. A cop who kills. Get it?'

71

The play had so far spun out perfectly, the plot twisting and turning in on itself, the actors themselves as surprised at the ending as the audience. Now was the time for the grand finale, time for him to gather up all the dangling strings of the dozen balloons that he had floated about, and pull them all together into a neat and tidy bunch. A Hollywood ending for everyone. So the frightened citizens could go back to leaving their doors unlocked at night.

Or not.

He leaned against the car, thinking, turning the red apple in his hands over and over again, wiping it with his shirt till it shined in the warm sun.

He *could* leave it just as it was, a real *Who Shot J.R.?* cliffhanger. Or a dark *Twilight Zone* ending, where there are no 'to be continueds' and there are never any answers.

He could let her live.

The public had a short-enough memory. A few months from now and Black Jacket wouldn't even be small talk on an elevator. Instead of, 'Can you believe another cop was cut up in Miami?' it would be a scratch on the head and a, 'Weren't there a couple of cops who died on the Beach a while back?' The task force would disband and he would eventually end up in cold case, forgotten. Another new detective might come on and vow to continue the search, as he worked his way up the promotional ladder and out of the squad. Then the cycle would repeat itself as the file gathered dust for another twenty years.

Or he could wrap up every end but hers, just let one balloon float away from the neat and tidy bunch. And, of course, that could prove to be an ending that was just as twisted as the one he had dreamed of. Let her live now to simply wallow in guilt and self-loathing for the rest of her life, let the responsibility she shared for the deaths of five people eat away at her, with a sixth, Bantling, waiting in the wings. The guilt alone, he was sure, was like a death sentence unto itself. Eventually, it would consume her.

Her death was not really necessary, because he knew she would never talk. If there was ever a time or an opportunity for her to have come clean, it had long since passed with the filing of Bantling's latest Rule Three. She'd had no qualms standing back up in that courtroom and doing it all over again, sending the wrong man to his death. No, her death was not so much necessary, as it was justified. It was payback time.

Taking the knife he would use to kill her, he sliced off a piece of the apple and popped it into his mouth. He was too busy for a real lunch, chasing leads down in the brilliant sunshine. He watched the little kids play in the small park across the street, their degenerate mothers chatting amongst each other or on cellphones, oblivious to their own children and the many faceless strangers that lurked behind a friendly smile around the sandbox and the swings.

But *she* knew. She knew death was out there, waiting for her again. Like a twisted video game, she had dodged it twice before, killing one enemy, feeding another into the chute, but they still kept coming at her, and she was running out of lives.

It was best to end it now, take out all the trash at the same time, he thought as he pulled out the throwaway cell. He only had to dial the number that would set it all in motion. Wrap it up in a pretty red bow for the police to sum up in a final report and dispo.

The line was ringing in his ear when he heard the small voice.

'Are you a policeman?' asked the brown-haired boy who had snuck up next to him, looking at the undercover car quizzically. A little girl of about five stood next to him, rubbing her sunburned nose. Little sister, probably.

Like taking candy from a baby. If he wanted it. 'Yes,' he said, flipping the phone closed. Mom was nowhere to be seen, of course.

'Where's your gun?' asked the boy, wide-eyed.

'It's in the car. Do you want to see it?' he asked.

The boy nodded.

'Mommy says don't talk to strangers,' said the little girl, hesitantly. She fidgeted with her skirt and looked back at the playground.

'Oh, no. I'm not a stranger. I'm your friend,' said the man with a smooth smile. Then he reached into his back pocket, and, as if to prove it, took out his shiny badge.

72

Ricardo Brueto looked at the number on his cellphone and his heart began to pound. He hesitated for a moment, letting it ring, knowing what it meant, knowing that the future would indeed change when he picked it up. Maybe he wanted to hold it off for just a moment longer.

Then it stopped.

He wiped his mouth with the back of his hand and looked around the club to see who might have been watching. But there was no one, just a couple of bartenders who had stopped by for their checks, and the crew who was cleaning Channel's dance floor and bar for opening. He stared at the phone in his hand, then moved to the stainless steel fridge behind the bar, grabbing a Bud and popping off the top. He chugged half the beer in one guzzle, wishing he was already drunk, wishing he was in that state where decisions could be made easily, without thought or care for the future. But he hadn't drunk enough. Yet. He finished the beer on the second chug, and poured himself a shot of Jack Daniel's.

He sat back on the barstool, just waiting for the cellphone he still held tight to vibrate, for the phone to ring again. He knew full well that it would by the end of the night, and he knew he couldn't just ignore it a second time. No, he couldn't do that. He had a choice to make, and that was that. Just picking up the phone would be the decision. These people were sick motherfuckers, and he could not refuse what was asked of him. And then he could never turn back and he could never leave.

The DJ did a soundcheck overhead, but Rico didn't hear it. Instead, he heard only the cries of his new son in one ear and Angelina in the other, whispering how they needed to make a new life. Go to Chicago and stay with her sister. Start clean, before he was arrested again or worse.

Two hundred thou. That was a hell of a lot of money. It would buy him a fucking nice car, and maybe a house for Angelina and a lot of damn diapers for Rico, Jr. It would buy him respect from those who did not already fear him. He poured himself another shot of JD, and wondered why he had put off answering these fucking questions until right now. Why he was making the biggest decision of his life between telephone rings.

He knew Angelina was right. If they stayed here in Miami, history would repeat itself. His kids would bear his scars. They would be in a gang by twelve, fighting on the streets for themselves, packing a Beretta with their lunch money the next year, raising their own kids at seventeen and wishing they had never been born sometimes. They wouldn't go nowhere, they wouldn't become no one. They would never escape, because no one could. Now was the time. If he was gonna do it, if he was gonna try and make it better for everyone, he would have to leave now.

His head was starting to cloud, the alcohol was making him breathe easier. He didn't feel so fucking jumpy. He poured another. Just an hour till this place started to hop. Only it hadn't been hopping as much as it should have been lately. Ever since those cops got whacked, it had been freaky quiet on the streets, nothing moving in or out, people heading north and out of town to get what they needed. Everyone was really nervous, so he should have guessed that the call would have come already. Besides, if this drought lasted any longer, and with the cops riding him day and night, Rico was getting a bit nervous himself that his ass just might become part of a package peace deal. That was another reason to pick up the line. At least he knew it wasn't him that was gonna suck the barrel of a Magnum when nighttime came.

He had a name in Miami. He had cash flow. No one fucked with him. Taking out some motherfucker who deserved it was no big deal. The world could live without one more scumbag, and he could live with that. Even if it did start a war that would never end.

The music started to pump up, DJ Ivo spinning away in the little booth. The floor became electric, flashing lights catching the shadows in the far corners of the club. This was a strange time, Rico always thought, waiting for the night to begin, watching people slowly trickle in.

His hand vibrated first, and then came the ring. Insignificant under the loud music, Rico still heard it. He looked at the number and quickly sucked down what he thought might be his fifth JD. The clock had suddenly moved past eight and he realized he still hadn't made a fucking decision. He took a deep breath and stared again at the phone. On the third ring, he flipped it open.

'I'm here for you,' he said finally.

Then he stepped outside to finish the call.

73

'Let me tell you something, Mr Lowell. I don't mean to tell you how to run your case, but I'll sure as hell tell you how I run my courtroom. No bullshit.' Judge Guthrie turned to the court reporter in the corner of his chambers and gave her a little wink, to make sure that last expletive didn't end up in the record. 'Your serial killin' *victim* goes on a rampage in a courtroom, wrestling with five correctional officers and you still want to hang the lead detective for a slap in the face?'

AUSA Nick Lowell cleared his throat. He didn't like being in this position, his credibility in danger, being questioned by a sitting federal judge while the powers that be – who'd made the decision for him to push this case – were sitting in their comfortable offices, three floors above him and nowhere to be seen. 'There's a video, Your Honor,' he said.

'Yes. I've seen the video. It's grainy. It's blocked out and it's, to me, a simple slap. Not that I'm saying it's right, but I'm asking you, do you think that's gonna get you a conviction? Do you really? Look at this man!' he said, holding up a copy of yesterday's *New York Times*, where a picture of William Bantling strapped to his wheelchair and being wheeled out of the courtroom in cuffs and shackles with a bite belt in his mouth had made the front page. 'I'll tell you right now, you can call him a victim till the cows come home but a serial killer is not coming into *my* courtroom unless he is decked out in his finest, I can assure you that. I will not have what happened in Miami happen here. So be prepared, Mr Lowell, because *this* is how your jury will see him. This is how *I* will see him. Now I ask you, do you still think you will get a conviction on this detective, or can we all just agree that the man was simply doing his job and took it a little too seriously? Let his department scold him.'

The message was clear. Nick Lowell would be pushing this case uphill by himself the whole time. The judge would make sure he didn't win.

Les Barquet was nodding up and down like a preacher. 'I think a jury might just wish Agent Falconetti had gotten a few more licks in,' he chuckled. 'And, let me remind Your Honor that four state prison correctional officers with the best of records will testify that Mr Bantling's *injuries*,' he said, holding his fingers up as quotation marks around the word, 'were not as bad as he now maintains. There is certainly a question of credibility, Your Honor.'

'I can tell you right now who will win that tug of war in my courtroom. Even if he is from Miami,' said Judge Guthrie, and the room tittered. 'So if you are still wanting to go forward, Mr Lowell, you better be prepared not to waste my time. And we'll be picking a jury in the morning.'

'The morning?'

'Yes. Mr Barquet says his client can make it up here and is ready to go. You and the US Attorney just better hope your jury pool don't read the papers.'

'Your Honor, this is a bit more complicated for me,' said Lowell, rubbing the back of his head like it smarted.

'I'm getting rid of this case tomorrow, Mr Lowell.' The judge's eyes narrowed, and Nick Lowell understood that his career in front of Judge Guthrie was going to be mighty unpleasant in the future. In fact, life for the entire US Attorney's Office was going to get rough for the next few weeks, if not more. 'I won't have it languishing. It is a serious miscarriage of justice to do so.'

'Please give me a moment, Your Honor. I need to make a phone call,' Lowell said after a moment, standing up. *Screw this.* He knew the deal and he was not going to let his career and his conviction record get fucked up by a bureaucracy hell-bent on avenging someone's bruised ego.

'Take all the time you need,' said Judge Guthrie, as Lowell ducked out of his chambers and into the back hallway. 'Oh, and tell your boss I said not to send me this shit no more,' he finished with a smile and another wink at the court reporter.

74

The Nextel at his side chirped to life, a sound Dominick never thought he'd actually welcome. But today – and maybe just for today – it was music.

'Falconetti,' he said.

'Congratulations,' said the voice on the other end softly. With the noise in the room, he almost hadn't heard her. It was C.J. His chest went tight.

'Congratulations yourself,' he said quietly, walking out of the squad bay and into the hall.

'Where the hell's he going?' yelled Marlon Dorsett.

'Two minutes back on the job and he's taking a fucking break,' laughed Manny.

The voices drifted off behind him and he found a quiet corner.

'No congratulations for me just yet,' she said. 'Nothing's appeal proof.'

'Chaskel seemed pretty thorough. I watched it on Court TV. I couldn't believe the news on Rubio. What timing.'

'Yes.' She cleared her throat before continuing. 'You probably know more about it than me, watching Court TV. It was a robbery.'

'So they say. No suspects, though, yet.'

'Anyway, Manny called me to say you weren't going to have to go to trial,' she said, quickly changing the subject. 'It's great news.'

'Not everyone thinks so.'

'Did de la Flors okay the nolle pros?' A nolle pros was slang for the Latin *nolle prosequi* – the official dropping of criminal charges by the government.

'Are you kidding? He would rather see me go broke trying for an acquittal at $350 an hour. My attorney says de la Flors had a coronary when he heard what the judge said. The conversation ended, I'm told, with a crude expletive. Geyer told his colleague from the Southern District to fuck off.'

'I'm sure Mark Gracker wasn't too pleased either.'

'He'll get his. One day. Right now, I'm supposed to play nice. Everyone's watching.' He paused. No matter how much he didn't want to care, he did. No matter how much he tried not to worry about her, he always would. He wished he could stop himself. His voice lowered. 'How are you doing? I saw what happened at the hearing.'

'No more Court TV for you. I'm okay. I've got a trial coming up. Are you back now?'

She had changed the subject once again. Running away from another issue, and it frustrated him. 'Yeah. First day,' he said quietly. 'I'm not leading the task force anymore. Fulton is.'

'How's it coming?'

'We've got some leads, but they're stretched out now. Fulton's still working a gang war theory, because that makes the most sense, even though no one's talking except to say they're happy that four cops are dead. Valle is dirty, no doubt. He's washing big numbers through his clubs, we just can't get anyone to say so. And Black is hoping we can at least make him on money laundering charges before the feds try to.' He paused, knowing what she was thinking, who she was thinking about. 'I don't

318

think you'll have to worry about Bantling on this. That statue – even though he never admitted sending it – was from him. It's all just a game for him, to drive you crazy. He already knew when he sent it that he was gonna get to see you at a hearing. Rubio had already forwarded him her letter pledging her support and he's no fool. With new information like that, he had to know a hearing and a trip down to Miami were pretty much guaranteed.'

She wouldn't let him protect her, but, still, he found himself trying. He didn't tell her about Bantling's last-minute futile attempt to elude the chair and his allegations that Chambers had a partner out there somewhere just itching to keep witnesses quiet. None of what Bantling said could be substantiated. Masterson had found nothing on the internet leads, no complaints lodged through, or investigations started with, either Postal or Customs. Nothing through Interpol, the international police agency. Nothing at all to corroborate Bantling's claims of a bizarre international snuff ring.

'I'm sorry, Dominick,' she said slowly. 'For everything. I want you to know that.'

'Let's not do this, C.J.,' was all he could say. *I didn't ask you to be my hero.* And so he wouldn't.

'I didn't want to drag you into anything—'

'You didn't. That's our problem.'

She felt her chest suck in, her body recoiling, when his words hit her. 'I just wanted to say I'm sorry,' she said, choking. Her eyes closed tight, wishing she could go back in time, back to a Sunday morning in bed with the paper spread between them, back to that weekend in Key West, his hand firmly locked on hers. There were so many moments. She wanted to feel just one again.

'Me too. But there are some things you just can't fix,'

he said. He closed his eyes and slapped his hand hard against the wall above him. He had nothing left to give. He heard her sniffle in the background. 'Okay,' he said finally. 'Don't work too hard. Good luck on the trial.'

'Dominick,' she said, her voice a tired whisper now. She watched streaks of rain weave their way down her office window. 'I was wrong. I need you,' she managed to say at last.

But it was too late. He had already hung up the phone.

75

Waist-high weeds covered the yard, both front and back, hiding discarded propane tanks and rusty car and bicycle parts in their midst. A dilapidated wood fence blocked the back door of the rickety green house with the sagging roof from the sight of its Liberty City neighbors on either side; the parking lot of a closed and boarded-up food market bounded the back. In the cloud-filled moonless night, it sat abandoned, back from the street, graffiti-painted plywood covering its windows and doors. An occasional breeze or invisible small animal crept through the weeds with a soft rustle, but other than that, it betrayed no signs of life inside.

From every angle, the house was invisible. Even if someone stupid enough to be nosy were to crane their curious neck and try to see in, they couldn't. Not that it really mattered. Liberty City, the birthplace of the 1980 race riots that left Miami burning for three days, was still an economically depressed, crime-ridden neighborhood. And in this hood, no one saw anything even if it happened right in front of them.

He blended with the dark in the back of the house, his fingers quickly finding the waiting deadbolts in the blackness, the crowbar efficiently popping them open one at a time. The wood splintered with a soft crack, like the rustle of the weeds, and then the door let him in.

In the black of the room that was obviously the kitchen, he flicked on his flashlight and made his way quietly down the hallway. He stood outside the door and listened for a moment, the sound of his own breathing screaming in his ears. He wondered if he could do this after all. Inside, he heard the jabbering voices and then the quick, concentrated flutter of laughs, followed by more voices and another bout of canned laughter, and the flashes of bright light from a television appeared under the door, dancing across his sneakers. The house was otherwise silent, as it should be. He slid the key into the lock and brought the Magnum to his side, ready to go, should things go wrong now.

The knob turned with a click and he pushed the door in hard. With a creak it opened, hitting the wall on the other side with a slam and bouncing back slightly.

Jerome Sylvester Lightner, aka Lil' Baby J, aka LBJ – the most wanted man in the entire state of Florida – sat on a pile of dirty pillows on an old couch. He stared blankly at a rerun of *Seinfeld* on the television in front of him. Dead bottles of Colt 45 and plastic liters of Parrot Bay Rum littered the windowless room, along with empty fast-food wrappers and chip bags and more than a few bent metal spoons and crushed, converted Coke cans, tinged black and tarred with yellow goo. The room smelled of piss and shit and burnt crack, a bitter, pungent stink. The 21-year-old who topped the FBI's Most Wanted List looked a lot smaller, at the moment, than his reputation.

It took a good five seconds for LBJ's stoned brain to tell his ears that the door had opened, that someone was now in the room with him. He turned his head slowly toward the door, his glazed brown eyes narrowing first perhaps in anger, then catching on the gun pointed at his face and softening in surprise. 'What the fuck?' he tried to say, but even those few words got tumbled, the crack dulling his senses. That might be a good thing later on, Rico thought. Maybe he would feel less. LBJ fell off the couch and onto his back, his bare feet scrambling beneath him like a cartoon character, scattering the used Coke cans and Burger King wrappers. He pushed backwards toward the open door, hoping to find a miracle behind him, to escape the fate which even in his drug-induced stupor he knew was to become his own.

'Shut the fuck up and move into the bathroom, and it won't be so bad,' Rico said, pulling out the pair of latex gloves from his pocket. Using the butt of the Magnum and the heel of his boot, he nudged LBJ away from the open door and into the small bathroom.

But the badass with the reputation as a cold-blooded killer knew that it *would* be bad. He started to cry. 'Shoot me, man,' he pleaded.

'No can do,' Rico said. 'Live by the sword . . .'

'He said I would be safe here,' he whimpered.

'He lied,' Rico said flatly. Then he closed the bathroom door and took out the special knife and the devil's handiwork was begun.

76

'Wake up, Sleeping Beauty. This is the Bigs calling,' Manny said over the Nextel. 'Welcome back to the game.' Then he started to hum 'Take Me Out To the Ballgame.'

Dominick picked the phone off the dresser and spoke into it without ever opening his eyes. 'Damn, I'm glad I don't have to wake up to you every day. What time is it?'

'It is 3:07 a.m. Do you know where your children are? I'm insulted. I thought I sounded sexy in the morning.'

'Alright, I'm awake now. And now that I am, what the hell are you doing calling me?'

'Listen up, 'cause even I get confused. IMPACT's money laundering strike force did a money pick-up tonight using a borrowed DEA paid source out of Colombia. Guess who this courier delivered two hundred thousand to? Freddy 'Fat' Mack with the BB Posse.'

'Fat Mack?'

'Sound familiar? Another fucking nickname is what it is. It's the same Fat Mack who's been running the club Maniac for Roberto Valle ever since his Posse bro Elijah Jackson decided to take that long swim with the fishes. The same Fat Mack we got up on wires running Valle's operation right out the back door and dissin' the Latin Kings. Six degrees of separation. Well, facing forty years now on first-degree money laundering charges and money transmitter charges, as well as a host of trumped-up RICO charges, big bad Mack ain't so big and bad after all. He rolled, Dommy, right over the one person whose name and location might actually shave some time off his sentence, if he lives long enough to see a courtroom. Guess who he gave up when Masterson made him cry? Okay, this time you can guess.'

'I am glad I don't wake up with you,' Dominick said again. 'Roberto Valle?'

'Better. America's Most-Wanted Asshole, Dommy. LBJ. Lil' Baby Jerome. Black Fucking Jacket. That badass cop-killer Posse brother who started this whole thing by taking out Victor Chavez. Then Fat Mack handed up operations at Maniac, told Chris where the books were and corroborated the wires. At that point he stopped and thought about how short his lifespan was probably going to be now, and started crying for a lawyer. We've got an address where LBJ's at. Masterson's sitting on it. It's in Liberty City. Fucking Liberty City, Dommy. This pans out, and he's been under our noses the whole goddamn time. Right down the fucking block.'

'Who's working it?'

'Fulton called out SRT. But it'll take them thirty to forty minutes to organize. I'm heading there and now so are you. I chirped Dorsett and Grim.'

'Give me the address,' Dominick said, rolling quickly out of bed now and heading for the closet. 'I'm on my way.'

77

Rico wiped the sweat off his face with the back of his hand, but it still ran down his head and neck onto his tee shirt, already soaked with perspiration. His nylon Nike sweatsuit was splattered with blood now. So much fucking blood. He looked back down once more at what he had done in the tub and swallowed hard. His tongue felt heavy, his mouth dry and coppery. He fought back the urge to vomit and wondered for a minute if the bitter taste that lingered in his throat would ever go away.

In the windowless room behind him, Jerry Seinfeld said something funny and the studio audience laughed.

There was no time left to think about what he had just done for money. That time had come and gone and he had ended up here, trapped in this hard moment forever, whether he liked it or not. He thought about the alternative – how it could have been his body lying in that tub. Then he flipped open the cell and made the call. 'Done,' was all he said when the line picked up.

He made his way back through the kitchen, not bothering to close the door behind him, letting the light of the television illuminate the hall. He noticed that his hands still shook slightly, and he wondered how long that would take to go away. How long it would take for him to accept what he had done and move the fuck on. He pushed open the door and stepped back out into the black night, hearing it close with a thud behind him.

'Freeze, motherfucker!'

The light blinded him, pushing him up against the back of the house, and Rico raised his hand to his eyes and squinted hard. His head darted around, looking for a place to run to, but the blinding light made it impossible to see. The fingers of his other hand touched on the cold steel handle of the Magnum, stuffed in the front of his pants.

'You heard me! Don't fucking move! Police!'

Rico knew then that he would never make it better. That his son would grow up without knowing his father, that he would never change history or beat a statistic. Just an hour ago he had thought $200,000 was a lot of money to kill for, but at this very moment he would give up every last penny.

He heard Angelina's wails, saw his mother's disappointment as she stood shaking her head over his casket. And right before the hail of bullets tore through him, he silently prayed for God to forgive him all his sins.

But, by then, even he knew it was too late for that.

78

'Shots fired! Shots fired! Report shots fired in the vicinity of Northwest 58th Street and 5th Court!' Jimmy Fulton's words exploded over the Nextel. Then the radio sprang to life in Dominick's car, the dispatcher sounding too calm and too composed for the words that she was saying. 'All available units, there is a report of shots being fired at the location of 5750 5th Court. Repeat 5750 Northwest 5th Court at 58th Street, Liberty City. FDLE Officer requesting immediate assistance from all available units.'

When a call comes that an officer needs help, everyone drops everything and goes. No matter what zone they were working or what speeder they might have been ticketing or what fight they were breaking up. Shouts erupted on Dominick's Nextel and over the radio. From everywhere. Sirens simultaneously sounded around the city, cruisers racing down streets and highways with flashing blue lights.

The front of the house became a mass of cop cars and confusion. Neighbors had begun to seep out of their houses to see what all the commotion was about. The presence of a cop car or two on their block was nothing to blink an eye over. The presence of fifty, with still more coming, meant something big. Uniforms spilled out of cruisers, guns in hand, radios squawking, looking for direction. Dominick spotted Fulton, barking orders into his Nextel, at the back of his car, a small crowd around him.

'Where the fuck is the team? Where is SRT? I want in that house, now!' he yelled, looking frantic. SRT was the FDLE Special Response Team.

'What happened?' Dominick said, rushing up and pushing past uniforms.

'We got one DB on the outside.' DB was a dead body. 'No ID, but looks like Brueto, the gang-banger who heads up the Kings. Surveillance lost him tonight, thought he was tucked in safe and sound at home. He pulled a fucking Magnum! Masterson saw him coming out of the house and took him down. Don't know what's on the inside, but I'm not waiting anymore to find out. The City can go in with us.' Years ago, Fulton had headed up the SRT, and he was damn good.

'Alright. Let's do it,' Dominick said, nerves rushing adrenaline to his lungs and brain. Going into a house under hostile fire always caused you to stop and think. 'Let me get my vest.'

'I've got flash-bangs in my trunk,' said Fulton. A flash-bang was a distraction device used by the Special Response entry teams.

'I'll take the back team,' said Manny, who had just run up.

'Alright, I'll hit the front,' said Fulton. 'Have Dorsett set up on the north windows, Dom you're on the south. Take five each. Have a uniform get that plywood loose. Dom will toss the flash-bang in on my count. Then we go in. No one comes out. Got it?'

Less than three minutes later the bang went off, and flashes of bright light exploded under the plywood window coverings. The wood muffled the otherwise deafening boom.

'Police! Police! Get down! Everybody down!' Fulton and Manny both screamed as the teams moved through the house, calling and then clearing each room over the radio.

'Living room! Clear!'

'Kitchen! Clear!'

'Bathroom, front hall! Clear!'

Manny found the back room first. 'We got life! Back room. TV's on,' he crackled over the radio. Then there was a slight pause before the yelling began as the team moved into the room. 'Police, get down!'

'Clear!'

'Closed door!'

'Right behind you, Bear.' Fulton's voice. 'Take it!'

Dominick heard the crack of wood over the radio and voices yell, 'Police!' at the same time. A sudden, eerie silence swallowed at least a second. 'Oh shit!' someone yelled. Another, 'Jesus Fucking Christ!'

'What's happening? Someone talk!' Marlon came over the radio.

'Motherfucker,' Manny said with disgust. 'We got a mess in here.'

'We found LBJ,' said Fulton. 'But apparently not before the Kings did.'

'Oh, shit! Is he dead?' asked Dominick.

'Hold up. I think we just lost one to the sink,' Manny said. Then he yelled, 'Don't fucking barf in here, man! This is a goddamn crime scene! Fucking go outside!' He paused for a second then said in a quiet voice, 'Dead just doesn't describe it, Dommy Boy. I never seen so much blood. The fucker is staring at me from the tub wide-eyed and wearing a necktie.'

'He's been shut up,' broke in Fulton. 'Dom, get your ass in here. I think we might not have a case no more. We got a war.'

79

'You gotta be kidding me, Andy,' Dominick said, a week later. He followed ASA Andy Maus out of the courtroom doors of 4-10 and into the crowded hallway. 'Four months of work and you're just gonna let them take it?'

'I have no choice, Dom,' replied Andy, walking fast toward the packed escalator, probably hoping to get lost on it and end this conversation. 'The feds have the right of way. They've got jurisdiction and they have a federal indictment. I won't be able to try Valle now in state court until the feds decide to finish him up, and there's no way Judge Surace is gonna let me languish on his overloaded state docket with a case that's already being handled by a US District Court. You heard him in there. I can't even get Valle back over to state court now to say as much as hello without a writ and a time limit and a host of federal marshals. The juice ain't worth the squeeze, boys.'

'So they get to cherry-pick the money laundering and RICO charges and the headlines and all we get left with is the dead bodies and a lot of reports to write?' said Manny. 'That just sucks.'

'Why are you guys so upset? It's not like you're losing the case.' As if on cue, Mark Gracker appeared out of 4-10, right behind the AUSA who had been sent by de la Flors to babysit in the back of the courtroom. The Cheshire cat smile was back, his eyes searching the hallway – probably for Dominick. He wanted to gloat. Dominick knew that some things were worth giving up his job for, and Gracker wasn't one of them, but if their eyes made contact right now, there were no guarantees he wouldn't snap. So he looked only at Maus.

'It's just going federal,' Andy continued. 'Money laundering and RICO charges are pretty good on a major player in the cartels. If he's convicted, he'll get slammed and he'll probably go somewhere not so pleasant. They sent Gotti to Leavenworth on racketeering. Look, you almost got nothing. Who knows? Maybe Valle will talk. Maybe he'll give up who ordered the hits. If he even knows.' He stopped at the escalator and turned around, his face crinkled in frustration, either at them or at the situation. It wasn't clear. 'Listen,' he said, his voice lowering a decibel. 'Let me be frank, guys. Black Jacket is dead, as far as the investigation goes. Both Brueto and LBJ are gone and Fat Mack is no more since someone left him in the general population with a target on his head.'

'Corrections was supposed to put him in solitaire,' Manny began.

'But they didn't, so he's dead. Thank God Masterson took his statement and you got the books to corroborate the wires, or Valle wouldn't be behind anyone's bars right now. I would have liked to have kept the state money laundering charges, but that's the way it goes. There's a bloody war on the streets right now and no one is talking. They're shooting. Every single night. There's no one left, no witnesses to take a stand. We've gone through the Dirty Lists, IA is sitting on every off-duty. We did what we could.'

'That answer sucks,' said Manny.

'It's the only one I have, fellows. Let Gangs work this, and pat yourselves on the back for getting Valle this far. No one else has been able to until now,' he said, as the escalator carried him down. He turned and straightened his suit and gave a short wave, then almost ran to the next set of escalators below.

Dominick could feel Gracker's eyes homing in on his back across the crowded hallway, the smile spreading on his pudgy red cheeks. There was no way he was going to turn around and give the fat fuck the satisfaction. That would happen in federal court for the next goddamn two years while the feds worked out their deals. Gracker would get his, but like Dominick's Italian relatives liked to say, revenge was a dish best served cold. The thought kept him sane.

'Let's get out of here, Bear,' he said to Manny, following Maus's exit down the escalator.

It was on two that he saw her. Manny actually saw her first.

'Counselor! Hola!' he said.

The only attorney Bear was ever happy to see was C.J. Dominick turned around on the escalator and suddenly there she was.

'Hi,' she said softly. She looked tired and rail thin, clutching an armful of file folders to her chest. Dominick knew that when the nightmares were at their worst, she simply refused to close her eyes, going weeks seemingly without any sleep and surviving on twenty-minute catnaps throughout the day. To relax her, he would put on her favorite funny movies and rub her back for hours.

'Hey,' he said back. Manny sensed the moment and took off.

'I heard about the feds taking Valle,' she said. 'Sorry.'

'You win some, you lose some, I guess.' He looked up and met her eyes finally. 'Are you sleeping?' he asked.

'Yeah,' she lied, looking away and pushing her wire-framed glasses back up the bridge of her nose, presumably to hide the dark circles. 'I'm in trial. You know how that is.'

'Again? Well, good luck.' He looked back down at the fast-approaching lobby below.

'I miss you,' she said softly behind him.

'Me too,' he replied. Then he walked off the escalator and into the crowd, making his way to the front glass doors, and disappeared into the warm afternoon.

80

C.J. walked slowly out of 6-7 to the elevator bay, dragging behind her another set of file boxes for another defendant on her metal dolly. The bailiff said goodnight and locked the doors behind her with a heavy click.

The courthouse escalators had long since stopped running, the cleaning crews come and gone. She maneuvered her cart around a yellow WET FLOOR! sign, and took the elevator down to the lobby. She made her way out the back of the courthouse and down the handicap ramp, past the looming mass that was the Dade County Jail.

Tonight she had convicted a 20-year-old of two counts of first-degree murder, and watched in an empty courtroom as the judge sentenced him to two consecutive life terms. Tomorrow at ten she had a next-of-kin meeting on another homicide and then all next week she had pre-files scheduled on an old murder that the City of Miami had just solved with a cold hit from the FDLE DNA database in Tallahassee. The rest of her day timer looked the same for the next six months. Only the names changed.

She nodded at the uninterested State Attorney security guard who sat reading his *People* magazine by the metal detectors in the empty lobby and made her way to the elevator bay. Her head ached and her shoulders sagged, heavy with the invisible weight she carried all the time now. It was almost 10:30 at night and she was the last one back again from battle, pulling another carcass behind her on her collapsible cart. Work had become her prison, but it was also her only refuge. It was her penance.

She knew with a deadly certainty after Bantling's outburst in court that no matter how much she wanted to run, she could never leave this job until his death sentence was carried out. She would devote her life to keeping him in, to finishing the job she had set out to do. And while she was at it, she would put some more bad people behind bars. This office defined her life now, it sealed her in, just fifty yards and a few steel doors away from murderers, rapists, thieves, drug dealers, burglars, batterers. Just fifty yards separating the keepers from the gray concrete, iron barred zoo across the street.

The halls of the State Attorney's Office were as deserted as the courthouse she had just come from. She made her way through the Formica maze of the Major Crimes secretarial pool, the motion-sensor fluorescents picking up on her presence and lighting her path sections at a time, awakening with a faint electric buzz. On Marisol's little corner of the world, she spotted an eight-by-ten picture of Manny Alvarez on his graduation day from the police academy some twenty years ago. Apparently he'd never had any hair. Smiling across from him in another frame was a Glamour Shots photo of Marisol herself, feather boa and all.

In her own office, she flicked on the desk light and sat down at her desk, shuffling through a hefty stack of mail and messages.

Black Jacket might be closed, but it had not been solved, even though Dominick and Manny and Andy Maus tried to assure her that it was. And although the rest of the team had packed it in and moved on, she could not. Someone had sent her those monkeys for a reason – as a message. Someone who wanted Bantling behind bars. Someone who knew the truth about that night on the Causeway. Someone who knew the truth about Cupid.

Someone who she feared was still out there.

Just then, as she skimmed through a thick motion – this one to suppress a confession – her beeper went off. Her body jumped and she unclipped it from her waistband and tossed it on the mass of papers on her desk. The tiny bright screen glowed in the semi-darkness of her office, as it danced across her desk with every vibration, beeping.

Damn, that thing made her jumpy. She hated it. She ran her hands through her hair and after a moment, picked it back up. It wasn't her homicide week, but she was on police shooting duty 24/7. She could feel the adrenaline pump into her heart and she took a deep breath. She dialed the number and it picked up on the first ring.

'This is C. J. Townsend with the State Attorney's Office. Someone beeped me—'

'C.J.? It's Chris Masterson,' said the almost breathless voice on the other end. 'Shit. I'm glad I got a hold of you. The girls at Intake won't give out your home, and they only had this beeper. Look, I've already called Andy Maus, but he's out of town at some seminar. Jesus, I'm sorry to call you, I really am, but . . .' He hesitated, his voice shaking, trying to find the right words. 'Damn, C.J., we've got another one. It's bad, it's so freaking bad.' He paused.

'C.J., it's Dom . . .'

'Goodnight, Ms Townsend,' said the security guard as he unlocked the front glass door that led to the parking lot. 'You sure you don't want me to take you to your car?'

But C.J. waved him off, dashing across the empty parking lot, heels clicking on the gritty pavement, one hand buried in her purse, praying that she had taken her keys with her, the back of the other brushing away the tears that streamed down her face and blurred her vision. In her rush to get out, she'd left her files and laptop behind and forgotten her jacket. She heard the guard mumble something unflattering underneath his breath and then he closed the door, locking it behind him once again.

In the day, this part of downtown was bustling and parking was at a premium. But at night, it was a black paved desert that sat abandoned under the overpass of the Dolphin Expressway in a desolate part of town.

She felt her heart crawl up into her throat, and she tried to swallow it back down as she raced to the car. She needed to think, not panic. Maybe it wasn't true, maybe the ID was wrong. The tears fell again. *God, please let the ID be wrong . . .*

Her assigned parking spot was in the main lot off of the State Attorney's Office, but wrapped around the side of the building, and pressed up against the deserted one-way street of 13th. Away from the view of the brightly lit lobby, it was hidden partially by the fronds of a droopy palm tree. Across 13th was the black paved no-man's-land of jury parking, which butted up against thick, tangled underbrush and the overpass of the Dolphin.

Her fingers finally found the heavy jumble of keys and key rings at the bottom of her purse. Next to them was the cold steel tip of the .22 caliber pistol her father had bought her years before. The one she now never went anywhere without, with the exception of a courtroom, where they were not allowed.

She pulled out her keys and clicked the door open, her fingers hovering over the red panic button on the key chain. Self-defense tactics and fourteen years of horrific stories had taught her that a woman is most distracted and therefore most vulnerable as she actually enters her home or her car. C.J. made sure that woman was never her, even in a crowded supermarket parking lot on a Saturday afternoon.

She quickly opened the door and climbed in, throwing her purse onto the passenger seat. She slid behind the wheel, her fingers immediately finding the automatic door locks to her left, locking the night out. She caught her breath and reached for the ignition. With trembling fingers she started the car.

The crisp hum of static and recorded 'dead air' filled the Jeep Cherokee for a moment. She looked to the stereo console. There was a tape playing in the deck.

A ripple of goosebumps raced across her flesh, and she felt the tiny hairs on the back of her neck rise up. The too-calm voice of the 911 dispatcher finally broke the dull, electric hum of recorded silence.

'911. What's your emergency?'

'There's a car. A late-model black Jaguar XJ8. Right now he's headed south on Washington from Lincoln Road. He's got two kilos of cocaine in his trunk and he's headed to the airport. He's going to take the McArthur to MIA, just in case you miss him on Washington.'

'What's your name, sir? Where are you calling from?'

The line clicked dead with a flat hum.

Paralyzed, she sat perfectly still for a moment. The next sound she heard stopped her heart. There was a rustle of fabric from the back seat, and then the familiar face rose to life in her rearview mirror.

'Hi, C.J.,' he whispered from the darkness behind her. 'Or can I call you Chloe tonight?'

82

Dominick shut down his laptop and closed the thick case file in front of him. Green-jacketed Investigational Reports and accordion folders marked *Black Jacket FDLE 03-0566492* still littered the cherry conference table, but not for long. The task force had officially been dismantled, everyone sent back home to their own departments. Tomorrow was the scheduled move date for the Fraud Squad to come back from their extended exile down the hall. The copiers would go back, the extra computers and secretary reassigned. The pictures of four dead police officers had already been taken down and placed in their respective files, where they would remain in perpetuity, ensnarled and suspended forever in Florida's Sunshine Laws as a public record. It would take the constant and vigilant care of the FDLE records custodian and Regional Legal Advisor and the records custodian at the State Attorney's Office to make sure those gruesome pictures were never actually disclosed to the public, printed on the pages of some newspaper or posted on the web. The bounty for an autopsy picture of either Gianni Versace or Andrew Cunanan topped out at $250,000 at the height of the media feeding frenzy in '97. The pictures of a mutilated dead cop in uniform would unfortunately fetch some big bucks as well.

He sat back in his squeaky old chair, the one he had brought down with him from the Bronx PD fifteen years ago, and rubbed his eyes. He lit a Marlboro to go with his microwaved coffee, sucking the harsh smoke deep into his lungs, feeling himself relax just a bit. He had lost count of how many times he had quit smoking in his life. He thought it almost funny how he had picked the habit back up now, *after* Black Jacket was over and his career salvaged. After the stress in his life was officially declared over.

For at least the tenth time that day, Dominick thought about C.J. and the way she looked that morning in the courthouse. Loaded down with files and legal books and thrusting herself into another high-stakes trial, she remained confident and composed to the rest of the world. But not to him.

Dominick's thoughts went for a moment to his father, and the day he had told Dominick and his mother that he was not going back to the beat. The day he had lied and told them with a confident smile that everything would be fine, he was sure of it. *The case's nothing – a simple misunderstanding, was all. I'll be back on the job in a week or two, tops.* The next afternoon, Dominick had found his body in the bathroom tub when he came home from school for lunch.

It was the sound of hopelessness that he had heard in C.J.'s voice today, that he had recognized. That had reminded him of his father. That he now feared. He had promised her once that everything would be okay and it wasn't. And he hated himself for breaking that promise. Maybe he had been too harsh, too emotional, too final when he ended it.

The ring of his cellphone pulled him out of his thoughts. It was Manny.

'Dommy Boy. You headed this way for a drink, or do I need to say yes to furniture shopping tonight?'

'Tonight?'

'Rooms To Go is having a midnight madness sale. Lucky me. I get all five pieces for one low price if I buy before the clock strikes twelve.'

'Don't do it, Bear,' Dominick said with a shake of his head. 'There, you've been warned.'

'We're gonna live together first. I told her she ain't seeing no rock till I see dinner on the table every night at five,' he chuckled. 'Like that'll ever happen. I think the last thing Mari made was reservations. And she ain't too good at that, neither.'

'Careful. There's always takeout. And microwave.'

'How come I can't get me some hot *mami* who likes cooking *picadillo* in the kitchen in an apron and G-string?'

'Stop. I'm picturing.' Marisol Alfonso decked out in her finest pink spandex thong, sweating over a stove, was not an image he needed tonight. Or ever, for that matter. 'Look I'm heading home to the Beach now. Thought I'd go to the Big Pink. Get a little late dinner. Where you at?'

'I'm still at the station. And that's what we need to talk about.'

'Let me guess, you want a job with FDLE now. I don't know how much pull I have at the moment, my friend. Call back in a few years when Tallahassee has forgotten that I was once an indicted man.'

'While I think it would be fun to hang with you, Dommy, my pension's better and I get real OT, unlike you cheap state dogs on your month-long work week. I'll stay right here with the City, thanks. But speaking of your fucked-up agency, I was gonna save this for dinner, but I gotta share. I'm back behind the desk now, and of course my LT is riding me like shit. He's still pissed over what I said about his daughter. Anyway he's all on me about what happened last week, how it went down. His brother's IA upstairs. Says it's great we finally did our jobs, but he don't understand what took us so long, why we didn't just put Lindeman under surveillance when Elijah Jackson cracked and started spewing names months back. Might'a saved the guy's life, he's got kids, blah, blah, blah. You know, everyone's got an opinion and everyone's gotta be Monday morning quarterback. Especially this prick.'

Dominick felt his anger grow. City IA had sat on that Lindeman issue for weeks. Black Jacket had already killed two dirty cops by the time Elijah Jackson was busted. If no one in City IA thought to tell anyone on the task force that one of their own had just been named by a flip, it just might be what had cost him his life. 'Tell your LT and his brother that maybe the next time IA should be a little more forthcoming with information. And a little faster.'

'That's what I said. And that's when he said they had. Said the communication problem is with FDLE and the task force, not IA.'

'Bullshit. No one handed us Lindeman's name till after he was six feet in the ground.'

'He said that ain't true, Dommy. Said they didn't need to give you his fucking name, because we already had it. Hope you're sitting, bro. On the day Jackson was popped for trafficking by the City, guess who it was came in and finally helped the dope squad talk him into giving up a few names? Including that of his boss, Valle, and the esteemed family man, Sonny Lindeman?'

'Who?'

'Chris Masterson, that's who. Jackson was supposedly

an IMPACT target. It was Masterson that told Jackson he was facing a 25-year min-man. Masterson who got him to flip after a closed-door session. Masterson who got him to name Valle as his boss and Lindeman as the muscle. He told the City to take credit in the reports because he didn't want to compromise an IMPACT investigation and a source.'

Manny paused, before adding his final thought quietly. 'At least, that's the reason he gave.'

83

Dominick ran his hands through his hair, trying to piece together events in his head. Questions flew at his brain like pesky mosquitoes, demanding to be swatted down, to be answered.

Why would Masterson not have told the task force about flipping Jackson? Why would he not have told them about Lindeman being dirty when he first came to the scene, the night Lindeman was killed?

In the file cabinet behind him he pulled out the mass of classified documents stamped IMPACT – OPERATION SNOWSHOE. His fingers raced back through pages he had practically memorized and he found nothing. Nothing that said Elijah Jackson was ever an IMPACT target.

His mouth went dry and he sat back in his seat, pulling down at his goatee. *You just had to know where to look.* He reached behind him for another file box. This one had over a hundred reports on officers who had made the MDPD Criminal Conspiracy Section's Dirty List for the past five years. His fingers flew through the files, finally catching on the thick internal for Officer Bruce Angelillo. The complainant was a doper with a history, pissed off and running for his life, who claimed that after Angelillo pulled him over on 36th Street for a traffic violation, he ripped off the six kilos in the back of his trunk. That started an internal that lasted six months before it was closed as unfounded in April of last year when the doper disappeared. Unfounded in this case was another way of saying 'we just can't prove it.' He scanned the pages and picked up the phone and dialed.

'Lynn,' said the voice over the phone. It hadn't even rung.

'Marty, Dom Falconetti here with FDLE. Sorry to bother you at night.' Marty Lynn was a lieutenant with CCS. Dominick knew him well.

'Nah, no bother, Dom. What's up?'

'I need to talk to one of your detectives.'

'Now?'

'Yeah, if I can. Haskill, Bobby Haskill. I'm cleaning up a report.'

'I'll get him for you, Dom. What number you at? I'll have him call you in a minute.'

'I'm still at my office. 305-470-5512.'

'You got it,' Marty said, then added, 'Oh, and Dom, congrats on closing Black Jacket. That was a tough one.'

'Yeah. Thanks, Marty,' said Dominick as he hung up the phone.

Five minutes later his phone rang.

'Agent Falconetti? This is Bob Haskill, Miami-Dade PD.'

'Hey, Bob. I know that a couple of months back you talked to some guys on the Black Jacket Task Force about Bruce Angelillo. I'm just closing it out now and—'

'Congrats.'

'Yeah, thanks,' he continued. 'I'm closing it out and I've got a question or two. That report on Angelillo. It says here that after the complaint came in, CCS tried to set up a sting.'

'Yeah. IMPACT helped us out. They supplied us the dope we used as bait. Like it says in there, Angelillo knew something was up, though. He didn't go for the cheese and then the complainant disappeared. We couldn't make a case.'

Dominick held his breath for just a second before he asked his next question, fearing, perhaps, he already knew the answer. 'Do you remember, Bobby, who worked it over at IMPACT?'

'Yeah. One of yours. Masterson. Chris Masterson.'

His stomach dropped. 'Thanks, Bobby,' he said absently and then hung up the phone. He stared out across the conference table where Chris Masterson had sat a dozen times before, during meeting after meeting. Never once had he mentioned working a sting on one of the Black Jacket victims.

Masterson knew *before* Lindeman was killed that he was on Miami's Dirty List, because it was his interrogation of Elijah Jackson that had put him on it.

Masterson had crossed Angelillo's name one year earlier on an IMPACT case and never told anyone.

Masterson had the narcotics experience. He wrote the wire applications on Valle and Brueto, based on IMPACT investigations he had run, based on information he already knew.

Masterson was DEA. He'd done stints in Bogotá, Cali. He immediately recognized the Colombian necktie and its symbolism.

Masterson had gotten Fat Mack to roll on Valle. To give up LBJ's whereabouts. Fat Mack had been killed in the general jail population that same night.

Masterson had pulled the trigger that killed Brueto.

Dominick ran his hands through his hair. It was all coming together, the missing pieces of the puzzle that were starting to fit. *You just had to know where to look.* In this case, someone had been trying to get him to look in all the wrong places, at all the wrong people. Now he thought of what Manny had told him after Bantling's evidentiary hearing.

Cop Killer. Bantling says Chambers' phantom partner-in-crime took that name not because he kills cops, but because he is a cop. A cop who kills.

Cupid. Masterson had worked the Cupid task force since its inception. He had access to all the original Cupid reports. He worked the investigation, the interviews. He had worked the crime scenes of the dead cops and the Cupid victims. He had searched Bantling's house three years ago. He had found his sadistic porn tapes. He had bagged the evidence. And after C.J. had stumbled out in the middle of the night from the offices of a madman, Masterson had worked that scene, too. He had been one of the first to arrive at Chambers' office. One of the first to find nothing to corroborate C.J.'s initial statements that there must be at least one more victim.

Jesus Christ. His chest tightened. *Was he stretching this whole story in crazy directions? Was he seeing things, making leaps just because they were there?* If what he was thinking was right, then his next question had to be why. Why would Chris Masterson want four cops dead? What would he gain from it?

Dominick knew better than anyone that sometimes there was no why that made sense. The Tamiami Strangler killed prostitutes because he thought they were dirty. Jeffrey Dahmer ate his victims so they would be part of him. Ted Bundy never bothered to offer any rationale and none was ever found that would satisfactorily answer the question. William Bantling had never admitted his guilt. But those were all serial killers.

Then Dominick thought of something else and his

blood chilled. He heard Manny's gruff voice, sitting in his living room a few weeks back.

A snuff club. Like the sex pervs who deal in kiddie porn, these are guys who like to trade pictures and stories, too, but instead of swapping kiddie pics, they trade snuff. Pictures of people getting whacked. Not already dead, but getting dead, got it?

Nothing had turned up on the snuff clubs because it was Masterson who had run that info.

And Dominick now knew why no lead had come back.

84

'Chris, it's Dom. Pick up.'

Dominick tapped the steering wheel with the back of his hand. The Nextel chirped again, but there was still no answer.

Come on, come on. He looked around the deserted FDLE parking lot, wondering what he should do with this information. The information that he struggled to make sense of. He couldn't shake this sudden, over-whelming feeling of bad that had come over him. Just bad. As soon as the light bulb had switched on in his head, he now saw things that he hadn't in the dark. Things that frightened him. *Hear no evil. See no evil. Speak no evil.*

Instinct told him to talk to Chris, to try and find a rational explanation for a strange series of what were probably coincidences. IMPACT often ran covert inves-tigations with other departments. Maybe info sharing would have compromised a larger operation.

If he was on another line, the chirp would come back as *user busy.* He was there, he just wasn't picking up. Maybe he didn't have it on sound. Maybe he had stepped into another room or left it in the car and couldn't hear Dominick calling him. He locked Chris's number on alert, so that the system would keep chirping him, freez-ing him out of making any other calls till he picked up Dominick's alert. Then he chirped Jack Betz, the FDLE Tech Agent.

'Dominick, back on the job ten minutes and already bothering people at home again,' Jack said with a laugh. 'Tell me you don't need something tonight. I just rented T3.'

'Maybe. I'm trying to reach Chris Masterson and he's not picking up.'

'Did you alert him?'

'Yeah, but he's still not picking up. I need to get in touch with him bad. Any way we can track him?'

'I'm glad I'm not in your squad. It's almost eleven. You're a ball-buster. Is he in his car?'

'I don't know.'

'But he's got his phone?'

'Can we track that?' asked Dominick.

'Nextel can. It's a new feature. What's his number?'

'305-219-6774.'

'Hold up. Let me call them. I'll call you back.'

You just had to know where to look.

Victor Chavez. Sonny Lindeman. Lou Ribero. Lourdes Rubio. The clues had been out there, only Dominick hadn't wanted to see them. He hadn't wanted them to make sense, so he had ignored them. Ignored the obvious relationship between the victims. Ignored what Bantling had told Manny about Chambers and death clubs and cop killers. Ignored even his own instincts going back to the Cupid investigation when he had long suspected a cop connection. All those Cupid crime scenes had been linked back to undercover police investigations, homicide scenes, drug busts. But it was easy after Chambers' death to accept Bantling as Cupid. There had been no need to look any further. Even if it was for the truth.

He closed his eyes. Because he didn't want C.J. to be involved. Not then. Not now. He didn't want to believe that she would manipulate a case. So he had ignored all the clues and he had conveniently closed out Black Jacket to gang violence and drug wars and Roberto Valle. Then he had grumbled about passing on the prosecution to the feds and he hadn't looked any further. Again.

Three minutes later the phone chirped in his hand. It was Jack.

'Dominick, we got a lock on the phone. Chris must be working late. Don't bust his balls too bad. He's still down at the State Attorney's Office.'

85

She reached for the handle but it was too late. His left hand had come from behind and wrapped around her headrest, holding her back against the seat. She let out a small scream, her fingers still scrambling in the air to find the door handle.

'Hey, there,' he whispered. 'Something tells me you weren't expecting me. At least not tonight.' Chris Masterson's boyish face emerged from the darkness behind her, pushing between the front two seats. 'Sorry about the false pretenses. You're a tough woman to nail down, C.J.,' he said with a smile. 'Never a pattern. I noticed that. Of course, you have good reason. I think you knew your past would come back to haunt you. And now, here I am.'

She felt his hand, firm against her throat. It was not choking her, but it could. For some reason, she remained eerily calm. She took in a deep breath and sat back in the seat, her heart pounding, her brain racing.

The Nextel chirped in the car. 'Chris, it's Dom. Pick up.' Dominick's voice filled the Jeep. Just to hear his voice and know that he was okay, was overwhelming, and she bit her lip to stop from crying.

'Isn't that ironic?' Chris said, taken aback for a moment. 'What timing.'

'Why?' she asked. It was the only word she could think of.

'You're a smart woman, C.J. I won't be the one to underestimate you this time.'

'I don't know,' she said, shaking her head. 'I swear I don't know!'

He moved closer, his face in hers. She could feel his fingers on her, closing in on her throat. He could crush her now, if he wanted to. 'What's the body count up to now? Four? I threw in that prick Angelillo for free, so he's not really on your tab. But they're all gone, C.J. Everyone who was in on your little secret. All dead and gone and telling no tales. Soon Bill will be nothing but a memory, too. Now there's just you. And me.'

He spit his next words at her with a hiss. 'I know what you've done. I know that you're no innocent, so don't fuck with me.' Something shimmered in his right hand, catching her eye, and she looked down. It was a jagged knife he held in his latexed fingers, hooked at the end. Images flashed into her brain. *Victor Chavez. Sonny Lindeman. Lou Ribero.* All those crime scenes, all that blood.

It was strange. Part of her almost welcomed the end of the fight, the end of the dreaded wondering. Like so many stalking victims that had come through her office, it was the fear of the unknown that had paralyzed her, transformed her these past few months. Now she wanted it over with. The others had gotten theirs, paid for her sins. Now, maybe, it was her turn to step forward and place her head on the block.

'I know the questions must have been there all along, C.J. I know that you must have woken up in the night wondering why all the facts never really fit, even with Greg dead and buried six feet under. Why there were pieces still missing, but you couldn't ask anyone for an opinion. Couldn't go back to the guys and say "help me out on this," because you had your own agenda. Did it keep you up? Make you look out your window, wondering when it would catch up with you? Or did that start only when the body count rose?'

'No, no . . .' Her brain stumbled over itself, trying to see the connection that had Chris's face in it. She heard the tape end with a click before the deck spit back out its telling contents. 'You . . . it was you who called in the tip.'

The tip that had set it all in motion. She saw Chris in her office, after she'd sworn him in and taken his pre-file statement, telling her how he had searched Bantling's house on LaGorce, about the porn tapes he had found, about all the evidence he had seized. She saw his initials on the sealed evidence bag of miscellaneous pieces of ladies' jewelry that he had seized from Bantling's bedroom. The bag that had held, what C.J. personally knew, were little precious keepsakes from Bantling's many conquests. His trophies. It was Chris's smiling, concerned face that had led her back to the empty conference room in the old FDLE building, where the evidence had been set out neatly before her like candy before a hungry five-year-old. It was Chris who had left her alone with that evidence in violation of police procedures and FDLE policy. He knew she was no innocent, because he had set her up. And he knew that Chavez and Ribero had lied on the stand in Bantling's trial, because he was the one who had called in the tip. From working the scene that night, he must have figured out Lindeman's involvement.

She started to choke under the strong pressure of his fingers.

The Nextel chirped again. 'Chris, you there? Come on, man, pick up.'

'Now the light is on. Or maybe your ex didn't tell you?

Maybe he didn't bring you up to speed before he walked out of your life?' Chris said, watching her eyes. 'The good doctor Greg had a friend, C.J. A very good friend. A very close friend. Do you hear me? Is it fitting now? In fact he had several, all of whom were really fascinated with his work. And now, I get to finish what we all started.'

He looked around the empty parking lot and back at the Graham Building, which seemed, to C.J., to be miles away from where they sat. She had just been in there. Behind locked doors, in the light only minutes ago. One decision ago. She had tried enough cases in her life to know that that was what most victims thought, in the moment they realize they're in trouble, the moment they sense a truly life-defining second fast approaching. She was a victim herself. When the headlights cross the median from oncoming traffic and bear down on their car: *If I had just stayed at the party a little longer*... When the crunch of footsteps sound behind them on the deserted footpath they took through the park: *If I had just not taken the shortcut*... When the distraught, crying ex shows up unannounced in the Home Depot parking lot waving a gun: *If I had just lied and told him we could be together*... Victims always spent their final minutes thinking back on how they could have and would have changed them. One decision sometimes made all the difference. *What would she have changed?*

'Seems Dom has some pressing business tonight,' he said when the Nextel chirped again. 'He's got me on alert. It might be interesting, listening to him yap on about a case while I have your throat in my hands. It'd make for great video, too. I could get a fortune for it. I figured out early on, C.J., that Dom has no idea what you've been up to. You never told anyone what you and those cops did. He's a pretty smart guy, and I knew that if the little present that I sent you at the office didn't ring any bells in his head, then there were none to be rung. Poor guy gets arrested trying to find out the truth for you and you knew what it was all along. I bet that's what broke you two up. Secrets and lies.

'Now,' he said, looking around, 'sometimes the security around here does actually work. And for what I have planned, we are going to need our privacy. After all, there's a few people I know who are gonna love to see your face again.'

86

Oh God. It made no sense. No sense. A friend? Chambers had a friend. A really good friend . . .

A lover?

In fact he had several, all of whom were really fascinated with his work.

Her brain scrambled back to a time she had struggled for the past three years to forget. Back when it had been her alone with a monster. A monster disguised as another familiar, friendly face. A monster that smiled at her with kind and understanding blue eyes and a soft, round face. A monster that knew all her thoughts, all her nightmares, all her fears, all her desires, all her innermost secrets. Because she had told them to him. Once a week for ten years, she had told them all to him on soft leather chairs behind the closed doors of his quaint Coral Gables office.

Dr Gregory Chambers, MD still appeared in her nightmares, seated in his yellow and blue waiting room, complete with Mexican tiles and lush potted plants, the soft hum of classical elevator music playing overhead. With his antisocial, psychotic patient Billy Bantling at his side, they both reached out their latex-gloved hands to touch her in the middle of every night, laughing at her in concert while she struggled uselessly to get away.

Bill Bantling had raped her body for four torturous hours. But for ten years, Gregory Chambers had raped her mind. And she hadn't even known it. That was what had been so disturbing, so unbelievable, so treacherous.

She hadn't even known it was happening. In weekly sessions, he had nurtured and watered and encouraged her feelings as her therapist, cultivating her mind like a needy garden, manipulating her thoughts to play out in his sick fantasy, in his twisted game. She had walked out of his office feeling better about herself sometimes, feeling drained and emotionally exhausted, feeling cleansed, feeling that a part of her might finally be healing. In reality he had just taken what he wanted. And she had paid him for it with a check and a thank-you. For years she had struggled to understand why. *Why was she chosen?*

Now she thought back. In the darkness of his death room three years ago, strapped to a cold metal gurney — the smell of old champagne caught in her matted hair, the scent of her own fear heavy on her skin — her brain struggled against the heavy drugs he had given her to understand words that made no sense. Troubling words that she could never forget.

I must say, C.J., that you and Bill were a perfect case study. A great working thesis. The rape victim and her rapist. What would happen if the tables were turned? What if the persecuted became the prosecutor? What road would she take, and how far would she go for retribution?

Now she understood. Answers she had purposely stopped looking for were right in front of her, dangling precariously before her the whole time.

Chambers had engineered the murders of eleven women to test his theory, his thesis.

All of whom were really fascinated with his work . . .

Chris Masterson had helped him test that theory. He had set up what he knew would be a bad stop by calling in a legally insufficient tip. *To see how far she would take it.*

How much would she bend the rules to make sure justice was done? He had seized the evidence that would tie her irrefutably in police reports back to Bantling, and then he had given her the opportunity to make it all go away when he had left her alone with it. *To see how far she would take it.* She would tell Greg what she was thinking in a weepy session, and then he would tell Chris. And the obstacles were put in place. Or removed. *Just to see how far she would go for retribution . . .*

All along, the manipulation of her sanity had been more than just a twisted game to Greg Chambers. It had been his work.

And he had a following.

87

'See? Sometimes they do work.'

C.J. looked in the rearview mirror. The front door to the State Attorney's Office had opened and the security guard had walked out to the front overhang of the building, stretching lazily and yawning. Then he sat down on a planter and lit a cigarette, taking in the night around him. The air was humid and the smoke hung about him like a dirty, wispy cloud. He craned his body and looked again at the parking lot where her jeep stood.

Chris's left hand gripped the back of her head. At her neck was the silver knife, the jagged teeth of its pointed hook smiling up at her.

'Turn on the lights and back out of the spot carefully. We're not going far, and then I'll take over. If you drive anywhere or do anything but what I tell you, this goes in your neck and it will be painful. This is not the movies. You won't live to find a policeman or a good Samaritan reaching out to help you. I won't give you a second chance. And if you try and alert the security guard, I'll add another body to your count when I'm through. Do you understand? Contrary to what you might have once thought, I'm not a nice person, C.J.'

She nodded slowly. She felt the knife at her neck, the jagged, hooked tip scraping her skin. Her hands shook, knocking at her extra long jumble of keys that hung from the ignition. She thought of her purse, and her father's gun, just a mere foot away, but she would never make it. She flipped on the lights and put the car in reverse, backing slowly out of the spot. The security guard sat back on the edge of the planter and looked back at the building.

'Drive out of the lot and make a right on 14th. Obey all traffic signs. We're just going to pass back under 836 and go around the block. Then you'll make a right and I'll take over.'

The electronic security arm swung up, letting her out of the lot, and she turned right onto what was, during the day, busy 14th Street, right in front of the parking garage for Cedars-Sinai Outpatient. She pulled up to the 12th Avenue intersection and waited at the light, her body shaking. Next to her she heard his breathing slow and she knew he was trying to read her thoughts. He pushed the knife softly against her throat and she felt the blood begin to seep out, running in small, slow trickles down the side of her neck.

Make a left and she would be down the block from Jackson Memorial Hospital and the Ryder Trauma Center and some of the best surgeons in South Florida. Surgeons who plugged the holes left by vindictive gang-bangers out to score some revenge on a Saturday night, who sewed back up the Hatfields before they went back to their shooting match with the McCoys, who re-arranged spleens and livers when a car kissed the guardrail on I95. Maybe, with a little luck, she could drive herself right into the ambulance bay, and they would be able to put Humpty back together once more. Dig the knife out of her neck and pour someone else's life into her veins. Maybe they could find all the pieces and cracks and stick them where they should be with some sutures and staples and new parts.

Stay straight down 14th for a mile and she could drive her own body right into the brick-faced offices of the Miami-Dade County Medical Examiner. Save the van a trip tonight.

Throw it in reverse, and she'd hit the steel barbwire fence that surrounded the Dade County Jail. Maybe that's where she really belonged.

Then there was the final option. Make a right and she would be driving into her own violent death at the hands of a trained killer. Once he was behind the wheel and in control, and driving her to some trailer in Florida City or some shack buried in the thick mangroves of the Everglades, she knew he would be able to use the worst weapon of all against her. Time. There was a golden rule in law enforcement, one that police officers told little kids at school Safety Day, right after they told them never to touch a gun. The same one that she herself had preached alongside detectives at community sex-offender notification meetings and heard repeated over and over again at women's self-defense clinics: *Never get in the car.* Let him shoot you right there on the street, let him chase you down the block with a baseball bat, let him drag your ass kicking and screaming into the back seat, but whatever you do, *don't get in the car.* Because once you're in, you're gone.

Silent tears streamed now from her eyes. It was over. She was already in a million pieces, maybe, and nothing and no one could put her back together again. Like a child that has been severely abused by a parent and then put into a foster system only to be abused again, some souls just couldn't be saved. The damage done was too much, too intense, beyond repair. For fifteen years she had been running from ghosts dressed in clown masks who still visited her every night. Even when the world thought she should be over it already, she still couldn't move on. Joining them was her therapist. The foster parent that was supposed to have saved her from her misery, had actually masterminded her mental demise and with a kind and patient smile, had manipulated her sanity for his own sick reasons. And now there was another one. Another friend, another betrayal she could not comprehend. Another one that she hadn't seen coming.

She made the right turn. The knife pulled back, as if he knew what her struggle had been and he also knew it was over. 'I'll make it quick,' he whispered. 'That much I'll promise you. For the record, I always liked you, C.J.'

The car in front of her pulled onto the expressway and disappeared. There was nothing between her and the overpass and no time to really think. Inside, she screamed at herself. *Do something! Run! Jump out! Find a cop! Hit a tree! Never get in the car . . .*

Then one final, sobering thought.

Don't let him end it for you. Don't you let him control that.

And so she wouldn't. Only she would make that decision.

She closed her eyes and thought of Dominick and papers in bed on Sunday morning. And then she hit the gas.

88

Bitch!

In a split second, he knew what she was going to do before she did it. His left hand hugged the headrest and the car lurched forward, the force of inertia pulling his body back in the seat suddenly.

There was no sound before the jeep slammed into the cement. No high-pitched squeal of brakes on pavement, no scream of tires as they tried to pull away at the last second. Just a deafening boom and then the crunch and shriek of metal tearing apart, crumpling like an accordion in on itself.

He felt his body ricochet off the seats, off the rooftop, and his face smashed into the seat back. The airbags exploded with a pop, like a hundred parachutes opening at once, and the windows shattered, raining pebbles of clear glass down on him.

And then there was the overpowering still sound of silence. But only for a moment.

He shook his head, trying to shake out the fog that surrounded him and get back his bearings. Somewhere, he heard her moan softly.

Fucking bitch! His head pounded and he looked around in the blackness. He touched his face and felt wet blood run through his hand. His fingers moved into the gash that pulled apart his forehead, littered with tiny pieces of glass.

The knife. It was gone. He only hoped he had stuck

it deep into her neck before she had taken her run at the wall, but that moan told him that just wasn't possible.

The whoop of a siren came upon the car, and he saw the flash of blue lights spill off the seat back in front of him. He moved his hand along the floorboard, searching in the darkness through the glass, but it wasn't there and he reached for his badge instead.

Then Dominick Falconetti shoved a gun in his face and told him to get the fuck out of the car.

89

Dominick had spotted the familiar black FDLE under-cover Grand Prix parked on 13th Court, in the *Police Parking Only* section across from the prisoner transport entrance to the jail and his stomach dropped. It looked like his own.

Maybe he's taken in a prisoner.

Maybe he's doing a late interview at the jail.

Maybe he's got a case going in the courthouse that no one knew about.

Dominick tried to work out all the maybes in his head, but none seemed to make as much sense as the one he didn't want to see. The one that had driven him here at ninety miles an hour down the Dolphin, lights on, sirens wailing. The one that had his eyes now quickly canvassing the many parking lots adjacent to the court-house and the State Attorney's Office for signs of her car.

Her voicemail had picked up at her house after four rings, so he knew that she wasn't on another line, but, rather, she wasn't home. Or she was screening his calls. She wasn't answering either her cell or her office, and his beeps to her had gone unreturned. She could be in court, he had thought. Beepers and cells weren't allowed in the courtroom. Maybe she was still in trial. Maybe she was out to dinner. Maybe she didn't want to take his calls, after how he had walked out on her the other day in the courtroom. But he knew in his heart that that just wasn't the case. He knew something was wrong. Chris Masterson's car confirmed it.

And now he couldn't find her. *Damn it, C.J.! Where the hell are you?*

He turned onto 14th from DCJ and saw the back of her jeep, then, just as it made the right onto 12th Avenue, heading toward the expressway which would take her back home. For just a moment, the fear that had been building in his chest eased up, releasing the tension that had seized his heart. That had caused him to rethink so many things on the way over here. *She must be out of that trial. That was it. She must be ignoring my beeps because of how I left things, because I haven't been there for her, because I haven't forgiven her.*

He ran a hand through his hair and blew out a quick sigh of relief. He flipped on his blue lights again.

He would pull her over. He would warn her about what he had learned tonight, about monsters disguised as friends that he knew now were real, about underground snuff clubs and death squads, about men who were evil. He would tell her that he understood what she had done to put Bantling behind bars, and that he should have told her that before.

Then he would put her someplace safe and then go back and hunt down another killer. One of his own. He would tell her that when he was done, that when this was over, he *did* want to go to that place with her – California, Hawaii, Hong Kong – anyplace where misery wasn't. Where she wouldn't be scared anymore and dead bodies wouldn't wake either of them up at 3:00 a.m. Somewhere where the past would not follow them. Someplace where he could fix her, if she would only let him. Because he didn't want to feel like he did when he lost Natalie.

He approached the light at 12th and turned to follow where she had just been, seconds earlier. Then he watched, seemingly in slow motion, as her Jeep Cherokee slammed head-on into the concrete overpass of the Dolphin Expressway.

90

'Get the fuck out of the car!' Dominick said, his firearm pointed at the figure in the back seat of the mangled jeep, while his head strained to look back to the front.

Her face rested against the exploded white airbag, her eyes closed. *Blood. There was so much blood* . . . Next to her on the front seat was a jagged hunting knife with a wicked curved blade, smeared red. The jeep had hit the overpass at about fifty miles an hour, crushing the front end. White, hot steam poured out of the mangled radiator, and the air smelled of gasoline and burnt rubber.

'Dom, man, you don't understand,' said the thing in the back seat that used to be his friend, his colleague. One of his own.

'Yeah, I do, Chris. Do exactly as I just said. Put your hands where I can see them and get the fuck out of the car!'

She made a sound, as if she were trying to speak.

'C.J., the ambulance will be here in a second! Don't move!' Dominick shouted, his hand not moving from the position. He knew enough not to take his eyes off the back seat.

'I don't have my weapon, Dom. I don't have nothing. Don't freak,' he said, sliding over on the seat toward the driver's side back door. Glass crunched under him.

'I know what you've done,' said Dominick.

'Done? I haven't done anything. She was just giving me a ride.'

'I know about everything, you piece of shit! I know about it all. I know about how you set up Lindeman with IA and Elijah Jackson and Fat Mack. I know you worked Angelillo, and I'm figuring his death was maybe payback for ripping six kilos' worth of Valle's money off. I know it was you and Ricky Brueto who took those cops out.' Brueto's nylon sweatsuit might have been bathed in LBJ's blood, but Masterson would have been the key. He would have had access to a cop's schedule. He would know the radio calls, the zones, and his badge and familiar face would easily open a cruiser door. 'Cops, Chris!' he screamed. 'They were fucking cops!'

Chris's face grew dark. Like a frazzled husband caught with lipstick on his shirt, he had pushed his story about as far as it could go, backed himself into the farthest corner. Now he bared his teeth in the back seat. 'Oh, I'm willing to bet you don't know it all, Boss.'

'Get out!' yelled Dominick, pulling open the back door. 'Before I shoot your ass and drag you out!'

'I don't have a weapon, Dom,' Chris said, raising his hands before him as he stepped out. Dominick threw him, hard, up against the side of the car, wanting to do to his face what he had done to Bantling. 'I'm unarmed. So go ahead. Do what you have to do,' he said, his cheek pressed hard against the roof of the car, Dominick's hand firm on the back of his neck. 'Take me in. And while you're at it, slap the cuffs on your girlfriend in the front seat, 'cause she's coming too. Tell me, what's the penalty for Attempted First?'

Dominick said nothing, but his eyes darted back to the front seat of the car.

'If you know everything, then you know what she's done, Dom. Those lying cops? They were *her* lies. She's

373

put an innocent man on death row. Sacrificed his life so she could have her revenge.'

Dominick had stepped back slightly, taken his hands off the back of Chris's head, as if he were suddenly electric. He wiped the sweat that had collected above his lip with the back of his sleeve, while his other hand held the Beretta. It shook slightly. He hadn't slapped on cuffs yet, so Chris knew he was thinking, chewing on what he had just told him.

'That sounds like a crime to me,' Chris continued, turning back slowly now to face him, his hands raised. A wail of sirens sounded somewhere in the not-so-far distance. 'That sounds like Attempted First-degree Murder. Good for a dozen or so years behind steel. More if they want to make her an example. And if the feds get her . . . Damn! That's civil rights violations. That'll run consecutive, I'm sure. That's almost worth going to jail for myself.' He chuckled, watching the reaction play out on Dominick's face, as he envisioned all the things Chris had just said. C.J.'s pitiful, pretty face wearing an orange shirt and shackles sitting on the wrong side of a courtroom she used to practically command.

'Move to the back of the car!' Dominick said, pushing him forward. Yelling almost too loud. Loud enough, perhaps, to drown out all that Chris was telling him. Because he knew it wasn't just words.

'Not that I will go to jail, Dom. If you know everything, then you know I got a lot of shit to sell to all the right people,' he said as he walked, hands still raised. 'I know all the right names from Colombia to Mexico to fucking Singapore and I know who's dealing and I know who's dirty. I know names that you wouldn't believe. And that's not all I can do. I can point our good friends

374

at the FBI to a group I bet they don't even *want* to know exists. Guys who live and work just like me. And think like me, Dom.'

At the back of the car, Chris turned to face him. There were more sirens now, mixed with the squawking honks of a Fire/Rescue truck. All fast approaching. His eyes locked on Dominick's and he lowered his voice. 'Guys that have money and power and fame and like to watch people die, Dom,' he continued. '*They like it.* They get off on it. And they'll *pay* for it. Some of the most wanted men in the world, and some whose crimes have yet to be discovered, but when they are, Jeffrey Dahmer will seem like a fucking kitten. And I'm willing to wager that information will buy me a new life and a new identity somewhere cozy, Dom. Somewhere where I can read all about your girlfriend as she comes up for parole.'

'Face down! Spreadeagle on the ground!' Dominick shouted, his firearm trained in front of him.

'Maybe I'll pay her a visit if she does make it back home in a few years,' Chris said as he began to kneel. He looked past Dominick, back to the front of the car.

His face froze when he saw her standing there.

Dominick turned his head and followed Chris's stare. C.J. stood, dazed, by the rear bumper on the passenger side of the car. Blood ran down her face from a large cut on her head, streaking her dark-blonde hair black, and splashing her clothes red. She was covered in tiny pieces of glass that sparkled under the streetlights. She stood slightly hunched over, with one arm folded in against her stomach. The other dangled at her side, hidden by shadows.

'Shut up! Face down on the ground!' Dominick shouted at Chris, but his voice hesitated for a second.

His gun stayed trained, but his head jerked back again to where she stood. 'C.J.! The ambulance is coming! Go sit down!' Then the shadows moved, and the gun she held down at her side came into view.

'Jesus, C.J.!' Dominick yelled.

Chris's eyes opened with alarm, but then quickly melted back into defiant slits. He knew she'd heard everything. The gun twitched in her hand.

'I know the system as well as you do, Dom,' he said, but his eyes did not leave C.J.'s, as he knelt down in the street. 'So take me in. And we'll see just how far this goes.'

Dominick knew at that moment that he was right. That Chris would beat the system because he knew exactly how to play it. He knew all along what it would cost him to make a deal, what it would take to expose her, and he had carefully stowed that information away for a rainy day, like money buried in a wall. Secrets that he would only give out portions of, juicy tidbits that would take him to all the right places. And he realized then that the truth would never really come out. That the whys would probably never be answered. Not on this night.

The moment happened so quickly, that years later, Dominick would still never quite be sure how to place the order of events. He heard C.J. scream. He saw the quick flash of movement as Chris knelt down, and watched as his hands went behind him. He heard himself shouting, but, strangely enough, could not remember the words. He felt the adrenaline rush him, grab his heart and shove it up into his throat. He heard the deafening blast of the gunshot, and smelled the acrid powder, tasted it as it burned the back of his throat.

But Dominick wasn't quite sure what happened first. Which one event set all the dominos tragically in motion. It was an instant, a simple second in time. But even as it happened, he knew he would spend forever replaying it.

91

There was complete silence, all sound suddenly tolled by the blast. Dominick felt the beat of his heart throbbing in his raw throat, pulsing to a crazy, off-beat rhythm, and the ground beneath him seemed to shake and bend. He blinked and slowly the sound began to filter back in, the ringing from the gunshot melting into the scream of the sirens, getting louder and louder, as if someone was by a radio, raising the volume knob.

He looked back at C.J. who stood frozen in the moment as well, tears running down her bloodied face, her trembling mouth open. Without a word, he holstered his firearm and moved to the body that lay dying in the street. He knelt over it and quickly frisked it, finding the weapon he knew was there. He hesitated for just a second, and then, using the tail of his polo shirt, pulled the .36 from the unclipped ankle holster, and placed it next to Chris's outstretched hand. He was careful not to step in the blood that was beginning to pool under his neck, seeping out of the top of his head and spreading red and slick into the dirty street. Chris's eyes stared out at the curb next to him, seemingly watching the blood as it ran down between his eyes and off his forehead and past him into the gutter. His foot twitched slightly, an involuntary reflex.

'He was going to kill you because you had found out about his connection with Ricardo Brueto,' Dominick said as he moved over the body. He did not look at her.

'Brueto was running dope and helping Valle clean money. Masterson was the go-between with the cartels. You were going to expose him. You called me. You wrecked the car to stop him. I pulled up and took him out. He pulled his weapon. I shot him.'

He stared down at the body. At least the last part was true . . . *wasn't it?* Dominick had seen the 'furtive movement' – as it was always called in police reports and close-out memos – that split-second clandestine move that tells a reasonable officer the subject may have a weapon. The move that will justify the use of deadly force. Chris had moved his hand back toward his ankle as he knelt down. Dominick knew he carried an ankle holster. He should've frisked him when he pulled him out of the car, but things had happened so fast . . .

But why was the .36 still holstered? Why wasn't it in his hand?

The sirens screamed.

'That's it. That's all there is,' he finished. He wiped the sweat off his face and moved to where she stood, motionless.

'Give me the gun, C.J.,' he said.

He held his hand out, his fingers finding the .22 in her shaking hand. He gently pried her fingers loose, and taking it, flicked the safety back on and tucked it in the back of his pants. He wrapped his arms around her trembling shoulders and walked her away from the body, away from the blood that ran into the street, away from the dying secret that was now theirs to share.

He placed her back on the edge of the front seat of her mangled jeep and knelt beside her. Gingerly, he moved her hair to touch the cut on her head. It was deep, still oozing red and dotted with fragments of glass. His fingers moved over her right arm, which she kept cradled in her stomach. The wrist looked broken. As did her cheekbone and maybe her nose. She might even have internal injuries, the way she was hunched over.

'Where's my ambulance?' he barked into the Nextel. 'I need that ambulance! 1350 Northwest 12th Street. In front of the State Attorney's Office. 12th Avenue and 12th Street!' He looked back at Chris Masterson's body, which wasn't twitching anymore. 'I've got a man down. There's an officer down.'

The words tasted bitter in his mouth. *Officer down.* The man in the road was not an officer. He was not worthy of holding the title, of wearing the jacket.

He closed his eyes and tried not to think of what he himself had just done, of the many lines he had just crossed. The ones he could never erase, never cross back over again. And he thought of his father, and that dark moment in the kitchen so many years ago.

'Why?' she asked quietly, tears streaking her face, when she finally looked up at him.

He thought about the question. There were so many questions he could ask that of. Then he took her hand in his and held it tight, knowing he would never, could never, let it go again, as the sirens finally descended onto 12th Avenue and the blue uniforms all ran from their blue and white flashing cruisers to help.

'Sometimes,' he replied softly, his words a throaty, choked whisper, 'I guess there is no why.'

Epilogue

'You're gonna need at least two engines if you're going out into the ocean,' said the salesman named Buddy with the rumpled tie and sweat-stained dress shirt. He squinted into the sun. 'Don't want to get stuck out there if one goes on you.'

Dominick nodded, looking around the bridge of the 26-foot Sea Ray Sundancer. The boat smelled like plastic and new carpet.

C.J. watched him from her spot on the stern's bench. He moved about slowly, carefully looking at all the gadgets and high-tech equipment. 'And this is the perfect place for you to entertain, Mrs Falconetti,' Buddy said, finally addressing her. 'Look, you can put your drinks right here in these cup holders. They're built in.'

'Ooh,' she said, and stole a smile from Dominick. Over the past year, there hadn't been too many of those. Maybe now there would be. The Broward State Attorney's Office had finally concluded their investigation and released the close-out memo this morning on Chris Masterson's shooting death. No charges would be filed.

In Florida, anytime an officer discharges his firearm while in the performance of his duties, it must be determined if the use of force was justified. Did the officer reasonably fear his own life or the life of another was in imminent danger? The State Attorney's Office in the jurisdiction where the shooting took place conducts an investigation, no matter how justified it may look on the outside, and even if his bullet didn't hit anyone. Because of the obvious conflict that had existed at the Miami SAO with Dominick's shooting, at Tigler's request, Broward had been called in, and a special prosecutor was assigned.

Over the years, C.J. herself had been asked to answer that same question in more than a few close-out memos. The police are given guns and instructed to use them if necessary. They have all the power. Average citizen does not. To ensure that the power has not been misused, as soon as the bullet is fired, the officer automatically becomes a suspect, and the investigation becomes criminal. If the use of force is deadly, the scene becomes a homicide scene. The police shooting team is alerted, the prosecutors and PBA lawyers are called out, and the sides are taken. The two allies – police and prosecutor – now become adversaries.

Dominick's shooting was no exception. In fact, it had been much worse, given that the victim was also a police officer and the only other witness was his fiancée, who had since become his wife. The circumstances were automatically suspect. And while he had been able to keep on working at FDLE and continue to carry his weapon, she knew that the investigation itself had hung over him like a thousand-pound piano.

Today, though, he had shown up in her office, right after she had gotten back from court, with a smile and a copy of the memo in his hand. Then, without telling her where they were going, he had put her in the car and driven her here, to Marine Max, a dockside boat dealer in Pompano Beach. She'd read the memo during the car ride.

For all its fifty pages of facts and conclusions, C.J. knew that some questions just would never be answered, though, because there was no one left to answer them. Through IMPACT, Chris Masterson had been linked to both Angelillo and Lindeman. But the full dynamics of their relationships would never be known. Because the feds wouldn't cut even a minute off any proposed plea recommendation for Roberto Valle, he, of course, refused to open up about his relationship – if any – with Chris Masterson. Based upon the totality of statements taken and evidence gathered, it was finally theorized that Masterson had been running money for the cartels, but no one with either Domingo Montoya's North Valley Cartel or the Colombian FARC revolutionaries could be tracked down to actually verify that supposition. The roads dead-ended. C.J. knew they always would.

'So what do you think, honey?' Dominick asked. 'Do you like it?'

C.J. looked at him, at the funny way he smiled at her. She knew the question he was really asking.

Buddy sensed a sale. 'If you come down to the cabin, I can show you the lovely kitchen. It has a stove and a microwave, for cooking up some nice meals for your hungry fisherman.'

'Why don't you give my wife and me a minute alone, Buddy? I think I've surprised her.'

'That you did,' said C.J., after Buddy had finally climbed back down to the parking lot.

'Are you ready for this?' he asked, looking around the bridge.

'I didn't know you were ready yet.' She had seen the stack of boxes in the back of his 4Runner on the ride over here, but hadn't said anything. His entire desk, neatly packed up and hauled away. 'Especially today, Dom. They just cleared you.'

He shook his head and said quietly, 'I can't go back anymore. I waited *until* today, but I can't go back. There's nothing for me.'

The people were the same, but for Dominick, the job was different now. The lines had blurred. He had waited a year to hear the final verdict, knowing all along that a finding of not guilty wouldn't make him innocent. He had spent that year replaying a split-second decision over and over again in his head, knowing he must have done what was right, but finding himself still hitting the mental replay button on the drive home just the same. He didn't want to do that anymore.

'Fulton and I decided to give the snuff investigation over to Postal. They're better with internet investigations, anyway,' he continued. 'Maybe they'll get lucky.'

Nothing had turned up on the search of Masterson's house or computers. He probably had a stash house, but fat chance anyone would ever find it. Chris was too smart to have ever let that happen. And, as he had told C.J., there were others out there, others who would want to ensure that never happened.

Dominick sighed and looked around him. 'It's time to move on. It's been time.'

She was quiet.

'*This* will take us to the Keys,' he said, looking around the bridge again, then he nodded across the lot, out onto the dock, where the sailboats and boats big enough to be called yachts sat. '*Those*,' he continued, 'could maybe take us around the world. We could get something used. Sell it all and become nomads.'

Her eyes followed his to the marina. A new beginning. A fresh start. A way to leave the criminals and midnight beeps and bad dreams they both now shared behind. Dominick's timing was not entirely coincidental. Bantling's execution was scheduled for next week.

'So, what do you say, Mrs Falconetti?' he asked with a whisper and the hint of a smile, taking her hands in his. 'Is it your time, too?'

His hands felt so good in hers. To see him smile again was priceless. If this was what it took . . .

'Yes,' she said after a long pause. She put her head against his chest and looked out onto the blue water. 'I think it finally is time.'

Down the row of empty cells, a faucet dripped with the incessant accuracy of a clock's second hand. After almost a month in this dark, mildew-infested cement pit, Bill Bantling thought he would go crazy listening to it. Absolutely crazy. *But, of course, that was what they wanted, wasn't it?*

They had come for him on Q-Wing about three weeks ago. The Governor had finally signed his warrant, and within a matter of hours, the prison was placed under Phase One of the watch, an execution date had been set, the press releases sent out. He was immediately brought down to the basement – to a holding cell next to the execution chamber itself, while security tightened and the prison readied for the all-important day.

In his years on the row, Bill had seen many men head downstairs. A dry erase board next to the guard station at the end of Q listed the name of every man on the row, and the specific crimes that they had been convicted of. A separate section on the board listed the names of those brought down to the basement. The ones on death watch. Some of those names had made it back upstairs, stayed at the last minute by an appeal or a sympathetic governor. Some were just erased.

Yesterday had marked the start of Phase Two. The final week. Sergeant Dick and the warden had staged a dry run with the team of COs who would work his execution. He had heard them down the hall all afternoon, fiddling with the different injection pumps that hung inside, checking the backup generator, and testing the phone line to the Governor's mansion to make sure it worked. All the while making coarse jokes that he was sure they wanted him to hear.

Now he heard the familiar jingle of keys down the hall, footsteps coming his way. He felt a strange jolt of adrenaline rush his body: perhaps today was the scheduled dress rehearsal. He would tell them to go fuck themselves. Find a mannequin to practice on with their straight pins.

The jingle stopped. 'Hands in the hole,' barked Sergeant Dick through the bars. Three COs stood behind him. The sergeant's eyes locked on Bantling's and didn't move. After a long moment he finally spoke again. 'Must be your lucky day, asshole,' he said finally, as he spat a wad of yellow onto the floor. 'We're gonna clear you out of here. Looks like you're headed back down south. The Governor's Office just called. They granted you your appeal. You're getting a new trial.'

Acknowledgements

I would like to thank the following individuals for their invaluable assistance on this project, some of whom have been called upon many times before and yet still continue to pick up the phone – even when they know it's me: Dr Reinhardt Motte of the Broward County Medical Examiner's Office; Miami Beach Police Officer Bruce Songdahl and the Miami Beach Police Department; Sergeant Travis J. Baird and Lieutenant Andrew P. Smith of the Florida Department of Corrections, Florida State Prison; Special Agents with the Florida Department of Law Enforcement, particularly Special Agent Ed Royal, Special Agent Chris Vastine and Special Agent Larry Masterson and ASAC Mike Mann; Esther Jacobo, Division Chief of the Domestic Violence Unit, Miami-Dade State Attorney's Office, Gail Levine, Sr Trial Attorney, Miami-Dade State Attorney's Office, Ivonne Sanchez-Ledo, Division Chief, Miami-Dade State Attorney's Office, John Perikles, Assistant State Attorney, Organized Crime Unit, Miami-Dade State Attorney's Office, Howard Rosen, Assistant State Attorney, Public Corruption Unit, Miami-Dade State Attorney's Office, and Priscilla Prado, Division Chief, Miami-Dade State Attorney's Office; Assistant Legal Counsel Marie Perikles, Office of the Inspector General, Miami-Dade County; Assistant Statewide Prosecutor Julie Hogan, Officer of Statewide Prosecution; Anita Gay, Assistant US Attorney, US Attorney's Office,

Southern District; Michael McManus, Chief of Operations Mexico/Central America, US Drug Enforcement Agency (DEA); Ed Hogan; and Rose Marie Antonacci-Pollock, Esq.

I'd also like to thank a few very special people who offered me their precious time and insight without hesitation or reservation, and for that I am particularly grateful: Lynn Broder, Esq., Marie and Julie and my brother, John Pellman, Jr.

I also need to thank my editor, Jennifer Hershey, for her hard work and tireless encouragement, and my agent, Luke Janklow, for his dedication and unwavering support.

And, finally, I would like to take this opportunity to thank all of my friends and family who have cheered from the moment I picked up a pen, especially my incredible husband, my children, my siblings and my parents, John and Thea Pellman. I am phenomenally lucky to have such an amazing and devoted support system – one that encourages me and inspires me on a daily basis, and one that I will never take for granted.